THE STUMPWORK ROBE

Book One

Published in 2008 by YouWriteOn.com

Copyright © Text Prue Batten

First Edition

The author asserts the moral right under the Copyright, Designs and Patents Act 1988 to be identified as the author of this work.

All rights reserved. No part of this publication may be reproduced, stored in a retrieval system, or transmitted, in any form or by any means without prior written consent of the author, nor be otherwise circulated in any form of binding or cover other than that which it is published and without a similar condition being imposed on the subsequent purchaser.

Published by YouWriteOn.com

For RJB

ACKNOWLEDGEMENTS

A number of people helped me with this book. Without the friendship and instruction of consummate stumpwork embroiderer Jane Nicholas, I would never have had the idea. She has graciously allowed me to use her designs as Adelina's own throughout the novel. My daughter Clare, of Salt Design and Peppercorn Papers, was my muse and responsible for the cover design and book layout. Cathy McAuliffe managed to find time between changing nappies to go into her studio and design the map of Eirie. My son Angus taught me the powers of observation. Thanks also to fellow writer Greg Johnston for constant support and witty repartee. To Helen, Kathryn and Alison from Cornerstones Literary Consultancy UK, thank you for your critical advice and patience over the last eighteen months.

GLOSSARY:

Stumpwork	A form of raised embroidery. Motifs include birds, beasts, flowers, fruits, flies and fish. Gold thread, silk and chenille threads, metal purl and beads are used in thick embroidery with a three dimensional aspect.
Cabyll Ushtey	Celtic folklore. A shape-changing waterhorse that eats mortals, leaving only the entrails.
Shatranj	A chess-like game from the east which pre-dates chess.
Sarbaz	Pawn-like piece in the above game.
Glamarye	Magical power.
Wight	Enchanted person or creature.
Ganconer	Irish folklore. Known as the Love-Talker. A fatal seducer of mortal women.
Lian-shee	Manx folklore. Fatal seductress of mortal men.
Veela	Balkan folklore. Could be benevolent or malicious, causing men who sighted her to pine and die.
Korrigan	Folklore of Brittany. A beautiful wight who enchants mortals at nights and leads them away from their path.
Washi paper	A cobweb-like Oriental paper.
Aine	In Irish folklore, a Faeran princess. In this novel, the Goddess-Creator.
Siofra	Irish folklore. Tiny faeries that are generally pranksters but can be benevolent.
Muirnin	Beloved, darling
Nökken	Finnish folklore. A water wight who may drown mortals.
Trow	From Orkney. Melancholy, potentially malicious Other dressed perpetually in grey.

Seelie	Benevolent.
Unseelie	Malicious.
Eldritch	Enchanted.
Mesmer	Enchanted or magic act.
Lig amach do ghreim!	Let go!
Each Uisige	Water-wight, the same as the Cabyll Ushtey.
Grindylow	Shape-changing waterwight from Northern England who will drown mortals.
Bain as!	Piss off!
Ymp trees	Rows of trees where branches have been grafted and pruned to form a long unbroken line. Believed to be one of the Gates to Faeran.
Dunters	Inhabitants of English peel-towers who cause disaster.
Iontach!	Breathtaking!
Mach an cheanna	Favourite son
Cantrips	Charms.
Bitseach!	Bitch!
Breitheamh na trialach	Trial Judge
Welkin Wind	An Other breeze

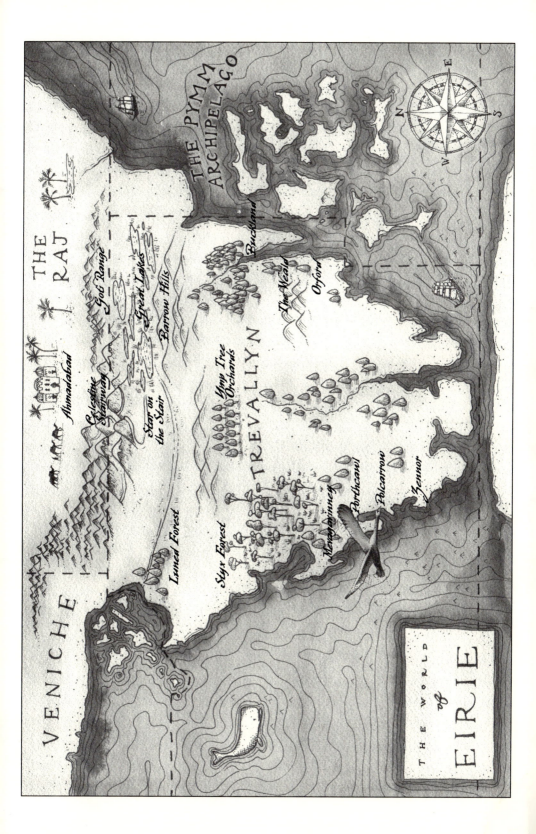

THE PROLOGUE

My name is Adelina. I am an embroiderer. I am the best in Trevallyn, possibly the world. I'm not a braggart nor arrogant about my skill, but when the most important people in the land employed me to embroider their robes of state, their everyday clothes, even their underwear and slippers, then I believe I'm right when I say I am good at what I do.

It's amusing really. I had no address and yet they always found me. You see, I am a Traveller, we of gypsy persuasion. Travelling wherever the seasons and our own sensibilities dictate. So if I had a home in the past, it was a caravan, pulled by Ajax, my equine friend. He of the gold coat and the ebony mane and tail, with delicious black frills flouncing around his fetlocks and a back broad enough for him to be mistaken for the unseelie Cabyll Ushtey.

I have an address now – of sorts. And I am angry, bitter and depressed.

I am a prisoner. Because of that self-same skill I have just mentioned. And whilst I am a prisoner, I embroider stumpwork so rich and full of colour and life that the very thread seems to jump off the fabric of the robe I am decorating.

You see, this is my story. The things that have happened to me and mine must be told as an excoriation of a pus-filled wound. I will write these words on tiny pages and sew them under the stumpwork embroidery of the robe that hangs before you.

Sometimes I wonder if my friends had not met me, become involved with me, with my life, would tragedy have gone elsewhere? Ah, but it's all rhetoric anyway. Because the reality is that it happened and I changed. From carefree to careworn in the time it takes to move the sarbaz across a shantranj board.

I wonder, did you find the robe at the Veniche Museo and did you run your fingers over the berries as they tantalised you with their realism? And did you find a bump or two that required further investigation? It's like a treasure hunt. Onward to find the next piece and the next...

Likewise, onward I must move – to another sheet of paper. You will find it lying beneath the raised embroidery of the fig tree. I shall tell you where you will find the next part after that. I am, if nothing else, efficient.

So you found the fig tree with its luscious fruit. The deep purple-black silk with which the fig is embroidered came from a Faeran market right across the other side of Trevallyn – the most unique market – enchantment floating in gauze clouds of glamarye. But that's something I shall relate later.

You noticed by running your fingers down the violet seed beads I applied to the embroidery, that the fissure opened, revealing this page. And you no doubt wonder how I made it so small.

In our travels, we have found those unseelie creatures who would sell their spells for a pittance... a cap of lace or a ribbon, some frippery. All I always wanted was to make things small, because I collected so much silk, satin and thread on my travels, my caravan was filled to the brim. The shrinking spell I secured helped me tidy up and all it cost me was a raw silk tail-coat.

Ah, such a beautiful thing! Turquoise silk shot with waves of amethyst. And all over, I embroidered dragonflies with wings veined in black and green. I piped it in violet silk and used cabochon amethysts for buttons. It was such an expensive coat but an indulgence to make and the wight who took it did it no justice at all. He was bent double and had knobbly legs as thin as dandelion stalks. His face was – plain. But I mustn't be rude because he gave me the spell and it's a very handy and somewhat precious thing to have. Besides, if you are discourteous to a wight, their anger may know no bounds. But I tell you, when that sprite put on my coat I had to turn away. Seldom has my work been so sorely draped. Ah well, I got the spell. And now it helps me shrink a story and hide it from my gaoler.

But to continue...

I'm sure you are aware of those most exceptional of the Others, the Faeran. Beyond description in their beauty, beyond belief in their way of life, filled with music, food and love. And beyond belief in the way they treat mortals who stumble across them. But then many Others are the same – wagering, prevaricating, toying with mortals – the purpose being to entice, deceive and kill.

Some are openly murderous – like the pretty waterhorses who offer friendly rides only to stick one to their hides and jump into deep water, to drown and then eat the unfortunate. But to my thinking, the most hideous of all are those that toy in the name of love – the Ganconer, the Lian-Shee, veelas, korrigans and many Others who through their singular beauty, attract, kiss and cause the poor love-lorn mortal to be filled with the pining sickness... a grievous death of starvation, exhaustion and painful heartbreak. All for an hour or two of physical gratification.

Love? Never! Perhaps now you see how bitter I am!

But I've run out of space on this page, so you must look to the embroidered casket below the rose arbour. You'll see the lace-stitch lid actually opens and inside there is a book with tissue thin washi pages, paper that my gaoler no doubt purchased from a souk in the Raj. Take the book out and pass the tiny slim wand secreted in the bottom of the casket over the book.

Say the words: *grow bigger and be, pages to see.* Then you will see why I became so full of grief and hatred. And you shall be the judge. Is it that those who knew me were doomed by the acquaintance? Or is that Fate played games with us all?

My story shall begin with Ana, a beautiful young woman who threaded her way through my life like a damaged piece of Pymm silk, breaking at every stitch so that it must be laced into the back of the work, joined and begun again. She is the first to enter my tragedy, thus making it hers as well. But there were others too, indeed one who was to become... ah, you shall see.

CHAPTER ONE

Ana Lamb stared at the earth as she walked up the field with a tan and white Trevallyn terrier in accompaniment. The sky bled with deep apricot and indigo and violet shadows edged Ana's path – funereal colours that suited Ana's mood. With each step she remembered her father's large footsteps covering the ground beside her. Joffrey Lamb had died six months before from a lung wasting disease and life for his attractive daughter had tumbled to the ground, blackened and soiled in an instant.

She likened the grievous mood she suffered to walking in mud – cloying, exhausting. Initially when Mr. Lamb had died she was numb, passing through hours and minutes oblivious – deaf and blind to all but the most basic interaction. Time meant nothing as each day was spent encapsulated in a bubble of grief that even the barbed comments from her mother could not prick.

Her dog barked sharply and ran up the hill. Looking up, she spied her mother standing with her brother Peter at the verandah post of the house. She knew they watched her with impatient misunderstanding and wished wholeheartedly that they didn't. If there had been a hole in the ground, she would have crawled in and curled into a ball, to be able to indulge her loss without scrutiny.

'Traitor', she muttered after the dog's fast disappearing rear and flicked her gaze to a spiral of dust at the end of the lane. Squire Bellingham's smart trap clipped away around the farthest bend.

Aine, what would that hateful man be doing here? Ana loathed him for his cruel, impatient arrogance. Indeed she detested the whole family, sired as they were from such misbegotten bloodlines. And how she hated his brutal son Jonty! She was angry – no, livid, Bellingham should so disrespect her father's memory to even set a toe on 'Rotherwood', because Pa had been twice, three times the man Bellingham would ever be!

Behind her, the Weald at the foot of the long field sank into black shadow as the sun eased itself behind the Thumbs, the range of low hills in the distance. Immediately a silence fell. Momentarily. And then the demented babble and shrieking laughter of the eldritch inhabitants of the woods burst forth.

Making a protective horn sign, thumb and little finger extended, middle fingers bunched in her fist, she continued walking to the barn in order to feed the horses. The Lambs were renowned for their small herd of Trevallyn thoroughbreds, Ana as proud of the bloodlines as her father had been. She opened the back of the barn, lit warmly inside by a lantern, and rattled a bucket of oats and lucerne. From the creek a shrill neigh filled the dark and the mob cantered toward her, hooves drumming on the pasture, heads and tails held high, feet thrumming their three-part rhythm. She slipped the rails across each stall as they filed in and leaned her elbows on the smooth wood, watching and smelling. Outside, she heard the patter of tiny feet like mice skittering, and then high pitched giggles and she knew the siofra from her mother's fern garden were about.

Her father had shown her the minikin wights. One quiet dusk, as they returned from the long field when she had been little more than a young child, Mr. Lamb and his daughter had heard the giggling and holding a finger to his lips, he crept to the side of the massive tree-ferns which dominated his wife's shady glade. Grasping the lacy foliage of the shorter plants, he allowed Ana to see the sprites dabbling their toes in the rill which bubbled over smooth pebbles and under fishbone and maidenhair ferns. Ana's eyes danced as she looked up at her father, he smiling and making buttoning motions at his mouth, she nodding in acknowledgment of their silent shared pleasure.

'I miss him, Tarkine.' She took up a body brush and slicked it over the smooth coat as the horse blew down his nose and continued eating. 'I ache like I have an ague and sometimes I feel as if I look at the world from a dark hole.' She moved to the horse's other side and clicked her tongue to shift him over, a trickle of thoughts becoming a flood of words.

'I should be stronger, so Ma says.' She had heard her mother one day and the words stayed in her mind, playing over and over, increasing her misconceptions.

She threw down the brush with a clatter and the horse's head arced up, ears back. Patting him with one hand, she picked up a whisk of rags to burnish the copper-bay hide. As she dragged it down his neck, it fell to her side and she rested her forehead tiredly against the smooth muscle, feeling a ripple every now and then as the horse chewed and swallowed. The rhythmic movement comforted her and she was reminded unwillingly of the smooth stroking of her father's hand through her hair when she had been very young. It followed that she remembered his hands guiding her around the farm as she grew up. She could feel them now and curled her palm a little tighter around the whisk, giving a small moan against the equine neck. Outside, the siofra laughed unkindly.

'Perhaps it *is* a pining sickness. It comes in waves: intense, black ones. And I feel filthy with it, as if I'll never slough it away. Sometimes I'm scared that I am going mad and sometimes I'm afraid that if the sadness disappears, I'll have forgotten Pa. But all I have left are memories and it's those that send me mad!'

She picked up a comb and began pulling it through his mane, dislodging crackling thistle leaves. The horse moved against her and swung his head to nuzzle, the soft mouthing across the surface of her hand prompting her eyes to fill. Tears crept down her cheeks and she gripped the mane comb to move to the horse's tangled tail, brush out the knots and pack the grooming tools in their case.

'That's the thing you see – everywhere there are memories. I'm going insane with them and I want to scream, and yet if I don't have the memories I have nothing. And I cry, constantly.' She lurched from one thought to another, rationale packed away just as the grooming tools had been. 'Perhaps I should leave it all behind.'

The words hung around her like a prophecy, almost tangible, as though she could look up and see them suspended in the sky, an exquisite aurora.

She envisaged herself walking away from 'Rotherwood', her mother and brother unaware. The image had something to recommend it but she couldn't, in her unclear frame of mind, put her finger on what it was.

She blew out the lamp, latched the barn and walked along the path towards the house. In the window, by the mellow interior light, she could see her mother and Peter talking as Marte moved around the room.

Something she'd not quite grasped had been going on for days – brother Peter morose, not just at herself but at Ma too. And Ma? By the heavens above, she was distanced so far from her daughter, she might as well be in the Raj. She pushed the door of the house open just as she heard her mother say 'this will help.'

'Help what?' she asked, unaware she had made Peter and Marte jump like conspirators. Marte pressed her hand to her chest.

'Ana, you will kill me with fright if you creep like that.' She turned away to the table. 'Peter suggested we put sheep on the pasture in the valley field. It's long and we risk it becoming rank if it's not grazed shorter.'

Sensing nothing more than the norm with her mother's clipped response, sunk deep in her own filthy misery, Ana washed her hands at the large wooden sink and sat at the table to eat her meal. Marte served herself and sat by her daughter.

'Did you remember it's the Stitching Fair tomorrow? We need new clothing and all the tailors will be there. We have just enough gelt spare.'

Ana nodded, sensing a bitterness in her mother's tone.

'Yes I remembered. And I remembered Squire Chesterman was bringing his mare to be covered by Tarkine in the morning, so I groomed the horse.'

Peter looked at his mother and gave an ironic lift of his eyebrows. Ana caught the glance. Saying nothing, pushing her food around her platter, she knew she hadn't imagined it – 'Rotherwood', her loved family home, now a symbol of sadness and despair, held no place for her at all.

These were the miserable thoughts of the young woman I would come to know so well – well enough to consider her part of my 'family'. Perhaps with a few more summers under her belt, she would have been able to rationalise her grievous loss, for it was grief which consumed her, have no doubt, that dark melancholia that could swallow people whole. Indeed I was to find myself swallowed soon after Ana, as if the Barguest, the black dog of doom, sat at my side.

But Ana was hurting and misunderstood and blind to everything but her own distrait and she had no idea an Other had overheard her in the barn and was now watching her with dark, burning eyes, musing on her private words with deliberate care and thinking on a masterful game.

CHAPTER TWO

The tents of the Stitching Fair resembled some vivid, gaudy rainbow. They stretched along the bank of the Prosser estuary, the river that flowed through the village of Orford. Ana breathed in the heady aroma of brackish water, seaweed and river-flats, all combining with the smell of roasting chickens, pork sausages and any manner of spiced potatoes. Jongleurs and musicians in gay clothes wandered through the crowd with its hubbub of dialects. Raji traders, Travellers, marketeers from all round Trevallyn and weathered, salty merchants from Pymm called to each other.

Ana felt her heart lift for the first time for weeks. She gazed at the flying pennoncels undulating in the light morning breeze. She had an obscure feeling bubbling away inside that this was going to be an odd day, a remarkable day. The feeling alone was unusual because for weeks now she had despaired.

'Ana, will you come with me now or would you like to wander and we'll meet later for lunch and choose our garments together?' Marte tucked a leather wallet in the folds at her waistband.

The pale face that had dominated Ana's appearance the last few weeks was tinged with a rosy tint and for once breeches and grubby shirts had been cast aside. But should one forget her father had not long since died, Ana had tied a cameo, brought from a Veniche merchant by Mr. Lamb, on a black satin ribbon. It nestled discretely in the hollow of her throat. She had twisted her hair atop her head but mahogany wisps fell about her lovely face.

'Can I wander? I'd like to see the Travellers' embroidery.'

'If you wish, we'll meet at the Tavern at midday then. Take care.'

Ana watched her mother stride off into the crowd, her straight shoulders and no-nonsense garb swallowed up by the dust. Aine, she's so removed, thought Ana. It's as if I'm an acquaintance now, not her daughter, the one she dandled on her knee! What will it take to make her Ma again?

She bit her lip, a cloud drifting towards the lighter feeling of earlier, but a loud groan disturbed her troubled reverie and she turned quickly to find a brown camel bearing towards her, loaded with rolled rugs and mats, placing one calloused hoof in front of the other and staring disdainfully down its cambered nose.

'Praise be, lady, we do not wish to run you down. Come to the Corner in a while and Kholi Khatoun will display all his wares for your pleasure.' The speaker greeted Ana and grinned, revealing bright white teeth.

'Thank you, I will. Have you come all the way from the Raj?'

She stared at the exotic, indigo tattoos stretched across the man's cheekbones. The curiosity that had died the day her father passed away resurrected itself just a fraction, testing the waters.

'Indeed mistress, from the Kosi-Kamali. I have been there through the Symmer Season for it doesn't pay to wander the Amritsands at that time.'

Kholi Khatoun flicked back the corners of his grubby travelling cloak. Thick, black hair sprung out in fierce curls from underneath the brim of a rolled and fur-trimmed caplet crammed on his head.

'Then did you come across the Goti Range and down the Celestine Stairway?'

'Indeed princess.' He smiled and the camel spat over the top of Ana's head. 'But Mogu gets impatient. She would rid herself of her cargo and rest. Namaste, lady, namaste.'

He folded a tanned hand across his midriff, and urged Mogu on.

She watched the camel's rump swaying away, trying to imagine the huge hooves negotiating the vertiginous, freezing paths of the Celestine Stairway and then wandered on, freedom tugging and pulling at her atrophied spirit. Like the night in the stable, as she unburdened herself to the stallion, she felt a twinge of something, some eldritch goad perhaps, saying *go on, keep walking, keep walking.*

Turning a corner she came across the site she had hoped to find. Travellers' vans were lined up in a row, horses tethered and grazing and tents pitched in front with wares laid out on trestles.

There was something special she thought, about having all one possessed in a van on wheels and pulled by a horse that was as important as one's next meal. To be able to uproot and go wherever the spirit led. No ties, to be free! Such a thing!

The Travellers were renowned for their knitting, weaving, for their various embroideries: crewel, cross-stitch, bullion work. Beautiful pieces in pastel colours or brights, in silk and wool, on velvet or silk or damask. But the most astonishing of all was the raised and padded embroidery the Travellers called stumpwork. And there was only one embroiderer of such splendid skill.

Her van was positioned under an old elm tree and Ana gazed at it, filled with a lascivious, bursting envy. The hues of the sea — pale blue, turquoise, mazarine blue, viridian — spoke to Ana of far distant waves and sea creatures. Above the tent fluttered a banner exquisitely embroidered in goldwork, with the initial 'A' wrought and embellished with leaves and flowers. The Traveller's wares were laid out on trestles amongst swathes of silks, satins, and pearlescent gauzes, along with finished goods… pincushions, mirror frames, music boxes, caskets, vests, tailcoats and beauteous gowns.

Ana approached the table and stepped out of the way of some satisfied customers, women chittering like sparrows in high-pitched voices. The Traveller, embroiderer extraordinaire, looked up as Ana's curious fingers reached for a tiny music-box which fitted into her cupped palm.

'You can wind it up if you like.' She smiled and Ana admired the attractive face with its crown of cascading copper hair. She could hear the Traveller's garments whispering as she moved, marveling at the topaz silk shot with mauve like a dusk sky and with embroideries of leaves, berries and bees.

'May I?' She turned the key, her joy as transparent as a child's as a sweet tune tinkled forth, filling the space with its chimes and cadence. Tiny rosehips, glinting blackberries and copper leaves decorated the lid, with a perfect ladybird crawling across, and underneath the leaves a silver cobweb sparkled with a tiny spider nestled in its centre.

'Oh, it's exquisite,' Ana whispered, a moment of wanting to share it with her Pa flicking across her heart.

'Then you may keep it.'

'But I couldn't afford to pay.'

'No, you mistake me,' the Traveller laughed. 'I give it to you as a gift.'

Ana's eyes opened wide at the offer and she experienced such a rush of pleasure, her cheeks coloured like a rose. The Traveller began wrapping the objêt in fine tissue.

'You see, I remember you. You come every year to my stall and it's obvious by the way you look at things that you value my work. You appreciate the time and effort. And I think touching the threads and fabrics stirs you the way it does me. Trust me, it is my pleasure to give you this as a token.'

The prophecy that had hung above Ana, now settled over her like a gossamer net. She reached for the small parcel and as fingers touched she failed to notice the embroiderer flinch. She thanked the Traveller who brushed aside the overt gratitude.

'Fiddle dee dee... it's nothing. I'm glad you'll have it. When you play a tune, think of me. By the way, I am Adelina.'

So! That is how I met Ana. As I felt that frisson when our hands touched, I looked up quickly, for it was an unusual feeling, quite eldritch in its sensation and yet I knew this young woman to be an ordinary mortal. My eyes spied a figure leaning against a tree opposite my van and I instinctively knew the feelings emanated from this strange individual.

The man was tall, impossibly well formed and graced by a face that could have been painted by a master. Titian hair had been impatiently drawn back at his nape and he crammed hands into the capacious pockets of a long black coat underneath which I could see dusty boots. His dark as night eyes did not flinch in their intense scrutiny of my client. He reminded me, the way he stood, of a black panther I had seen in the Raj... sleek as it lounged around but with teeth and claws concealed in the ebony satin package.

I knew straight away, by the fear that made my heart jump, the man was Faeran. You may ask why was I scared? Well, does the word 'Faeran' not translate in our language to mean fear? We mortals seldom see Faeran but if any of us are unfortunate enough to cross their path, it seems we are doomed to a life of pining and grief – if not death. They are an unknown quantity, these people, with their own dubious morality, their questionable antics.

Quickly I checked the faces of the crowd walking past to see if they had spied this man, to see if they felt the manifestation of his eldritch personality. No one had. And I realized he had used Faeran glamour to hide his nature from all bar me. Why? I wish I knew. Perhaps he wanted Ana and I to be friends, as unlikely as such a Faeran view would be, because ultimately that is indeed what happened.

I wish with all my heart and soul that everything had not happened and as I watched him examine her, I felt his study of Ana meant something devious. I was sure! Fear for the woman shivered through me and I longed for a warm wrap in which to swathe my trembling body, for suddenly I saw a shatranj board with a life-threatening game underway. Do you know shatranj, that game of black and white shah, vazir, rukh, alfil, asb and sarbaz? The dark stranger would manoeuvre like an aliyat or grandee, the most serious of players, with a great stake at play. The stake would be the sarbaz and I knew who that pawn would be. The question was, my friend, who would play the white shah and queasiness tickled my belly as I wondered if it might be me.

You will notice you are now reading the last of the washi pages. So I would like you to place the small wand on the book and say: *That is all, be small.*

Take the little book and place it back in the casket and close the lid, keeping the wand with you. Follow the tiny black and gold bee past the stitching of Queen Ann's Lace and amongst the rosebuds and ladybirds, you will find more bees – follow them and you will arrive at a hive. I tell you, that hive took me weeks of weaving honey coloured thread in and out until I achieved the semblance of a real willow bee bothy!

Put your smallest finger in the door of the hive and feel for another tiny book. Those that are unaware will think I've padded the hive thickly, one of the techniques of stumpwork. They will have no clue as to what really hides there.

See now, you have a buttery silk-covered book in your palm. Use the wand, say the charm and read on...

CHAPTER THREE

A wave of sound rolled down between the aisles of stalls and broke around Ana's head causing her to look up at the Traveller with a rare sparkle in her eyes.

'It's the boat races! Oh Adelina, I must go! My brother is racing in our coracle! I'll see you later though, my mother would buy clothes for us and I'm positive you have things we'll love. Oh and by the way, I'm Ana Lamb!'

Adelina smiled.

'Good day, Ana! Now get you gone or you'll miss the fun!'

Ana turned in a flurry of moleskin skirt and sped off in the direction of the riverbank, her falling hair and a fragrance of lemons streaming behind, unaware a tall stranger followed at a discrete distance, to all intents and purposes part of the crowd who did not want to miss a minute of the water races.

Those already positioned on the bank had secured the best spots and were cheering and laughing as each race ran its course. Ana squeezed and ducked under people's arms, trying to get closer as friendly banter surged around her.

'Here, Lady, would you like a hand... it's a good viewing platform.'

A voice shouted above her and she followed the line of the outstretched palm, up to a shoulder and a pleasant face framed in dark titian hair. Hearing the crowd yell again, Ana put out her hand and allowed herself to be pulled onto a broad log from where she could see head and shoulders over everyone. A breathless thank you, more as an aside, was tossed in her tall benefactor's direction as she frantically searched the oncoming craft for her brother.

Coracles could hardly be called the fastest and most graceful craft on water. Built of pitch-soaked calico stretched tightly over wicker frames and like a soup bowl in shape, they were deftly propelled by the rower leaning precariously forward and sweeping with one blade around the curved sides of the quaint vessel. The strength and fierce purpose of the competitors made for an unstable lurch as each craft wobbled down the course, the battle spreading white wavelets across the water. To add to the difficulty of the race, the spectators flung small sacks of flour and dried cow dung at the competitors, calling and jeering, urging the rowers on.

'Peter! HARDER!' Ana yelled encouragement.

'Which is Peter?' The stranger spoke over the yell of the crowd.

'There, the blonde head, – oh, come on Peter! Put your back into it! Go!'

The stranger bent down level with Ana's shoulder and followed the line of her arm, hand and finger. Her soft-as-satin hair blew back and a tendril caressed his cheek. In that instant, what had been a plan of quick dalliance changed to a far more serious game of strategy and manipulation.

The timbre of crowd noise began to alter on the breeze and Ana's gaze sharpened as hissing began to fly across the surface of the water, her angered cries adding to the rest, fists balling.

'No, NO! Ooh, you lousy swine, Bellingham!'

'No,' the tall companion said. 'Watch... your Peter will come to no harm.'

Jonty Bellingham, livid at Peter's skill, had powered in close by and raised his paddle to club his competitor across the shoulders. He lifted the make-do weapon, took aim and had brought it viciously forward. The paddle swished towards its target and then, with a loud smash it hit something solid and unseen, foiling his aim, and with the whack, the paddle fell from his grasp, his craft lurched and Jonty flailed backwards. The crowd screamed with delight as he slid under the river surface. To vociferous catcalling, his pugnacious face bobbed up again, red and angry and streaming with brown riverweed. Some fool began chanting 'wet, wet, wet, wet!' Within seconds the crowd had taken it up and the miscreant had swum to the shore to beat a dripping retreat. Peter meanwhile had continued on gamely, crossing the finish line, paddle waving above his head to the applause of the crowd.

Ana crowed. Cheering, her face radiant, a tiny piece of her realized it was the happiest she'd been for months. She turned to her companion.

'Well sir,' she flirted ingenuously. 'You were right. He came to no harm.'

'Indeed. And what does he win for being the victor?'

'A kiss from the Stitching Queen – she's pretty mind, and Peter and she are betrothed and will be married in a fortnight. And a hundred gelt. Which Ma will no doubt purloin for seed or some such. But it doesn't matter. He beat Bellingham and in my eyes that's all that matters.'

'Not a nice person then?'

'No!' She edged along the log, eager to leave, and the gallant stranger jumped down, to reach and swing her off. His hands circled her waist and he swung her in an arc, secure and balanced.

The world slowed. His eyes and the ink blackness of them dragged her down into their velvet depths, as surely as if he had weighted her with boulders. Nothing existed but the swing of her skirt, the air swishing passed her ears. Her feet touched the ground but the man's hands stayed encircling her. He spoke.

'I am Liam.'

Ana nodded, her heart skipping, stomach light.

'And I'm Ana.'

'I know.'

She floated in the dark comfort of his gaze until her brother's shout broke the crystal clear moment, shattering it with a whoop that all around could hear.

'I must go...' she hesitated, the man's hands still encircling her, a feeling of dismay crowding in as he let them drop.

She went to run to her brother's call but stopped to stare again. And then she was off, brown skirt kicking up, falling hair flying. Ana was now under Faeran thrall, her heart and her soul belonged to the aliyat, the game-player who would move her wherever he wanted on his shatranj board, until the opposing shah was forced to declare.

I WAS TO FIND OUT THE TWO had shared this crucial moment because I spent many hours in the company of Ana and she related her first meeting with the Faeran, her feelings and other things to me as we journeyed in close quarters. That's why

I felt so shattered with what eventually occurred. Events on this day, the day of the Stitching Fair, conspired to propel her toward a destiny she would never have imagined for herself.

Myself? It was my skill with the needle that brought me in touch with the Faeran world. Can you imagine I was a better stitcher than the best of the Faeran? Fiddle dee dee… it hardly matters. What matters is that I became a player. And as my friendship with Ana grew, I needed to draw up every ounce of tactical skill to try and equal my opponent, the Faeran aliyat.

There I was on that fateful day, sitting at my stall with a birchwood hoop in my hand and tiny strips of green basilisk skin, fashioning the thoraxes of goldwork beetles. The gold thread, small skeins of tightly plied fine metal, lay cut to lengths in front of me. My needle slipped back and forth through the taupe silk in the hoop with a shushing sound, anchoring the basilisk skin with tiny stitches. Occasionally, as the roar of the crowd surged around my ears, I would turn the screw at the head of the hoop and stretch the fabric as tight as a drum, tapping to test for a hollow resonance, indicating the perfect tension for my work. As the needle flew in and out I mused on Ana.

You know when you meet someone who will be a kindred spirit, don't you? Bells don't ring loudly, but maybe they tinkle a little, as if some sort of eldritch harmony could occur. That's what happened when I met the woman from Trevallyn. She reacted to my embroidery in a way that delighted me and I felt a common bond as if she wanted to know so much more. But more than anything I saw a sadness which intrigued me and I wanted to see her again – to pass the time, to delve into the shadows of her melancholia. But the thing that pricked every one of my senses to a state of alarm, was the entry of the Faeran stranger into her life. Being sad, she was weak and being weak she was vulnerable… a perfect pawn.

CHAPTER FOUR

'Oh, Peter, well done!' Ana ran to her brother, grabbed him in a hug and then stood back as Fiona, the Stitching Queen and Peter's betrothed, moved to his side. 'Fee, good-day to you, didn't he do well? Oh, Peter, I think the river spirits were with you today as something stopped Jonty for sure. He meant business!'

'Aye.' Peter pulled a shirt over his muscled torso. 'I don't know what was wrong with the git but I was never so glad when I saw him tumble. By Cuachag, but I detest him. I hate that he's about to be...'

'What? About to be what?'

Ana heard the distress in her brother's voice and would have pushed him further had not the Mayor called Peter to take the stand and receive his prize. She watched her brother walk forward and glancing at the town clock, saw it was well past the meeting time for she and her mother. Sucking in a worried breath, cognisant of potentially further disapproval, she hastened away in the direction of the tavern, turning sharply into Quickstep Lane as a shortcut.

Two shadows stood half way down the shaded, gravel path. At first, Ana thought they were dark stripes cast by the spreading gum tree that towered over the high stone walls of the houses backing onto the lane. But then the shades moved toward her and she recognized Riddle and Peebles from the village, the flaccid and easily led offsiders of Jonty Bellingham.

Her footsteps slowed. Memories of schoolyard bullying loomed overlarge, her knees like jelly. She acknowledged the fellows briefly, not quite meeting their taunting eyes, and went to skirt around them. They moved with her and blocked her. She stepped the other way, they moved again like a macabre dance pattern. She could smell their body odor, rank and sweaty.

Deep in the middle of the lane, the sound of riverbank revelry dwindled and the shadows of the tree and the high walls threatened darkness.

Ana thrust against the lads ineffectually, trying to push out of the shade enclosing them all, desperate to get away from the threat that hung heavily amongst the leaves and branches.

'Let me past! My Ma waits at the Tavern.'

'Oh, really?' Peebles pushed hard against her, driving her to step backward, turning her ankle on a large stone. Anger flared briefly, her fragile emotions forever on a knife-edge. She raised her arm to push him away but it was grasped from behind and yanked fiercely back above her head and she was forced to swing around to relieve the searing pain in her shoulder. Bellingham stood facing her, the size of his bulk blocking any exit.

'Your Ma can wait.' Fat lips curled as he reached forward and ran a hand lasciviously up and down her side.

Ana flinched as the pig-like face, ruddy and flushed with an ugly excitement, pressed closer. He was taller than her by far and very broad, as if he could stand square to a stampede of black bulls and never be knocked down. His greasy hair was slicked back but locks of it fell forward over the slit eyes. For all the money of the Bellingham family, Jonty had no polish, no finesse, a hoodlum to the backbone of his loathsome body. She dragged up spirit, compressed and hidden since her father's death.

'No she cannot! Now get out of my way, Bellingham!' She used all her strength to push at his hand with a dismissive thrust, at the same time lashing out with a knee to try and catch him in the groin.

Jonty pounced on her like a ferret with a rabbit, grabbing her and flinging her back hard against the wall of the nearest house. A sharp pain shot down her back and the air inside her flew out in a violent cough. She sagged with dread as she saw how corralled she was in the iron cage of Jonty's grip.

'What in the name of the Napae do you think you are doing?' Each word came out in a breathless spurt, fear prickling her armpits. Peebles and Riddle guffawed and urged Jonty on.

'Go on, Bells, tup 'er. Tup the daft chit. Give it to 'er 'ard!'

'Shut your gobs, you two, shut it!' Jonty shouted back, spittle spraying over Ana's face.

'You touch me and you'll have the whole Trevallyn Marshalls' Corps on your neck!' Her voice was shrill with angst.

'You think?' Jonty spoke half way between a smirk and a sneer. The expression on his face changed like water before the wind. And with the speed of someone far less bulky, he thrust one hand around her throat and the other he twisted in her hair and pulled. She gasped with the pain, her scalp stretched taut as if her hair could lift in one bloody piece.

'Listen you little whore, who was the sod you were with on the log.'

'No one!' She smelled sour whisky on Jonty's breath. His bloodshot eyes had dilated and the grip on her throat immediately tightened as she answered. Her breath sucked in and out, her pulse vibrating in her temples, her face turning red.

'Jonty, you're cho...king...me!'

Momentarily he relaxed the pressure on her throat but still holding her hair, began a frenzy of ripping at her shirt, pulling it out of the waist of the skirt. Two buttons burst and fell to the gravel at Ana's feet and Peebles and Riddle burst out laughing, excited by the sexual threat. She tried to anticipate his actions, her heart crying out for Peter, for Ma, for her father, for anyone! Rape crazed his eyes and his fat tongue ran over wet lips. He reached out to her breasts and began to squeeze, grunting like a rutting bull.

'You let him touch you. He held you. I saw.' Between each statement, he wrenched and pummeled and terrified tears formed and began to trickle down Ana's face. He thrust a leg between her thighs, driving it up hard, a pain shooting through to her hips as if a hammer had crashed against her.

'Are you well, my princess?' An accented voice emerged from the shadows. Soundlessly shifting forward, Kholi Khatoun stepped from the dark of the lane behind them.

'Bugger off!' Jonty growled, his hands still grasping urgently at Ana's breasts.

'Why sir, of course, if the lady wishes.'

Kholi threw back a voluminous black cloak, cleaner and heavier than the earlier one and fingered a huge scimitar tucked through a blood-red sash at his waist. Within seconds the curved weapon had swished to rest against Riddle's throat. As he squeaked, Kholi Khatoun threw him aside. The two louts sprinted up the lane, leaving Jonty exposed and alone.

Kholi moved with the agility and grace of a tiger. His scimitar flashed and Jonty's hands let go of Ana as his trousers fell to the ground, a glancing swipe having cut through the leather belt without harming a cell of Jonty's bulk.

'Do you wish me to go, lady?'

Ana grabbed her shirt and folded it over her aching, bruised chest. Where she had hit the wall, a branch had scratched her temple and a carmine stain trickled over blanched cheeks. She shook her head silently from side to side.

'On your way, scoundrel. I am within my rights to truss you like the overfed chicken you are and bury you in the sand to your white, fat neck and with one swipe...'

The blade whistled sideways and a thistle was beheaded, it's flower lying on the cobbles, mauve petals broken and scattered.

Jonty pulled his trousers up into his crotch and turned to Ana, his wide jowls trembling with anger at his emasculation.

'This isn't finished, beloved. Next time this sand savage won't be around! I have rights now. Betrothed men always do.' Ana's eyes opened wide with horror and he sneered. 'Oh by the Spirits, your Ma hasn't told you!' He pealed into hysteric giggles. Ana's protector pricked him with the end of the cruel, curved weapon.

'Enough, lard-face. You try me.' Kholi stood close to Bellingham. The exotic robes blew around him and his dark eyes glinted, the face which Ana had thought engaging, appearing strange and threatening as the scimitar was weighed and measured. Jonty turned with a wilted attempt at nonchalance.

'You and I, Ana – we are betrothed now. Your Ma and my father have signed us together. To be married the week after your brother. So till later, love of my life.'

He sauntered awkwardly away to the corner at the top of the lane leaving Ana bruised, bloody and aghast.

Kholi quickly undid his cloak and wrapped it around the girl as her shivering worsened. The brightness and expectation of Ana's day had completely cracked as the words 'we are betrothed now' spilled forth. The desert merchant placed an arm around the girl and pushed her gently towards the Tavern as a figure hurried into the lane.

'Ana! Gracious, girl! I've been waiting for half an hour. Jonty said he saw you just now, that you had an accident.' Marte eyed the stranger suspiciously.

'Indeed madame, she has.'

'Well thank you kindly sir, I'll take my daughter now.'

Something about the protective tone in her mother's voice jerked Ana from the silent place to which she had retreated. She threw up her hands and brushed her mother away.

'Did you betroth me to Jonty Bellingham?'

Shrill tones dropped like glass splinters onto the ground at Marte's feet. She looked despairingly at her daughter. Ashen-faced, blood trickled down Ana's cheek and her blouse was torn under the cloak.

'Ana, please... you have to understand. The farm... Fiona's dowry...'

'DID YOU BETROTH ME TO BELLINGHAM?'

Her mother stood fingering the wallet at her waistband, silent, face frozen. Ana sucked in a breath and turned sharply, picking up the folds of the cloak, to run as fast as she could, as if distance from her mother was the only thing she craved.

Kholi Khatoun slipped the scimitar back into the blood-red sash.

'Memsahib, I'll find her and see her to your home, don't fret.'

Marte nodded, pulling at a small, embroidered kerchief. Kholi coughed politely.

'Memsahib, I realize this is not my business, but the man to whom your daughter is betrothed, he just assaulted your daughter! I was witness! Such a man should be castrated!' He broke off, embarrassed. Folding his hand across his middle, he bowed slightly. 'Memsahib, forgive me.'

Marte's face betrayed no emotion as she stared at the Raji. The soft lips stretched tight, the blue eyes glinted like glaciers.

'Thank you for caring for Ana and I would appreciate it if you could send her home should you see her. Other than that sir, it is as you say, none of your business.'

No woman could ever understand how terrible Ana felt to be assaulted, unless they had suffered the same way. How filthy, how frightened! Ana's sense of self-worth plummeted to hell and beyond at that point. All she wanted was for her father to come – to rescue her, to tell her she was still his perfect girl. To make her feel clean again. Inside that poor damaged young woman was a hole that was achingly empty and her search for something to fill it was to be her downfall.

You have come to the end of this little book. If you would be so kind, do what you did before – the wand, the shrinking charm – and return the book to the beehive. It is very important the books are secreted again and that each is in its sequential spot, more important than you could ever believe and you must, absolutely must read them in the order I say. I beg you, on my life! You will see why eventually.

Find the small panel of peacock, grapevine and beetle? Very, very gently lift the peacock's tail and mark how I have used the end of a real peacock's feather, a clever conceit, I think. There, underneath, is the next book, covered in teal blue silk. And you are lucky this time, because if you also raise the embroidered metallic elytra of the beetle, you will find a copper silk book. Enlarge and continue.

CHAPTER FIVE

Adelina looked up from her work to see a black swathed figure walking past her stall. At first she was unsure if it was Ana – a cloak enfolded the young woman. But Adelina saw the dark mahogany hair and even though it was awry and almost covered a drooping face, she was positive it was her.

The Traveller waved her hoop with its trailing threads to attract attention, but her arm froze in the air as she glimpsed the stricken face turning toward her. Throwing the hoop amongst the goods on her trestle, she raced out and led her back to the stall to gently push her to sit on the cushioned chair.

'Your face, what happened? Here, let me take the cloak and clean you up.' She reached for the clasp and was about to pull it off Ana's shoulders when she saw the torn shirt underneath and yellow and blue striated skin. Sucking in her breath, she pulled the cloak tighter and with an arm under Ana's elbow, she pushed her gently.

'Come sweeting, to my van. Katinka, hey, Katinka,' Adelina called to her fellow Traveller on the neighboring stall, 'can you mind my stall? My friend needs to use my van.'

Katinka pulled the cheroot from her lips, gave a grin and then continued puffing as she measured off a length of fine navy wool.

Adelina's van wrapped around Ana like a womb around a babe. Oblivious, she followed where she was led and allowed the embroiderer to guide her through folds of silk-gauze cocooning the bed and shielding it from inquisitive eyes. The light within the van glowed softly, large windows at the sides having been hung with the same covering, creating a secret haven.

'Ana, what happened, muirnin?'

Adelina squatted down in front of the girl and tried to get her to focus. But she hung her head to allow her hair to shield her and two tears overflowed and trickled down the smeared cheeks. Adelina took a kerchief from beside her bed, dampened it and began to wipe the stricken face. She reached for the cloak and went to loop it off Ana's shoulders but trembling hands came up and held on tight.

'By the soul of Aine, what possesses you, Ana?'

'She has been assaulted.'

Adelina turned quickly to the door. The bottom half had been unlatched and a dark shadow filled the entrance, backlit, blocking the doorway.

'Kholi Khatoun! But how do you know this?' Shocked, Adelina reached an arm round Ana's shivering shoulders.

'I saw it.' Kholi motioned with his hand. 'May I?'

Adelina nodded and he moved into the van.

'She'll not speak, and no wonder, for she must be profoundly traumatised. Have you any liquor?'

'Brandy?' Adelina turned away to the compact galley that served her as a kitchen space. Hardly a galley, more a bench with a tiny set of travelling shelves holding kitchen utensils. Underneath, in two cupboards, were her food supplies, along with bottles of brandy, ale and wine, elderflower cordial and a sweet muscat she had picked up from a travelling merchantman from the Pymm Archipelago. She poured a small measure of the brandy now and dropped in some elixir of valerian. Ana's hand trembled as she reached for the drink, so Adelina cupped the shivering fingers in her own.

'Drink, muirnin.'

The liquid burned its way to her belly and she coughed but the warmth offered comfort enough for her to push back her head and stare at the Traveller, still saying nothing.

'Listen muirnin, lie down for a while. That's it. Close your eyes and rest. Then when you feel stronger, Kholi Khatoun here will take you to your home. Would you like that?'

Adelina eased the young woman back on the pile of creamy pillows on the bed and pulled a woolen shawl over her. Ana made no sound but two more tears slid out of the corner of her eyes as she closed them.

'Come on Kholi, let's sit outside and leave her to recoup. Would you like an ale or some wine?'

'Wine, Adelina. Thank you.' He backed out of the van, concerned eyes never leaving the prone form on the bed.

The two sat quietly and Adelina handed the Raji a goblet.

'So tell me, what happened?'

He detailed the awful events.

'He would have raped her, Adelina – he had lost complete control. I should have sliced the mongrel into kebabs and fried him over his own rendered fat!'

'Kholi Khatoun!' Adelina grabbed the merchant's hand. 'Quietly! Don't scare her! It's as well I have known you for so long or I would think you a cruel barbarian.' She sipped on her wine and spoke in a lowered voice. 'Mind you, your choice of punishment seems apt. But there's more, isn't there?'

'Oh, indeed! The monster, after I had relieved him of the weight of his breeches, proceeded to taunt her, telling her she was his betrothed. I tell you, I think it was that more than the rough handling which did for her.'

'Betrothed! But that requires her parents' approval and that of the cretin's family.'

'You're kind – cretin does him honour. But you see, you're right. The mother has betrothed the poor thing to him. By afrits and djinns! One would wonder why?'

They sat in an uncomfortable silence, musing on Ana's fate.

'You know, Adelina,' Kholi put down his glass. 'There is something her mother was not telling. I think there is trouble at home. The mother was icy and seemed unable to relate to Ana and the young woman was obviously in a dire way and needed her. What would prompt a mother to act so? And why would she betroth her daughter to such a brutal man? I spoke my opinion to her and my thoughts were unwelcome.'

Adelina leaned back against the doorjamb, casting an eye in Ana's direction. She hadn't moved and her eyes were closed. Thrusting a hand through her hair, the embroiderer eyed her friend.

'Well, I suspect it's too late. Betrothals signed under Trevallyn law are legally binding. The poor creature is trapped. By Aine, how sad! But you know, there's a thing! When she came to my stall this morning, she was already sad, I can sense these things. So yes, you are right. Something has happened in the home and affected she and her family.'

The two travelling merchants sat savoring their wine and musing on Ana's fate. It was almost upon Adelina's lips to mention the Faeran stranger but she decided against it. There was enough angst without introducing another problem. Instead she chose to pass the time of day with Kholi Khatoun. He was, after all, a very old friend.

'Kholi, how are things with you? Have you had a good Fair?'

Adelina leaned back and tipped her face up to the sun. The rounded cheekbones and aquiline nose were marvelously juxtaposed. She radiated ripeness – like a peach or an apricot filled with juicy promise.

'I sold everything,' the Raji smiled, eyes alight at his good fortune. 'Every rug and mat, in an hour and for good gelt too! And you?'

'Excellent. I have sold almost all the apparel and you know how expensive it is. All my mirrors have gone and the trinkets were dribbling off the stall. Some fabrics too, so I am happy. I need to purchase more threads, silks and satins, it's time for some serious re-stocking.'

Kholi grinned his approval. His blue-black hair, having been relieved of the squashing effect of the travel caplet, curled in smooth waves around the strongly boned face. His hands were strong and broad, deeply tanned with wide, clean fingernails and something about them appealed to her, as she envisaged them holding, stroking...

'So where shall you journey?' As he spoke, she detected a deeper interest than just mild curiosity and the discovery quite thrilled her.

'To the Raj I expect. Unless I can find a market to the north of here and before I get to the Celestine Stairway. My Ajax is quite scared of heights and therefore scares me as well.'

'We could travel together.' Kholi laughed. 'My Mogu is not at all affeared and she may keep your horse calm.'

'Indeed. If we can get over the fact that Mogu is a camel, then Ajax may cope.' When she smiled and leaned forward, her shirt gaping to reveal a smooth décolletage, she was aware of Kholi shifting uneasily on the steps and she stroked his arm teasingly with her fingers. 'Tell me Kholi, have you a betrothed back in Ahmadabad?'

The desert man's expression, lit bright with her touch, became solemn.

'No. Who would want a man who travels nine tenths of the year?' He sighed.

'Why, another traveller of course.' Adelina opened her eyes wide as he looked at her.

'But where to find such?' He was quite serious. 'I tell you my dear friend, because we've known each other these many years, I do get lonely. I love my Mogu, but a camel can't really take the place of a wife.'

'Poor Mr. Kholi,' Adelina giggled. 'No wife, no life.'

'You jest, but I am serious.'

'Oh Kholi, I'm sorry, I don't mean to hurt you. Look... I have known you since our parents carted us to all these markets and fairs. Let's travel together for a time! I would welcome your company. When do you leave?' She smiled her ripe, golden smile.

'Tomorrow at dawn.'

'Then I shall be ready. Collect my Ajax and me as you leave. Now let's see how Ana is. The sun's dipping and I fear it's more than time for her to go home, poor sweeting.'

Remember I mentioned when Ana entered my story, that she was like a piece of damaged thread that broke at every stitch. My Kholi was like thread also. There is a Raji thread, glossy and bright and it gives dimension when one uses it to pinpoint light. I find it a reliable thread, always the same but with the ability to lift my work beyond the mundane. Like Kholi.

No doubt you wonder about Liam. What is he in my thready analogies? Huh! He is Faeran, and Faeran silk is the most magnificent of all. Lustrous and unbreakable. Or so I thought.

But you have reached the end of this latest revelation and you know what you must do – charm, replace. And then, if you would like to continue this journey of words, I would ask you to make a traverse across the warp and weft of the robe.

Can you see a pavilion with small tassels hanging off the awning? Such a difficult thing to make, masses of needleweaving which is my least favourite stitch, but I think the effect is worth it. See how it's roomy enough to contain a stool and a basket of strawberries? Aine but that wretched basket required more needleweaving! However, it all sits on a blue checkerboard floor that was much easier to render. Satin stitch... I can do that in my sleep!

This is a larger piece of stumpwork, well padded and deceiving and most people focus on the strawberries. Feel around inside the walls of the tent and you will find a much thicker booklet than before. Fortunately this will enable you to continue reading for some time before you once again must amble on your treasure hunt across the byways of my embroidered countryside.

I must tell you that the pavilion was stitched as a gentle reminder. On my journey with Kholi Khatoun, he would rig a delightful tent, exotic and colourful, with tassels and bells all around the awning. The bells were to keep unseelie wights at bay. It was in this tent that our friendship transformed to love, amid the harmonies of tinkling cones of engraved silver.

CHAPTER SIX

When Ana left Liam to run to her brother's celebration, he was not afraid of losing her in the crowd or never seeing her again. He had already placed her on the board and in the manner of the aliyat, he was going to play her.

Momentarily though, in the mere blink of an eye as her hair had grazed his cheek, he looked at her in a different light. Not as a sarbaz but as someone he could share something with, learn from even. He wondered if she had innocently turned the tables on him, made him the game.

Never! Blatant arrogance curled the strong mouth. This is my game, played by my rules.

And so he wandered amongst the crowds, observing mortals, the happiness and the joy, the belligerence occasioned by drink and jealousies, mothers' love and fathers' discipline. All the while he knew it would be easy to find Ana in such a small, provincial town, he had only to ask. But somewhere in his consciousness curiosity hunkered. What if she should come to him willingly, without the glue of Faeran glamarye? The bored loneliness of his life shifted slightly at the thought.

And so it was, as the crowds broke from the boat racing and set about the serious job of denuding the food stalls and emptying the stitchers' troves, he entered the dark, shady end of Quickstep Lane. Hiding, blending himself with the chiaroscuro of shadow until he was merely another shade amongst the shifting patterns wafting on the river breeze. Stationed mutely. Just as Kholi Khatoun spoke so heart-rendingly to Marte.

'Ana must not marry that Jonty man. This man assaulted your daughter! I was witness... She is badly wounded in the spirit and the heart... Such a man

should be castrated.'

Berserk anger erupted in Liam. Ana was his! His trophy, his prize, to do with what he wanted! Not the possession of some over-fed mortal miscreant. Instinctively, his hand went to his stiletto... a way to emasculate Ana's assailant, just as Kholi had said. Splitting Jonty's legs open, reaching for his plump testes and slicing them off with one stroke, blood spurting, and then handing the offensive, flaccid bags to the wounded individual. Watching the horror and pain erupt forth from the mortal mouth. Good indeed!

But not enough!

Marte walked away and Kholi Khatoun turned the other way toward Liam, toward the black shadow that seemed deeper than the time of day would warrant. The breeze stirred the tree occasioning a peppering of gumnuts on the ground, their noise a subtle patter. Kholi stopped at Liam's feet to pick one up and sniff its sharp astringency. On the verge of revealing himself to the Amritsands merchant, Liam felt he would have a ready accomplice but he held back. A Faeran needed no help! Thus Kholi Khatoun walked away, unaware of the eldritch shade in the lane. No telltale frisson rippled in the air – Liam had cast himself invisible.

He hurried down the lane and round the corner to the Tavern, retrieving his dark grey mount from the stable and passing the groom a handful of silver coins.

'Oh sir! Thanks. But I 'ardly deserve it, 'e's such a good boy it were a pleasure to care for 'im.'

Liam tightened his girth and looped reins over the horse's head.

'Indeed, he's good and fast with it. Tell me, I'm seeking young Jonty. Can you help me?'

The groom looked at this elegant, friendly man, stranger though he was and wondered what anyone could want with that git Bellingham. Why, the way he raked his mount's flanks with rowelled spurs was criminal. Fella should be horsewhipped! But cognisant of a palm full of silver, he smoothed the grey's forelock as he answered.

'Lor, sir, you just missed 'im. 'E 'as 'eaded 'ome.'

'And which way is that?' Liam fixed the lad with his Faeran gaze and the boy, quite soothingly mesmered, was willing to tell him everything he needed to know.

Riding at a steady pace through the woodland shortcut, Liam was content that he would head off Bellingham at Buck's Passing, the stony passage across Buck's Beck on the main road. On either side of the Passing, the beck possessed deep waterholes, green and black and frilled with undulating weed. All the world knew it skirted the western edge of the Weald, inspiring fear in those who must go that way. Liam had no doubt Jonty would attempt the crossing at a cracking pace, coward that he was, in a desperate need to pass it by quickly. Ah well, he, Liam of the Faeran, had other plans.

He surprised himself at the fount of anger erupting on Ana's behalf. Real anger, dangerous anger – as if she really did matter, that this was not just a game. He allowed the emotions to carry him along: intrigued, excited, which only served to heighten his fury at Jonty Bellingham. Aine, the scum would pay!

The afternoon was sinking into the gold and navy shadows of evening and being the last of those clear autumnal days, it promised to be a longish dusk. The coin-like discs of the copperbeech rattled like the backbone of a skeleton and the horse trod on a fallen branch, the loud snap like the breaking of bone. Thereafter, silence grabbed and swallowed sound, the only noise the horse made was the occasional shush as its feet shifted through the forest detritus.

Ahead, light glittered silver on a shallow pass of water and Liam could hear the ripple and tumble of the beck as it flowed over the stones from one deep hole to another to continue its journey to join with the Prosser in a stony gorge called Paradise.

He reined to a halt and threw his leg over the grey's neck to jump to the ground – casual, unconcerned. Smoothing errant wisps of hair back with a hand, he led the horse to a deep patch of shade where it could be seen neither from the Passage nor the track. Despite the occasional skittering and the glint of amber eyes through bushes, despite heavy footsteps and coarse whispering close by, his horse was as eldritch as any other and neither sidled nor snorted nor laid its ears back. It merely cropped the low forest grasses, swishing an idle tail, knocking off the will o' the wisps gathering in the growing dusk.

Returning to the edge of the track to lean against a tree, Liam was not surprised to see a horse of great height and breathless beauty standing still, resting a hind leg. It pricked its ears and met the Faeran's eyes with its own glinting black orbs. He admired the sheen of the coat, so black it glistened like jet. Dangling from the horse's flowing mane was a piece of waterweed and twisted in its tail, the same grassy decoration. It snaked its head and gave a half rear, adding to the unseelie atmosphere swirling between man and horse, reins falling from a sparkling bit and bridle.

'I am not your prey today,' Liam whispered in Faeran. 'Be patient, there are better pickings than me.'

A thrumming rumbled underneath his feet, a horse at full gallop. He passed his hand smoothly in front of his body, like someone wiping moisture off a windowpane on a frosty morning. Immediately the drumming changed to the three beat of a horse cantering, then an uneven two beat as the horse trotted with difficulty, and finally a bad tempered shout, as the animal limped around the bend and to the edge of the Passing with a foul mouthed Bellingham astride.

'You bloody bag of dog meat!'

He raised a long whip in his hand, sawing at the reins with the other. In obvious pain, the horse laid back its ears and sidestepped, dropping its shoulder on the afflicted side.

'Ho sir!' Liam stepped out from under the autumnal shade. 'What's amiss?'

Jonty swung his horse toward the voice, missing the gliding movement of the Faeran hand in front of the body. With a mesmer laid, Jonty had no idea the man facing him was the same 'sod' who had swung Ana off the log. As Liam had planned, he was just a journeyman Jonty had run across as his horse went lame.

'The cursed nag has cast a shoe and I daresay bruised a sole, with me yet to ride three more miles.' The lout kicked at the horse viciously.

'I would sell you mine for the price of yours and some extra thrown in,' Liam grinned.

'Extra!' Jonty snorted. 'My horse would be worth twice yours and then some. Anyway, where's this nag you think so highly of.'

Liam pointed to the huge elm at the edge of the beck and the magnificent black beast he had so admired earlier strode out. Each step revealed rippling muscle, light shone on the glistening coat, the etched ears pricked forward and the tail was held high like the stallions from the Amritsands.

Liam knew what Jonty would be thinking, such a mind was not hard to read – prancing down Prosser High Street on board the superb mount with people running out of the way of flashing silver hooves. Jonty sucked in his breath audibly as he used his spurs to push his horse close.

'How much?'

'As much as is in your pockets now – and your horse.' Liam gestured with his head.

Jumping off, Jonty thrust his reins into Liam's hands. As he stood there, Liam smelled sweat and grime and other unappealing body odors and wondered briefly if his plan would work for the mortal smelled like offal. Bellingham grabbed at the handful of gelt in his pocket to throw in Liam's direction and stalked towards the beast by the beck, growling at Liam as he went.

'Help me mount!'

The horse skittered sideways as Liam and Bellingham approached.

'Steady my man, steady. You shall never have as a good a treat as the rider you are about to carry.'

The horse's eyes flicked open and closed, a shadow in them growing bigger and then reducing. Lips drew back over the beast's teeth but only momentarily, as they were overlarge and disturbing.

'Have you no saddle?' Jonty stood by the side of the huge animal, his hand gliding over the silk coat.

'Sir, this horse is so well bred and schooled, you could ride him without bridle or saddle and you would feel as safe as if you and he were melded together.'

The horse sniffed Jonty's hand and in a gesture Liam thanked the Nökken for, licked the outstretched palm, tasting the mortal juices.

'Come on then, give me a leg-up!' Jonty bent his leg at the knee and waited for Liam to heft him. In moments the job was done and he sat high, gazing along an arched neck at the perfect ears.

As the horse moved forward with low, smooth strides, Liam passed his hand again, breaking the mesmer charm, leaving Jonty fully and utterly aware of every movement, every nuance in the horse's body and of everything his eyes should alight upon.

'Trot him in a circle sir, and I'm sure you will find he's the ride of your life.'

Jonty nodded, not looking at the Faeran as he turned the beast to left and right. Then he urged the animal to a canter, heading him towards the Passing.

But the beast swerved away and Jonty swore, dragging at the reins. The horse began to canter in circles, tossing his head and lifting his hind legs in agitated bucks.

'What goes?' Jonty called over his shoulder. 'The swine won't turn!'

He glanced back at Liam who stood hands in pockets and for the first time recognized him! His eyes snapped wide, his mouth opening wider as Liam laughed, irony bouncing around the clearing.

'Indeed, sir. He does have a mind of his own!'

Jonty moved to jump off, sensing incalculable danger from this cool man before him. Guts twisting, breath coming in short spurts, he tried to swing a leg over the rump, pushing his hands at the neck to give himself purchase. But he was stuck. Firmly, irredeemably. As good as if a bookbinder had melded him with book-glue. The realisation of what his mount truly was blanched his face milk-white and he turned screaming to the Faeran, spittle frothing at the corner of his mouth.

'IT'S THE CABYLL USHTEY! HELP ME, HELP ME, IT'S THE CABYLL USHTEY!'

The horse began to gain speed and headed for the side of the beck. As Jonty screeched, so the black coat became greener and the fine head thickened and broadened. The eyes opened wide, filled with madness, and the lips drew back over teeth as sharp as those of the killer whales in the Pymm waters. The weed in his mane and tail streamed as he cantered.

The Faeran watched, a satisfied glimmer around his lips and a coldness in his eyes, reminiscent of the glacial cool of the ice plains in the Goti Range.

Jonty's screams had degenerated into a mad burble of hysteria as he struggled and writhed on the broad back, the reality of his plight lending vigour to his actions. But to no avail as the more he howled and contorted, the angrier the malevolent horse became, twisting its evil head and taking bites out of the legs stuck to its sides, with Jonty screaming like a stuck pig. Already blood dripped and as the beast tasted, so it hungered for more. Circling in front of Liam, it spun quickly, snapping Jonty's head, almost breaking his neck, to launch itself at one of the dark ponds.

Abruptly, the unintelligible yowls of fear ended with a gurgling shriek as the unfortunate man disappeared on the back of the water monster, the beck closing over him, bubbles rising in a maelstrom.

Liam moved to the side of the pool, a sauntering action that did him little credit. He watched the fizz and waited, counting. In a passage of five moments, the bubbles became pink tinged and then a red-brown stain spread up and out across the surface of the pool. Small pieces of carcass drifted in the stain.

Liam had seen enough. Bellingham would never assault Ana or any other mortal again. He caught the exchanged horse and ran his hands soothingly over the damaged beast, over bloody scorings on its sides, over the sore leg. He unlatched the bridle and threw it into the beck and then cast the saddle after it. Whispering, the horse having lowered his head into the kind hands, he bade it track through the Weald and away. It would be safe.

He called for his own mount and with nary a backward glance, trotted away whistling. Uninterested in the bloody wavelets that stroked the banks of the beck and in the offal that floated back and forth.

Because whilst the Cabyll Ushtey devoured all mortal flesh, it never ever ate entrails.

CHAPTER SEVEN

Ana shivered, sporadic trembles shaking her bed as she refused her family's entreaties. Her bruises ached far deeper than a mere ague, right through to her heart which beat a solid tattoo against her chest. As she tried to think, to assimilate, she felt as if she walked a narrow path on a foggy day, the mist thickening like soup all around. The occasional shriek issued from the Weald accompanied by the call of owls as they hunted for mice to pad out their bellies. From the long field a bleat funneled upward – deep, laborious, as a solitary wandering ewe called to the rest of the flock.

A dark shade of navy coloured the night-sky, the stain unmarked by sparkle or glimmer. A crescent moon like a piece of bitten fingernail had risen earlier and tracked west. At the moment it hung delicately in the sky, a lone adornment in the vast firmament. Bad weather approached, the edges of the lunar landscape blurred as if a large and careless hand had rubbed at the outline.

Ana could only see Jonty's eyes, smell his breath, hear his voice... *betrothed, betrothed, betrothed!* Everything merged with the sight of her father as he lay lifeless on the bed. Then her mother's voice saying 'this will help.' It cascaded over her head threatening to wash her sanity away.

The prophecy, that eldritch feeling, pulled at her: *start walking, go on, walk!*

She stood up as if stung and began to cram clothing and a rug in a tote, rolling the few things tightly. A small miniature with a deft pencil sketch of her father followed, slipped down the side of the bag. Her dog Hector watched her sleepily, yawned and turned in three circles, to collapse and tuck his head firmly against his side. Ana went to kiss him, but something made her turn away – if she was to do this properly even he must be excluded from her life!

'I will not stay to marry Bellingham, and I can't stay in the same house as Ma and Peter. I can never forgive them.' Her muttering disturbed the dog and he grunted and burrowed his head deeper. She turned away propelled by hurt, to grab the bag and climb through the open window, clambering on stockinged feet across the iron roof to the horse-chestnut tree by the back of the house, to jump and land like a cat on the ground. Creeping as quiet as a shade, she let herself in the kitchen door and set about piling some food into a cloth. Muslin bags filled with some flour, a little salt, dried meat, some cheese, some windfall apples, a mug, the bread-knife. Time to be gone.

She pulled the door shut and as carefully as possible picked up her father's rowan crook with its collar of silver bells, her most suitable weapon against attack from unseelie wights, and wrapped it in her jacket so it would be silent until she was behind the stables. There was a slight tinkle that seemed to ring like the chimes of the Veniche campanile bells on the night air. She sucked in her breath for a moment, expecting Ma or Peter at the door.

Nothing!

With relief, she pulled low riding boots over the black breeches she had chosen to wear. She had knotted her hair and dragged on a dark woolen cap of her brother's – she truly was a nightshade.

A matter of moments and she was past the stables and in the middle of the long field, feet a little wet from the night dew, but surely only the first of many discomforts she must endure. Not the least of which was the hurt she felt at her family's shameless treatment of her. She would never understand, never!

Then, as she hefted the bag onto her back, having unwrapped the crook and put on the coat, her bruised breasts pulled and tugged, utterly blue and yellow as if a horse had thrown her and stomped all over her. As sharp as a goad, the pain prompted her to put her head down and continue through the pasture a quarter of a mile to the hawthorn hedge which separated 'Rotherwood' from the wildness of the Weald. She could hear the wights and trows, their eldritch voices even now casting shivers down her arms. Throwing a last look back at the shape that was her home, Ana put a foot on the stile over the hedge and began to climb.

Immediately the forest silenced. The total lack of sound crashed around her ears, more disconcerting than any noise, because for all of her life, Weald-wailing had run as a continual counterpoint to normal night sounds on 'Rotherwood'. She grasped the crook firmly and with a tinkle of the collar of bells, she jumped to the ground and doggedly continued the journey she had begun.

She had a plan. During the evening as she sat alone in her room, intermittent shivers shaking her body, she had dwelt on her mother's perfidy. Unaware of the farm's heavy crop losses, of the knife-edged finances, her grief had kept her insulated. Had she been more cognisant, she may have understood her mother's fear-driven actions a little better. Certainly she would never have countenanced a marriage to Bellingham but she may have understood the desperation. As it was she knew only that she must leave. Get as far from her mother's perceived disloyalty, from the assault, from the memory of her father's death as possible.

Whilst lying in Adelina's van, she had heard her friend and the Amritsands merchant talking of leaving at dawn. That was the solution! She would go with them. They would agree, they pitied her! She could use their sympathy as her ticket of leave and travel as far as the Raj because by the Spirits, she never wanted to return to her home. Ever! Having planned her escape, hoping to meet them on the other side of the Weald, she left no note for her family. Her loyalty was done.

The black boles of Weald trees surrounded her, leaning down over her, suffocating and ensnaring as they marched in dark, shadowy lines. Many were in the throes of discarding summer leaf and Ana's face was brushed by falling foliage, like moths on her face, or spiders. The floor of the forest crackled loudly under foot in the uncommon silence and she cast tentative glances sideways, the flick of amber eyes and the moving shape of a shade keeping pace behind the shrubs of yew and holly.

Gloom pervaded. Ana longed for lunar brightness to illuminate her path but the snippet of light which had guided her to the Weald was long gone, buried beneath the swathes of cloud drifting across the sky. A light drizzle had begun and whilst the heavy canopy of evergreen verdure protected her like a vast umbrella, every time she stepped from the shield of evergreen to the broken spaces of deciduous, her face was moistened with the lightest wetness, a kiss, a promise of weather or something else to come.

Footsteps sounded behind her, to the side of her, in front of her and her heart clanged in her chest, mouth drying. She tried to be mindful of the Weald, its tricks and vagaries. Of course there would be footsteps... the Others knew she invaded their domicile. They would track her, trick her, deceive her, grieve her. But, she thought, they can damage me no more than I have already been hurt this past month. So she tried not to care, the benefit of suffering a deeper pain blunting the edge of fear of the unseelie. To be safe, she stopped and pulled off her coat and hat, turned them inside out and put them back on again. Almost immediately she heard disgruntled whispering and the padding of feet away from her.

She longed to rest, to light a fire, to ease her remorseless aches, so she halted under the thick branches of a spruce and felt around for twigs and pine needles, kept dry by the resinous canopy. Scrabbling in her bag for the flint she had grabbed from the mantel as she left, she stroked sparks off it with a knife. Within minutes she had a tiny flame burning, the smoke hanging abjectly under the branches, adding even more to the moist fug of the night.

She chewed a windfall, mindless of the overtly sweet, autumnal flavour, staring out into the dark with her back firmly against the tree, knees scrunched up and held by one arm. The Weald had begun to speak up again, a vicious invective, but more familiar in its tone than the silence. Words flittered in the dark. Snickering, the occasional howl and eerie whispering. Ana listened, trying to determine a word or a sentence. Mostly it was an indefinable hiss, a message designed to increase paranoia and fear. Occasionally out of the sibilance, she heard *'go home, go away, begone. Or you'll be lost and forlorn.'*

'Oh, BE SILENT!'

The blackness swallowed her shout and she heard laughter, but she had the fire and the rowan crook with its precious collar of silver bells and she banged it on the ground. Its tinkling tones sent shivers over the sniggering spriggans and sprites whose task it was to unsettle her. For an hour she sat ignoring their games, defiantly shaking the crook like some odd, nocturnal morris-dancer.

Footsteps behind her jerked her head around. Close now, it sounded as if someone was infinitely weary as the steps dragged. She held her breath, lips bitten and chewed. The drizzle created a gauze like curtain of the smoke and pushing through it, seeming as if all the woes of the world sat on his shoulders, a small wizened man shuffled under the tree, offering no harm, nothing really as he neither acknowledged Ana nor asked permission to share her warmth, but merely sat himself quietly on the other side of the fire.

The Fir Deac, she thought, elated and anxious to be in the presence of an Other, oh – of small stature with long grey hair, a faded coat the colour of a raspberry and a dented black hat, it's him! Wet and shivering, he repeatedly wiped a dripping nose with a dirty scrap of fabric.

Prudently she left the little man to warm himself. If a mortal allowed him to sit unmolested in his insular pleasure in front of the flame, it was believed good luck could only follow.

He rested briefly and then stood and faced her. Saying nothing, he lay twigs on the ground and then turning, tapped his ear. Knowing to acknowledge him would destroy any beneficence, she began to stow things in her tote. The Fir Deac shuffled silently away, his eyes not having once met Ana's. She raised her eyebrows in perplexed and awed astonishment at such a strange confrontation and bent to scoop up the twigs to throw on the fire. It was then she saw the shape – an arrow and pointing away.

Puffing out a grateful breath at her good fortune, she almost forgot what else the seelie wight had done – laying his finger on his ear as though listening for something.

Ana stood still, head cocked away from the spruce tree. The Weald had lapsed into pregnant silence, waiting – and then sweet and clear, the trill of a starling, more melodious than could be imagined and harbinger of the dawn. She ducked under the spruce foliage seeking some sky. To be sure, there the sky had lightened imperceptibly. There was east!

In her room, in her grieved and injured state, Ana wondered if the Weald might be the death of her and she hadn't cared. It would have been an end after all to everything. She had certainly never imagined good will coming from this odd place. What a quaint little man she thought, full of eldritch gratitude because he was welcomed to wipe his nose in front of a fire! She pulled the tote over her shoulders and picked up her crook to head easterly, knowing Others were an intrinsic part of life and could not be avoided, just treated with cautious care.

The rolling heaviness of the Weald began to give way to clearings and spinneys. She glimpsed fields and green hills in the distance as the sun arose in a sluggish, drab way. At the foot of the green downs, she could see the grey ribbon of the Barrow Highway.

She entered a dappled glade, full of ferns and mosses – an eldritch place. A small stream tinkled over pebbles and despite the grey day, the water sparkled with invitation. Balm to Ana after the potential menace of the Weald, she wandered to a small pool, a crystalline loop to the side of the rill. Around the edge, like the perfectly scalloped hem of a Veniche robe of state, were waterlilies – moon shaped discs upon which alighted leggy leaf-dancers, their bodies and wings iridescent in the gloaming.

She knelt at the water's edge, trailing her fingers back and forth, and splashed a handful on her face. The ripples she caused reached to the outer edges of the pool, to becalm, and presently a mirror-like surface reflected an image of the surrounding elms and beech of the coppice, alight with autumnal hues.

Languorously within the deeps, a paler colour floated, filling the expanse of gold until Ana saw a white face, dark waving tresses and a sinuous body. It smiled at Ana – enticing, beguiling. And in her present state of calm, she looked deeply into the green eyes drawing her to the very edge of the pool.

She leaned closer and the face floated immediately beneath the surface and she could discern the jaw, the mouth, the cheeks and nose... of her father.

'Pa?' She whispered as she reached out a finger and traced it over the water. Her father's image smiled back lovingly. Two ripples set out in concentric circles as tears fell from Ana's cheeks into the water.

'Pa, is it really you?'

The image nodded and she blindly reached out a hand the better to stroke the face she so loved. As her hand reached down, cold, strong fingers laced around her wrist and dragged.

Mesmered as she was, she neither struggled nor shouted, merely relaxed into the deadly grasp drawing her closer to the watery grave. The visage of the figure, fully satisfied it firmly held its prey, reverted to a pale as death woman's face. Only as it smiled and revealed its jagged teeth would anyone have realised it was one of the deadly grindylow.

But the peace of the coppice broke as a masculine voice rang out. 'Lig amach do ghreim! Let go! I will destroy you!'

AS KHOLI AND I LEFT ORFORD TOGETHER, *we had no idea Ana had run foul of the deadly grindylow. If I had any idea at all of her travail, I would never have had such great excitement in the pit of my belly. For Kholi was such an attractive man! And he was so erudite, such experiences and viewpoints did he relate! I found I warmed to him as we rode along.*

A great part of our early conversation was indeed about Ana. How the young woman had obviously been tipped over the edge by her assault and run away. We believed she had run away, other doom sayers in the village felt she had left to take her own life, her state of mind a subject of great conjecture. We were asked to keep an eye out for her and of course we did, but we saw nothing and eventually concluded she had passed in another direction entirely. My heart broke that she had left her home in such circumstances, for there was a fragility about her that worried Kholi and I. We wanted to find her because we felt we had a vested interest in her and in a funny way, I felt if it hadn't been for Ana, then perhaps I wouldn't have connected with Kholi so firmly on that day at the Fair.

But it is time now to hunt for more books and you must move on, following the trail of tiny bees until you come to the tawny owl on the oak branch. He was such a rewarding enterprise with much bullion stitch in mixed silks, and buttonhole stitch around tortoiseshell beads for those wise, wise eyes. Worldly wisdom, lucky bird! Oh that we all, my friends and I, had a quarter of that wisdom. But hindsight, they say, is a useless thing.

You must, in a good light, carefully slit the stitches holding his body to the silk and underneath, you will find another book with which to continue your journey.

CHAPTER EIGHT

Liam slept soundly. Unlike a mortal, there were no profound feelings of guilt or sadness running through his head. In the typical Faeran way, he simply moved on, having removed one piece from the shatranj board. He had put his head on the pillow in his room at the Tavern, closed his eyes and slept. And would have remained so, if an accursed ruckus had not begun downstairs about an hour before dawn. Voices shouting and cursing, doors slamming, feet running. He swung his booted feet to the floor, for he hadn't bothered to undress, and opened the door of the room.

Light gleamed from the bottom of the staircase and noise levels rose. A maid ran past.

'Mistress, what goes below?'

Liam smiled engagingly at the maid, who simpered and tucked loose hair behind her ear with a spare hand, the other holding a bundle of towels.

'It's the Bellinghams, sir, something bad has happened.'

'TARA! THE TOWELS, C'MON LASS!'

The girl looked apologetically at Liam and swung away down the stairwell.

Liam followed casually, assuming that necessary Faeran skill, to see without being seen. He could waft in and out of a crowd, listening, asking questions and no one would remember him after they had answered.

A fug of smoke and steam smelling of wet wool, tobacco, horse and dog filled the room. People gabbled and shouted and asked questions, and a roar soared as a bear of a man yelled above the rest.

'QUIET, THE LOT O' YER!'

Bruin the pub-keeper stood his ursine bulk on a table. The crowd hushed on seeing his ruddy face with its long sidewhiskers. His eyes sparked with impatience.

'Let the poor men have a sup and then Jimbo, can yer tell us what yer know?'

Jimbo flushed as heads turned but he took a long swig of his ale, wiped his head vigorously with Tara's proffered towel and stood on the table next to Bruin.

'Jonty Bellingham's gone!'

Those of the muttering crowd who had been with Jimbo out in the night, nodded in agreement, burying their faces in their tankards. Everyone knew and liked Jimbo, even if he was the Bellingham's ostler.

'Go on,' Bruin nudged him.

'He didn't come home and by dark the boss were worried. So he got a group of us estate workers together and we followed the track from the farm, we took the dogs an' all.' He stopped, took another slug of his drink and wiped his mouth with the towel. 'The boss were dead set the young fella would have come home 'cos they had to organise the big announcement fer today. Anyhoo, we searched the paddocks and the hedgerows and finally got to Buck's Passing and there were a melée of horse prints as though someone had been through and the boss made us get down and search on foot and it were me...'

He stopped again and paled and put the towel to his eyes with a shaking hand. Bruin put his arm along the lad's shoulders.

'Come on, its orright.'

Jimbo smiled tremulously.

'Well you see, I found him. Well, it weren't him, it were...' he swallowed. 'Bits of him.'

A sharp intake of breath from the crowd sucked the atmosphere of the tavern dry. Liam leaned against the wall, arms folded and tapping his biceps with bored fingers.

'You see, it were the Cabyll Ushtey. Everyone knows Buck's Passing is his lair. We all take it at a gallop. Anyhoo, I didn't just find bits of him...'

'What bits?'

Someone earned a savage glare from Bruin as Jimbo's shoulders shook with a stifled sob at the question, but he bravely answered.

'His innards. You know how they always say the Cabyll Ushtey don't eat innards.' The audience nodded sagely as if they all had intimate knowledge of the water monster and his habits. 'Anyhoo, I found bits of his clothes and you could see blood washed up along the shore and not a sign of his horse.'

There was a ghastly silence filled only with the crackle of the fire and Tara swishing past Liam, and muttering under her breath.

'What did you say?' He whispered just loud enough to gain her attention and she coloured as if caught in a misdemeanor. She glanced around, surveying the otherwise engaged crowd and then leaned purposefully closer to the Faeran.

'I said no loss, sir!' Her angry eyes turned on the crowd and Liam raised a prompting eyebrow. 'He raped me. I hate him! What if I'm pregnant with his bastard? The Bellinghams'd kill me to kill the babe! Good luck to the Cabyll Ushtey I say!' Her agitated whisper hit the walls and bounced back. Liam reached out a hand and ran it down her arm, so that she relaxed as if she had honey and spirits poured into her veins, thick and warm. She continued more calmly. 'But you know, it's a blessing and a sadness in a way. The announcement Jimbo mentioned? Well, that monstrous louse was due to be publicly betrothed to my friend, Ana Lamb. Aine sir, I tell you – she's as gentle as her name and she would definitely have died under the Bellingham's care. And now she's gone and run away, all for nothing.'

Liam's interest concentrated itself fully on the girl and Tara melted like butter in the summer sun.

'Run away, you say.'

'Aye, run off in the night. Her ma and brother heard her dog howling and broke into her room to see what was amiss and the girl was gone, a bag taken, food too, her father's rowan crook gone. And no trail, for the ground was covered with drizzle. As if they didn't have enough troubles at that farm, with Mr. Lamb up and dying and a crop failure and Aine knows what else. You know what farming's like.' Tara shook her head. 'Anyway, no one can find her. The Travellers have been told and they're leaving on their way soon and will keep an eye open.' She leaned toward Liam and he bent his head down to her. 'But do you know what? If I wanted to get away from someone like the Bellinghams, I'd hide in the Weald. No one'd find you there.'

He touched her forehead like a butterfly kiss and she turned around looking for the source, but there was nothing. Her memory of having talked to Liam was gone, as was her memory of his very existence. By the time her hand had come away from her forehead, Liam was in the stable saddling his mount. By the time she was in the tavern kitchen, Liam was galloping through the village outskirts to the road skirting the edge of the Weald. He knew Ana would make for the highway, as far from the village as possible and with the Weald in between her and them. He had no doubt she believed they would not consider her brave enough to tackle the Weald at night and would look for her elsewhere, giving her time to put distance between she and the searchers. He also had no doubt the northern reaches of Eirie with its mountains, deserts and exotic locales would appeal to someone who was fascinated by the Travellers.

By dawn, the black mass of the forest was in his sights and he put his horse at a low hawthorn hedge, jumping into a lightly wooded valley that fell lazily down to the Weald. Lacing through the green folds, with tinkles and chunterings, a small stream meandered toward the dark shadows of the woods. His horse picked its way carefully along the banks, finally pushing through wild fragrantissima to a coppice that glowed gold in the weak dawn light. Trees drooped under the weight of moisture from the nighttime drizzle and those that could, shed their leaves in showers of gilt. The horse stepped delicately over autumn crocus to stop dead, throwing up its head, eyes wide, a snort rattling down its nostrils.

Liam threw himself out of the saddle and ran toward the far edge of the clearing where the stream had opened out to form a dappled pool – the kind to please the eye of an ingénue, to trap the unwary – the home of a grindylow.

A figure in dark clothes was kneeling, almost lying, by the side of the leaf-bedecked pond. A pale arm poked out of the water, hand wrapped like rope around a mortal wrist. The unfortunate anchored so maliciously was a whisker away from the watery surface. Soon the face would be under water and the unseelie wight would hold it there until the victim drowned. There would be no struggle. The wicked wights of Eirie could entice and slaughter their prey with the minimum of fuss.

'Lig amach do ghreim!' Liam shouted and the grindylow turned a snarling face toward the Faeran as his hand began a mesmer sweep, the waterlily pads curling, browning, the water beginning to steam and bubble. The water monster opened its mouth in a silent howl, letting go of Ana and swimming to the far side of the pool to grimace with jagged teeth. Kicking up a spray of water, it disappeared into the dark green depths, leaving a shaken and faint Ana kneeling at the edge, whispering 'Pa? Pa?'

'Come away. It's a charm from the grindylow.' Liam slipped a hand under her elbow.

Ana lifted a wretched face to him, eyes filled with a wracking sadness. 'But I saw him...'

'You saw what the grindylow wanted you to see so it could entrap you. Ana, you are still in the Weald. It is the playground of the Others.'

She sat on the ground, head hanging forward in her hands. From the muffled space came an enquiry.

'But you are Other, aren't you?' She looked up then, her face pale and wan.

'Yes.'

'And you won't hurt me?'

Liam stilled, a momentous silence in which his fingers moved the pawn backwards and forwards across the board. And then,

'I think not.'

She allowed him to help her up and he hoisted her bag over his shoulder. He saw her crook on the ground but unable touch it, he gestured.

'Ana, your crook. I can't...'

She bent and retrieved the carved staff, the shiver of bells casting a twin shiver over Liam. Ana saw him flinch, awed that her father's stick should have such offensive power.

'I'm sorry,' she muttered, whipping off the woolen cap, tendrils of hair flying around her face. She wrapped the head of the crook in its soft confines so the bells were silenced. 'Could I have used it against the grindylow?' She ran her fingers down the smooth wood as if touching her father's hand.

'You could if the wight hadn't put a mesmer on you. After that, you had no control over anything you did. Your crook, even though it was lying by your feet, was no protection because you couldn't hold it. Now come, I'll take you away from here.'

Liam had been guiding her gently toward his horse but she pulled back from the masculine hands, as if his touch had become repellent and repugnant in an instant.

'No!'

The Faeran eyebrows rose in response.

'It's kind of you.' She stood still, brushing the loose hair out of her face. 'But I must meet my friends on the highway in an hour.'

Her eyes dwelt on Liam's face. As he had retired the evening before, he had stared at his reflection in the mirror and wondered what she saw when she gazed upon him. Not handsome, there were prettier fellows. But the planes of his face were equal and strong and his nose was long and well-shaped and when he smiled he could charm and he believed she would feel drawn to him as iron filings to a magnet. He grinned.

'Of course. I realise you had to be here in the Weald for a purpose. Let me take you to the highway on my horse.'

She bit her lip. He could imagine her tremulous thoughts: yes, no, should I, could I?

'Come now, Ana. I am no shape-shifter. I am Faeran but my offer is harmless.' He held out the hand that yesterday had swung her off the log and noticed a faint blush on her cheeks as she reached forward with cautious fingers. 'Right then, if we can just work out how to deal with your crook, we can mount my horse and go.'

He began tying her tote to the pommel of the saddle and then turned as he caught sight of her wrestling the crook in the corner of his eye. She had taken off her coat and slipped the crook through the armholes and then re-buttoned it at her neck with the top button. It hung down her back like an absurd mantle, the arms horizontal and stiff like a scarecrow. Liam laughed.

'Well if nothing else you're resourceful. But I can't haul you up behind. Climb the fallen log over there and slide on behind me.' He jumped on his horse and guided it to the side of the temporary mounting block. With only slight difficulty, Ana slipped over the dappled back to position herself astride, arms tentatively holding Liam's waist, trying to keep the crook clear of his body.

The journey up the valley proceeded gently, the horse happy to amble with its added cargo. For a little while there was no sound from either Liam or Ana until she shifted and he reached behind and slipped a hand over her arm. She flinched.

'You're alright?'

'Yes, I'm fine.' She gave a sigh. 'I often rode like this with my Pa.'

'But I'll wager not with a crook sticking out of your shoulders.'

'No, Pa had a special sling made and it hung down his horse's shoulder so he could grab it in a hurry if needs be.'

'Ah. A Faeran horse wouldn't cope with it at all, let alone his rider.'

'What does it feel like?' Curiosity, the mortal weakness, began to assert itself.

'The crook? Well, it's rowan wood and that's a guardian timber for mortals, so it's almost like a bane for any wight. Add to that the silver bells and it feels like a flash of lightening. It burns and shocks, an anathema!'

'Can you feel its proximity?' Ana swayed with the stride of the horse, her body touching Liam's and he relishing every minute.

'Indeed. It's apparent.'

'Does it hurt?'

'Not especially,' he lied. 'Now tell me, why are you here on your own?'

Her initial silence smacked of cautious prevarication and he wondered if there was a stronger will than he had thought, perhaps not quite the easy game he hoped. Finally she replied.

'To meet my friends. I had thought to shortcut through the Weald. I was almost there.'

'Where do you plan to go?' His questions nibbled away.

'Wherever my friends wish to go. The Raj, Veniche, I don't mind.'

Liam listened to her quiet voice, enjoying the pressure of her body behind him.

'What about your family?'

Her body tensed against him, a withdrawing, a curling of the fingers at his waist, a straightening of the spine.

'They won't miss me,' was all she said.

He knew better than to prevail any further and felt her body subside. But as they reached the side of the highway, she called out in a voice filled with light.

'There!'

The Faeran's fingers clenched on his reins, face scowling briefly. He glanced down the grey ribbon of road and saw a vehicle pulled by a large horse and alongside, the shambolic shape of a camel. In his own tongue he cursed the approaching caravanserai as the nuisance he felt it was.

Interference, conversation. His lip curled. He wanted her to react to his voice like that. Bain as! Bain as!

*A*NOTHER BOOK HAS BEEN FINISHED *and you must shrink it and replace it. We must read on because there is so much I must tell you. It's as well this robe is so commodious or I would never be able to conceal the whole story.*

Move to the depiction of the fruit, the two branches arching with gooseberries, oranges, rosehips, blueberries, and raspberries. Embroidering fruit is immeasurably colourful and tactile and such pleasant stitches are used – veniche knots, satin stitch, trellis stitch and many more. As one applies the individually wrought elements to the silk of the robe, it is like attending a fruit market and picking the best, and in my current situation that becomes a small measure of comfort.

Fluttering amongst the fruit, you will see a butterfly of terracotta silk thread with aqua Veniche knots on the wings. Very, very carefully, peel the applied wing back and there you will see another book. Read on!

CHAPTER NINE

'So, Ana!' Adelina's face cooled like a weather change. Meeting up, heeding the Faeran presence, transferring Ana and her luggage, crook included, to the van was all done in a matter fact, slightly gritty way by Adelina who cast combative looks at Liam. He meanwhile, smooth as can be, kept up a pleasant patter with Kholi Khatoun, the latter fully aware he was in the presence of an Other and not unimpressed by the fact.

'Don't be angry,' Ana smiled tentatively at the Traveller.

'Angry!' Adelina slapped her hand against her thigh. 'Ana, you have no idea how worried we have all been! Aghast! When we left Orford, the whole town was about to begin a search for you. Everyone was mad with fear because... because...' she looked sideways at the Faeran stranger who chattered away to Kholi. Some dark, black notion filled her whole being and she turned quickly back to the younger woman. 'Because it was the middle of the night and everyone thought you may be dead. I really must turn round and take you home.'

'No!' Ana grabbed Adelina's arm. 'No! I am never going back, never! I just want a lift away from Trevallyn. If it's not with you, then I'll get it with someone else.' She glanced at Liam, a glance Adelina could hardly miss and her need to chaperone the woman and keep her safe from harm's way became greater than the need to overly chastise.

'Ana, there are people at home who ache with loss for you. How can you do this?'

Ana sat for a moment watching Ajax's huge shaggy mane blowing in the cool morning breeze. His ears flicked back and forth at the voiced inflections from behind him and his **tail** swayed from side to side in an equine version of a Raji dance of the seven veils.

'I can do it because I ache more than they do.' Ana spoke through gritted teeth. 'I can do it because they abrogated any familial right to my respect and affection with their actions.' She sighed and looked directly at Adelina, eyes glistening. 'And I can do it because my father is dead and I have been assaulted. Adelina, I ask you as my friend: accept my decision to leave and be my highway kin.' She touched Adelina's hand. 'Please, I can't go back!'

The Traveller put her own hand over Ana's, her face softening.

'Alright, for now. We'll talk again later. And what about him?' She jerked her shoulder in Liam's direction, hands bunched into the horn sign.

'What about him? He's Liam. He saved my life. I suppose he's a friend too.'

'Ana,' Adelina looked scornfully at her friend. 'Liam is Faeran. Yes, I realise you know this. But do you understand what Faeran means in our language? Let me see, how much time do you have? Oh, that's right, plenty!' Sarcasm fell from her lips like droplets of water onto a tranquil pool, the purpose being to set up uneasy ripples in Ana. Adelina stared at Liam with dislike, certainly disdain. 'It means danger, peril, ambush, harm, distress, deceive, terrify, frighten. All those words translate to 'Faeran' in the Travellers' tongue. I am horrified you journeyed with him.'

'Oh stop it! Look at him!' Ana glanced toward the Faeran. Liam and Kholi who were laughing together at some shared joke, so deplorably normal that Adelina's attempt at unhinging Ana's view of the Faeran looked doomed. 'He saved my life. I was by a pool and had been mesmered by a grindylow. I was a hair's breadth,' Ana measured with her fingers, 'from being drowned. He saved me, just the way Kholi saved me from… from Jonty.'

'And did he tell you that if he saves you three times, he can call in the debt. That you must live in Faeran for all eternity?' Adelina's voice stung.

'Well, so what? It must surely be better than my life has been of late.' Ana rubbed her bruises.

'Oh Ana, I am so sorry to bully you! You've been through the worst of times and it is unforgivable of me to harass you, I apologise, but it is just that Kholi and I are worried. To have an Other in such close quarters is extremely disturbing for us. Anyway, you must sit and rest, there will be time later to talk.'

As Ana took her place on the van stoop, none of Adelina's reservations eased. Ana was behaving like a hurt animal – fleeing to survive and without rational thought, for surely to have run so far from her hearth and in the presence of an Other smacked of irrationality. Adelina shook the reins over Ajax's broad back – the back broad enough to be that of the unseelie Cabyll Ushtey. And that is something else I must tell her, she thought, not relishing the task of explaining Bellingham's gruesome demise.

As they continued on their slow journey, Ajax's weighty hooves matching the ponderous stride of the camel's, Liam's fine stallion danced alongside the sapphire and emerald coloured van.

'Adelina, your van is the only beautiful thing here on this grey morning, present company excluded of course. If only the heavens could match the colour, the day would improve immeasurably.'

'Aye,' called Kholi Khatoun from high up on the swaying back of Mogu. He was swathed in his grubby cloak, the travel caplet pulled down hard on his head. 'I swear I shall freeze before I get to the Celestine Stairway.'

Liam laughed.

'My friend, you are so much a creature of the north, aren't you?' He turned back to Adelina. 'Madame, you must make him a warming posset when you stop. Unfortunately I'll not be able to share it with him for I must leave you now."

'Really.' Adelina's caustic voice was as loaded as a brewer's dray with beer-kegs. 'Then let's not keep you. Thank you for delivering our friend safely and adieu.' The teeth of any lesser being would have been set right on edge.

'Adieu to you also.' He turned his eyes to Ana, black pools drowning, drawing the pawn away from the side of the white shah's board. 'Safe journey. I'll see you anon.' He clicked his tongue and his horse sprang into a canter as he turned off the highway and headed through the valley of North Tamerton.

Adelina was aware of the rigid person beside her who followed the shape of horse and man until they were dots presently swallowed by the dark shadows of forested hills. She sighed and shook the reins again over Ajax's back.

'Kholi, shall we stop at Buckland? There's a lovely tavern and they do an excellent roast.'

'No!' Ana piped up loudly before Kholi could reply. 'No, please could we go further? I don't want to be seen. Not yet. I must get away. Please.'

I COULD SEE THIS DAY was going to be overly long so I resolved to teach Ana the rudiments of stumpwork as we trundled along, something to take her mind away from her tragedies and from thoughts of the unsettling Faeran she was patently attracted to. Kholi tied Mogu to the van and took to my bed to sleep and we swayed up the highway, seeing nothing bar the exceptional beauty of the emerald green valleys of Trevallyn. No man, nor wight, no beast nor bird bothered us. We were quite, quite peaceful. How I wish it had stayed that way forever. Fiddle dee dee, if wishes were horses and such.

CHAPTER TEN

The Barrow Hills reminded Kholi of a woman's breasts: soft mounds which in the light of the dusking afternoon took on a subtle skin colour. Immediately he began to think of Adelina and resolved to invite her to his tent when they encamped. He was a man after all... with needs, and she was a nubile woman who had indicated she found him attractive. He smiled to himself and gazed fondly at the Hills.

But there was Ana. A gooseberry? No, she could sleep in the van, a perfect solution! He mused on Ana. She reminded him of how much he missed his sister, Lalita Khatoun. She was like Lalita – beautiful, impetuous, every mood flashing across her face for all to see and he could hardly miss the way she looked at Liam. But there was still that underlying melancholia. Even now, as she sat behind him on the camel to see what it was like, he could sense a part of her withdrawn, defensive.

And Liam... a Faeran, no less! Adelina seemed almost fearful of him – she who had the courage of a war-queen! He moved his fingers in the sign of the horn, an automatic action because one should be cautious of an Other, whether in the Amritsands or not. His horn hand unfolded. But this Faeran, he seemed such an engaging fellow.

Bare moors climbed steadily higher until they opened out into the marsh-ridden territory of the Great Lakes. The occasional red-leafed tree lit up the slopes of the hills like a ruby in the cleavage of some magnificent chest. In autumn, the bright fire of that blood-red hue would have made an afrit proud. They were, after all, sprites of flame in the Raj.

Scattered across the hills were tumbled towers of some ancient defensive sort. Weathered and broken, they were decrepit remnants of times when Raji hordes were aggressive and incursive. Ana, trying to relax into the odd loping stride of the camel, stared at them.

'They remind me of my Pa's shatranj set. He had little ruhks, battlements wrought of ivory and ebony. He bought the set from a Pymm trader who had been in the Raj and he and Ma used to play at night. Every time Pa took one of her pieces, he would hum a little tune.'

She hummed against Kholi's back and he could feel the grief bleeding through to his spine. So, he surmised, it is her father who has caused this deep sadness, it is the sadness of loss. And having lost his own parents when he was younger, he could understood the awful emptiness, the fear.

'Kholi, where shall we camp?'

Adelina's rich voice called from her seat behind Ajax, causing shivers of desire to ripple through Kholi. They had come to an unusual fold in one of the hills, displaying a full circle of the ruby-leafed trees and amongst them a small stream chuntering down to the van.

'Here I think,' he looked around, surveying the glade as Mogu entered, moaning in her pitiful way. 'We'll be kindly sheltered by these trees. And the stream has no unseelie air. Do you agree?'

'No unseelie presence?' Adelina sighed with tiredness. 'Then let's stop! My rear is melded to this seat and I can't sit a minute longer. Whoa, Ajax, whoa!'

Ajax hardly needed to be bid twice, the sheen of sweat glistening under the harness. Mogu, with much groaning and spitting, folded herself to the ground enabling Ana and Kholi to ease their stiff bodies from the high horned Raji saddle.

Filled with Adelina's appetising stew and bread, chewing at a dried fig, Ana caught herself later, marveling at her good fortune. To escape, to be a Traveller, even if by default! She turned over the tiny pincushion she had embroidered that afternoon. As the needle had pushed in and out with its flaring tail of threads, she felt a small wave of happiness spreading to the dead, dry places of her soul.

Kholi erected his pavilion and Ana could hear the little bells that skirted its roof as they tinkled in the evening breeze. Melon coloured tassels swung energetically on the corners of the tent and the striped fabric ruckled and puffed as the draught teased it. Kholi wandered over and sat next to her by the fire.

'Well, my princess, there's weather coming. I can smell rain on the breeze. Early in the morn, I suspect, so we must to bed soon and be off at dawn.'

Ana didn't reply immediately, just turned the pincushion around in her hands. Then she spoke, so quietly Kholi had to sit closer to hear.

'You know, this is the only thing I've done since Pa died, of which I feel remotely proud.'

'What do you mean, shrimati?'

'My father took twelve months to die. In that time I help to wash him, feed him, I talked to him for hours, read to him, played shatranj – things which were important and practical and of which I was proud. Then he died and with him went my purpose and my identity. When he was alive, he made me feel special. Do you know,' she looked at Kholi with eyes diamond bright in the light of the fire. 'He used to call me princess too. And blossom, pet and a whole lot of other silly names that made me feel unique. But with Ma as the head of the house, I ceased to exist as a person, special or otherwise. I suffered such pain, Kholi. I liken it to being drowned in a murky swamp. Darkness everywhere. You see, Pa was my friend and wherever he was on the farm, I would always help him, even when I was tiny. Ma and Peter had no patience with me after his death because I seemed paralysed with loss. But the truth of it was that I had a cloud around my head as if I walked in a fog. I was so tired – miserable and tired and no one seemed to understand, least of all me. I just wanted someone to say I was normal, that what I was feeling was normal, but no one did. And then I just wanted to think of nothing because if I thought, it would be of Pa and this pain would crush me,' she hit her chest with a bunched fist, 'and sometimes my thoughts seemed like a donkey harnessed to a grinding wheel, going round and round.'

She returned her eyes to the pincushion.

'When I was embroidering, nothing else pierced my brain. And it was the same when I left home. I had a purpose, to get away. And I thought of nothing else. So you see, leaving was the best thing I could do, for me.'

Kholi took her hand and rubbed it.

'Indeed, my princess. But demons have a habit of riding unseen on your back. It's best you acknowledge your grief and love your father, don't run from it. I think that's what your mother is doing. Run, run, run!'

Kholi made pumping motions with his arms as if the Wild Hunt were behind him. 'She won't acknowledge how threatened she feels by the loss of her husband.'

'My mother!' Ana's voice scalded the cool night air. 'My mother has run from nothing! She is Mrs. Lamb, landswoman! She didn't even run from the horror of betrothing me to Bellingham! Any normal mother would have run a million miles from that!'

'But Ana, let's think on that for a minute.' With a swish of her skirts and tossing of hair over her shoulder, Adelina had joined them, passing each of them a glass of muscat, which glowed gold in the firelight. Pausing to light a cheroot, she sucked on it and then blew out a perfect smoke ring occasioning a lift from Kholi's eyebrow.

'The Bellinghams are rich, aren't they?'

'Yes...'

'Was your farm in trouble?'

'No, I don't think so. I'm not sure.' Ana looked down, disconcerted. 'I didn't listen to Ma and Peter at night. I would go off on my own. I know we had a spell of footrot and I think there was a crop failure and I suppose Fiona's dowry won't help that much because she's the daughter of a landsman and she has three other sisters, so the dowry chest would be fairly small.'

'So?' Adelina turned up her hands enquiringly, the cheroot glowing as the breeze brushed past its tip.

'We were unable to hold our sales at the beginning of summer because of the footrot. And sales on the wheat came to nothing because we had no wheat to sell.'

'And I am guessing,' Adelina took another puff and then flicked the exhausted cheroot into the fire, 'this would involve the loss of substantial income?'

Grudgingly Ana nodded. She flushed, irked to find guilt pressing heavily as Adelina unconsciously pinpointed her disinterest in her family's trials, that lost as she was in her own grief, she had neglected to wonder how Ma, Peter and her father's legacy of 'Rotherwood' were coping.

'Well then, you can understand why your mother would betroth you to a wealthy family in desperation, can't you?'

'To a point.' Ana spoke sharply. ' But not to the Bellinghams! There are other wealthy sons in our district.' Anger flared. 'Honestly! The man was set to rape me and would have if you, Kholi, had not happened along! Why are you taking my mother's side? What about me?'

'But Ana, maybe Bellingham made an offer too good for your mother to refuse.'

'Too good?' Scorn sound like a cymbal clash. 'Too good to ignore me being assaulted? Too good to ignore Jonty's reputation? Do you know he raped a friend of mine? Aine, Adelina, how could she do that to her own daughter?'

'Because I suspect she was utterly desperate and afraid she would lose her family's farm, her home, her loved husband's legacy, that she, you and Peter may end in the Poorhouse. And now she is even more desperate, having lost you. I am not condoning her choice, muirnin, not by a long shot, but I think I can see what she was trying to do. As Kholi says, I think she is mired in her own grief and is thinking only as clearly as her emotions will let her. As you are. Please Ana, will you not return?'

'Never! To marry that... that...'

She fell silent and her hands shook. Kholi reached for them and held them in his own large ones, aware the assault was even now coursing through her memory.

'But, my dear princess, you would not have to marry him. You see, he's dead.'

The fire crackled and spat and lines of sparks drifted into the night sky.

'When, how?' Shock reduced Ana's reply to a faint whisper.

'Last night.' Adelina replied, shifting herself to sit on a convenient log, closer to Kholi. 'He didn't return to his home and a search party found his remains at Buck's Passing.'

'What do you mean, his remains?'

Adelina sat for a moment, visions of her dark, black notion and the ugly water horse filling her head.

'It's believed he was a victim of the Cabyll Ushtey.'

Ana's hand flew to her mouth and her eyes widened in horror. But then a grey shadow passed over her face, eyes as cold as iron, mouth bitter and grim – like watching a winter frost harden, Adelina thought.

'It's no loss. He deserves his end. Besides, it just happened quicker than fate would have decreed had I married him. Because by the Napae, I would have killed him myself, I tell you. I hate him!'

'Ana!' Adelina admonished.

Kholi raised his eyebrows and scrutinized the young woman's eyes, seeing a desperate hunger for vengeance. This girl was troubled, and no wonder, he thought as he reached for her hand. Abuse of any sort bruised a tender psyche.

'See, little shrimati,' he said kindly. 'There's no need for you to stay away from your family now. You can return.'

'No!' She was adamant. 'If nothing else this whole event has just propelled me to be a master of my own destiny, not my family's. Don't you see?' She looked at her friends, her eyes pleading for understanding. 'My family don't respect me, they have ignored my hurts. They have! I so desperately needed them when Pa died, let alone after Jonty,' she shuddered. 'And anyway,' her voice softened. 'I am a woman. Whatever happened, ultimately I would have left home. To marry, perhaps to work on another estate. I have just brought the leaving to fruition sooner. And without the entanglement of an unsuitable match.'

CHAPTER ELEVEN

Around the campfire, the companions brooded. Then Kholi shifted and slapped his thighs with his palms.

'You shall stay with us, sweet Ana. We'll mind you, won't we Adelina? For the moment, so rest easy.' He cast a look at the woman he wanted to love and saw her eyes narrow but then she nodded as she reached for the young woman's shoulder and gave it a rub. Ana looked at them both and gave them a tentative smile.

Kholi clapped his hands together.

'Enough of this soul-baring and heart-creasing talk! I'm going to tell a story. Would you like that, my sweet ladies? Kholi Khatoun can turn his hand to stories as easy as he can sell rugs. We have a collection, we in the Raj, of the most wonderful stories called A Thousand and One Nights. I am going to tell you the one we call The Historic Fart!'

'Kholi Khatoun!' Adelina laughed with delight, her eyes glowing in the light of the flame.

Kholi began.

'In the Amritsands there lived a wealthy merchant called Abu Hasan whose money was made selling rugs and mats. Hmm! Just like Kholi, don't you think?' His eyes sparkled and then he looked wistfully into the flaring red and yellow flames. 'But Abu Hasan tired of the nomadic life,' Kholi looked down at his hands and then cast a long glance at Adelina. 'Just like Kholi.' But then he grinned.

'So he became a wealthy town merchant with a prosperous shop, a beautiful wife and a big house with a view over the town all the way to where the Amritsands glimmered in the distance. He was young, Abu Hasan, and would always offer up thanks to the spirits of good fortune when he sat on his roof on a Raji rug, smoking a hookah and enjoying the spoils of wealth.'

Kholi shifted on the log on which he sat and turned to the two women.

'But life is never simple, is it?' He looked directly at Ana. 'Just when he thought things were at the peak of perfection, his lovely wife died. Just like that.' He snapped his fingers. 'And Abu Hasan fell into a black pit of despair, grief stricken and lost. His friends worried for him and after a suitable time had passed, chivvied the young widower to marry again. The town matchmaker was put to work and she found a lovely woman who, whilst not competing with his first wife for sheer beauty, was nevertheless somewhat of a desert bloom.'

Kholi stood up and walked around the fire, assuming a position in front of the women, like a bard in front of an audience. His hair shifted in the lazy breeze and his robes blew and creased gently around him, creating the image of some exotic man of legend – perhaps even Abu Hasan himself.

'Abu Hasan organized a massive wedding feast whilst the bride, whom he had not yet seen, went into seclusion where she was fêted and served by the women of the town. They would come from her chambers and taunt Abu with florid descriptions of the desert flower's attributes. He found himself looking forward to the wedding greatly.'

'Kith and kin came from all across the Raj and Abu Hasan provided a wondrous feast in the biggest tent the town had ever seen. There were five different types of rice, sherbets, curries, goats stuffed with figs, dates and almonds and sprinkled with cumin and cardamom. There was lamb tagine and fish stuffed with walnuts and pistachios. Everyone ate until robes and cords, tassels and sashes had to be undone and re-girded as middles expanded.'

'Finally it was time for the groom to be summoned to the bedding chamber. He rose from amongst the guests at the table, pulling his silk robes around, the epitome of dignity and assurance. But as he stepped away from the tables, he let fly with the biggest, loudest, most ripping fart that had been heard in all of the Raj. In fact it was said that even the camels at the Kosi-Kamali oasis stood up with concern as it flew on the air.'

Adelina and Ana chuckled as the images of the desert merchant's embarrassment filled their heads. Kholi looked at the woman he adored and he wondered if she had any idea of how seductive she appeared. He raised his eyes to the skies, offered a small prayer and then continued.

'The guests, hiding smiles and guffaws, talked loudly, pretending not to have heard. Abu Hasan was mortified, excusing himself as if to go to the watercloset. Hastily the poor man ran to the stables and saddling his horse rode away from the town, weeping copiously.'

'He took ship for the far away coastlines of the Raj and was employed by a kaffir for ten years as his most trusted bodyguard. But finally, desperate homesickness got the better of him and he slipped away, to return to the town of his previous life. To see if people remembered the Abu Hasan from before the fart, not after.'

Again giggles filled the encampment, but Kholi held up a hand for silence and continued.

'On the long and arduous travail, he endured a thousand hardships of hunger, thirst and fatigue and a thousand dangers from lions, snakes and afrits. If I detailed them all, my ladies, we would be here for the passing of one or two more nights, I can tell you. Suffice to say, in every travail, his strength and honour prevailed, but at great cost to his body and maybe, just maybe, even more to his spirit.'

'Nearing the town, he was unrecognizable. He looked very different after ten years and more, as well as with his most recent trials, and so he had occasion to wander unknown and unmolested for seven days. Finally as he leaned against a wall, tired but remotely hopeful, he heard a young girl talking to her mother.'

'Mother, tell me what day I was born so that I may have my fortune told.'

The mother answered. *'My child, you were born on the very night when Abu Hasan farted.'*

Ana and Adelina exploded. Even Kholi, who knew the story as well as he knew the lines on the palm of his hand, chuckled. The very air around the fire sparkled with conviviality and good humour

'The poor man fled, crying to himself,

Verily my fart has become a date! To be remembered forever and ever. And so Abu Hasan, the great merchant and then the famed and esteemed bodyguard returned to the lonesome, singular existence he had experienced as he had journeyed back to his town. He travelled all around

Eirie, in self imposed solitary exile, never speaking, never spoken to, until he died somewhere in the dry Amritsands.'

Kholi folded his hand across his middle and gave a theatrical bow.

'Kholi,' Ana clapped her hand delightedly, 'you have missed your calling.'

'Indeed.' Adelina's eyes darkened and her face flushed as she looked at Kholi. He watched her pull gently on Ana's arm and wished on the djinn of good fortune that his prayers would be answered.

'Come now Ana, it's time for sleeping. I propose for you to use my bed and I have a wish to sleep in Kholi's tent. I have never slept under canvas and I have often wondered if it should suit me.'

'Oh no. I couldn't force you from your bed, Adelina. I shall just roll myself by the fire,' Ana walked to the van, 'I'll get my blanket.'

'No, I insist. Sleep in my bed.'

'But what about Kholi? He'll be forced from his bed.'

Kholi shook his head vehemently.

'No he won't.' Adelina looked steadily at Ana.

'Oh... oh! I see. I'm sorry!' In the light of the fire it could have been a blush or the light of the flames that spread across the young woman's cheeks. She hastily kissed her friends on their cheeks and went to the van. As she left throaty chuckles followed, not unkindly. Her cheeks flamed even brighter.

AND THUS KHOLI AND I BECAME LOVERS. Little more needs to be said just now because you must move to the next piece of embroidery, the next part of the hunt. Have you spotted the second group of arched branches? You must follow the berries until you reach the palest gold gooseberries. Very, very carefully lift the wired leaf under which is the spiders' web. If you carefully feel beneath the leaf, you will find another book. See how I bound its covers in washi paper from the Raj in exactly the colour of the leaf? There is a reason.

This whole task has been an exercise in subterfuge and camouflage. Perversely, despite my current predicament, it gives me pleasure. To be cunning, to be capricious... to tell my story. Thank Aine, because life would be intolerable otherwise.

CHAPTER TWELVE

The morning dawned. Pale light wound under Ana's eyelashes – probing, awakening. She washed away the last remnants of sleep with cold water from the jug on the counter and opening the door to the van, was confronted with an oyster coloured morning, the sky beyond the trees like a piece of Veniche taffeta. Swathes of grey veined the sky as if someone had poured a darker shade over the lighter shade and dragged a marbling comb through. Kholi was right – it would rain before the morning was past.

Approaching the pavilion quietly for fear she would wake the occupants, she need not have worried. Adelina's husky voice, thick with the passion with which it was becoming more endowed by the minute, murmured forth.

'Kholi Khatoun, would you give me breakfast in bed? After all, you gave me supper in bed last night?'

Kholi chuckled. The pavilion was lit softly from within as he struck a tinder and lit a small lamp. Their figures became illuminated like a shadow puppet show.

'Like this you mean?'

His standing figure lowered itself over the reclining woman, who in silhouette, reached arms up to grasp the man.

'Indeed. I shall have shaslick and you shall have oyster.' Her laugh was cut off as the pair kissed.

Ana turned away sharply. Her face put the glowing autumn trees to shame. As silent as a wraith, she hurried away from the clearing, heading up the Barrow Hills and as far from the encampment as possible. She needed time and space to think, to decide if she could continue the journey with this couple who obviously found themselves in the throes of new lust, if not love. What else would she be but a nuisance, a third wheel, a gooseberry?

Puffing as the incline steepened, she stopped briefly to survey the globe-like hills. Rumour had it in Trevallyn, that the hills were actually sidh, home of the Others. Looking down at her feet, at the stubble and the unprepossessing tussocks that spiked the ground here and there, Ana could hardly imagine the Others occupying such a plain home. Certainly not the Faeran anyway. Folk-tales told of being able to find a gate to the Faeran world – by passing a coat between one's self and the view of a likely place. Or by finding Ymp trees, those lines of peaches and apricots that had been pleached together to form long twisted bowers, pruned beyond natural growth and therefore the perfect gateway to Faeran.

Ana was fully aware of the price of venturing into the Others' world: the loss of one's self, belonging neither here nor there, but dimmed by the longing for both. But she would, she knew, long for nothing if she was with Liam – absolutely nothing! She wondered if he would ever display the uninhibited devotion of Adelina and Kholi toward her and a tiny part of her became anxious at the thought that perhaps Liam merely lusted after her. She was after all only a mortal, surely only a plaything of the Others, and Faeran seldom exhibited long-lasting devotion.

Such staunchly held life-long emotion was what she missed with her father's death. Truth to tell, it was why she was on the road. She was searching for someone to fill the gap in her life. There could never be a replacement for her father but was there not someone special for everyone in the wide world? It was what her Pa had told her once whilst describing the breadth of his love for his family. She turned her gaze up the hill and spotted one of the tumbled peel towers that so reminded her of the ruhks in her father's shatranj set. Its walls crumbled and folded onto the ground but there was enough to see it was once a handsome little building, castellated as it no doubt had been.

As Ana approached the door, drizzle tickled her face, what her father had called 'wet rain', which Ana as a young child had always found amusing.

'But Pa,' she would giggle, 'all rain is wet.'

'Ah, but pet,' he would reply running a hand through her damp, frizzled hair. 'Mizzle-drizzle seeps and sighs right into the very skin. Until it makes one puckered and wrinkled as a dried out old prune!'

The drizzle on the Barrow Hills was becoming more determined, fogging the landscape with a wet wash. The first drop of something heavier hit Ana's forehead and she decided to shelter for the moment in the tower. Her hand reached for the wrought knob of the old door but as she grasped it, a singular puff of wind slid past – dragging wetness and damp with it and blowing open the growling door.

She jerked her fingers back quickly as if burned and stood tentatively surveying the glum shadows. But the windswept rain pushed her further through the entrance, her footsteps echoing around an interior that cloaked her in shadow. Shafts of grey daylight squeezed through arrow slits in the walls. She negotiated her way across a stone and beam-strewn floor, shrieking as a rat scampered past her feet and her face brushed some lacy, sticky web.

Backing away, feet disturbing a cloud of dust and shards of stone, she located a stair clinging with determination to the weeping walls and began to climb. Her hands grazed the supporting walls, mildewed and spongy under her fingers. Creeping centipedes and millipedes no doubt haunted the deep cracks where aged mortar had crumbled to dust and she shuddered with distaste, imagining them sliding across her fingers in the gloom.

Another cobweb brushed her face, a spider sliding moodily away to the other side of the web to glare at her. Ana jumped up two steps to get away from it, her heart racketing like a moth's wings against glass.

A sound ground out faintly from above and the moth's wings froze briefly.

'Hallo... who's there?'

A crushing noise filled the tower subfusc, as though wheat were being crushed rhythmically by a quern. Ana thought someone must be on the floor above her.

'HALLO!' She called again, louder. The grinding stopped momentarily and then started again almost above her head. She could imagine a pair of hands rolling the round stone back and forth, back and forth over the grain as it lay in its shallow bowl. She jumped up the steps quickly and rounded a corner of the tower as the milling noise continued, looking above rather than at her feet and failing to notice one complete step had crumbled so that she fell, cracking her shins. Swearing and rubbing her leg, she rounded the next bend. Reason told her this dark, crumbling tower was no place to pursue idle curiosity. Dim light and damp air were hardly the stuff of interest. But then Ana was mortal and curiosity has ever been a mortal's downfall and the young woman was so very incautious and naïve.

The milling now was as loud as if she were in the presence of a dozen bakers' wives as they patiently ground millet or wheat. Despite the precarious nature of the tower, Ana's head filled with the delights of fresh flour and hot bread, blotting out caution as her stomach grumbled. When she placed her hand on the door timbers she felt the vibrations of grinding through her fingers. Somewhat fruitlessly, she called again, in the vain hope someone would be there and she could talk, pass the time of day, maybe have breakfast as the rain continued outside.

'Hallo there, can you hear me?'

The vibrations continued.

The handle to the door in front of her was curiously wrought to represent a hand bunched into a fist and in the weak drizzle-filled light slanting through the arrow slits, it glistened dully with the patina of aged bronze. Ana's hand reached forward and she grasped the knob.

'DON'T, ANA! DON'T TOUCH!'

But too late! The bunched metal fist had sprung open and the cold fingers grasped Ana's hand tightly and the cramped, tumbled room echoed with a scream. The latch clicked and the door began to move outwards allowing a chink of oyster light to slide through.

'HELP! HELP ME!'

The momentum of the opening door dragged Ana to a sheer drop some hundred or more precipitous feet off the wet ground outside. She glanced down in terror, toes gripping the floor, feet sliding and leaving a trail behind in the dust as she glimpsed the glistening saw-toothed stones lying where they had landed as they crashed from the decrepit building. Spread-eagled across the rocks lay white-washed bones – the remains of a back that had been cracked and broken from where the curious living mortal, like Ana, had been dragged by the door into the ether beyond. The harsh snap and crack of her own frame as it landed on the boulders filled a head empty of everything but the need to struggle.

'OH PLEASE! HELP!'

Her toes hung over the edge of the tower as the door kept up its remorseless tugging, her free hand trailing desperate fingers on the door frame, dragging splinters and dirt to fill her fingernails. She screamed again as an arm snaked around her chest and pressure pulled the other way.

'LET GO!' Liam shouted in Faeran to the malevolence dragging Ana to a shattering death.

'Never, no, never more!
See what happens when you open the door!'

Liam's arm came up sharply and an amber flash filled the door space. A shriek dropped from above and there followed a spattering of sharp footsteps running across the old shingles of the tower roof.

He pulled Ana's body back hard against his chest, dragging her on her feet away from deathly space. As the footsteps and the yelling faded away, the bronze fingers of the doorknob fell open and released Ana's hand. The door slammed shut and the hand was seen to give a lewd gesture to the pair before rolling itself into a bunched, inanimate doorknob.

Ana sagged in the circle of the Faeran's arms, her own curling over his as they wrapped tight around her. From behind, she felt his chin rest on her head and then…

'Alright?'

She nodded and was sure she felt a kiss through her tumbled hair, burning into her scalp. The timbre of her heart rushed as she bent her head and rested her own lips on the damp moleskin of his coat. The heady intimacy of the moment was not lost for a minute on either of them and a fulsome silence filled the damp space.

Finally, Liam took her hand and pulled her towards the stairwell behind him. She followed like a dutiful child.

'They were dunters,' he said over his shoulder as they made their descent. 'Unseelie beings whose sole purpose is to entice the unwary and curious to their deaths from the top of any tower they inhabit.' They reached the entrance to the tower without Ana uttering a word. 'Why were you here and where is your rowan crook?'

Despite the shock, Ana sensed an edge to Liam's voice, not unlike Ma when she was concerned the child Ana may have put herself at risk in some activity. In those days, Ana felt wanted and cherished by her whole family. Wanted and cherished. Perhaps Liam…

She replied hastily, before a blush coloured her frightened cheeks too much.

'I forgot it. I left camp in a hurry.' She sat down on a pile of stones, legs folding and Liam sat down beside her.

'Why did you do that?'

'Um... Adelina and Kholi...' Ana blushed again.

'Yes?'

'Were... making love. I saw them!'

'Did you, by Aine! Did they see you?' Liam laughed with apparent delight. Ana jumped up, indignation rampant.

'You're laughing! How could you? IT WAS SUCH AN INTIMATE MOMENT! As laden with sex as anything could be!' Humiliation, reaction, anger, all touched the taper.

'Ana, Ana.' He grasped her shoulders. 'It is the most natural thing in the world for two people who are so attracted to do what they did. Don't take on so.'

'So easy for you to say! No doubt Faeran do it all the time, willy-nilly! I however, was embarrassed, profoundly so! And because of their little love-nest I feel I shall have to leave and that goes a long way to spoiling all my plans! Aine I hate this world! Everywhere I turn people I trust fail me! Pa, Ma, Peter! And now I can't even trust my only two friends. This whole world is immoral and obscene!' She pushed her hair away from a red face.

'Have you finished?' Liam raised his eyebrows.

She growled at him, a rising crescendo, and stormed off towards camp.

CHAPTER THIRTEEN

Adelina and Kholi lay comfortably side by side, the drizzle making a shushing sound on the canopy of the pavilion.

'Ana is very quiet.' Kholi offered the few words into the soft ambience.

'It will do her good to rest. She's had momentous times.'

'She's a sweet thing, Adelina, but she is not world hardened, is she?'

'You're so polite, Kholi.' Adelina laughed, a throaty chuckle. 'Naïve, young and immature are better words. And fragile. There is a brittle shell to her, as if one more tap will be all it will take to smash it to pieces. She just seems to have been unable to rationalize all that has happened to her.'

'And why should she? The death of a parent, then the assault. I think you expect too much.'

'Maybe. But that is what causes her fragility and she lurches from one bad idea to another – running from her home, joining up with the Faeran. Aine, the Faeran! I have tried to impress upon her the dangers of Others and she almost laughs in my face. And all the time, that Faeran gets closer and closer to her. Her life now depends so much on her growing up very fast. And to be honest, she has no one but you and I to teach her. She certainly won't return to kith and kin.'

'Is it so bad that she has Liam as a friend?'

'A friend! Huh! He wants her as a plaything, mark my words, and what happens to a Faeran plaything, Kholi? Tell me that!' Adelina poked Kholi in the chest, whereupon he grasped the offending fingers lightly, kissing them, as she tried to wrap herself in a robe.

'Don't be so hard on him, Adelina. I believe there is something deeper than play in his eyes. Amusing, isn't it? That a mortal should so ensnare a Faeran?'

'Ah, my Kholi, you're such a romantic! Amusing? Fiddle dee dee! If only it were amusing it would save a lot of angst, we could just sit back and watch! But just say you are right,' Adelina continued as they walked to the van, 'and he does care for Ana. Even so, in my heart I feel a doom if they continue on such a path, an intuition, and Kholi, you can't deny Travellers' intuition, we have a reputation for it. As Ana's friends, I think we must do all we can to protect her and teach her to protect herself.' She raised her foot to step into the van.

'Then you had best teach her about every single unseelie being in the whole of Eirie!'

'LIAM!' Kholi's face split into a grin that vanished faster than water on the Amritsands as he looked at Adelina's face. Disgruntled to see the subject of her dislike standing before her, she was furious when the subject of her concern walked out from behind the black clad body.

'Ana! We thought you were in bed. Where have you been?' The Traveller swung around in a blaze of copper and fixed the Faeran with a fiery eye. 'What have you done, Faeran?' Her gaze intimidated, daring him to play the next move. Unaware of the opposition between Adelina and the Faeran, Ana fired back.

'He saved my life, Adelina. That's what he has done. So get off your high horse with him, because you weren't around to save me, you were busy making love to Kholi!'

Adelina flushed red at Ana's bald argument. For a moment she was tempted to shout the chit down. How dare she? Am I her keeper? But then yes, maybe that is exactly what Kholi and I are, she thought. By default. She looked at Ana through eyes that had closed to slits. Perhaps not the innocent little lamb we imagined! She raised her eyebrows and shrugged, giving in graciously.

'So what happened?'

The story of the dunters was related and the part Liam had played in returning Ana to her fold. Kholi, to underline what they had just heard, recounted a poem:

*Invidious rust corrodes the bloody steel
Dark and dismantled lies each ancient peel.*

*Afar, at twilight gray, the peasants shun
the dome accursed
where deeds of blood are done.'*

'Oh exactly!' Ana shuddered. 'I shall never look at the ruhks on a shatranj board again, I swear!'

Adelina, thinking strategically, busied herself preparing breakfast and then sat beside the Faeran whilst Kholi and Ana harnessed the animals and packed up the encampment.

'It was fortunate you were there, Liam. One wonders whether you actually left us at all yesterday.'

'I did. But I returned.' He offered nothing to Adelina to explain his comings and goings and she hated not knowing. Still, he was Faeran – they made an art form of secrecy.

'You have saved her twice now.'

'Indeed.' The Faeran eyes betrayed little at all as they gazed back at Adelina. It was as if Ana's flagrant support of him in the face of the Traveller's dislike added grist to his mill and she could see he was determined not to let her disturb his equanimity. She worried on though, like a dog with a bone.

'Once more and you are within your rights to demand your forfeit. It is the way of the Others, is it not?' Acid tainted her voice.

'Yes. It is the way.'

'Shall you then?'

Liam sighed, ever the bored dilettante.

'Well, Adelina, that depends on two things. Firstly that Ana should need saving. And secondly, that I should want to call in the forfeit.'

'Oh come now! I've seen the way you look at her. There can't be any doubt.' Adelina's voice held a touch of scorn.

'You may think so.'

She ground her teeth. Still no point to her, not yet anyway!

AND SO, MY FRIEND, for I think you are that now you have come this far with me, you can see how the game began to sharpen, that the Faeran and I had truly sized

each other up. And he was good, so good!

But you and I, we have come to the end of this latest book. Conceal it in its hiding place and seek the little Raji man with his hand upraised and curled as if to hold something. He of the striped red and yellow silk pantaloons and the red fez.

I shall tell you something. Ana made him. It breaks my heart to see the Raji because it reminds me of her and of Kholi. You see, Kholi Khatoun had told us the story of Aladdin's Lamp and Ana decided to make a stumpwork Aladdin and of course she used Kholi as the model. Although I must say Kholi is... was... much more beauteous.

You will notice I speak in the past tense about him. Remember that. It is why I sigh and cry as I tell you to gently remove the little fez and feel inside for another book. It is a red one. Red silk. Red, the colour of marriage in the Raj...

CHAPTER FOURTEEN

The journey took on a rhythm for Ana – gathering food, cooking and cleaning, whilst Kholi and Liam fed the animals and made camp each day. Then as they travelled along the tracks and trails of the Barrow Hills, she would take her own sewing basket, a gift from her mentor, and assist in basic embroidery.

The Traveller had unfolded a length of rose coloured taffeta and cut it into the pieces of a gentleman's vest and she and Ana were now working a design of fruit and beetles down the lapels on either side. The beetles of course, needed intricate skill beyond Ana's simple expertise but she was quite able to stitch the beautiful fruits and leaves Adelina required. And many an hour was spent in quiet contemplation of wires, silken threads and needles.

But sometimes the two companions sat together on the van's wide step, embroidery lying in a heap by their sides, watching Ajax's vast bay rump swinging from side to side, their eyes straying further afield, to admire the men in their company or to admire the scenery. Both activities engendered feelings of contentment.

It was almost possible to forget Liam was Faeran. He had not disappeared since the episode with the dunters and he set about chores just like a mortal, complaining if the animals were unobliging or if he himself was hungry, delighting in the food given to him at meals, telling stories of his travels. He carefully removed any mystic references in the telling, it seemed to keep Adelina calmer, and he chatted in a typically masculine way with Kholi, about horses and races and money and 'get rich quick' schemes. It was believably normal.

Adelina and Kholi slept in the pavilion at night, Ana slept in the van and Liam, by his own preference, slept rolled in a black swag under the night sky, by the fire. If it drizzled in the evening, he would roll his swag under the van and sleep there.

For the first time in a long while Liam was content.

This night he lay gazing at the diamond light playing in the heavens. Beside him the fire crackled in a desultory way, sparks drifting skywards. From the pavilion came the sound of whispers and Liam could not help listening to what he presumed would be the mortal language of love. Rather disturbingly, it proved otherwise.

'I tell you, Kholi, I am still concerned. There's something about him...'

'Hush now, Adelina. You don't want him to hear.'

She lowered her voice further and Liam stood up and crept closer to the pavilion.

'How many stories do I have to tell you about Faeran to convince you that he is no different.'

'Quite a lot it would appear, shrimati.'

Kholi's dry response brought a faint curve to Liam's lips. By the Spirits that woman was a worthy adversary! Liam's eyes sparkled in the firelight as he thought of the game of possession. After all, in essence that was all that shatranj was. He listened again as Adelina ploughed on regardless.

'Then have you heard what happened to the Baron of Pymm? He was married to the one love of his life and the day before their wedding anniversary, he rode out into the forest of Fenian on Pymm to find white fritillaria that he knew the Baroness adored. He rode for two or three hours and became thirsty, so stopped by a Fenian rill to drink. As he sipped the cold, clear water a korrigan appeared and you no doubt know they are the Pymm family of Faeran and like all Faeran she was beyond beautiful and brought all her persuasion to bear. For drinking her water – the korrigan always claim the lakes, streams and fountains are theirs – she desired him to sleep with her. He of course, being desperately in love with his wife, angrily refused and the korrigan cursed him as he rode away, dooming the Baron to his death within three days. He choked, poor man, on a fishbone at his anniversary banquet and the distraught Baroness herself succumbed to a broken heart and was buried not long after, next to husband.'

'A sad story, shrimati.'

Liam heard Adelina take a huge breath.

'My point is the korrigan is symptomatic of the rest of the Faeran – selfish, cold and infinitely dangerous.'

'Adelina, I can see you may be right. I had heard vague rumours of the Baron's death. But I do think we would be hasty to attribute such mannerisms to Liam as he has done nothing yet of which we can accuse him. Time will tell, don't you think?'

Liam heard Adelina humph and he returned to his place by the fire. She was right – the korrigan had damned the Baron to an early death, it was well known. Part of him couldn't give a fig for the love-lorn man, but then part of him wanted these mortals into whose lives he had inveigled himself, to trust him just a little, maybe to like him... to believe that he could never act as the korrigan had done – an odd series of thoughts and ones he swiftly turned away from.

He wrapped himself in his swag and lay back. From the van came the sound of Ana's tiny music box, its exquisite tune tinkling out into the night air. It sounded like a Faeran gittern and Liam was dragged much against his will to remember the people he tried so hard to banish from his life.

Liam was a second son. One would think under normal circumstances that being a second son is an undemanding thing – there is no inherited sinecure, so there is no pressure.

Not so for Liam. Born into a noble Faeran family, the family must bear itself in a certain way. If that wasn't enough, Liam's brother had vanished as a babe. Nothing was said, but Liam had heard the lesser Faeran talking maliciously. His mother had partaken of one of the Faeran progressions, a rade, through Eirie. Tired of the demands of pregnancy and the new babe, desperate to play, she had been determined to join this progress. And so she had, against her husband's orders, stowed the infant in one of the panniers carried by the musicians' horses.

In the beginning she had been quite resolute, feeding the child, seeing to its needs before her own, all the things a good mother would do. But the Faeran are selfish and soon she began to neglect the infant in favour of good times. This little babe, Liam's sibling, was placid beyond belief – rarely crying, and thus the mother all but forgot about it. Which culminated most sadly in the babe being left behind one day as the progress continued.

It is a common enough event amongst the Faeran – for self-indulgence to cause children to be misplaced. Liam's father was wrathful and searched fruitlessly for the child. But like any of the Others in Eirie, it truly seemed to have vanished into thin air, so in a fit of rage he got another child on the mother, to her despair and horror.

It is well known that all Faeran have banes, be they met at fifty years or five hundred. If they did not, considering they are immortal, the world would be over-run with these exceptional people. It was the mother's misfortune to have as her bane, her second son. She died in childbirth, mourned only by her own vengeful mother. The heartless husband cared only that he had another son to carry the family name. This babe was Liam and his father, to make up for the dilatory behaviour of the mother, would watch the son like a hawk, till Liam felt like prey – tracked and trapped. Thus as a grown man, he would disappear as often as his father's back was turned. To wander the mortal world of Eirie and seek some amusement and compensation to give his life the dimension he felt it lacked.

He strayed from Faeran for long periods, disinterested in the fecklessness of his peers and on his return would engage in a fruitless and violent brawl with his father over nothing and everything. Most recently he had stayed away longer than ever, distance proving a panacea to his ills, and found on his return that his father had met his own bane. A moth alighting on the man's hand had left some of its precious wing dust behind… and that, by virtue of its poisonous qualities, did for his father. Unusually, because in Faeran there are no moths, only butterflies.

Liam walked away from his father's death blandly, no sense of love or loss distorting into grief. Which was why he felt such prodigious amazement at the sensations he was experiencing in the mortal world. He endeavoured to see things through mortal eyes, pushing his senses to experience everything in the mortal way. The extremes, from pain to love, were almost masochistic. He reveled in them. For to be a Faeran was surely to have one's senses dulled forever by excess.

And here was the nub of it and why he wanted to keep Ana in his sights. She fascinated him. Her dark pensiveness in the face of loss, her excitement at traveling, her innocent disgust at the sex so lately enjoyed in camp, it set a fire in Liam's soul. The flames were fanned further by Adelina's blatant opposition. It was akin to the perfect game of shatranj. He was leading two down, with the added excitement of removing Jonty from the board. Come the third move and Ana required rescue again, he would indeed call in the forfeit.

CHAPTER FIFTEEN

Journeying through the Barrow Hills took some days as the formations undulated to the very edges of the Great Lakes. Winding down off the final Barrow, the companions found themselves by the edges of a mirror-form watery swathe. Scattered and dotted like so many puddles across the landscape, the pools seemed at once eye catching and troubling. They reflected the sky in its turbid, grey glory and it seemed to the travellers as if they stared down on holes ripped in the fabric of the earth, that a window on an entire other world was displayed. Behind the Lakes, like the painted backdrop in a theatre, was the beginning of the Goti mountain range and hidden in its jagged confines, bedecked by frost and snow, climbed that most famous of roads, the Celestine Stairway.

'Ana,' Adelina grabbed at Ana's sleeve. 'These lakes are renowned for the Nökken, for all manner of water sprites, mostly all unseelie. And there are the Cwn Annwn, the Brag, urisks – Aine help us! You must promise me you will have your rowan crook by your side constantly until we make the safety of Star on the Stair. Promise me!'

The Traveller brooked no argument. Her fine brows drew together with concern and she squeezed Ana's hands in her own, despite the fact Ana was working with a birchwood hoop, needle and thread at the time.

'I will, I promise.' The young woman laughed at Adelina's protective angst. 'Aine knows you have been tutoring me mercilessly about the unseelie out there.' She gestured with her hoop. 'Anyway, how long will it take to get to Star on the Stair? Oh, Adelina, I'm so excited! To be at the foot of the Celestine Stairway! I never thought to reach this far in my whole life. It was always somewhere that held my imagination in Pa's stories, some eldritch place where one could climb to the very stars.'

'Trust me muirnin, the heights of which you speak are truly vertiginous and one wrong step and you may well be in your very own land of stars. And to answer your question... we are far enough away for you, indeed for us all to be in mortal peril wherever we turn. Now pack up your sewing. I need help to unload my silver charms and my special talismans. We must hang them all around the windows and doors of the van and over Ajax!'

Kholi-Khatun had heard this exchange and commented in a voice as dry as the desert sands.

'My shrimati, I'll wager you have more bells and whistles than a Raji orchestra in that van of yours. Why do we worry though? Have we not got an Other with us to protect us?'

He bowed towards Liam and touched his forehead and his chest as he did so. His cream and blue striped robes fell in folds down Mogu's sides and wound themselves together with the saddle tassels into thick twists, forming ropes of thread and colour.

Liam gave a courtly bow in return, looking sideways at Ana and winking.

'Huh, yes, well...' Adelina grumbled and swept up from the seat behind Ajax into the van with her basket of threads trailing over her arm. By afrits and djinns, Kholi thought, she draws me to her like water to a sponge. As he stared at her, seduced by the hint of a shapely calf disappearing into the van, he realised Liam had been talking to him.

'A thousand pardons. What were you saying?'

'You are badly struck, aren't you?' Liam laughed.

'And you are not?' Kholi responded as he gathered up the loose reins on either side of Mogu's hairy neck.

Liam was silent, feeling the customary Faeran secrecy flush forth, but a faint desire to please the Raji surfaced for air and he smiled.

'Perhaps. But it is difficult. We are not of a kind and to be truthful, she rarely shows me any more than mild favour.'

'Come now. I have seen more than mild favour when she has cast glances at you, surreptitious though she thinks they are.' Kholi looked at the Faeran riding beside him, at the other-worldliness of his bearing, his looks, the depth of his eyes, the aura of strangeness and yet not about him. Stealthily, Kholi pinched himself, something he did a dozen times a day, to remind himself he was in the presence of an Other. In the Amritsands, few would believe him.

'You think? She is more disdainful than a Faeran!'

Kholi ran his fingers briskly back and forth through the black hair that curled freely whilst on the road. He welcomed the thought of bathing in warm water at Star on the Stair and lathering his head to release its curlicews.

'Not at all, she is a fragile thing who is still grieving for her father, and dealing with the after effects of a brutal assault. In truth it is a wonder she allows any man to talk to her, let alone touch her! Her bravado is merely that... bravado.'

Liam said nothing, knowing that if he should touch her, she would melt into his body... if only Kholi knew!

They rode companionably along, allowing the honking sounds of waterfowl to fill the silence between them.

'Liam?'

'Yes, my friend?' The Faeran sat easily in the saddle as if he were glued to the back of the Each Uisge as Florien frisked sideways.

'Liam, Adelina and I have become fond of her. She is by default our family. Have a care for her and beware of hurting her.'

'I hear what you say, friend Kholi.'

With that the Faeran dug his heels into his horse's sides and set off at a canter, round the edge of one of the lakes, his horse looking as if it was floating just above the ground in order to miss the mud and mire of the swampy surrounds.

The journeymen splashed through tiny pools secreted under silver button-grass and grey tussock. Occasionally, they trod through a shadowed allée of stone pines, the trees arching their odd buttress shape over their heads and neither Ajax's nor Mogu's feet made any sound on the scattered pine needles. It was a stealthy passing, as though they travelled on tiptoe so as not to disturb the inhabitants of the waters, for the waters themselves inspired watchfulness and discrimination.

Kholi-Khatun and Adelina knew the dangers of the grey water – that hidden under the silvered reflection were any manner of water-wights who could shape-change and deceive and then drown the unfortunate whose luck had run out. Like the Cabyll Ushtey, or perhaps the Ceffyl-Dwr, that beautiful grey horse which leaped out of the water and grabbed any lone traveler and by gripping hard would squeeze the prey to death and then kick and trample on them.

The sound of silver bells tinkled and mingled with the mournful cries of duck and water geese. Above them in v-form, a flock of black swans flew in solemn procession. Kholi performed the horn sign and Adelina shook the whip covered in bells over Ajax's back. Ana merely remained quietly watchful, wondering more where Liam had gone than shivering at the ripples on the water or the sounds in the air.

A splash to their left engendered a heart pumping rush and heads turned in time to see water flick up in a spray of diamond drops. Something had dived in. Kholi sent a plea to the urisks to ask for their patronage, and where, Aine help them, was Liam?

The mournful cries of waterfowl echoed out of the greyness and in the future Adelina would forever be reminded of the keen of the Caointeach – the small woman dressed in green, washing bloodstained linen by a stream, her woeful wails the harbinger of death and doom. The embroiderer shivered on the stoop of her van, the spasmodic cries setting her teeth on edge, little goosebumps racing each other up her arms to seethe in a cluster under her armpits. Her grip on the whip tightened and she could see Ajax's ears laying flat against his skull, as the normally mesmeric tail lashed left and right.

A sound cracked into the air, echoing like a harquebus shot. The van lurched sideways and Ajax skittered as the vehicle dragged precariously, the wheel split and broken. Kholi hissed and hustled Mogu to kneel, chafing at their position in the middle of this watery plateau, as cold as a cemetery. A cry behind them curdled blood as Adelina leaped from the stoop. Time was of the essence and the day began to draw in as if someone pulled a drape across a window, blotting out light, depositing them in the middle of a shadow that smacked of things dangerous and dark.

'Adelina, it will be impossible for us to fix this! And I cannot leave you alone here while I get help.' Kholi rubbed a hand over his face.

'And I do not intend for you to move an inch away from us, Kholi.' She looked over her shoulder, checking, surveying. 'But I have a jack under the van, we can move the broken wheel quickly and then be ready to place the spare at first light. Oh, Aine, why did this happen? This is a terrible place!'

She cast a look at the lakes vanishing into the spreading darkness, her eyes a little wider. Sounds emerged from the water. The odd cry, a garbled call. She was sure the sounds weren't avian. She felt they were watched, could feel eyes burning into her as Kholi began to work.

The sounds from the lakes had accumulated as the dusk darkened. Adelina rolled her eyes and made the sign of the horns but Ana merely smiled and raised her eyebrows. Unaffected by the screams and moans beyond the camp, child of the Weald that she was, she reflected how far she had come in such a short space of time. Loss, grief, anger, even hate for a moment had receded to a comfortable distance. For the first time she was an individual of her own making. Not her Pa's, not 'Rotherwood's'. Not an item to be bargained with. She was far enough away from it all to test the waters of objectivity. She poked and prodded like someone with a scab, wanting to see if it still hurt. Only a little, she thought. If I am afraid of anything at all, it is that I may forget my father as I move forward, and I must not! But it's a new world and I'll not go backwards. Besides, there is Liam.

Liam! She drew her arms in tight to her body and sighed as she thought of his face and remembered the feeling as he kissed the top of her head and how she had felt as she laid her own lips on his arms. In that instant in the peel tower, as his arms had pulled her back against him, she felt she had been pulled into the slipstream of some fast-moving bird. Dragged along, buffeted by the power of emotional and sexual attraction. Her stomach filled with soft fluttering as if a flight of butterflies tickled its walls, delicious and disturbing. The same kind of feeling occurred when Liam brushed against her or when his eyes met hers. She tried to pierce the darkness beyond the stone pines. Where was he?

'We must be up early, Ana. Before dawn. As soon as the new wheel is on we must be gone to Star on the Stair. I'll not stay another night here by the lakes, it makes my skin crawl.' As Adelina spoke, she wrapped her arms around herself and shuddered. Kholi pulled her against him.

'Don't fret. We have fire, silver bells and talismans. We shall retire to sleep and sleep with our clothes back to front and inside out if it will make you feel better and we shall allow no one,' Kholi leaned forward and eyed Ana, 'to convince us to open our doors to them all night. Shall we?'

'Oh of course not, you silly man. I'm not stupid.' Unconcerned, Ana laughed, picked up a cushion and threw it at Kholi.

'Ana, I am serious! Shape shifting is the forté of most unseelie water sprites. Keep your door barred and open it to no one, for Adelina and I will not be leaving the pavilion until daylight. To remain safe inside with our talismans is our only protection. If you open the door, you meet them on their terms in their territory. Do you understand?'

Ana thought Kholi was over-stating things. After all, she had lived her life surrounded by the Weald's unseelie worst and she had survived. But she agreed anyway and kissed both her friends on their cheeks as she beat a retreat to the van. Looking back, she saw Kholi hold back the door flap of the pavilion for his ladylove and presently they were just faint shadows preparing to sleep. Ana watched the wheel glowing on the fire, its rim and spokes sparking red as a faint breeze blew over the campsite. And then she turned and locked the van door.

CHAPTER SIXTEEN

Liam had cantered back to Faeran, through an ancient and secret gate hidden in a dense orchard. He had avoided returning to his peers for he would not be quizzed or patronized, but he went back to Faeran to find a quiet corner where he could think. To ruminate on the burgeoning comfort he began to feel in the mortal world, and on the obsession with the woman with cascading, dark hair.

Sitting by the most sublime stream in an exquisite glade, he was unmoved, bored even, by his surroundings. The air was crystal clear, the temperature perfection. There was no stimulation. He felt he was a man with no sensory perception and surprised himself with the bald thought, is mortal life better? He strode back and forth, sleepless and agitated.

Sleep was not hasty in finding Ana that night either. She fretted and tossed in a lather and hungered to be in the presence of Liam. She wondered if he had cast a net over her heart as Faeran were rumoured to do. But no, he wouldn't! She could trust him, she was sure.

She threw her legs over the bed. Still dressed, ready for that early departure, she gathered up her embroidery. A stitch or two would settle her. She rummaged amongst the threads, searching for her stumpwork music box. A tune, softly played, would help sleep come as she sewed.

But it was not there.

In a fever, Ana tipped the basket on the floor and searched fruitlessly. The box reminded her of Pa, because she could remember as Adelina gave it to her, the immediate need to show it to him! She had decided every one of Adelina's expert stitches would be a token to his memory, just in case Aine forbid, she should forget him and need help in remembering. She would NOT lose it! She searched feverishly, tipping this, pulling that. Tears pricked her eyes. Apart from her cameo and the sketch of Pa, it was the thing dearest to her heart. Damn it! Grief raised its head again, always in the background, never far away, ready to pounce, to drag her down.

'Ana, look here, look what I have.'

She heard Liam's voice, sighing with relief that he had come back, positive he had found the box at the foot of the van. Gratefully, joyfully, she turned the key in the lock, because if the box were in her hands, then memories of Pa would stay with her, never to be lost. Liam understood this, he knew her!

'Ana... Ana. Look!' A voice whispered from the other side of the trees as she slipped barefoot onto the ground.

'Liam?' She hastened round the tree trunk.

'Here, closer to the lake. See?'

'Wait,' she whispered. 'Wait for me.'

Above her an owl hooted and she stumbled as she looked up. The lamp slipped out of her hand as she hit the ground and its friendly glow was extinguished. The dark settled on her like a shroud.

'Liam. Where are you?'

No one answered. She sat very still and looked around, aware of an ugly emptiness. Even the campfire appeared to have gone out, everything swallowed in the blackness. No sound of the animals could be heard – only the slap slap of wavelets on the shoreline and the honk of a lone goose calling for its mate. The uneasy quiet of a graveyard surrounded her.

She turned to go back the way she thought she had come and a light sparkled through the trees. The campfire! She hadn't realised she had been holding her breath until it gushed out in a big sigh. Angry with Liam now for playing with her, teasing her, she cast a look over her shoulder.

'Liam! Don't do this!' The anger implicit in the threat was leavened by the whisper and the whole was swallowed by the night. She headed for the candle-like glow, arms a little outstretched to avoid colliding with tree trunks and vans.

The gleam flittered and danced in front of her and she followed its path, believing she was moving toward the caravan. But after five minutes of toes sinking into watery puddles and feeling splashes of moisture dance on her calves, she stopped, concern and the faintest ripple of something-else pulling at her consciousness.

'Liam?' A scared whisper sighed out as she turned in a circle, confusion erasing all sense of direction. The dribble of fear that had rippled earlier now became a raging torrent as sweat began to gather across her body. Her mouth dried and she swallowed rapidly, taking shallow breaths. She ran straight ahead, terrified and barefoot into blackness until she spotted a pinprick of light dancing far ahead.

Sobbing with relief in the sucking silence of the lakeside night, she ran faster. Water splashed and tussocks bent as she wound through the lake-land. Always equidistant, the yellow gleam enticed her on. Soon her whole focus was that golden sheen. When she stumbled and fell to her knees amongst the puddles she noticed nothing but the light which waited mesmerisingly whilst she picked herself up and struggled on, Liam's voice calling occasionally from a muffled distance.

As she gasped for breath, her chest sucking greedily at the night-air, something gripped her arm – cold talons whose stiletto nails hooked into the fabric of her jacket. Phantasms rose from amongst the tussocks, growing like some malodorous grey waterweed, to tangle and trip. She screamed as hollow eye sockets bent toward her sucking her into their bottomless depths. Hands brushed at her hair, dragging at her, pulling her toward the marshy shore of the lakes. As they touched her she imagined her skin puckering – shrinking and dying. She fought them off hysterically, shoving and kicking like a gazelle pinioned by pride of lions.

Her breath gushed in as she sobbed, mumbling words that had no meaning. Pushing at the phantasms, turning away from their shriveled, grey faces, from the weed and snails that bedecked their hair and clothes. Always keeping the light in sight.

For what seemed hours, Ana had described circles and squares and always that fateful light had kept her far from camp and fire, the wretched Teine Sidhe – cruel will o' the wisps, dragging her to the point of exhaustion where her legs gave way and she crashed to knees on which she began to crawl. The phantasms pushed her forward, all of them contained by circle upon circle of the dancing yellow light of the Teine Sidhe.

The water surrounding Ana had thickened like the black curd of her grief. Her legs bogged down in the mire and her hands found little purchase. But with the effort of the truly doomed, that final heroic push which mortals make when faced with disaster, she heaved her exhausted body up and took a last desperate step.

Her feet hit bottomless murk, squelching up between her toes, and she fell after it, buried to her knees in the sucking quagmire. The swamp began to exert pressure on her body, squeezing, strangling, and she floundered little as inch by weakened inch she sank.

In the distance a lone rooster crowed in some cosy backyard at Star on the Stair. Above, in a sky that changed from ink black to deep navy, a dark shape flew over the doomed mortal. Looking down, the black swan shook its elegant head and flew on.

CHAPTER SEVENTEEN

'Where in the name of Aine have you been?' Adelina flung around at Liam, shrieking as he rode into the copse. 'SHE'S GONE!'

'What?' The smile on Liam's face vanished as if he had swiped it away.

'It's true.' Kholi spoke sharply with a knife-edge to his voice. 'I thought we could trust you, Liam, to be there for us. You were our friend. We welcomed you as such. And in this wretched place you leave us and what happens? I asked you to have a care for Ana, didn't I? And now she's gone! Been spirited away – the van is a mess.'

Adelina moved like a wildcat. She advanced on Liam with teeth bared and eyes narrowed. If she had a tail it would have twitched dangerously from side to side.

'You feckless, arrogant bastard! I don't agree with Kholi! I swear she would still be with us if you hadn't happened into our lives!'

'Adelina, stop!' Kholi shouted. 'This achieves nothing.' He turned towards the Faeran. 'But in truth Liam, I don't know where to begin to search.'

'Show me.'

Liam pushed past Adelina to the van and Kholi preceded him inside. Drawers teetered open and baskets of embroideries, fabrics and threads tumbled out. Ana's bedding was pulled back, the sheets ruckled. Her basket lay on the bed, its contents a rainbow of scattered colour.

'No Other has been here.' Liam turned to go.

'Is that all you have got to say? No Other has been here? By the spirits!' Adelina raised her hand to crack him across the cheek. Kholi grabbed her arm, full of intimidation and a quelling anger. Shocked she subsided as he hustled behind Liam down the steps, the Faeran stalking around the copse. He sniffed like a hound, casting wide.

'And none here either.'

He walked outside the ring of trees, turning this way and that.

'But here...' he paused and looked into the watery distance and then quickly returned to the van. 'There have been Others here. And she has gone after them, I think she has followed, not been taken.'

Adelina threw down the nosebag she held for Ajax, the grain pooling in a honey coloured heap on the ground, full of fright at Ana's predicament.

Liam avoided her and spoke directly to Kholi.

'Get the wheel fixed and leave immediately for Star on the Stair. I will find Ana and bring her to you.' He grasped Kholi's forearm and gave it a shake. 'I will find her, I swear.'

'Yes, friend Faeran,' Adelina spat the words like so many shards of ice, cracking in the morning air around them. 'But alive or dead. I tell you, if one hair of her head is damaged, I will seek you and curse you until you are dead yourself.'

Liam glanced at her briefly, a look that said 'don't cross me,' and turned away and flung himself on Florien. Leaving the copse at a gallop, he flung divots of soil in his wake.

Momentarily there was silence and then Adelina picked up a fallen branch and flung it, followed by a string of invective after the departing Faeran. Kholi shook his head and as he bent to pick up the spare wheel to slip it on the axle, he spied something lying half buried in the disturbed soil and pine needles by the side of the van. He curled his fingers around it and brushed at it, holding it to the ever-brightening sky to get a better look.

'Adelina! Look, it's Ana's music box. How did it get by the wheel?'

Adelina had been striding around the copse, hands on hips and breathing hard. She attempted to calm herself as she took the box from the merchant's hands.

'I imagine it fell out of her sewing basket when the wheel collapsed. We had our work on the step as we journeyed.'

She rolled the petite objêt in her hand and Kholi watched her struggling with very real fear of Others and what they may do. He reached over and pulled her to his chest.

'Come my shrimati, he will find her, I have faith.'

'Oh yes,' she uttered, macabre thoughts racketing through her mind. 'He will find her. But alive or dead, Kholi. That is what I am afraid of. This is the work of Others and you know as well as I, what can happen. This is the home of many shape shifters: the Teine Sidhe, those evil will o' the wisps, and worse Kholi, it is the home of the Limnae, the spirits of the Marsh. They are unseelie, they are dead spirits.'

'Adelina, stop!' Kholi shook her gently. 'You only have two choices in this. To trust the Faeran – or not. For myself, I shall trust him. If you have faith in me, do as I do.'

His dark eyes opened wide and she stared into them, a tear trickling down her cheek, catching the dawn strobes as they flashed through the stone pines. Perversely, the sun had rolled into a clear blue sky and the day would be beautiful.

Adelina nodded her head silently.

Kholi picked up tools and continued to work at the wheel, desperate to be away to Star on the Stair where they could wait in safety.

Liam followed the trail at a gallop, the smell of mortal quite overt to the Other: a sweetness in Ana's case, and to Liam it was like pollen to a bee. Ana's track meandered: looping, curling, retreating, advancing till Liam felt he was creating a vast Faeran calligraphy... a rune of flowing, curving curlicews telling a story of murder and mayhem.

All the while his mind gnawed at the emotion he was feeling: mortal emotion. An overpowering fear – fear that someone he wanted, that he obsessed about, that he could almost love, would be lost. Why did it matter, because he had only ever really wanted a game, an experience? It was as if some giant prophetic hand had moved all the pieces on the board so that he must really struggle to win.

Perhaps it was something he had done so that some Other cursed him. His father's soul? No! Perhaps a mortal then, maybe Adelina. She hated him enough and wanted him as far from Ana as possible. He could die in the attempt at goodliness and the copper-haired she-devil would remain unmoved.

His horse flew – as if by galloping, Liam raced away from the dark shadow of his former life and by finding Ana and sweeping her into the saddle with him, he would be resurrected, reformed and revived. Maybe it was a game. With the winner taking all!

He careened to a halt by a stone-pine bending over a knoll and overlooking a lake. A silver ruffle of buttongrass and sedge edged the shore. As the sun rose, seeping over the horizon and stretching gold and silver light across the landscape, the lake became a bowl of molten metal, as if an alchemist strove to create something magical in a steaming cauldron. In the dawn air, the gauzy mist lacing in amongst the shrubby shoreline created mystery and mesmer.

The lake edged around a small promontory and as the cocks crowed far away at the foot of the Goti range, a lone black swan flew in a circle over the lake, gliding smoothly onto the surface, legs skimming, ruffling the water and then allowing stillness to resume as it shuffled and folded rich black wings across its back. Paddling idly, it approached the shoreline and as it took a step from the shallows, it shape-changed, becoming upright. The feathered covering dropped over the being's arm to drape, shining like satin. The white swan face smoothed and elongated to become a woman's visage... a woman starkly and palely beautiful with lips the colour of blood and cheeks the colour of blossom. Her form was clothed in a black gown falling in pliant folds to white, narrow feet and she walked to the shrubs and laid her cloak of plumage carefully. Everything about the woman was starkly graceful and she returned to the lake to enter its shallows as any normal woman would, bending and washing her face and sinking below the surface to lie like a star: floating, arms outstretched, eyes shut.

Immediately Liam dismounted. Laying gentle fingers over the horse's mouth, he ran to the shrubs, to the heap of glistening feathers. As he touched the cloak and gathered it to his arms, a hiss flew from the water and the woman turned to the shore, raising herself, a column of black fury.

'Faeran! Leave it!'

'It is mine, Maeve Swan Maid. And you are now mine. Again as I recall, and this time you will do my bidding to get your cloak back!'

The swan-maid ran out of the water, her robe clinging to her perfect form. Her chill face was filled with mocking anger as she stood in front of Liam.

'Faeran, thy memory is good. Apparently though, thou has no humour or thou would have taken that moment, so long since, as youthful foolery?

I asked for my cloak then and thou did give it to me. Thy misfortune! Hast thou brooded of thy weak-minded idiocy since? It is surely history.'

'You owed me favour. I had lifted your cloak, you owed me, it is the lore of the swan-maids, is it not?' Liam fixed a gaze filled with loathing on Maeve.

'Thou tell of the truth. And I would ask thee, if I do thy bidding now, wouldst thou then give my cloak willingly? For thou seems inordinately angry at my own self.'

What passed for a smile and a faint attempt at charm flashed across the chill face. A mere lifting of the corners of the mouth, no answering lilt in the eyes.

'I asked for your favour, Maeve. I was young. I wanted to have you. I should have taken favour first and then given the cloak back. One lives and learns. Besides, I am glad you were not my first, there was another and she was, shall we say, warmer and more willing than you would ever have been!'

The maid hissed and spat at him.

'Maeve, Maeve, can you not bear a little truth?' Liam mocked but then plucked a feather from the cloak and as he did, Maeve Swan Maid gasped and grabbed at her shoulder. He plucked again. She grabbed for her arm, moaning and crying. Again, despite her pain, perhaps because of it, he plucked at the cloak. And she writhed, casting hissing cries at the Other who towered over her. He held up three black feathers.

'Three reasons for you to do my bidding. I don't trust you, so the insurance will work admirably. You know as long as I have these you are in my thrall. So you can no longer promise the world and an oyster to have your cloak back. I would not have you fly off this time before my wish is carried out.'

'Faeran is cruel!' Maeve grabbed at her throbbing arm and shoulder as though she had been pierced with red-hot splinters. 'So much pain! What is it thou wishes?' Her voice moaned, like a nasty little breeze.

Liam held up one of the feathers.

'Tell me the truth Maeve, have you seen a mortal woman in these lakes, last night or this morning... remember, I can crush this feather.

'Liam of the Faeran, thou heart is hard.' She wrapped her arms around her shivering body. 'I did see a mortal. But for the hair, I would have thought it was a boy.'

'Where?' Liam curled his fist over the black quill.

'What carest thou for a boy?'

Liam began to squeeze the feather.

'No, cruel man, no!' Maeve took a step forward. 'To the southeast. At the Bog. And the Limnae were there. The mortal had lost its reason. Eyes as vacant as a swan's nest out of season.' She stifled a satisfied glimmer as Liam gasped at this last. 'Dost thou have affection for this boy, Liam?'

Liam would tolerate no arch levity from the bird-woman, his voice rapier sharp.

'Be quiet, Maeve! HOW FAR?'

'Why, tis a she!' The swan-maid expressed surprise. 'And thou feels love for her? Poor Faeran man, poor mortal woman.' Again she mocked. Unwisely. 'AAH!'

Liam had closed his fist unapologetically on the feather.

'How... far?' He spat the words like cherry stones between gritted teeth.

'Less than half a mile as the swan flies.' The swan-maid's face paled, small beads of sweat glistening above her lip.

Liam held out the cloak. It shimmered in the daylight and the tips of the feathers ruffled in the soft dawn zephyr. Maeve Swan Maid grabbed it in taut fingers. Tearing it over one shoulder, she hissed at the pain of the plucked plumage, turning a bitter face toward Liam as she sneered.

'And so thy first ever was a mortal.'

'As it happens, as well you know. So?' He fingered the feather.

'Liam of the Faeran should remember what eventuated before he seeks most recent lost mortal woman.'

'Why?'

'Thy lovemaking destroyed thy mortal plaything. She was insensible in her home, neither eating, talking nor sleeping. One night she left, wandering the countryside seeking her Faeran love.'

'Maeve!' Liam warned and took a step forward but the swan-maid swung her head towards him, hissing.

'Listen Faeran and learn! She was overtaken by a Faeran rade, the radiant progress thy people make into mortal territory. Thinking every Faeran male was you, she became utterly mind-shot. She died where she lay days later, of hunger, thirst and with heart broken. That is what happened to thy first mortal love, Liam of the Faeran. What shall happen to this one?'

Liam was momentarily speechless, cut in half by warring emotions – distrait at the death of the innocent girl and fury at feeling such distress. Then fear. That Ana, the sought-after prize and possession may so end her days.

He stared at the sharp face of the swan-maid for a moment only, holding the feather up.

'Show me, Maeve. I will follow you and remember, I have the feathers. I can crush them, cut them or burn them. Each pain you will feel as if it were you that was incinerated or stabbed and it will diminish you and make you weak and ill, so that you can neither feed nor fly. You will die. Go!'

The maid cast such a look of humiliation, anger and pain on Liam, a small wave of guilt rippled. But reason stepped in. I am Faeran: we feel no guilt at all, he thought as he watched the beauty paddle into the shallows. She pulled the cloak up over the other shoulder, shape-changed and launched herself to the skies with a gutteral cry.

Liam leaped for his horse, thrusting the feathers in the pocket of his riding coat. Two wishes left, or maybe two weapons. Either way, he knew he would find Ana.

I KNEW THE MOMENT LIAM set off after Ana that I was indeed the other player in his game. The way he had looked at me, just for a minute, as I said I would curse him. I could see him on the other side of the board with his black entourage, strategising, as I, poor white shah as I was, floundered with the details of a game I had played but once in my life. But enough of this, you and I are at the end of this tiny book so you must find the next embroidery, retrieve the installment and enlarge.

But of course you ask which embroidery? I am sorry but I am tired and my gaoler has been very demanding. The design I am working on is not to the woman's liking and I must unpick and begin again, so my mind is not as sharp as it should be.

You may ask, when do we hear about this prison and how it happened? But you see I am telling you. This whole story, my story, is how it happened. So you must be patient and read on.

Find the deer, infinitely fat and well fed in Eirie forests. It sits beneath an oak tree laden with lace and satin stitched acorns, all expertly applied with lace-

stitched oak leaves.

There is a tiny fawn suede booklet under the flank of the stag. You must unpick very carefully. And I have a special surprise! You are going to receive two for the price of one, because you will notice a peacock sitting on the bough above the stag. Beneath the turquoise tail of the peacock is another book. I beg you lift that tail with sensitive fingers. The real fringe of feathers is exceedingly fragile and the wire of the tail-shape more delicate still. Read on.

CHAPTER EIGHTEEN

Star on the Stair bustled. After a week in the wilds, unvisited by journeymen of any sort, Kholi's and Adelina's senses reeled under the bombardment of people and noise from this perfect place.

The town angled sharply skywards, lanes and paths cobbled and narrow, certainly not made for dragging caravans and camels around. Thus a very large mews existed at ground level, at the point where roads converged. A journeyman could leave his beast of burden in the mews and for small cost have it well tended for the duration of his stay in the town.

Enormous and grandly positioned, the mews dominated the foot of the Stair. Arched wooden beams spanned the width of the halls and motes of dust and straw floated in the golden beams that streamed down to the cobbles from the high fenestrations.

It reminded Adelina of the story of Noah and his Ark from Travellers' tales. The mews housed not merely camels and horses but elephants, donkeys and oxen, alpacas, llamas and yaks. The place hummed with the sounds of many hooves on cobbles, of camel groans, the bubbling rumble of contented pachyderms and the low nickers that indicated horses at peace. Adelina never tired of it and had been known to walk for hours with a bag of apples and nuts, feeding any friendly animal whose head turned her way.

She and Kholi had stabled their animals and left them in the care of the ostlers, and with a bag each they began to climb the lanes into the town. The day glittered brightly blue and quaint cottages and shop fronts climbed up the inclines by their sides, stone walls whitewashed and window frames painted black, with window boxes full of tumbling scarlet and pink pelargoniums. Doorways coloured red, bright blue or black invited journeymen and merchants inside and each small inn had its name on a swinging sign with an appropriate design: the Pig and Whistle, the Ox and Cart, the Goat and Cheese. Kholi and Adelina made for the one place their families had always used – the Inn of the First Happiness.

Its sign swung joyfully in the breeze, occasioning a musical, if faint squeak. The depiction of a fat little man sitting at the table with one glass of ale in front of him and a beatific smile on his face was well known in Eirie. Not the least because as the Celestine Stairway climbed up and over the Goti Range, the only comforts any journeyman could count on were from the chain of inns bearing this sign, so that subsequently there existed the Inn of the Second Happiness, the same fat little man sitting at table with two glasses of ale. Then the Inn of the Third Happiness and so on until at the Raji end of the Celestine Stairway and at the foot of the Goti Range and just before one began one's interminable journey over the Amritsands, there squatted the Inn of the Sixth Happiness. The fat little man sat with six ales spread out and if one could smile even more beatifically, he did so.

The two friends pushed open the bright red door and entered a small room with chairs and tables squashed cheek by jowl and where a bar tender, fat like the man in the sign, stood polishing glasses. He beamed.

'Well! Well, well, well, well, well! Aren't you a sight for sore eyes!'

'Hola, Buckerfield.'

Adelina stretched over the bar and kissed the ruddy cheeks. Kholi reached out a hand and shook the meaty palm.

'On your way back, then?' Buckerfield held the tankard he polished up to the light and satisfied it had the required sheen, hung it from a hook on a beam alongside a dozen others glistening like stars.

Kholi nodded as Adelina butted in.

'We need a room, Buckerfield. We might need it for a while. We are waiting for two friends.'

'That's fine. I have two rooms yet. You can have 'em.' He grinned as he uncorked a barrel, tapped it and then picked it up as if it were a piece of sugar floss and placed it on the end of the bar.

'We only need one room, Buckerfield. A double.' Kholi spoke quietly, almost shyly.

'Oh ho! So that's the way of it then. Well that's alright, a double room you shall have and I couldn't do it for two nicer people.' He boomed with the kind of voice one would expect on a landsman or a longshoreman, preferably not on a publican where a whisper would sound like a shout in the confined space of the Inn. Kholi looked around. The clientele had listened to the loud exchange and were smiling, raising their glasses, joking coarsely but kindly, as pub regulars do. He shrugged his shoulders, occasioning a cheer.

Buckerfield edged his bulk around the counter and showed them to the stairs.

'Second door up there,' he jerked his head sky-wards. 'You know the one! Towels on the bed, you look as though a bath's worth more than a beer right now.'

They thanked him and clattered upwards, the cosy whitewashed walls touching their shoulders until they came to a narrow passage and the second door wide open before them, allowing a strip of golden light to shine across the bleached floorboards of the hall. They entered and Adelina threw her bag on the bed and rushed to the window, whilst Kholi pushed the door shut and leaned back against it, wearily swiping off his travel caplet and running agitated fingers through hair.

'You know,' said Adelina, 'my mother said this town was built by a man from the coast far to the south of Trevallyn. People there live in little villages that cling impossibly to rocky coves and shorelines and they are all painted white and have names that sound like the lyrics of a Faeran song... Porthcawl, Porthkerris, Polcarrow. Have you been that far south, Kholi?'

As she talked, she gazed out the window at the town spread-eagled precariously against the mountainside. Across from the walls of the Inn, the cobbled Celestine Stairway climbed doggedly skywards. The Inn was in a perfect position, its steep walls forming the town ramparts and lining the edge of that noble path.

Kholi came across and put his hand on the nape of her neck under the warmth of the heavy copper hair. She didn't move.

'No, I have never been there.'

'Then shall we go together one day?'

'Yes we shall.'

He felt her tension under his fingers.
'She is out there somewhere, Kholi.'
'Faith, my shrimati, faith.'
And he rubbed her neck softly.

The black swan flew as high as it dared, neither wishing to be too close to the Faeran, nor wishing to tempt Fate and have him squeeze another of her feathers. As she flew she scanned ahead, her black eyes opened wide, afraid to miss a thing. The wind pulled teasingly at her and she felt the updraughts and gusts stroking and pushing. Her body stretched in a long black line from beak to tale and it undulated with each flap of the midnight wings. From his place far below, Liam could make out the red beak and the white face. She flew on.

The Limnae had vanished as daylight brightened – their hours were the darking hours. If the mortal was doomed as Maeve believed, the Limnae would wait patiently until the mud, muck and mire had filled every crevice and orifice of her body. Thus embalmed, they would spirit her amongst them, to become one of the snail-bedecked, grey and rotting phantasms who lured more and more mortals to their foul world. A spirit of anger and hatred festered in the Limnae for they resented any who bloomed and walked in living light. They had one aim: to besiege and drown any mortal who crossed their path and then absorb them into their mouldering fellowship.

The swan mused. It was not such a bad death. By the time they drowned, mortals had invariably lost their reason. They felt nothing. It suited her to forget the marauding terror beforehand, before reason left. Such callow forgetfulness was always the way of the Others.

A movement ahead caught her eye. There, a flap and a splash! By all that is impossible! She banked and flew lower. Her harsh, gutteral call fled behind her, dropping to the ears of Liam as he galloped across the buttongrass and puddles.

Maeve began to circle as the mortal woman sank and her chin rested on the mire as it bubbled and fussed around her. One arm lay across the turgid surface of the bog, flapping weakly like the broken wing of a marsh hen. It was almost within the heart of the swan to feel sorry for the mortal.

But then she remembered she would not be in this invidious position if the mortal had not been in trouble. She hissed as she flew over Ana's muddy head, spying the chit's eyes. Empty, vacated of all life. A shell, the kind the Limnae crave.

Maeve flew round and round as Liam drew closer. Why does he want her? She is dirty and ugly. Look at her! Empty of thought and sense. He will never repair her. Why waste himself? If he wishes to join with a mortal woman there are plenty more. Stupid man!

Liam had seen the flapping arm and the horror of its weakness propelled him out of the saddle to land at Ana's side, water splashing high in diamond drops. He waved his hand and shouted a preventative charm, something to stop the drag and crush pulling at her. Around the two of them, Limnae began to rise uncharacteristically in the daylight, like a filthy grey fog. Angry with the Faeran, furious their prize may leave their midst, they moaned a banshee wail, pulling at Ana's hair and at her arm. Morbid visages scowled and screamed, the kind of thing to tip any mortal over the edge. Snails and slugs crawled out of ears, leaving a silver trail as they entered mouths and empty eye-sockets, whilst lank hair hung wetly in the mouldy folds of wrinkled skin.

Above this mob, Maeve Swan Maid circled tightly, shrieking as if to wake every waterfowl in the lake-land. Liam motioned again and an invisible barrier sprang up around he and the girl as he pulled her, inch by inch, from the muddy confines. The bestial army howled, their black, empty eye sockets portraying an endless horror of ghastly ruin.

Ana flopped like a rag doll, offering no resistance. Her head lolled on Liam's shoulder as he hoisted her into his saddle, leaping behind. He wafted his arm again, snarling a further spell and the barrier fell away. The Limnae rushed in to grab at the horse and its passengers but the animal leaped over the dank heads to clear them and land on firmer ground on the lake bank. They cried out in frustration but began to recede into the muddy waters until presently the lake was calm and quiet and no sign of Ana's life and death struggle existed.

Liam allowed Florien to stand for a moment as he shifted Ana to a more comfortable position in his arms. He watched her sightless eyes slide back and the lids shutter down. There was no hint of recognition, of anything. She breathed to be sure, but that was all.

Maeve glided onto the shore, her wings folding and her tail feathers twitching.

Once again the cloak slid down her white arms and she began to transfigure. Florien snorted loudly, backing away.

'Thy lover is mind shot, Liam. What dost thou plan to do? Thou canst hardly care for her thyself.'

'She can be mended.' He smoothed muddy hair from the girl's forehead as if she were a baby.

'Thy head must be addled by thy heart, Faeran. Too much time will it take. Leave her where her friends can find her. She is not thy concern.' Maeve hissed, her distaste for the mortal evident in her curled lip.

'I shall take her to Jasper.'

'Ha! Thou wastes time on this mortal. Methinks thou has departed from thine own senses.'

'Silence! It is not your business. But this is!' Liam reached into his pocket and grabbed a black feather, squeezing the end hard and relishing the sharp intake of breath from the swan-maid.

'Second feather, second duty. Go to Star on the Stair and seek out the Traveller Adelina and her friend the Raji merchant, Khatoun. Tell them I have found Ana and that I take her to a Faeran healer and that I will return as soon as I am able. Tell them, she is… tell them she needs treatment for a wound. And give them this and say it is on my honour.' He held out a pin that had been at the neck of his shirt. 'The merchant knows what it represents.'

Maeve stared at Liam as he leaned down from the saddle, her eyes narrowed.

'Honour? Since when do Faeran pledge honour to mortals.' Maeve sneered. 'Why dost thou want to heal the chit? What prompts thou to do such a strange thing?'

'It's a unique experience, Maeve. Something different to do.' Liam's face emptied of all emotion. 'Life can get damnably boring sometimes.'

He lifted his reins and touched Florien's flanks with his heels, calling back, squeezing the feather again.

'Do it, Maeve!' The horse and its cargo walked away as if Florien knew the life of the mortal hung by a thread so slender the slightest jolt would tear it asunder.

'Feckless Faeran!' The swan-maid hitched the plumage over her shoulders and this time launched into the skies silently, banking and heading northerly to the mountains.

The journeymen had slept, waking only when an insistent banging at the door had rendered their peace shattered.

'Hey, you sleepy heads! It's almost mid-afternoon. Love aint that grand, surely!'

Buckerfield's voice bounced achingly off the whitewashed walls of the hall. Pulling on his striped robe and belting it, Kholi opened the door. Buckerfield took in the tired eyes and the grey pallor.

'Well, good grief! You have been asleep. My apologies.'

Kholi smiled and stepped aside as Buckerfield entered the room.

'Ah, methinks you've had troubles on the road, for you look done in. Well never you mind. If you want to talk I'm here and if not, well that's alright too. But I bet it were them bloody Others, weren't it? Anyway, you're safe here and it won't be long before your friends come. Aannnd...' he drew the word out to indicate he had something special to announce. 'Tonight is the Fire Festival, because a Traveller has just arrived from up top and the first snows are falling. Aannnd...' his eyes twinkled and the double layer of chins shook and jostled. 'Tomorrow is the Fire Festival Market!'

At this Adelina's face lit up.

'Yeesss! Thought that'd brighten you. But there's more!' The folds and wattles of his face creased in an excitement he wanted to share. 'The Faeran will be selling their wares. And whilst I don't take much with them Others, the Faeran do have some beautiful stuff and honestly I reckon it'd be once in a lifetime they'd bother to mingle with mortals in a market of their own making. I don't think they do it for the money, that's for sure. I reckon it's for the game. And Adelina, a group of traders has just arrived from the Raj with some stuff that'd be right up your alley and Kholi, I bet you know half the folk anyway.' He paused for breath. 'Anyhoo, my lovelies, I must get back to the bar, very busy it is. But I think you need a bit of relaxing, so get you up and out and be a part of it, eh? I'll see you later.'

And before they had a chance to thank him he had departed on soft light feet, and closed the door gently behind him.

CHAPTER NINETEEN

Liam slowed Florien to a walk as he negotiated the foot of the Barrow Hills. He had travelled back over trails already covered by the foursome in earlier days until he had found a track that was barely a defile of broken grasses leading to a fold in the Hills. Sequestered in a quiet vale was an orchard of peach and apricot trees, the last of their jeweled leaves dangling. They waved, miniature pennants undulating in a Welkin Wind whereupon some detached to flutter and land between the trees, forming a carpet which crackled under the horse's hooves.

The trees were twisted into espaliered lanes, and the tortuous results became the infamous Ymp trees... gateways to places outside nature and one of the gates to which Liam had retreated so often over the past few weeks.

Florien walked down the first lane and then up the second before turning carefully into a third, so that Ana would be neither jostled nor jolted. The reins hung loose over his neck and all the while as they walked along, Liam had been stroking Ana's forehead, smoothing her dried, muddy locks back, away from her catatonic face. Had a mortal been watching their progress into that third lane, he would have thought himself bosky as the horse, his rider and cargo vanished as if they had never been.

'So you are come at last.'

An elderly Faeran leaned on a stick, the Ymp trees sporadically unloading their plunder around his shoulders. Some landed to mix with his white hair which was cut short, closer to his head than the fashion. It showed an elegant forehead lined with a wealth of grooves that indicated kindness and a goodly dose of humour.

'You knew I was coming.' Liam gazed flatly at the Healer. Jasper was wise, possessed of the ability to seer, to scry – one of the privileged few.

'Indeed, Liam. Watching your progress these last few weeks has been somewhat of an entertainment, my boy. My my, if your father were alive, he would flay you for the turn you appear to be taking. No, no... don't look so. I am not your father, in fact most Faeran think me very strange indeed. I have always thought kindness in anyone, mortal or Other, will bring its own reward. But come now, I can see the girl needs attending.'

He set off between the Ymp trees, using his stick more as a scythe than as a support, his swagger indicating an agility belying his years.

Here, through the gate to Faeran, the colours were richer, the fragrances more overpowering. Where peaches and apricots had dropped, so they rotted and fermented, wafting a heady odour. Liam had become more used to the subtle tastes of mortal life and found the scent of Faeran clogged his nose and fogged his senses. Birds chimed and chorused, butterflies flitted, touching Ana's head with soft wings. And everywhere was the sense of richness and excess. Liam grimaced. Jasper called over his shoulder.

'Mortal life suits you then, more than your own home.'

Liam wondered if the old man had eyes in the back of his head and responded gruffly.

'There are things I prefer.'

The hauteur in his answer caused Jasper's eyebrows to shoot for the sky, as if he found something amusing and ironic in Liam's reply.

They had wound their way through a dense knot garden full of thick privet and box hedges groomed to intertwine in some ancient Faeran way. A charm to be sure, thought Liam, to keep the unkind and unkempt away. Cypresses stood at each corner of the garden, reaching to the sky like sentinels. In the middle of the knot, right where the privet and box met in a controlled explosion of tightly pruned branches, a white dovecote stood proudly. The paunch-bellied doves swaggered around, dipping and curtsying to each other, the feathered parody of a Faeran Court.

They had reached the forecourt of a stone house. Long and sitting on a gravelled terrace, the sandstone dwelling looked as if it had been dipped in honey, the colour dripping onto the gravel. Jasper tapped on a deeply carved door with his stick and Liam had a moment to observe the carved runes curling, presumably telling only Jasper the charm to use for the thresh-hold to be safely traversed. The massive piece of cedar swung noiselessly back to reveal a light, sun-washed interior.

Liam sat aboard Florien, nursing his bundle whilst Jasper chivvied Folko, his ostler, to help. The stocky servant reached up and Liam placed Ana gently in the wide, tender arms and quickly dismounted to loosen Florien's girth and follow the party inside.

The interior smelled of beeswax and herbs. Tellurions and orreries glinted in the beams of sunlight falling through the large oblong windows, globes, spheres and discs rolling, swinging, rotating silently in movement of eldritch propulsion. Shelves exploded with all sizes of books and those not shelved were marshaled into ordered rows along the walls. Vast rugs covered polished floorboards and at the far wall, where a stone fireplace stretched from floor to ceiling, a woman was setting kindling and logs and brushing the hearth with blacking.

'Margriet! We have our company at last and I need your help! Folko, bring the lass to the back bedroom.'

Jasper walked rapidly ahead, his boots making no sound on the rugs and his long black damask coat sweeping behind him. Through the high centre-vent at the back, Liam glimpsed Jasper's breeches, dirty with a saddle mark. The man had obviously been riding early that morning.

Liam glanced at vast tapestries telling great stories as they passed down the hall to the back of the house, and at lecterns holding illuminated books, a lifetime of Faeran history at which he shrugged a shoulder.

Folko proceeded carefully through a door into a sparse room where a large bed stood in the centre. A huge silver framed mirror was propped on the mantelpiece and had Liam looked he would have seen an image of himself following Ana, as she walked around a pool. It played the same scene over and over. But he glanced at nothing bar the woman being laid on a brown rug. The mirror returned to its normal, reflective form.

'Will she be well?'

'Not sure just yet, my boy.' Jasper placed a hand on the mortal's forehead. 'Folko! Carry the bath in and then, Margriet, bathe the girl in warm water with lavender and camomile oils and light the lavender candles. Try to be as calm and gentle as you can. Methinks that while she may not feel you touching her, any sudden move may cause her to break even more.'

'What do you mean 'break even more'?' Liam moved to Ana's side. She was as limp and lifeless as a corpse.

'I doubt her physical injuries are much at all. But she is catatonic and I think all the events she has experienced these last few months have finally pushed her into a deep depression. And yes, I know all about her Liam, so don't prevail too much upon my good humour!'

'Can you heal her?'

'I will try dear boy, but she is mortal.' Jasper looked around the room, searching for something.

Liam concentrated on manifesting impartiality, for the feelings that curled tight fingers into his soul were unfamiliar and disturbing.

Jasper was distracted. He pushed at the door of the room beside Ana's. Capacious, lined shelf upon shelf with manuscripts and folios, the workroom smelled of herb and vellum, parchment and oil. A massive table extended along the room covered in an array of alchemical glassware. Mortars and pestles marched along the windowsill. A low fire glowed in a hearth overhung by an iron trivet. Ranks of drawers filled one wall. Liam watched him go immediately to this fine piece of cedar furniture and fling open one drawer after another to place herbs and petals on the table. Then he turned and stared at them, fingers to his expressive mouth. The night-sky blue eyes looked up at Liam, unfocussed.

'What are you doing?' Liam picked up a crucible and turned it this way and that before returning it impatiently to the table.

The Elder grabbed the dried flowers and stored them again. He spoke to himself, ignoring the man closeted with him, each sentence underlined by a small slam of a drawer.

'No, this is all useless. I need fresh flowers.' He grabbed a small basket and placed a bottle of clear water and some glass bowls wrapped in cloth, gently inside. 'Come quickly out to the garden!'

The sun saturated the walled garden at the back of the house and the whole was suffused with the overpowering scents of flowering shrubs and the drone of bees. Jasper immediately headed for the far wall, mantled in a swathe of clematis. Beside the climber, a wrought gate stood open, giving a glimpse of the Ymp trees and their fragrantly rotting fruit outside.

His liver-spotted hands reached up to the flower heads and he deftly plucked a small number with a pair of pincers, then turned to order the man at his side, who stood, hands in pockets.

'Liam, fill the glass bowls with the water and dear boy, don't allow your own skin to come in contact with the interior of the bowls or with the liquid. Ana's sensibilities depend on your care and must not be tainted by your own juices. Clematis, you see, when steeped in water and allowed to heat in the sun and pour out its properties, is a marvellous medic for unconsciousness. But there are other things too.' He deftly picked up the clematis petals with the pincers and dropped them into one of the bowls Liam had prepared. 'I need some golden helianthum for extreme shock and some gentiana. Altogether, the three flowers will insulate her from the terrible mental injury she has sustained and allow her psyche to re-build.'

'How long? Is there not a charm, some form of incantation?' Liam stared at the few paltry flowers, unimpressed.

'No my boy, there is only this. And patience.' And love, he muttered to himself but the young man didn't hear as they went about their pruning. Mimulus was picked and scleranthus and the feathered white blossoms of the cherry plum. This last to prevent loss of mind. And then sweet chestnut to cure the mental anguish the young woman sustained.

Throughout the garden, the water-filled glass bowls continued their distilling process under the warmth of the sun until presently Jasper gathered them all, passing the basket to Liam and returning to the sickroom.

Ana lay clean and smelling sweetly of the fragrant oils on her skin. Her hair, still damp from Margriet's tender care, was spread on the pillow and mahogany strands of it glinted in the light coming through the wide window. Her skin shone pinkly, more healthily, although Jasper spied two spots of bright carmine on her cheeks. He placed capable fingers against her forehead.

'Margriet, open the window and pull back the covers, she is a little warm. I shall return forthwith.'

At this last, he turned in a flurry of black, the damask silk hissing against the cedar door as he brushed past. Forgotten by the Elder, Liam walked to Ana's bedside and ran his fingers into her open hand. Margriet, watching covertly, had never seen such a tender moment. She felt embarrassed as his fingers slid slowly and almost wantonly over Ana's palm to curl her inanimate fingers in his own.

There's a thing, she thought and turned away.

Adelina and Kholi stepped along the cobbled streets of Star on the Stair. Excitement about the coming Fire Festival fizzed around them, but they felt insulated from it all, slung deep in worry.

'What if he can't find her?' Adelina walked with a thick padded coat wrapped around and tied with a Raji cord, to exclude the cold. A chill breeze blew down the mountainside, bringing with it the smell and feel of the approaching snows of winter. But she knew her own cold was more than skin deep, it came from a heart and soul filled with anxiety. Kholi put his arm across her shoulders and pulled her close.

'Liam is Faeran. He has many ways of searching and Others to help him.'

'But I told you Kholi, she's fragile and I am so worried. I don't want to lose her, she has become family. I hadn't realized how much I have missed family since my own parents died. I honestly always felt I was a self-contained person and content with it, but I can see I am not.'

They had reached the small lake at the far side of the town. It filled from the mountain streams that would soon be frozen. Now it eked a sluggish overflow into a narrow waterfall that could often be seen from parts of Trevallyn, a glistening gold and copper ribbon in the rays of any dawn sun.

Kholi led Adelina to a bench under a bare willow. The branches undulated in the breeze and the two lovers tipped their faces to the sun as it moved westward. The day had begun to darken as the sun slid down towards the precipitate crags.

The lake ruffled here and there as the breeze danced across. Small green ducks with curled tails and upswept tufts of feathers on their wing tips floated past, saw the strangers had nothing to offer, quacked in a dejected fashion and moved on. Their white ringed necks made them look bureaucratic, reminding one of the collars of the suited clerks in Veniche. A movement to Adelina's left caught her eye and the waving willow branches parted as a pair of swans glided through. White and graceful, they rested their eyes for a moment on the mortals and then with a hiss of warning to stay away, swept regally on. Kholi's arm draped over Adelina's shoulder.

'You won't lose her, Adelina, I swear. And in addition, you have me.'

Adelina looked up at him and kissed him as a black swan paddled through the twiggy willow veil. It approached the shore and stepped onto dry land – to transform, the cloak sliding down to rest on the slim white arm of Maeve Swan Maid.

The lovers untangled with a gasp. This unexpected Other, in her singularly chill fashion was breathtaking.

'Kholi and Adelina. I come from Liam. He has found the chit. He said to tell thee he takes her to Jasper. She is wounded, but...' she paused, her sibilant tones shivering to a halt.

'But what?' Adelina had quickly buried her awe of the swan-maid and become agitated. She reached out to grab Maeve's arm, but with a hiss and a sweep of the elegant neck, the long midnight hair describing an arc, the swan-maid stepped back out of reach.

'She is wounded but can be repaired.' She closed her beautiful lips as if to say 'that is all'.'

Kholi, prescient in the extreme, desperate not to offend, stood and gave her a bow.

'Thank you, Swan Maid. We are grateful. But can we prevail upon you a moment longer?'

Maeve looked at him and heaved a sigh. He continued, choosing to ignore the compressed red lips and the black eyes closing to slits. He also grabbed hold of Adelina's hand with one of his own in an effort to impose some order on his lover's behavior. Her dislike of Maeve had tainted the air like a fog from the minute the woman uttered her first words to them.

'Who is Jasper?'

'Ah, thou knows nothing.' Maeve looked at the two contemptuously. 'Jasper is a Faeran Elder, a healer. Everyone,' she looked down her nose, standing tall like a black lily above the seated traders, 'knows the healer.' Her sibilance gave her the sharpness of a knife.

'Will she be well?' Kholi persisted.

'Thou asks many questions. Yes. Now, I bid thee adieu.'

Adelina watched the fingers begin to pull the luscious cloak up the flexuous arms. Her concern for Ana burst its straining banks.

'Is that all? Is there nothing else from Liam? How long?'

'Thou pushes too hard, mortal. Ah, but yes.' Maeve dug into the pocket in the side of her black gown and withdrew something. She held it out to Adelina who stepped closer.

'This is for thee. Liam said thou would understand the intent. And as to time? As long as it takes. But he did say he would bring the chit to thee when she is well.'

As she spoke, Maeve pulled on the cloak and walked to the water. A swan again, she pushed off with a flap of the gracefully stretched wings and flew away, a harsh cry swooping lakewards.

'The chit is called Ana,' Adelina muttered as she turned over the object in her hands. A silver pin, it was exquisitely wrought in an under and over rune. The opening and closing ends of the rune depicted horses' heads, manes flying back in the unseen breeze.

'It is the Faeran rune for honour.' Kholi examined the brooch. 'Liam explained it to me once. See, my shrimati? He has found her, she is hurt but she is to be made well. And he will bring her to us.' He grasped Adelina and shook her gently. 'On his honour.'

Adelina rolled the brooch over and over in her hand, trying to believe the Faeran was helping Ana. That this wasn't just one more move, the final move in his gameplay. She could spend hours trying to explain to Kholi how she believed she and the Faeran were locked in some sort of combat with Ana as the prize and he would think her mad and if not mad then difficult, certainly wrong. So she kept silent, hinting by other less satisfactory means that Liam was not all he appeared to be. But Kholi could not be convinced and she hated that they had this one bone of contention between them, because in every other way they melded together perfectly.

Sometimes, as Kholi lay asleep next to her, she would lie staring into the dark and wonder at how her life had changed these last few weeks since Kholi had appeared. She had never loved so completely before. If she lost the focus of her love then she would die too, she was sure, or if not die then go mad with grief. It frightened her because she knew the other side of love was loss. As a solitary Traveller, uncommitted to anyone, she believed her life had balance. Now her life was like a mountain track, exhilarating, exciting, but one never knew what was around the next precipitate corner.

CHAPTER TWENTY

It was dark. Margriet had lit the lamp by the bed and as Ana's fever had dissipated and the night air was chill, the fire had been re-kindled. Liam had gone to eat at Margriet's behest and Jasper sat by Ana's side. He tipped his head back and watched the mirror as Ana walked alongside Liam around the pool, with the width of the path between them. Each time she came to a small arched bridge, she would turn toward it as if to cross. But then a look of fear would enter her face and she would fling away, Liam hurrying to catch up. Each time she came to the bridge, the Ana on the bed would twitch and her eyelids would flicker rapidly as if she were about to wake.

Such significance in such small actions, thought Jasper. As she lay with her lips slightly apart he drizzled drops of the distilled flower essences. Certainly she seemed less corpse-like. He watched as she began another circumference of the pool, but snorted like a horse exasperated with its rider and leaning forward, gently took Ana's cold fingers in his own and rubbed them softly. The girl in the mirror turned away from the pool with a start.

'Ana, have no fear. I am Jasper and I can help you to leave your anxieties behind. Trust me, my dear. Next time you come to the bridge, you will be calm and positive about what lies beyond. And by crossing, you will be able to leave the horrors of your past behind. It is, my dear, what bridges are for. Trust me.'

Ana had reached the bridge. She stopped and looked at it, biting at her lip, her hands clinging together, the bones white. She stared across the bridge and then back over Liam's shoulder, almost as if she would prefer to stay in the past with its harrowing memories.

Jasper saw a wounded creature who had lost all sense of trust, who could make a decision to neither move forward nor step back, frozen in the iciness of her pain.

She took a step away from Liam and placed a foot on the bridge as he watched intently and then she began to walk cautiously forward as if she trod on a single rope cable that swayed and dipped over an endless abyss. Softly, softly, step by step.

On the other side she turned and looked back at the Faeran, her face clear and radiant, the anxieties smoothed out. Her eyes sought Liam and she looked at him from underneath shy lashes, the glimmer of a smile playing around her mouth. Liam took a step forward and it was that very action that caused Jasper to sweep his hand in front of his body in the Faeran way, to fade the mirror to its normal form. Without turning, he spoke.

'Come in, Liam. And shut the door.'

Liam did as he was bid and with a cool expression, moved to sit in the other chair by Ana's bed.

'What were you doing, Jasper? What was Ana doing in the mirror? What was I doing?'

The young man looked at his Elder with only the merest hint of respect. So this is what he is like when he is disturbed, thought Jasper, watching the smouldering of the volcano.

'It's a dream mirror. Ana was having the same repetitive and defeating dream, it was distressing her and had the capacity to keep her locked in her despair. I merely helped her move through the dream.'

'But you stopped it when I started to go with her.'

'It was a dream, Liam. The only important thing was that she crossed the bridge.'

Liam sat tapping a leg, jig, jig, until Jasper put his hand down hard on the appendage.

'So she will be well?' Liam pushed up from under the Elder's grasp and strode around the room and Jasper gave a sigh.

'I believe she now sleeps quite normally and that she will wake and be quite well.'

Liam turned such a look of excitement on the Elder, the old man's heart skipped a beat. Ah, he thought, now we get to the nub of it. I'm right. A fool can see Liam has given his heart to a mortal. He grimaced.

'In the name of Aine, will you sit down and stop that confounded pacing! Pass me a goblet of wine as you do and you'd best pour yourself one. It may calm you a trifle.'

Liam picked up the glass carafe of wine and poured enough to fill two goblets. Had his mind been on the task in hand, he would have noted the soft chartreuse colour of the liquid and the fragrance of peach that drifted as he poured. He spilled some on the rug as he carried the goblets to Jasper and sat as he was bid.

'You make me feel as my father did,' he grumbled after taking a long draught of the wine.

Jasper gave a wry bark.

'You may well laugh. But if you know so much, you'll know my father treated me brutally.' He toyed with the fine stem of the goblet, turning the glass this way and that with such tight fingers, Jasper worried the fine crystal would snap.

'Is that why you went away so much?'

'What was the incentive to stay? I was supposed to fill the loss of his first son but so help me, most times he blamed me for the loss of the babe, abused me... I have marks on my back and arms that will be with me for eternity and you can guess the strength of such punishment to gouge a Faeran skin so. So Jasper, tell me, what in Aine's name was the point in staying?'

'I think you'll find that you reminded him over much of your mother, you have her eyes and a similar hauteur. And he hated her for losing your brother. He was... a difficult man.'

'Difficult!' Liam scoffed. 'So much that I sought refuge away! I hated him!'

Jasper shifted in his seat, the leather creaking as Ana slept on. The fire crackled softly.

'But why away from Faeran, Liam? There are plenty of your peers with whom you could have progressed around Eirie far from your father. Why spend so much time away from your own sort?'

Liam drained the wine and set the goblet on the table by Ana's bed and stared at her so intently Jasper flinched. *What a mess this will be, mark my words,* he thought.

'My peers?' Liam responded, quite direct. 'They were no better than my father: mocking, deceitful, bored, cruel. Faeran is about surfeit. About taking more and more so you can feel more and more. Outside of Faeran with the mortals, one gains an interesting perspective. One starts seeing things through other eyes, to feel things differently. And such a relief to be away from the demands of a bastard of a father. My heart leapt with delight when he met his bane and my life improved from that minute.' He shifted in his chair. 'In the beginning there was a mild interest in mortals and that became a fascination. And then I met Ana.' He leaned forward, a wisp of excitement passing across his face. 'Aine, she was like a book begging to be read. I just wanted to turn the pages to get to the next chapter. She is tragedy and comedy rolled into one. I became quite absorbed with the whole mortal thing because of its very unpredictability.'

And that became infatuation and then obsession, thought Jasper, looking at the cavernous shadows under Liam's eyes.

'How long since you slept?'

'A day, maybe two.' Liam shrugged the broad shoulders.

'Then sleep now. There is room beside Ana. I am going to stay here until she wakes so set you beside her on the bed and sleep.'

He wafted a hand in front of his chest as Liam closed his eyes to yawn again. Shedding boots and walking to the other side of the bed, he looked back at Jasper. The Elder sat smiling kindly and nodding his head, waving the goblet at him and encouraging him to lie down. A wave of tiredness crashed over Liam's head and he wondered for a moment if he had been mesmered. He was asleep before his head touched the feathered pillow beside Ana.

'Now, we shall see what we shall see.' Jasper stood up, a steely look of intent in his eyes. He walked to the flask of wine, poured more and then wafted his hand again and the dream mirror resumed focus. What Liam had not been told was that the mirror was one of Jasper's ways of reading futures, so lives would be revealed before him, unfolding in a series of scenic images. Chief amongst the information he secured was that of banes.

As the hours of night drifted by and Ana moved closer to the world of the wakeful and as Liam slept heavily beside her, Jasper's heart sank as more and more information was laid in its plain glory. He sighed, realising there was nothing, absolutely nothing he could do to prevent the outcome.

If I had known that someone else shared my own misgivings, that someone knew violent outcomes could be heading our way, then maybe, just maybe the tragedies that beset my life could have been prevented. But it was not to be.

So let's not waste time... to the new book and the next piece of embroidery! Follow the bees away from the oak tree. You will see they make a handy trail to a pear tree. Lovely leaves, lots of wiring and stitching, the kind I enjoy – stemstitch and satinstitch. Can you spy a tiny nest with a precious oval Veniche glass bead as an egg, sequestered inside. Flying away from our tree is a delightful robin with a proud red chest. Underneath his inky wings, and here I must ask you to bend the wire carefully, is a book of the same ink colour. Bound in Raji silk – silk I found at the stalls of the Fire Festival market.

Once again you will get two for the price of one. There is a squirrel sitting in all his caramel coloured finery. See how his tail is an absolute brush of Raji knots? Part them carefully, you will find a tiny sand coloured book covered in silk.

CHAPTER TWENTY ONE

Star on the Stair froze and glittered in the bitter cold. Across the face of the peaks above as the sun had set, swathes of heavy grey cloud swirled angrily. Adelina sat at the window of their room watching one fire after another spring up along the town ramparts, whilst Kholi carefully shaved his chin with the blade of a dagger. He had generously lathered his face in soap and Adelina looked back.

'At least I know what you will look like in your old age, Whitebeard.'

Kholi stood up, wiping off the lather, and walked to where she sat, to bend and kiss her with sweet tasting lips. He stood looking over her shoulder as the moon rose over Trevallyn. The lady moon, as he liked to call it, ascended shyly, dragging a pale wispy cloud behind. He whispered to Adelina.

'When moonlight,
near moonlight,
tips the rock and waving wood
When moonlight
near moonlight
silvers o'er the sleeping flood
When yew- tops
with dew-drops
sparkle o'er deserted graves;
tis then we fly
through welkin high
then we sail o'er the yellow waves.'

'Iontach!' Adelina whispered, eyes bright.

'I like poetry, 'he smiled. 'And many poets share campfires and we all entertain each other. I try to remember them all. That is one of my favourites, it came from someone who had travelled through Faeran and said it aptly described a time when one might see the Others.'

'There is a word designed to spoil anyone's joy,' she shivered.

'Come, my shrimati. Fire and flame await us. You must not dwell on such a thing tonight. Tonight is for celebration. Ana is alive and I believe she is well! No! Not another word! Come on you she-devil or I shall throw you over my shoulder and carry you outside as if I would ravish you!'

'You wish,' she smiled softly, depression and anxiety barely shifting as she allowed herself to be hurried outside.

Clusters of people rolled down the alleys and steps, their bodies rounded and fattened by layers of heavy insulation, faces shining in the light of the torchères they carried. Children ran chittering, their high-pitched excitement overlaying the rumble of their more adult companions. Some people carried lamps and these swung in their hands, the light travelling from side to side over the quilting of their warm outerwear.

The town-square was awash with the crowd. For a stretch of a minute, Adelina could have believed she was in the halls of the unseelie as noise and shrieking and flame stung faces surged around her. She tucked her arm tightly through Kholi's and clung to his side, the anxiety of the previous days heightened again by the dark shadows of the unlit square.

There were perhaps two minutes of silence grating on everyone's expectation. Adelina felt the crowd building to a mute frenzy, the atmosphere stretching her taut nerves tighter. Since they left the Inn, she had felt her scalp prickling, and goosebumps underneath the padding of her coat. Her instinct was to turn and survey the crowd and the ebony shadows because there was something, someone, out there, she knew it, her Traveller's intuition was rarely wrong. As the paranoia surged over her shoulders and around her neck someone called 'look'!

Hundreds of heads craned back to gaze into the heavens as a flaming arrow flew downwards from the belfry of the townhall. The trail glittered like the after-burn of a comet, streaking to embed itself in a deeper than black shadow in the centre of the square. In seconds the flames had exploded into a pyre of vermilion and gold as drums began to thunder through the night and a squad of red and yellow-garbed youths strode into the arena.

The evening licked and burned with tongues of flame as jugglers and tumblers threw, swallowed and flung fire, momentarily ridding Adelina of her worries. As the final fireball was dowsed and the world descended again into the blackness of night, she smiled at Kholi.

'Iontach,' she sighed as the crowd maintained a silent awe. The town clock began to chime... a succession of beautifully tuned bells played a melody reminiscent of sleighs and with that, in the flickering light of hundreds of lamps, snow began to fall and the people cheered and clapped. It was the finale they had wanted... a shower of white flakes drifting and fluttering to glance off hoods and hats, lashes and lips.

Kholi turned to Adelina. Her copper hair was laced in snowy finery. He wanted to run his fingers through it and kiss her wildly, so deeply had the insistent beat of the drums stirred him all evening. He grabbed her waist and lifted her high off the banquettes, swirling her round to face the exit. In his excitement, he neglected to see a woman close by and knocked her sideways as he placed his lover back on the ground. The female staggered and turned to berate him but caught up short when she spotted the woman in his arms.

'Ah, Adelina!' The female's voice was shallow and sharp. 'They told me you were in town!'

'Severine.' Adelina dug her hands into Kholi's arm as if it were the woman's throat she was squeezing. This then had been the someone in the crowd, this spawn of the she-devil who stood right here in front of her. Her neck ached with tension.

'Indeed. It is I. It has been a long time.'

A black quilted coat with a hood edged in spotted lynx fur draped the woman's body and snowflakes trembled amongst the nap of the fur and glistened like diamonds in the light of torch and lamp. The sharp-featured face betrayed nothing to soften and charm. Which was not to say the woman wasn't striking. Of that there was no doubt as male eyes passed over her and lingered longingly.

Adelina became aware of her own escort as he stood beside her, his interested gaze resting on this darkling woman.

'A long time indeed, Severine.' Inside, a feeling of dislike and unbridled concern slid like oil through her stomach. 'May I present my friend, Kholi Khatoun. We are journeying together. Kholi, this is Severine, another Traveller. She and I grew up on the road. You may possibly remember her.'

Kholi smiled and held out a hand.

Severine's eyes glanced at the olive skinned Raji merchant, taking in the indigo tattoos across his cheekbones and the wavy, black satin hair. She acknowledged him with a flick of her eyelids but turned ostentatiously away from his friendly gesture.

'I do not recall Mister Khatoun. But then I did leave our little band of gypsies quite a long time ago, Adelina. And I am Severine di Accia now.' She gave a sharp laugh. The embroiderer was reminded of two crystal goblets rubbing together... a honed laugh, full of knife-like edges like the woman. 'Actually, it's Contessa di Accia. I married.'

'I thought as much, Severine. Was that the decrepit old man we met on the road all those years ago, the one who seemed charmed by you? The old Count from Veniche? I thought I had heard it was. My, my he must be ancient now.'

Severine tipped her head slightly to the side and gave Adelina an appraising look.

'Sadly, my beloved husband is dead. I now run his estates. I can see though that you are still a Traveller. Still hawking your wares. Behir, but I am glad I no longer have such a life. Too arduous by half.' Severine ran a dismissive eye over Adelina's apparel and smoothed the snow away from the expensive fur edged plaquet of her own coat.

'Oh, I don't know, Severine. I think there is not much difference between you and I,' Adelina spoke the words as if they were tainted by lemon juice. 'You must travel for your husband's affairs and presumably you buy and sell. It is different but the same.'

'Hmm! Well I can see you have not changed. Always ready with the last word.' Severine drew herself up to eye-level with Adelina and gave a twist of her lips, what passed for a smile of sorts. 'Perhaps I shall see you on the morrow at the Fair. Good evening to you.'

She swirled her flared coat around and swept off, ignoring Kholi completely.

'By Aine, not if I see you first!' Adelina muttered a Traveller's curse after the swift vanishing back of the woman.

'You don't like Severine then?' Kholi took the taut hand he held and tucked it into the warm crook of his arm.

'No,' Adelina continued walking, looking straight ahead. 'Kholi, tonight was magical. Tonight went some way to easing my angst. Please let us not spoil the rest of the evening by talking about that virago. Do you agree?'

Dawn began to seep between the folds of the drapes covering the windows in Ana's room. The fire had long since burned down to glowing coals and the room had begun to chill.

On the bed two figures slept, one sideways with an arm draped over the waist of the smaller figure. In a red chair Jasper sprawled, legs akimbo, head flopped back and a stentorian snore filling the chamber. Loud enough it seemed, to wake himself but not the two in the bed. He jerked up with a start, giving the head with its high, intelligent brow a firm shake and wiping his mouth with a hand. He stood and stretched like an old dog rising from his basket by the fire – head up, chin stretched, arms and legs taut. Then he gently began an examination of his patient. He felt her forehead and encircled her wrist with his own fingers, checking her pulse.

Leaning down, he gently prised open her eyelids and seemed pleased with the result. Although he frowned after glimpsing Liam, he nevertheless carefully stepped around the bed and pulled the curtains open a fraction. Then with one last glance he walked to the door and exited, leaving a sleepy ambience that turned progressively more golden as the sunlight slanted in.

Nightmare after nightmare had swept over Ana, dragging at the cobwebs of her sanity. The night-ghasts, demons of the most frightening of dreams, pulled at her so that sweat poured from her body and her heart raced as she sought to outpace the fears that lurked behind her, waiting to pounce. She heard dunters and saw grindylows. Limnae's wrinkled fingers pulled at her very soul and the thought she could flee across the bridge was tempting beyond belief. But what lay on that other side? There could be Nökken, the Each Uisge, boggarts, all capable of maiming and killing. And there, in the distance behind her as she turned away from the bridge with wide eyes – Jonty, gory and foul, holding up a dripping arm with a fist missing. She turned to run away but caught sight of a titian-haired man, one who was so familiar.

In her dreams her heart beat as fast as if the night-ghasts continued their pursuit, but it was a thrilling beat, a feeling that she was more secure by being in the gleam of the Faearan's sights. The excitement flushed over her entire body and she longed to reach and put just a finger on him, just once. But something pulled gently at her soul, leading her forward, away from the Faeran and calmly to the bridge as a soft, hypnotic voice encouraged her to step up and over.

An overwhelming sense of freedom filled her to the brim as she stepped off the bridge and turned to stare at the Faeran on the other side. His black eyes burned after her, her skin feeling the static of a powerful yearning and she glanced shyly from under her lashes. She saw him place a foot on the bridge and then she fell into a deep, dreamless sleep.

She became conscious of light much later, as if day pushed at her eyelids and so she opened them slowly and dreamily, unafraid of her unknown surroundings and content as she stretched under the covers of the bed of clouds in which she was sure she lay. Something weighed down upon the blankets and impeded her and she turned in the semi-light to source the reason.

Liam! Her fingers crept to her mouth in uncertain delight.

He lay heavily asleep, unaware of Ana beside him as she tried to piece together the jigsaw in her mind. She lay and blinked at the golden light making patterns on the walls, feeling again the power of yearning that had manifested in her sleep. Her skin craved to be rubbed and her hair desired to be twisted in the hands of the man beside whom she lay. She could clearly remember the lost music box and Liam's voice, and the heady feeling of wanting to find him in the dark as she leaped from the van. As for the rest, all the horror and pain, it was as if it had been bleached from her mind, leaving her with a pristine sheet of paper on which she could write a new life.

Perhaps I am mesmered, she mused, perhaps Liam spirited me to Faeran. She lay still, feeling the rhythm of breathing beside her and the sensation filled her with a sense of wellbeing. Briefly she danced attendance on the thought that she was in bed with this man – in bed! Was she a victim of Liam's lack of probity, his Faeran corruptibility?

She had never deeply examined how she felt about Liam's reputation.

Oh, to be sure she knew all about the Faeran. Hadn't Adelina been drumming it into her for days. But Liam... he was different to the rest. He had saved her life... three times!

She heard the faint coo of doves outside but wrenched her attention to the face of the man next to her. He had only ever treated her with scrupulous kindness, with gentlemanly care. To the point where if someone asked her did she trust the Faeran more than her family, what could she say? It was obvious to the most dull-witted fool. He hadn't tried to sell her, barter her happiness for the price of a piece of dirt! Liam was a figure to be trusted. Implicitly.

She heard the man of her thoughts take a deep breath as he rolled closer to her. I want to touch him she thought, as the intensity of his presence swept all else from her mind. She eased herself onto an elbow and examined every inch of the face before her, the way stubble littered his chin and underlined his high cheekbones and the way his cheeks had a faint tawny glow as the coverings warmed him. His hair had come untied and strands of it stretched across the linen of the pillows. His mouth was slightly open and Ana could see teeth gleaming between the lips. Without a thought, she traced fingers as light as thistledown along the chin and up to the cheek. Instinctively she leaned forward and pressed her own lips to Liam's, at first softly but then, as she felt her body filled with a rushing and aching pain, with naked desire.

His hands snaked from under the covers into her hair and he returned the pressure of her lips, rolling her under him as he eased the linen of her gown from her shoulders. She gazed up at the strong jaw, at the hard, black eyes and felt as if she was falling into a dark oubliette and she knew that if he would just make love to her she would be happy to rot alone in that dark hole for ever, because the sensations would nourish her more than food or air.

Jasper, in his workroom, was attempting to scry using his crystal spheres. Most of the night he had watched the mirror and had discovered Liam's bane. He was depressed, angry at being unable to turn the tide of events. He rolled and palmed the balls in a lyric, flowing movement, mesmerising in its rhythm as the glittering glass eddied from one hand to another.

He had tried to intuit Ana's future in his mirror and whilst there were faded images, nothing had been clear enough to be sure. Surely the balls would help. But as images pervaded the crystal clarity of the instruments and as Jasper tried to grasp the message, the concentrated peace of the room shattered as first one and then the other of the two spheres cracked and fragmented and the pieces fell out of his hands on to the floor – by their own disintegration revealing a rebounding integration happening under his very roof. He growled and swept furious hands along the table, sending notes, apparatus and charts flying. He had never felt so impotent in his life!

CHAPTER TWENTY TWO

Such a Faeran sight, to be sure!

Adelina opened the drapes in the morning and gasped at the view laid out before her. Everywhere was sparkling white. As light danced off snow-clad roofs, tiny crystals sparked and spangled. It reminded Adelina of organza – the kind that in a certain light glitters with all the colours of the rainbow as one throws it about on a cutting table, measuring off lengths for a ball gown.

Below her, she watched children chasing each other with snowballs, ducking, weaving and exploding with laughter. Off the eaves above, sharp icicles hung like crystal stalagmites, not a drop of moisture splashing from their razor sharp ends, for the air was freezing.

'Kholi, come look!' Adelina huffed on the condensation on the window to clear it away.

Down on the Celestine Stairway, children gazed up as a fist rubbed at a fogged window in the Inn of the First Happiness. They watched as two faces appeared side by side. One copper haired woman and then one of those Raji men with the blue tattoos on the cheekbones. They waved to the children below and childish hands waved back and then there was a yell.

'Get 'em!'

A fusillade of armaments shot skywards to pound in cascades of fine powder snow against the windowpane, causing the two lovers to laugh at the youngsters below.

'Bullseye!'

The children were jubilant.

'I used to be just like that once.' Adelina rubbed the window with a wistful finger.

'And of course, now you are too grown up. Is that it?'

'I suppose. Life just seems a little more serious.' She turned away from the window. 'Especially now.'

'My shrimati, the sun shines! Be content! I expect Ana to be back in a day or two and I really think you should stop this perpetual agonizing. She is protected and cared for and we are here with a Fair to attend and we are warm and safe in our little Inn. We are fortunate, aren't we? I think we should just get on with our day. After all, Ana would want us to, wouldn't you agree? Besides, I'd venture to say if she is able and well now, she is relaxing and sparing us little thought. Yes?'

'I confess you're probably right. But you know Kholi, up until now my life has been totally carefree. Selfishly so. And now all of a sudden, I have the responsibility of this child.'

'Come now, she's certainly no child! And why should you assume the role of parent? She chose to leave her familiar environment so surely she must accept responsibility. No... I know what you will say. She is young, naïve, unaware.' Kholi dressed as he spoke. 'But I think she has learned a lot in the last few days and in the end Adelina, we have looked after her the best that friends can. We need not chastise ourselves at all. I think she must assume her own mantle of responsibility. And,' he pulled on a high buttoned, over-tunic which he belted with an embroidered scarlet sash. 'If her life's decisions include Liam, it is not up to us to prevent her. She must make her own choices.'

'Kholi, I dispute the joining of Ana with Liam.' Adelina's voice hardened. 'Mortals are not meant to align themselves with Others, it always ends badly. I feel it deep in here,' she tapped her forehead with her fingers. 'And in here.' She tapped her chest. 'I can tell you any number of stories from Travellers' tales and they are all true. Remember when Oisín met with Niamh? That was a love story but he, the mortal, died.'

'Yes, I know. But my love, we all die sooner or later. And isn't it better to have had the experience of such a love before you die than to go to your deathbed wondering? Listen, I'll tell you this. I would die tomorrow a happy man after the days I've just had with you. I swear on my sister Lalita's life!'

Adelina met Kholi's intense eyes and touched his cheek, defeated temporarily by his argument. He didn't understand – she had this feeling, an intuition that all was not well, that their lives would all change irredeemably and she was convinced it was because the Faeran would not leave them alone, would not leave Ana alone. The weight of that intuitive feeling weighed her down more and more each day and she just wished Kholi would believe her. She sighed, realizing he was as stubborn as his wretched camel and would not be moved. Wisely, she changed the subject.

'You know, I have a wish to buy such a length of fabric today. I am inspired to make a robe, Kholi, the kind no one has seen nor will ever see again. Come on, let's go shopping.'

At the house amongst the Ymp trees, Ana lay sleeping the sleep of the exhausted, full of surfeit and the seeds of a Faeran lover. Her skin glowed like Adelina's satin in the light from the window and her hair lay tousled across the pillow. Liam, dressed but with his shirt loose over his breeches and his hair untied, sat in the window embrasure on a bench full of cushions. He stretched a leg from one side of the window to the opposite, the other leg bent and hands resting upon it, cupping his chin, eyes unfocused as he stared into the walled garden.

He and Ana had made love. She had given herself willingly and he had looked down at her, black eyes swallowing her whole.

'Ana, I have saved you from death three times, I am now at liberty to call in the forfeit. I have the right to ask you to follow me to Faeran. You are unable to say no.'

For a while they said nothing: a silence filled with breath and sighing. Then he added, 'But I would not force you, Ana. I want you to make the decision willingly. So I revoke my Faeran right. You will not pine or suffer. You are free to make your own way.'

'Liam,' Ana's voice was croaky with tiredness, repleteness. 'Even if you had not taken away your right, even if I was bound to follow you, I would do it willingly. I want nothing more than you. Forever if you want me.'

Liam smoothed his hand over her back and she sighed and closed her eyes. As she drifted into sleep, she whispered so he had to bend to hear her.

'And forever is such a long time in Faeran, isn't it?'

Why did I encourage her, he thought. What provoked me? The heat of the moment? The desire to play a game with her or am I being played like a pawn? I don't understand. Look at her, she thinks she gives herself to me for eternity! Do I want her that long? Forever is almost forever for me.

He shook his head. There were times like now where he found this absorption with mortal love so difficult to comprehend. So often he had asked himself why this had happened to him. On those disappearances from his friends, fulminating in some corner of Faeran, he had tried to wriggle out of the obsession, out of the fascination, out of the inevitable commitment that mortals seemed to pledge. He had thought she would be so easy to open, read and discard. But like the worst addiction, he craved more. He turned his head to the door as he heard it open. Jasper stood utterly immobile, face filled with cold rage.

'You,' he said in a loud whisper. 'Out here! Now!

He preceded Liam at a prodigious pace to the gravel outside, swishing his whip against doors and walls.

'Mount up!'

The command was as stern as any Liam's father might have given. So he took Florien's reins from Folko, after tucking in his shirt and hastily tying his hair back. He barely had time to leap for the saddle before a whack on Florien's rump and a shouted 'hyar!' sent the horse into a bolt.

Jasper led out amongst the Ymp trees and away from the overblown beauty of the Faeran orchard. Hooves pounded the dry grass of the Barrow Hills whereupon the horses wove and bent between the wild trees, the last red leaves falling agitatedly in the mad slipstream as they sped past. Onwards and upwards until the snorting animals began to slow against the incline, the snorts marking the beat of the hooves. As they crested the highest hill, Jasper pulled back on his reins, his black horse sliding to a bucking halt. Florien spun around as Liam tried to calm him, the very air filled with the crackle of anger and impatience.

'I'm sorry. I abused your hospitality and your care of the girl. I should not have.' Liam leaned over his horse's neck, smoothing and patting, blushing a fraction, for he knew why Jasper was angry. To make love to Ana under the man's roof! An impertinence! And a mortal, no less!

Jasper said nothing as the two men dismounted and let their horses stand with drooping heads and resting fetlocks.

'It was a bit of fun, Jasper.' Liam attempted to fob off the event that had begun to resound with repercussions.

'Fun, mac an cheana? Well then, I cannot prevent you from having fun!' There was a slight sting in the scorpion's tail as Jasper hit the ground idly with his whip. He sat against one of the ruby-leafed trees, his coat pooling around him on the stubble.

'If you had tried, I may have told you to go to Hades.' Liam lowered himself by the old man.

'Ho indeed!' Jasper mocked the bravado. 'To no avail of course, I am a Faeran Elder after all.' He laughed the dry bark again. 'You do like your own way, don't you?' Then he changed the subject with such alarming speed that Liam's head spun for a moment.

'Why did you murder the mortal, Liam?

Liam looked down at his boots and brushed at the dust.

'I did not kill him. The Cabyll Ushtey did.'

'With your not insubstantial assistance.'

Liam shrugged. So what? No doubt Jasper knew why and that it was a just retribution. Anyway, it did nothing to lessen the moment he had just experienced with Ana.

'Does she know?' Jasper turned and looked Liam in the eye. The young man's gaze slid away. 'She will hate what you have done, Liam. Most mortals have a far different code, one they call benevolent justice. If it is at all violent it becomes so after the decision of an independent court. She will never understand how you could appoint yourself summarily judge and jury. And with the Cabyll Ushtey! Aine, man! You had best never tell her. It will go heavily against you.'

'Then we shall keep the secret, shan't we?' Liam now fixed Jasper with such a cool look, it was the Elder's turn to slide away from the frigid eyes.

They sat absorbed in their own thoughts. The birds in the trees whistled and trilled and were utterly contrary to the issue of life and its taking which had just been touched on. Liam leaned his head back against the bark of the tree. He felt its roughness against the back of his skull and longed for Ana's ivory smoothness.

'So my boy, do you fall in love with this pretty young thing?'

Jasper's question jerked him away from the dream of sexual favours.

'Of course not! It is a dalliance, a game pure and simple! Something to deter the mundane and titillate the senses!' His voice held a tinge of mockery.

'Aine man, don't chafe so,' Jasper sighed. 'If you have, then you follow other Faeran who have trod the same path. It's one of those thousand to one things that becomes the stuff of story and legend – the Faeran and the mortal.'

'I have not. You are wrong.' Liam's response pushed at the outer edge of respect. 'You imagine things in those balls and mirrors of yours, old man.'

Jasper smiled patiently.

'In my balls and mirrors, boy, I see more than you can ever imagine. Others come to me to be healed, to secure charms and potions, spells and incantations. But the chiefest thing they come for, those who are brave and stupid all in one, is knowledge of their bane. Sometimes, when I know, they will stop me telling them, realising it is better to know nothing and continue regardless than to know everything and continue life constantly glancing over the shoulder for the presence of the final Doom. Some don't want to know because it adds a spicy danger to their lives, wondering if this encounter or that will be the source of their demise. Sometimes I don't care what their bane is. I dislike them so much, I pile the truth upon them and send them on their precarious and gloomy way. But there are other times,' he turned away from the tree and faced Liam. 'Times where I know the person and I hate the knowledge I have.'

He lapsed into a deep silence. Liam waited but nothing was forthcoming. So he stood and went to Florien, to lean against the horse's neck and the animal swung its head around and nuzzled his hand.

'You know my bane.' Apparently unperturbed, he ran strong fingers through Florien's mane.

Jasper looked at the young man, marked the height, the breadth of shoulder, the engaging face. He could see the charm.

'Yes.'

To know one's bane – did he want to? Somewhere in the pit of Liam's stomach, worms writhed, for who would want to know how they were going to die or when? Then again, he mused as he looked across Florien's back, this could be the greatest game of all time! To forestall Destiny, to change Fate.

'So?' He confronted the Healer.

Jasper's mouth grimaced slightly and he took a deep breath.

'I have known you from afar and close since you were a tiny chap,' he remarked fondly, eyes softening so that Liam could see affection and care, something he had been privy to so little in his life. 'I watched your father misuse you and I hated him for it. Then I watched you as an adolescent closing up on yourself like my precious blooms when the sun leaves the walled garden. I saw you leave, at first for short times, then longer. But we have lost you. The minute you saw Ana, you were no longer a part of Faeran and you seemed governed by emotions that had no brake, no control. Simply, my boy, your obsession made you blind to everything.' Jasper's expression hardened. 'Liam, you willingly and cold-bloodedly facilitated a mortal death. We don't do that. If a mortal dies because of a confrontation with us, it is not because we wantonly murdered them or were accessories to murder. Generally they have died because of their own misdirected emotions. So what you did will have far-reaching ramifications. Of this I am absolutely positive.'

'How so? Is that my bane?' Liam almost scoffed. As if Jonty's death mattered!

'No.'

'So? I don't care! I will cope when it does.' Cocksure, he shrugged the act and its guilt away.

'Liam, you may not be able to. But all that aside, are you sure you want to know your bane?'

Liam nodded his head fiercely.

'Ah my boy. It is... it is...'

'Oh Jasper, for Aine's sake!'

'I believe it is Ana!' The words gushed like a geyser on the plains in the northern Raj.

'Ana? ANA?' Liam's eyebrows rose high on his forehead as his heart chimed a single beat. For a minute it felt like a death knell: so final, so loud was it, he thought Jasper would hear.

'How so? Will she kill me?'

'Not directly,' Jasper replied, beads of sweat glistening on his forehead as the sun climbed higher. 'She is soft, kind, in love, it would be hardly likely. No, she will be the death of you. That is all I know.'

'What if she died before me?'

'Before, together, after – it makes no difference. She is your bane.'

So saying the Elder approached his black steed and vaulted up. He waited while a perturbed Liam placed a foot in the stirrup and mounted Florien. They rolled in the saddles as the horses eased themselves one hoof in front of the other down the steep slope.

'And you saw this? In that confounded mirror?'

'Yes. I saw you deceased my son, and a slim, dark-haired woman stood over you with her back to me.

'Was I old, young? And anyway, it could have been any mortal. Why should it be Ana?'

'Because Liam, one of the painful things about my skill is that I can hear what happens and I heard what you said with your last breath.'

'Ana!' Liam whispered, unaware Jasper had not answered his first question. The game reconfigured beyond expectation.

'I'm so sorry, mac an cheana. So sorry. That is why I was angry. There was nothing I could do.'

'Nothing?'

'A darth a bith. A destiny is set in stone, muirnin.'

They rode on.

Books are being finished and concealed at a prodigious rate and the story begins to darken like the sky as a thunderstorm approaches and the air begins to crackle with lightning. I find as I write these journals that I feel ill, as the knife begins to carve close to the bone. So you must move on quickly.

There is a magnificent white lily, tall and gracious. With yellow silk stamens of wrapped wire and fine strappy green leaves. Can you see the beetle at its foot?

It is a Ruby Longhorn Beetle. Brick red Veniche silk and tiny black antique bugle beads from Bressay in the Pymm Archipelago. They mark its antennae beautifully. Lift the elytra carefully, just as you have done before and there is the journal.

CHAPTER TWENTY THREE

The Fair took place in the ancient roofed market place. Never sure of the vagaries of mountain weather, the forefathers built an area filled with arcades and spanned by huge wooden transoms, carved and wrought with flowers and leaves–the sculptural wonder alone, market notwithstanding, made the place worthwhile. High up, as in the mews, skylights allowed light to enter and sunbeams slanted down and pooled in brilliance on the floor: golden discs that could be mistaken for puddles of glamarye, the kind that someone could fall into and be trapped by the Nökken.

Faeran entrepreneurs occupied one arcade of the massive bazaar in a veil of mystique and the Raji traders had set up in the other, radiating brash and colourful exotica. Whilst sitar and tabla evoked souk, stone and sand, melodic Faeran harp and gittern created promise and the answers to expectation... a strange cadence which shivered down backbones but smoothed away the trills and tremors as it washed over the listeners – music filled with contradictions. Brilliance radiated – light playing off silks and satins, soft, bejeweled skin and fantastic raiment. Patrons touched things tentatively, overawed, wondering if they were destined to buy silk purses that were actually sows' ears.

Kholi and Adelina wandered, the embroiderer's nervousness on hold, her anxiety at the entry of Severine into her life, blotted out by the sellers who smiled, charmed, maybe even mesmered. The mortal crowd edged by, warily fascinated, observing the rules of care when dealing with the Others – wearing charms and amulets, palming surreptitious signs of horns, avoiding namegiving. Irrespective, the goods for sale glistened and sparkled like a treasure trove, the like of which few mortals might ever see again.

Adelina found threads she must have: a skein of the finest silver thread for the stitching of a stumpwork cobweb, silk gauze ribbons – gold shot with mauve, raspberry with green, white with silver – the perfect degree of flimsiness for insect wings. But she craved fabric and wandered until she smelt the silk stall.

Silk has its own fragrance – delicate, redolent of mulberry and sunshine and the perfume of flowers and leaves from which the dyes are taken, and it drew her as if she smelt the subtlest tang. The seller behind the counter watched her beadily as she advanced and with a flick of her wrist sent cascades of a pure silk flowing to the end of the table. It floated like a waft of a mist or cirrus cloud, entrapping the white brilliance from the skylight, whispering as it fluttered to lie in front of Adelina.

'Oh!'

She gazed at the fabric, reminded of the unblemished cream of just poured milk until the light changed and she recalled the inside of a shell, like the palest pink Veniche cameo. Its nacreous lustre flowed from milk to shell and back to milk, a constant play of light akin to the beams in the sky when an aurora is evident. It was so utterly unique, so completely Other, Adelina stilled with awe.

The Faeran woman beckoned. She held a fold of the fabric out to the Traveller in graceful fingers, enticing. Needing no second bidding, Adelina slid the folds through her palm, feeling the coolness, the faint texture as here and there was a slub or knot of the fibre. She could hear the seductive whisper as it rolled beneath her fingers: 'buy me, use me.'

'Oh Kholi, I can see a robe of such magnificence, so unique! A work of art!' She turned a glowing countenance to the merchant. 'Can you envisage it?'

'Indeed, my princess, I can. A work the Faeran will want to own.' He grinned at the silk seller and she smiled secretively back. Adelina intentionally broke the seductive moment.

'Seven lengths then, if you please?' She deferred politely to the Faeran, who questioned the mortal in amusement.

'Don't you want to know the price?'

'Faeran, whatever you ask, I shall double the amount. And pay *you* double again to make that robe for me, Adelina.' A sharp voice cut through the quiet negotiations at the stall. It reminded Adelina of fingernails on a panel of glass or the Symmer wind in the Raj, which could drive a man mad with its shrieking. She swung around to stare into the basilisk eyes of Severine di Accia.

Mentally she stamped her foot, glorying in the image of Severine's own being under her heel as she repeatedly ground that heel in and in. Aware she could never afford the price the Faeran would ask. But, she thought with a flash of pure venom, neither would she ever make her robe, her design, for Severine! Never! She turned a grim expression back to the Other.

The Faeran's translucent skin created a canvas for a perfectly drawn face – framed by mahogany hair in cascades of curls interlaced with gem and pearl. Loose twists fell around her face, over the alabaster forehead, sliding around her neck as she glanced almost mischievously from one to the other of the competing women.

'Your inspired robe sounds almost good enough to be Faeran, Adelina. As your handsome consort knows.'

She cast a look of such radiance at Kholi, the heat of sexual expectation warmed his entire body. Adelina stepped back knowingly on his toes.

'Thank you.' She tried to smile and be gracious, knowing the Faeran desire to toy with mortals, knowing the seller would see the naked lust for the fabric in her eyes, positive she would enjoy watching the disappointment and sadness as Severine departed with her prize.

'Come then, Faeran. Hurry and name your price. I don't wish to dally.' Severine's shrill voice acted on the Faeran as if a fierce weather change had occurred. Her eyes darkened like a night sky when the moon lies hidden behind layers of black cloud.

'Well now, Contessa di Accia.' The Faeran's voice shrivelled the air and Severine slid her hands into a sable muff. 'It seems today, I have no liking for straight black hair, grey as slate eyes and mouths painted redder than a drop of mortal lifeblood. Today I like copper hair. And eyes like dark topaz. And freckles. Yes, today I like freckles. And because I like freckles, I am going to give Adelina her seven lengths. And for you some advice. There is a Faeran seller of dyes further down the aisle. She does a good line in copper hair tint. Avail yourself of her services.'

Adelina's eyes opened wide. Quickly she glanced at Kholi and then turned her eyes on Severine. Hell and damnation burned viciously back, as if all the unseelie of the world had been sucked into the very soul of the woman before her.

Severine remained speechless, but Adelina felt such a stream of hatred rushing toward her, she knew the woman's thoughts would have ganched and flayed her to death. She turned toward the stall and buried her shaking fingers in the cool of the silk. When she turned back to Kholi, Severine had mercifully departed.

'Here you are.' The Faeran held out a thick parcel wrapped in cobweb fine paper. 'But I lied, Adelina, I do require payment. As you know, nothing is for free from the Faeran.' She leaned forward and wrapped soft fingers in a hank of Adelina's hair. 'I want your hair. Not much, a dozen or so strands. Then we shall consider payment made.'

Moments later, her parcel under her arm and a long lock of copper hair curled into the Faeran's palm, Adelina walked toward the Raji stalls.

'Aine I feel ill. Severine and I were mere playthings just then. That Other had a game at our expense. She was so livid at Severine, not caring the woman now hates me even more. Trust me, this is a terrible game that is only just begun. Severine will make me pay in the end Kholi, and all the while the Faeran will laugh at the outcome, that's for sure.'

The day sank behind the clouds of night and the couple returned laden with purchases to their temporary home. As they spoke, their words escaped in puffs tinged white and vapid with the freezing air.

'But it has been a good day, shrimati, excluding that last contretemps. The marketplace, the Faeran goods, the Raji stall holders?'

'Oh indeed.' Adelina hugged the parcel of silk to her chest, the urge to cut and stitch bursting. But in the back of her mind she saw an image that cast a dark stain over the folds of fabric. 'Except for Severine.'

'Adelina I insist, you must tell me why she agitates you. Your face folds into such frowns when you speak of her.'

'If you say I must, but later, yes?' She shuddered and hugged the silk even closer, lapsing into a puffing silence as the steady incline took hold.

They had reached the door of the Inn and as Kholi pushed, Buckerfield pulled it back to greet them, his cheeks flushed and pouched, the welcoming smile widening at the sight of them.

'Well, my lovelies, I can certainly see you have had a good time. You've been gone long and spent gelt too, it seems.' He eyed the arms loaded with parcels. 'Now, go to my little nook and I'll bring you some refreshment. You have visitors!'

He moved his bulk aside and as Adelina and Kholi squeezed past, they smelled the fragrance of grape and hop, a pleasant enough perfume. They stopped dead when they caught sight of the visitors. Dropping her parcels where she stood, Adelina ran across the room and threw herself into waiting arms.

'Ana! Thank Aine!'

CHAPTER TWENTY FOUR

Ana had woken dreamily whilst her lover and the Healer were galloping up the Barrow Hills. She had stretched languorous hands above her head and felt a slight chafing in unfamiliar places. Her hands flew to her belly as the early morning's delight flooded into her mind. Turning to the window, lying on her side and gazing out between the slightly pulled drapes, she felt a surge of coyness as she remembered what she and Liam had done – coyness coupled with rampant desire.

Momentarily she wondered what Pa would think. Disappointed at her looseness? Probably. But Pa, you are gone now. I trusted you to stay with me for so much longer than you did and now I must make my own way. And I choose to make my way with a man called Liam, who I believe loves me as much as you did, as much as I trusted Ma to love me. She sighed and missed the gentle opening of the door, in the midst of a resolution that it would be the last time she ever dwelt on trust and the lack of it!

'Ana?' A soft voice redolent of honey and spice eased her from her poignant reverie. She rolled over.

'Are you feeling well, muirnin?' A slim woman of indeterminate age moved to the window and pulled back the drapes. An ostler appeared with a tray of steaming breakfast food and an arm of trailing clothes. Having placed the tray beside the bed, a smile lightening the crooked and austere face, he laid out his other bundle on the bed.

'Jasper said you needed clothes. So there are some jodhpurs for you and a shirt and warm suede coat. The ewer is filled with warm water.' The woman wafted a hand in the direction of the jug and bowl and Ana heard the trickle of water, saw the steam.

'Liam and Jasper are riding. If you are ready before they return, you are welcome to take a turn in the garden. You will be quite safe.' The woman hustled the ostler in front of her and the two walked to the door. 'If you need anything, just call. We can hear you wherever we are.'

Ana slipped her legs over the edge of the bed, caution erased by the woman's matter-of-fact, easy manner. Picking up a triangle of steaming toast, she licked confit off her fingers and chewed as she walked to the window to gaze at the humming, blossoming garden.

Peace cosseted her almost to the depths of her soul. For the first time for months there was no suffocating grief, no confusion. For all that time, her energies had been directed to the sublimation of emotion, to the mere act of survival because if she let sorrow in with more than a foot at her door, she had thought it would completely overtake her. But of course, her efforts had been in vain because the misery had its own agenda, controlling her rather than the other way round.

Now though, she felt different, lighter. She was able to think of her father without the black dog of loss sitting behind her staring dolefully. She could see Pa's face with its slightly balding head and kind, brown eyes and she knew she could draw up his image without pain. Her mother had said in one of her rare moments that it took time. In Ana's mind, time equated with distance and the miles she had travelled serve to lessen the load.

She was reminded oddly of the oubliette, so recently in her thoughts – the dark, dank hole where people were imprisoned and forgotten, to rot into eternity. What a perfect place to jettison the awful memories she had! Of the way her father had died, starving for air, the rasping, the panic as he clawed at the bedding fighting for just one last breath. Of Bellingham and his outrageous brutality, of the Others who had wantonly, maliciously tried to kill her. She watched them in her mind, sliding into the hell-hole, and then she turned away to fill the emotional space so recently vacated by her father, with Liam.

The two Faeran steadily picked their way across the rolls of the Barrow Hills. For some time Liam had been quiet, brooding on Jasper's revelations. He flicked a section of mane from one side of Florien's neck to the other and broke the silence. So he was to die – at Ana's behest, somehow. As his heart once again found a rhythm, he wondered why she affected him so?

'Did you discover anything about Ana's future?'

Jasper had relaxed, allowing his horse to meander along, and took a moment to answer.

'No. Mortals are hard to divine. Their heads run at a million miles an hour with things they hold on to. And to be honest I was concentrating so hard on trying to get Ana to break free from the constraints of her emotional withdrawal, I did not give it the time it needed.'

His horse jogged a few paces and Jasper sat easily in the saddle, his posture hardly changing, hands relaxed on the reins.

'But there was a repeating symbol.'

'Indeed?' Liam sat straighter, the saddle creaking. 'What?'

'Quite odd really. A horseshoe."

'And so?'

'Well I'm not quite sure. To mortals, horseshoes are tied with good fortune and marriage.'

'Ah well, to be sure, we shall be married and live a long life.' At Liam's bitter tone Jasper grimaced, tightening his fingers on the reins.

'Did you ever seek my brother?' Liam wanted to get far from Ana and banes for the moment, it required a commitment in which he suddenly had no desire to indulge.

'In fact, yes. Every year for five years I spent time in the Pymm Archipelago, for that's where he was mislaid. I thought to find signs, but there were none. Not a solitary thing.'

'Do you think he died?'

'There are only two possibilities, Liam. Certainly one is that he died. I never spent time with the babe to be able to determine his bane. If I had, I would perhaps have had clues as to where and what to look for. At least I could have reported something definitive back to your father. The other possibility is he may have been found by a carlin... a mortal wise woman whose skills and abilities border on Other. Only one such as she would have known how to hide a Faeran babe from Faeran eyes. But there was not a sign. Plenty of orphaned children as there were hard times in the islands, but none were Other.' He turned back and looked at Liam as he raised his eyebrows and shrugged his shoulders. 'So there you are. Now!

What say you to a race, to blow away gloom? To home! HYAR!!'

He closed his heels hard on his horse and sat down firmly in his saddle. The horse flew into a gallop, sending clods of soil and tussock in its wake. Liam needed no second bidding. Faeran are renowned for indulging to excess when there is amusement to be had and besides he wanted so much to shake the uncharacteristic foreboding with which Jasper had filled him. He clapped the reins either side of Florien's neck shouting, and the grey animal sprang after their fast disappearing companions.

The duelling horses racketed through the Ymp trees and skidded abreast to a gravel-scattering stop outside the house. The noise of the snorting, the shouts and laughter and the shod hooves crunching over gravel as they plunged about, brought Ana flying around the side of the house. When she saw Liam she stopped and smiled and even Jasper could see the bloom and beauty on the girl's face. He watched Liam surreptitiously. The fellow smiled at the girl but there was nothing overt that one could construe as love, or even fascination. He wondered if the boy would ever admit to it openly, let alone face the reality himself because there was something of Fate in all of it and the one thing Jasper knew was that one could never change Fate, Destiny – call it what one will. He jumped off his horse.

'Well Ana, muirnin, you look so much better. Perhaps you can return with Liam to your friends. What do you think?'

'And so here I am.' Ana relayed an expeditious account of her trials and tribulations, with the occasional help from Liam, although the two carefully left out reference to the morning's dalliance. But Adelina knew immediately that Ana had given herself to Liam. She held herself a different way, as if she had discovered seduction on her journey... a glance with a heavy lid, a licking of the lips, a toss of the hair – this time she was no ingénue.

Adelina sat back as Ana laughed with Kholi. She held a glass of wine in her hand and tapped it thoughtfully against her lips. Liam sat down beside her and his very presence acted on the embroiderer like salt on a wound.

'She was fortunate beyond doubt, Liam. She could be living the murky life of a Limnae now. And all thanks to you.' She didn't look at Liam as she spoke, just began swirling the wine in her glass, trying to dredge up her long lost equanimity.

'Yes, Adelina. She is alive and well and here. Surely now you will trust me. I truly have nothing but her best interests at heart.'

At this she turned and looked at him.

'Yes, but why?'

He shook his head, laconic, dry.

'Ah, Adelina. Sometimes I think you are brave as well as unbelievably stupid. Do you forget that it is totally within my power to bewitch you or even Kholi and turn your lives upside down.'

He spoke to the air, not looking at her once, and she could feel the steeliness of the threat, as sure as if he held a poniard to her side. He continued, bending to flick a white thread from his dark breeches.

'But by all means have your digs and jibes. I allow them to pass before me, free of restraint. Because of this! I want Ana! Whether it is to love her, lust after her, dominate her, mould her...' he dragged out the word 'mould', his hand cupped, fingers closing as if on a ball of soft clay. 'It is my choice, not yours. So I care nothing for your approval or otherwise. All you need to know is that I will have her.'

He closed his fist with a snap. 'Besides, look at those two.' Kholi and Ana chatted amicably, the Raji's arm around her shoulder. He said something and she laughed, the embodiment of spontaneous happiness. 'Do you think with your perpetual carping, you will convince them I am anything other than what I appear to be?'

He raised an eyebrow, clinking his goblet against her own, the tink-tink sounding like the clash of swords in Adelina's overactive imagination. As he moved away, his voice returned to her.

'Your move, I think!'

Adelina turned away, for once speechless, but Ana called to her.

'It seems you've had your own excitements. Silks and satins and Faeran markets and what about Severine. She sounds dire!'

Adelina composed her face with speed, not wishing Liam or the others to see her distrait.

'Oh she's dire indeed! I've hated her since I was an infant. For some perverse reason, both our sets of parents flung us together as often as not. We are of an age you see. And neither of us had siblings, the difference being that my parents were quite young whilst Severine's were ancient, truly.'

She took a sip of her wine, remembering the jabs, jibes and joys of childhood.

'And because she was this wondrous gift from Lady Aine so late in their lives, they spoiled her, loading her with gifts and compliments till her ego was the height of Mt. Goti! What made it worse was that she really was quite a pretty child, itself amazing as her parents were nothing out of the ordinary. And I was so plain, a typical redhead, and she let me know it. She called me spiteful names behind our parents' backs and encouraged some of the others in our caravanserai to bully me, and I mean bully! You know how insidious children can be. After that, my hate for her knew no bounds and my red temper would pitch itself like a war-machine against the hateful bastion of her person. I sabotaged her life, pinching, pulling, stealing, destroying – anything and everything to get my own back on her.'

Adelina pursed the lips that Kholi loved so much.

'Then I heard the word 'changeling' and I decided she was one. She just didn't fit in our Travellers' world, the way she gave herself airs. I began to call her a changeling and the other children took up the chant and I hoped we made her life wretched but it was water off a duck's back. Inadvertently I gave her the tool by which she would re-shape the rest of her miserable, and let me say dangerous life. When she found out that changelings were exchanged Faeran children she began to see herself differently. Never mind that a changeling was usually a sickly Faeran babe – in her mind it was of no account. Hell's teeth! If she had given herself airs before, it was nothing to the way she behaved as we reached our more mature years!' She took a sip of the comforting liquor and continued.

'I blossomed a little as we grew up. My hair quietened down, I lost my puppy fat and I began to draw the male eye, a thing Severine loathed. All her life she had been the one who attracted the attention in the camp and now she had a contender – me. She pitched herself against me in everything – relationships, trading, embroidery – which I might add I trumped her on every time. What some saw as amusing competition, I knew was actually war. In her private moments, she constantly read about the Others and tried to emulate them and their ways, her belief in the changeling theory having rooted itself like an ugly weed. Her parents were devastated because as long as she believed such illusory stuff, she was denying her parentage but they were too feeble to gainsay her. And then something terrible happened.'

Her audience was still, even Liam who leaned against the wall in the shadows, sipping a goblet of red Raji wine.

'We had stopped in a glade we knew of, to collect fungi, truffles. It was something of a tradition when we passed through that part of Eirie. All of us, even Severine, set out and filled baskets of the stuff and then went about preparing our food and eating it, each family enjoying their own repast. But something stirred in my gut that night as I remembered a few years ago my dog, my darling little terrier and my shadow, had been poisoned at this very same time, the truffle feast. And next morning the memory was even more vivid as there was an unseelie shriek from Severine's family van and when we ran to investigate, she stepped back to show us her parents, their faces set in some agonizing rictus of death.'

She passed her glass to Kholi to refill.

'You can say what you like, but she murdered her parents! I had seen her spend time with a herb-gatherering crone and I shall bet my life she asked for details of botanical poisons. We all had an idea of what was poisonous or not but her unfortunate parents had more than a bellyful of sickly toadstools. They died in silent and most fearful pain.'

Adelina emptied her glass and rolled it in her hands.

'She made a thing of grief as we buried them, but a day later the Count arrived.'

'Di Accia!' Kholi broke in.

'Indeed. He was hugely wealthy, anyone could see that. Severine sold herself to him, everyone knew she seduced him on the first night because the next day she wore an opal with diamonds around her neck and left with him immediately, no sign of grievous loss or pain on that face, just an arrogant, cold smugness.'

Adelina finished with a sigh, not relaying that Severine had glanced back as she left that day and bestowed such a look on the Traveller. Cross my path, it said and you will pay. Be warned!

'So you see, she is dire... no, let us be truly honest here.' Her throaty voice resonated with unequivocal disgust. 'She is a murderer, as evil as the most unseelie Other!'

Buckerfield's large attic with its massive worktable became Adelina's studio, the room warmed by a quaint circular stove decorated with roses and birds, and she was content to work for hours with snow drifting down outside and the measured tick of an old mantel clock filling the interior space.

Ana took to joining her and she was set to work sorting threads, beads and fabrics because Adelina needed to know exactly what she possessed to begin this major piece, to have everything ordered and neat.

Butterflies darted against the walls of her stomach as she laid out the fabric ready to cut, as if something momentous might happen. So much so she wondered if the result would be cataclysmic! Would she ruin the fabric? Aine, it worried her.

Her hands shook as she took up the scissors and the blades squeaked as her fingers forced them apart. The fabric split apart with each cut, snip, snip snip, like ice cracking on a hoary pond.

Before long she had the pieces sectioned and stood staring mindfully– how to proceed? And then she thought that if she tacked it together, she would have a succinct idea of how the embroidery design should be and how each 'scene' could be linked to the next.

'Ana, come here. You shall be my dressmaker's dummy just for a moment. Twist your hair up and shed that bulky top. I want to fit this and your shape is a common enough one.'

'You do have a way with words, Adelina!'

'I mean you are of an average height and breadth. Now hold still.'

She began to drape and place and pin and the robe took shape over Ana's body. With her mouth full of pins she articulated garbled instructions.

'Turn this way, that, mmm. Mind the pins. Shift your arm that way, this.'

Under her fingers the cool silk responded, moulding and falling until she deemed it perfect. She stepped back.

Ana stood like a queen – she, the fabric and the design were made for each other and as Adelina studied her, it seemed she had become Other in her loveliness and quite simply the robe could be worn by no one else and Adelina knew that a masterpiece was about to be created and just for once, the awful blackness of her intuition faded away and left her with the creamy sheen of the gown.

The collar lay up Ana's neck, defining a swan-like arch. The shoulder fell away to cling to her full breasts, showing the rise and fall of the cleavage until the fabric flared in front and behind, cascading to the floor in an expanse of frothing cream, exaggerated by godets.

'Oh!' Adelina held her fingers to her lips. 'Turn and walk to the end of the room and then come back.'

Ana grabbed a piece of the silk in her fingers and twitched the folds around behind her as she turned, an unquestionably regal gesture as if she was born to the wearing of such a garment. She walked the length of the attic and stopped just as the door opened and two curious heads poked around. Turning in the same manner and seemingly oblivious to her audience, she walked back, the robe rustling, her head held higher, her shoulders straighter.

Liam pushed the door wider. His eyes darkened and his face stilled as he watched her, and Adelina could only think of iniquity and her heartbeat thundered like tribal drums. Ana's faraway gaze sharpened as she realised he was in the room and she met him glance for glance with libidinousness in her eyes.

Liam spoke into the explosive silence.

'Adelina, I will pay you whatever you want. Please make the robe for Ana. I want her to wear it when we marry.'

I CAN'T BEGIN TO TELL YOU how horrified I felt as Liam uttered those words. As you read on, you will see for yourself. Life just seemed to have pulled away from my control and I hated the feeling...

Anyway, we have travelled a long way around the bottom right hem band and followed bees and ladybirds into the first godet, haven't we? The godets themselves have provided almost their own page of detail, thick with stumpwork as they are. And we are about to follow the hem further around to the back where I have inserted another godet to increase that regal sweep. This time, I'm sure you will find the object of our search easily.

There is a lion, tawny and gold, not unlike my own colouring. He is worked in padded long and short stitch. Underneath the rich bullion stitch of his mane is a tawny suede journal which will expand to a thick read. You will notice our tawny king lies under a spray of mauve foxgloves and on a grassy mound made of green chenille thread. Entirely inappropriate of course, he should be lying under some vast Raji umbrella tree on brownish native grass. But I believe in poetic licence and I think the mauve is a perfect foil for his coat and the green chenille mound a nice place to hide another book under.

I wonder if you have realized yet, that the designs I created were my attempt at controlling something, something I contrived, something that I could make or break at my own whim despite my gaoler, maybe even because of my gaoler. Being imprisoned, one loses control of one's life completely. Embroidery and the writing of the journals gave it back.

CHAPTER TWENTY FIVE

Kholi grabbed Liam in a celebratory grasp and proceeded to shout his excitement in loud Raji dialect. He clasped Ana to his chest and hugged her, kissing the top of her head as her sparkling eyes smiled at the joy Kholi radiated. Liam watched almost paternally. Adelina felt there was a sense of complete ownership in his eyes and under her breath she muttered 'I knew it, I knew he'd take her!'

'What did you say, Adelina? Are you not happy for us?'

Liam fixed her to the spot. She felt like a fish caught on the hook and about to be impaled by the fisherman's knife. She busied herself with removing the pins from her mouth, transferring them to a tin and then placing the lid on, prevaricating.

'Adelina?'

'Well,' she began slowly. 'It seems to me, when any man wants to marry a woman, he is beholden to ask her family formally for her hand. And as Ana has foregone her blood relatives and as she named me her highway kin... do you remember, Ana... then I have not had such a question put to me. So I can't say how I feel just yet.'

'Adelina!' Ana's impatience crackled in the air.

'No, Ana. I would feel less than responsible if this were not carried out with proper protocol, I'm sorry.'

'Kholi?' Ana turned to the merchant whose brow was creased.

'Ah, my princess.' Prevarication again. 'Well, I'm sorry, but you are our family as Adelina rightly says and we would be reprehensible if we did not do this properly. If this were my sister Lalita, I would expect the same. You understand?'

Liam meanwhile had looked at the embroiderer, closed his eyes and shaken his head imperceptibly. Not a bad move – oh, she knew what he was thinking alright, but he walked over to her as she sat at the worktable. His plea when it came could be perceived as emotive and poignant or, Adelina thought, as underhanded, utter gameplay, nullifying her move immediately.

'Adelina, if I ask with my heart and my soul, swearing on my life that I will care for her, may I have Ana's hand in marriage?'

'Huh, it is pointless you swearing on your life, Liam. You are Faeran, you are immortal.'

'Adelina!' Ana hit the table with her bare palm.

'Ah, but you see, you are wrong. I am Faeran, yes. But while we were with Jasper, I obtained a potion. This...' he pulled a small stoppered vial out of his pocket, 'is the juice of the buckthorn. You know of the buckthorn?'

'Yes. The story of Gilgamesh.' Reluctantly Adelina nodded. She did indeed know the story of the buckthorn, how from that one tree, if one pricked oneself with the thorns, one could assume immortality. And how if one drank the juice of the fleshy leaves, one could reverse the process. No one but one or two Faeran knew where the shrub survived and Aine knows, many mortals had tried to find it.

'Indeed. And there is only one shrub in the whole of Eirie, hidden in Faeran.'

'And so?' Adelina busied herself at the table.

'I asked Jasper for this,' he held up the vial somewhat triumphantly. Inside, viscous liquid clung to the glass sides. 'I have been taking it each day for the last few days – the juice of the buckthorn. One more dose,' he drew the stopper and drank it down, 'and my immortality is gone.'

Ana and Kholi both gasped and stepped forward but he signaled them to be quiet.

'So you see, no more immortality. Faeran yes, immortal no. I ask you again. May I have Ana's hand in marriage?'

Such a pretty speech and so clever Adelina thought. And why would he do it? How can I trust he has really done this thing? She looked at him. By Aine, he was such a strong and fair-faced individual, there was no doubt about it, and if he has done it, then he truly must love her, just like Kholi and I love each other. She looked at the Raji, his hair gleaming blue-black in the light shining through the large attic windows, the tattoos stretching as he smiled.

Adelina raised her eyebrows and gave Liam a cool look.

'How valiant you are, Liam. I commend you. This must surely compare with Oisin and Niamh for devotion. You know the story? And in all honesty I can find no reason to spurn your entreaty. So, yes, I give you Ana's hand in marriage and charge you with her safety and surety.'

As she finished speaking, Ana hurled herself into the embroiderer's arms, the robe crackling and swishing around her. It was a little too much for Adelina and she pushed her away.

'Ana, mind my silk. If I'm to make this for you, I want it to be perfect. Remove the robe carefully and leave me, I must prepare for a full day in here tomorrow.

'As long as you promise to hurry downstairs when you've finished because I am going to get Buckerfield to have a celebration. Oh, Adelina I'm so happy!' Ana flung the words over her shoulder as she clattered down the stairs after the two men, leaving Adelina defeated, feeling the Faeran had won. And her intuition burned like acid into her belly.

The crowd spilled out, along with the light, from the door of the Inn of the First Happiness. It was a markedly euphoric crowd, reveling in the news imparted by Buckerfield, that there was to be a winter wedding. And to those nice young things Buckerfield had staying at the Inn. Good on 'em, I say.

Of course warming alcohol had a lot to do with the blithe crowd, but even so, Ana and Liam felt themselves the centre of excitement and joy. The feeling was a familiar, if not particularly recent one for Ana. For Liam it was another new experience to revel in. A Faeran wedding inspired nothing but grandiose largesse. There was no joy for the groom and his bride. Who cared? They would have multiple partners from now till forever. A constant search for another experience – stronger, longer, better, and so it went on. He raised a glass of the champagne Buckerfield had poured as another friend of the publican's clapped him on the back.

'Good choice, boy, she's a beauty. She were in my shop t'other day and my word but she were nice. Friendly like and respectful. I warmed to her, I did. I hope you'll be very happy. Now you come down and see me, cos

I'd like to give you both a gift.'

The noise from the Inn drew others to its doors and drinks were passed out as people stood round flaming braziers, sharing happy stories.

'What's going on?'

A figure swathed in furs had pulled up with a small retinue, on the edge of the crowd.

'A betrothal. Buckerfield's friends. A young girl from the Road and her handsome consort. The girl is a relative of Adelina the Traveller. You know Adelina? Yes, thought you would. Everyone knows Adelina.'

'Indeed. As you say, everyone knows Adelina.' The fur swathed person reached white hands to the brazier.

'Here, have a drink. It's mulled wine, beautifully spiced and I swear it will warm your cockles.'

A woman handed over the drink and the stranger took it and tipped it up. It was indeed warming.

'Better? I thought so. Bitter night but starry and pretty. Just the night for a betrothal. So you know Adelina. Did you know she's making the wedding robe? Supposed to be a work of art. Buckerfield reckons it'll look Faeran by the time its finished. She's clever, that Adelina.'

The fur swathed stranger finished the mug of mulled wine and placed it on a tray carried by a passing waiter.

'She is clever, I'll grant you that. Very clever.'

The words emerged quietly from the depths of the furs, because by now the gregarious conversant had moved on to others and the stranger stood alone. As she turned away to walk back down the street, flaring light caught the fur swathed face. A pale countenance, dark as slate eyes and blood red lips appeared briefly. Severine's expression was as cold as the air she breathed and as she followed the path to her own Inn, all she could think of was the fabric and the robe that would suit a Faeran. It was an integral part of her plan now, the robe. And by Belial and Behir, she would have it no matter what it cost.

Ana had spent the night on a wave of happiness, riding the crest for a long while as each person had come to wish her well. Now however, the wave had broken and she sat becalmed at her window, watching the last glow of the braziers as a small flurry of night-time snow settled in the courtyard.

'You're quiet, muirnin.' Liam ran his fingers through the mahogany hair that had bound him to her, was it such a short time ago? A month perhaps? He tried to forget the bonds, to erase the seriousness of what he had done. Asking her to marry him? And as part of a game? Aine! She inclined the head towards the sensual pressure of his fingers and turned to him, her eyes wide.

'Do you love me, Liam?'

He turned away to the bed, pulling off his coat.

'Why would you ask? Marriage normally implies something of love does it not?'

'I want to know that I can trust you, the depth of your feeling.'

He stood behind her, pulling her back against his hard body, feeling the need to make love, feeling the lust fizz over.

'Methinks you worry too much.' He lifted the dark brown hair and kissed her neck as if he were a butterfly. The mesmer he laid removed all taint of angst and she turned to receive his lips, silent, wanting more.

CHAPTER TWENTY SIX

Severine di Accia laid her head on her pillow in the Inn further down the mountain and stared up at the whitewashed ceiling. The drapes were drawn back and a fiercesome night sky – black, indigo and grey, swirled across the face of a moon almost as pallid as Severine's cheeks.

All her life she had craved to know of things Faeran. Wasn't she after all a changeling? In her youth, she had listened and absorbed the tales she heard on the road. For one such as she, attractive, different from her parents certainly, charming when she wanted to be, it was easy to presume she had Faeran links. And in very rare, more realistic moments, if she wasn't Faeran then it was possible to assume such likeness. And that is where the arrival of the Count di Accia had been fortuitous, taking her away from the 'death' of her parents. The man had money. Money brought knowledge and knowledge, as Severine rightly knew, was power.

It required no real effort on her part to seduce him. She had previously had one cheap, if informative night with an oily Raji reeking of garlic. The experience was just that – an experience, but one which she tailored to her needs and which served to put the old Count right in her pocket. When she left in his cavalcade the next day, she experienced no guilt. Her emotions were a perfect vacuum, space enough to be filled with more important matters.

Count Di Accia chose to marry the 'changeling' on the way from Veniche to the Pymm Archipelago. Privately thrilled at having her on his arm, the fact she was alarmingly younger was nothing. The sylph-like beauty gave herself all the airs and graces of a noble Other and he felt it reflected well on him.

He gave her gelt by the bag load and she brought clothes and jewelry and furnished their palazzo on the Veniche waterways in a manner befitting a man of his rank. What he couldn't understand was why she spent money filling a library with weighty tomes on Other life. Why she learned to play harp and gittern. Why she employed a strange wisp of a man dressed in cobwebs of brown and grey to teach her obscure languages. And why she spent long days and nights, sequestered in the library studying.

She smiled to herself as she lay on the bed. She had learned much. It wasn't hard to convince simple folk she might be Other in her skills. Not when she had such knowledge of occult law, such powerful comprehension at her fingertips. It was a quaint poem, one of four cantrips translated by her strange wisp of a man, that she chanted in her moments alone. Her mantra, her prayer for the future, her insurance, just in case. As she lay in bed staring up at the sky she whispered and the words sat in the air above her in ribbons of vapour as the evening air grew colder.

'*From caverns deep, abysses cold*
There lies a ring, so very old.
Through its eye the bearer sees
souls of Others which are keys
Keys to locks within a door
from which the bearer can expect more.
More life eternal, evermore.
'*The souls must part befront, behind.*
Till four of the same from two will wind
their power around, around and more.
More life, eternal evermore.'

It had taken her time to secure the ring. Her wispy man, an Other, found it for her after months of searching. The ultimate weapon – an artifact from the days of chaos when Other had fought Other. This battered piece of jewelry made by the worst of the goblin wights, had the power to kill the Faeran, sucking their souls into its sphere. And by some ancient glamarye, anyone who possessed the ring and the souls could have the power of everlasting life.

Ironically, not long after the find, Severine's husband, frail and unprotected by rings and souls, cast his mortal coil. Of course, lesser people could assume she had helped him reach the other side – no one would ever know. What everyone did appreciate was that she was now one of the wealthiest women in Veniche, in Eirie perhaps, as even Heads of State recognised her fiduciary power and treated her with cautious respect.

She stretched in the bed, reaching for a looking glass. Adelina? By Behir, the bitseach was nothing compared to the face staring back from the mirror. That common Traveller, her childhood combatant, looked like a whore and behaved liked a harridan. A laugh escaped, soaring to the rafters of her chamber and hanging there to echo in the stillness of a winter's night.

She turned her head this way and that in the mirror and in the soft light of a bedside lamp she was able to admire her complexion with its unblemished skin: the deep slate eyes so clear of guilt, smooth ebony hair falling down her back, not a wisp of grey. Despite the harsh words of that odious Faeran at the market, she knew her cool looks would last longer than the overblown, hothouse face of her childhood acquaintance.

But there was a rub to it all. Time waited for no man. And she knew that she would age, become heavy of body, wrinkled of visage and decrepit of mind if she was not truly immortal. Unless...

She was within days and minutes of holding her grail in her hands. And the robe? It would serve to fulfill a two-fold duty. One being a way to emasculate Adelina! And the other? The perfect place to sew the souls. She gave herself a smug grin.

She had one of course... one of the 'keys'. In truth, its deep blackness and its texture of freezing nothingness disturbed her. But never mind. It had been an easy capture that day, by the lake. The Faeran silk seller, she of the sarcasm and cruel wit had received such a surprise when Severine, coming upon in her in a solitary walk after the Fire Festival Market, had acted instinctively.

Whipping off the ring, holding it to her eye, she pulled the woman's soul into her grasp, leaving her a frozen husk amongst the feathers and bird-dung of the shore. The woman hadn't even time to cry out, only her eyes opened wide with horror as her soul tore free of its earthly anchor. Severine smirked. The speed and instinctive ease with which she had carried out the action without any forethought or rationalising thrilled her.

And now one more and then they would be parted 'befront, behind...

till four of the same of two' existed and she would force Adelina to sew them into the stumpwork of that robe and every single time she donned the garment more and more glamarye would seep into her bones until she was truly, indubitably, undeniably immortal! She stared fixedly at the mirror, into her cold eyes with their absence of guilt. There was nothing, absolutely nothing, she wouldn't do to secure this end.

I AM SURE YOU CAN SEE as you read, that what people are and how they act truly does affect their fate, does it not? Although Jasper would disagree. He would say one's fate is cast from the outset.

Remember too, my friend, back in the early days of this history I talked about kindred spirits? Ah! Kindred spirits are the glue that keep Travellers together. But Travellers are also able to feel the reverse, someone who is meant never to be kindred of any sort. The day I met Severine as a young child, the hair stood up on the back of my neck. I knew even then we would be destined to be at best, competitors. At worst, sworn enemies.

Ah well... shall we continue?

CHAPTER TWENTY SEVEN

'You still don't wish to contact your family, muirnin? Even now? With the prospect of your marriage and journeying to another life entirely?' Adelina shook her head infinitesimally as she asked, unhappy with the ease with which Ana had cast her family aside. Whilst she waited for Ana's answer, she had tried three times to thread a needle and three times her hand shook just as the thread nipped the eye. She had no doubt the tension was fired by anger at Liam's arrogant confrontation with her. And she knew she had been stymied by the marriage proposal. If she spoke to Kholi, he would never believe her, his experience of Liam so contrary to her own. And Ana? She was a lost cause! She put the needle and thread aside and picked up a length of fine wire as Ana answered.

'No. Liam is all I need.'

Adelina studied her and couldn't help noticing her assurance. It's as if by joining with Liam she has reinforced herself, re-invented herself, she thought. She glanced down to see she had been forming a wire shape for a leaf and thought how much Ana was like that fragile foliage. Without Liam's backbone, like silk thread without reinforcing wire, she was sure the woman would fold in a minute.

How deep does this new found confidence run, wondered the stitcher. What is she without the Faeran? Something better, something worse, weaker, stronger? She sighed with frustration. Faeran and mortal, mortal and Faeran, it ran around her head like a mouse in a wheel... a mouse in a wheel whose little axle was almost worn through. She tried to concentrate on Ana's voice.

'You know, Adelina, I am truly at peace. I trust Liam with my life!'

Adelina shifted in her chair, the mouse wheel racketing around and close to shattering apart.

'How much do you know about him, Ana? Do you really talk?'

Ana looked up, surprised.

'Adelina! Do you think we just stare passionately at each other and make love?' She cut away at pieces of lining, with each word the scissors snip, snip, snipped.

'Have you ever seen him use a mesmer or any of his special powers?' Adelina took a tiny pair of embroidery scissors, the ones with the blades shaped like a crane's bill, and cut a remnant of thread.

'Yes. When he rescued me from the dunters. If he used them at other times, I was mesmered myself and wouldn't have been aware. I am not sure if he even has those powers now he has lost his immortality. I haven't asked him. Does it matter?'

'No, I suppose not.' Taking a huge breath and feeling her heart thudding, Adelina faced Ana just as the mouse-wheel broke.

'Do you know if he has ever used his powers for ill?'

'Adelina, please!' Ana threw down her scissors and fabric, her voice as sharp as the implement that now lay partially covered by the slippery satin. 'Has he not proved himself to you? Sometimes you make me so angry! You're so opinionated, as if you have the right to say and think whatever you want! Have you forgotten this is the man I choose! And no, I am not suffering the pining sickness, he hasn't mesmered me. This is a choice I make freely. You hear? I make it myself!' She picked up the scissors again. 'I don't want to fight with you, not now, not ever. So I insist you give up this witch hunt and accept he is what he is: kind, caring, Faeran and my soon to be husband.' She banged the handle of the sharp tool on the table with a thump, glaring at Adelina.

Momentarily shamed, surprised at the vehemence of Ana's outburst, Adelina sat back.

'I apologise, muirnin. It was wrong of me. As you say, it's none of my business. But Ana, even though you are only my highway family, I am as fond of you as if you were my own and I only want the best for you.'

'Liam is the best, Adelina! I wish you could understand. Don't you want me to have the kind of love you have with Kholi? You wouldn't be so selfish would you, not to want that for me?'

Adelina could hardly gainsay the request.

'No, of course I want the same for you. Forget I spoke at all. Can you forgive me and try this on?'

Ana left Adelina not long after and hastened down to the door of the Inn to take a step outside. The glitter of snow and ice was so sharp her eyes closed to slits and she was momentarily blinded, walking carefully across the cobbles that separated her from the Celestine Stairway.

The road was empty of movement, sinister snow clouds sliding backwards and forwards over the sun, the wind taking cruel bites at anyone's exposed skin. Most journeymen had eschewed the frosted Stairway for the warmth of taverns and inns. An ugly gust sent a flurry of snow flying up the walls and buttresses and baffled away at Ana's unprotected ears. She shrank back to the shelter of the porch and as she gazed at the grey and white striated distance, she heard footsteps shushing toward her – the four beat of an animal pushing through the snowdrifts.

Her hair prickled on her neck, each individual follicle rising and separating, goosebumps racing up her arms as she tried to discern the whereabouts of the sound. To the left there was nothing, then to the right. Only hard shadows against the corners of buildings, impenetrable blocks of dark where neither shade nor movement could be detected. The padding came remorselessly on and she turned her head again, her feet horribly rooted through the snow to the very surface of the mountain.

A black shape detached itself from the corner and two amber eyes moved closer. A giant shaggy dog as dark as doom approached quietly, its eyes burning into Ana's, piercing her heart. She gasped with horror as the gaze slid into her soul. A tiny corner of that life-source within her crinkled a little more, as it had done when her father died. The Black Dog, the Barguest, harbinger of the victim's end, had marked her and she spun away, her hand scrabbling at the latch of the door, shoving it open and then slamming it behind, to lean against the portal, a shaking hand to her mouth. She winced as a shadow passed outside, rippling across the bubbled glass of the window. Violet, the tavern cat, arched a hackled back, spat and then ran hissing into the bar as if the Barguest would enter their tidy, happy world.

Ana closed her eyes and stood swaying as her world strained to re-orient itself. She pressed her palms against each other until everything felt right again.

She was overwrought with excitement, that's all! Of course there were shadows for Aine's sake and anyway, even if it was the Barguest, was not her own betrothed an Other? Against whom none could prevail?

She snorted like a tricksy mare and raced up the stair.

Liam had spent time alone, sitting at the window staring at the iced escarpments of the Goti Range. The forbidding edifice echoed the unease in his mind because the game had taken a turn, changed drastically as if the rule-book had long since been torn up and thrown out the window to be blown up to the crags.

He wanted to win, but win what? And against whom? Adelina? Himself? With Ana as the prize? A valuable enough trophy to be sure, but did he really want to marry her?

Then again he could do worse, her devotion knew no bounds. The thought of that unlimited affection, of the yearning that brought them together in a silent paroxysm shook him to the soles of his boots, making him doubt his own game-play. And when doubts crept in, it was those moments that caused marriage offers and such. As if he lost control of the game utterly!

'Liam, Liam!'

'I'm here!'

Ana flew in on wings. She grabbed him, sparking with a brittle light.

'Come on! Let's go out, take me to the Mews. I need to stretch my legs, they are wound tighter than a spring!'

She pulled him after her and he was struck by the frenetic edge to her manner.

'Ana, is anything wrong?'

'No! No! I have cabin-fever, that's all. All this snow and staying indoors. I need to breathe!'

They had reached the foot of the stairs, entering the bar on the slipstream of Ana's odd mood, the air crackling and shifting around the two. Onlookers could assume it was excitement and love as they informed their friends they were going out, reaching for the quilted coats they had necessarily acquired since taking residence in Star on the Stair. Bundled up, twice as rotund, with leather boots and fur hats, they called farewells and headed into the remains of the grim day.

'Ah well, kegs and beer to be shifted so I'll get on. Have a couple on me,' Buckerfield pushed over two goblets of wine.

'I knew I always loved you for a reason.' Adelina patted the big hand on the counter as he turned away to serve more customers. She picked up her drink and joined Kholi at a table by the window.

'You know, this really was my favourite place when I was young.' She spoke quietly to Kholi as the pub filled around them. Dulcit chatter, as yet unfuelled by alcohol, created a murmuring backdrop to their conversation.

'Buckerfield's not that much older than I, and when my parents stayed here on their journeying, he always included me with his local friends. After the horrors of Severine's company and not having a brother of my own, let alone a sister, Buckerfield was always special. I remember he taught me how to make snow angels. One winter we lay down and made dozens all the way up the Stair. We were wet through when we got back. It was such fun!'

'Life has its moments, doesn't it? I think Ana's will improve now she has Liam. Aine knows she deserves something good after her terrible traumas.' Kholi raised his glass in a toast.

Adelina gave a crisp little laugh frilled with the sharp timbre of sarcasm.

'And you think a Faeran can supply that? Kholi, you live in a dream world!'

A Raji expletive shot across the table, along with Kholi's hand as it grasped Adelina's wrist. She stared in shocked silence at the fingers pressed white around her wrist and then she shifted her eyes to his face. She saw anger where she had never expected it. Only once before had he shown such ferocity – at the campsite, when she had raged at Liam on Ana's disappearance. Like then, Kholi's calm constancy had changed, as explosive as a firestorm. With a sick heart she knew she had pushed his calm to breaking point.

'Adelina, enough! Let this whole matter go!' His eyes burned. 'You have had days of opinionated rhetoric pouring forth from your mouth till I swear I could sail away on it. And Aine it has become boring! He has done nothing wrong, do you hear me?'

'But I don't want her to marry him! Kholi, you have no idea! He is duplicitous and cunning. You have only ever seen the affable side, I have seen the reverse!'

Kholi's eyes bored into hers so deeply she looked away, just for an instant flushing with a surge of resentment that he should react so.

'I will not listen! He has proved himself more than enough to me! I would be happy if Lalita chose such a man. By afrits and foliots, Ana is a grown woman. I've said it a dozen times Adelina, she has made her choice. Let her! She deserves to have love.'

'You think maybe to compare what we have with what they have? Please!' Adelina spat back. Kholi's hand tightened further.

'You are her friend, not her mother, nor her sister, not even her mentor. To me, and it galls me to say this because I have loved you so much these last few weeks, you seem rude and insensitive. I compare nothing with nothing because right now, Adelina, that is what we have. I have no intention of tying myself to someone so mean-spirited. Not so different I think, from your vile friend, Severine.' He placed his drink down firmly and left the table, slamming the door behind him.

'Oh!' Adelina gasped. 'OH!' She felt nausea well up in her throat. Their journey had been remarkable for Kholi's gentility, support and unconditional affection. She had come to rely on his companionship, falling asleep cocooned in his broad arms and to wake as a finger trailed like a skein of silk down her backbone from her neck to her buttock.

She shivered as she remembered, reminded also of the intellectual span of his mind – his poetry, his prose. He was no dullard – as capable of assessing men as she was in determining her own view. So could he be right?

She growled. What was it about Liam that caused war-drums to beat and sabres to rattle? Fight me, he urged. Fight me and I will win.

She pounded her fist on the table. Kholi says I am wrong. If I say I am not and we dispute still, might he leave me? She shrugged her shoulders. So? I have been alone, I can be again! But then she remembered him touching her and drawing her along in exquisite passion, whispering how she would be the home for his heart, the key for his soul, the scabbard for his sword.

She ran to the door and wrenched it open.

'Kholi!' She shouted as she pounded up to their room, 'Kholi, wait!'

CHAPTER TWENTY EIGHT

The wind hurtled around corners and up and down alleys, cruelly pulling at buttoned up coats and rushing under fur trimmed hats. Every now and then a flurry of snow would draw its white veil over everything and one would be forced to take shelter in a doorway for visibility was impossible.

The two young lovers had been bowled down to the mews by the mountain wind, running furiously as the blast blew under their heels and against their backs. Returning was a different story, as bent double and shielding their faces with free hands, they twined their other hands grimly together. As they rattled around a corner, a flurry of snow obscured their view and they crashed into a woman being pushed down from the steps above.

'Oh, I'm so sorry!' Ana grabbed her fur hat and smiled apologetically at the tousled and snow covered woman, as a hand grabbed at a nearby handrail. They could see anger in her expression and expected an avalanche of vituperation to pour down but then the woman's eyes settled on them and gleamed with cool recognition as the snow flurry cleared.

'It's Liam and Ana, isn't?'

Ana nodded. The woman held out her hand, gloved in beautifully stitched black kid.

'I am Severine, Countess di Accia. I am a friend of Adelina's from many years ago.'

Ana shook the proffered hand reluctantly, after glancing briefly at the shuttered face of her fiancée. As the woman's fingers closed over her own she felt an ache surge up her arm, bone deep like the headache one gets when eating something freezing cold. Severine turned to Liam to shake his hand but as she turned, she stilled. Becalmed in mid-action, devoid of expression – like a waxworks figure – lifeless and yet not. Her heart thumping, Ana spun around to face Liam.

'What did you do, I saw you, what did you do?'

Ana's agitated whispering was less a question, more a panicked statement as she checked frantically to see who may be watching. Inevitably with the chill wind, the streets were deserted.

'She's mesmered, it's nothing, calm down. Ana, did you feel anything as you shook her hand?'

'By Aine, yes. My arm, it aches unbelievably.' She rubbed up and down the appendage, her gloved fingers trying to erase the pain. He nodded grimly, and Ana could almost feel the despair.

'I can hardly stand near her. This woman is evil.' He circled her, holding out a hand from which he had stripped a glove. 'See, watch my hand shake.' And indeed, as he held his hand beside Severine, it began to tremble and the fingers unconsciously crushed into his palm like the petals of a flower closing when the sun slides below the horizon. 'She is dark. She has done something utterly terrible.'

'Why should I feel it though? I'm not Faeran.' Ana stared at the glassy eyes, unable to believe they registered nothing. She was tempted to pinch the arm held out, just to see... but no, the woman discomforted her. She turned her attention to Liam as he answered her query.

'Some of my Otherness has rubbed off on you. Is it not the way with lovers Ana, that they feel each other's joy and pain?'

He prowled around Severine, taking in the slate eyes with lashes that were lined with tiny snowflakes. Strands of fur on her hat and coat trembled with the weight of the minute crystals. His face paled and his eyes filled with a pain that cut Ana to the quick.

'What', she grabbed his hand. 'What ails you?'

'She has killed. She has killed a Faeran.' His voice was low, growling like a dog thinking to bite.

'Liam! Are you sure? How do you know?' Ana stepped back hastily from the space in front of Severine, the fear of the Barguest and its portents forgotten.

'Because the monstrosity of what she has done has penetrated her so deeply she reeks of it. And I know! I know what she's done! She has stolen a Faeran soul!'

He looked at Severine and Ana saw something in his eyes that frightened her even more than the Barguest had done. He had said, we feel each other's pain, or words to that effect. Does he mean I feel his rage as well? Because that is what I see and feel now... thunderous rage: deep, dirty, surging to crash beyond the point of restraint. She bit her lips, wrapping her body in the protective circle of her arms.

'How do you know? Liam, let her go and let's get away please. She frightens me!'

But he continued angrily, ignoring her.

'And I know why.' He turned, brushing Ana away like a speck of snow, oblivious to her anxiety. 'Remember Adelina mentioned she had heard Severine was seeking immortality? This...' Ana could see he would plunge a knife through the woman's heart there and then if he had one. 'This aberration of a mortal has taken a step on that reckless path. She has taken a Faeran soul... only one, I can sense only one. Aine, one too many! She has murdered one of us on her journey to immortality and damnation!'

'What do you mean?' Ana's voice trembled with cold and fear as the terse, despairing man in front of her ranted and railed.

'Immortality can be gained by a mortal with possession of two Faeran souls.'

'But how...'

'The tales of old tell of a ring – an ancient gold ring. If one spies a Faeran through the aperture, the soul can be sucked through the circle into one's hands leaving the body a dried up husk... very, very dead. It's an old occult secret. We thought it was long gone, one of such foul secrets hidden or destroyed ages ago.' He continued to prowl around. 'Ana, take off her gloves.'

'Liam!'

'Please!'

Ana reached reluctantly for the hand still proffered. As she peeled the glove away, both her arms ached bone deep.

But Severine's hand was bare.

'Now the other!'

Ana cast him a look of anguish as she took the other hand in her own.

The black kid glove slid off smoothly. Severine's fingers were fanned out. Long and artistic like all Travellers' hands, she betrayed the creative heritage of her ancestors. The nails were beautifully shaped – pale pink, oval and with perfect white crescents at the nail bed. And there, glowing in the flickering light of a torchère, was a plain but dented gold ring on her middle finger.

Liam stepped forward and tried to run his hand over the ornament. But he pulled back quickly, hand flying to his mouth, a Faeran expletive escaping.

'What, what!'

He turned his hand over. In his palm was a burn, an arc, half a ring perfectly mirrored black and red in the skin.

'I can't touch the ring, I can't! No Faeran can. It is the ultimate bane!' His tone echoed with hopeless frustration. 'She can murder any one of us whenever she wants!' He stepped back, the reality of the horror filling his eyes.

'Unmesmer her, Liam. Now! Let's get away.'

Liam wafted his hand, the gesture so like someone wiping moisture off a window. Severine's eyes brightened with life... a cold sparkle, reminiscent of ice on the high passes of the Goti Range. She looked at her bare fingers, then surprised, at the ground, at the gloves hastily dropped by Ana. She bent to retrieve them.

'Such a pleasure to meet you both. You are indeed as beautiful as people say. I do wish you well.' She pulled the gloves on, sliding them over her freezing fingers. Ana and Liam nodded their heads at her and began to walk away.

'Ana, if you have a moment I do have something I wish to ask you. A business deal, shall we say.' Her slightly high-pitched voice followed them, a descant to the moaning wind scraping at windows and doors.

Ana waited, superficially polite, deeply afraid of this cold as ice woman.

'I would buy your wedding robe. I tried to buy the fabric at the Faeran market but Adelina was more successful, quicker in her dealings than I. I had my heart set on commissioning her to make such a robe for me, you see. And it is the fabric I covet, Faeran as it is.'

Liam's breath sucked in as Ana's fingers clenched his arm through his quilted sleeve, trying to prevent an outburst.

'Countess di Accia...' his voice ground out between clenched teeth, his jaw rigid.

'Come now, Liam. My friends call me Severine.'

'As I said... Countess di Accia,' his voice resonated now with undisguised hate. 'My fiancée's robe is not, nor shall it ever be for sale. Now if you will excuse us, we are deathly cold and wish to return to our home. Good evening to you.' He spat this last and turned his body away from Severine, dismissing her and pulling Ana after him, chivvying her into the wind, away from the accursed woman.

Severine watched them go, fury shaking her shoulders. She marked the well-formed body of Liam as he disappeared around a corner and in her mind's eye, saw his face as he spoke to her. She traced the image of that unusually striking visage with a mental finger: the high planes, the eyebrows, the distinctive hair colour underneath the fur of his hat.

The lines of his race were imprinted in her brain and she knew as she ticked off one characteristic after another, that Liam was Faeran. She smiled, a slow drawing up of the cupid's bow lips.

'Well well now, there's a thing.' She turned and walked down the alley, the wind pushing and pulling at her. 'The robe *and* a Faeran soul.' She gave a small chuckle and then laughed out loud. But no one heard her. She laughed like a banshee and the wind sounded the same, it was all of a piece.

Time again to move on. I have said before that my narrative is a purging of the emotions I have filled to the brim inside me and I shall continue this expunging until every trace of angst has been expressed across every page. So if you want to continue with me, follow the bees again.

You will come across one of my favourite pieces... see how I have inserted it in the godet at the back of the robe? It gives it weight and makes it flare even more. It is a creation of two Pymm thistles bending their mauve heads in some unseen wind. They are partnered with a dandelion plant, the white thistledown heads leaning and casting their seeds to the wind. They remind me of so much in their unusual partnership – maybe of Liam and Ana, of Jasper, perhaps Kholi and myself, even Maeve. And then of friends you are yet to meet because there is so far to go – Phelim, Gallivant and Ebba. But everything in its sequence, so...

Under the prickly thistle leaves, which I have to say took me ages bending wire and overcasting, you will find two little suede bound books. These are my next offerings to you, my friend.

CHAPTER TWENTY NINE

The robe hung on its hanger, swaying in the warm air that filled the attic, the little floral stove merrily burning its logs underneath the timber mantel. Adelina had moved the garment and hung it from a nail jammed into a central rafter so she could examine it from all angles.

She was alone. Ana talked downstairs with Buckerfield, which may help drag her out of the strange mood she appeared to be in last evening, she thought. Ana and Liam had rushed in the door with the wind behind their backs and some sort of discord had blown in with them. Liam's face was as dark as the clouds around Mt.Goti and Ana was heavily withdrawn.

Had they fought? Adelina didn't think so, although secretly she wished they had. Liam said they had seen some silly idiot belaboring a mule, trying to push it up the Stairway into the teeth of the blizzard. That would be upsetting, an answer for sure. But Ana had still been flat this morning. A bad night she said, fretting about the mule – it was certainly Ana's way.

But Adelina could barely spare them a thought because she inevitably blamed their relationship for the rocky night she had experienced. She could not, would not let Kholi go. If ever a kindred spirit had arrived in her life it was Kholi Khatoun and no amount of pride and posturing was worth the loss, if he should be so offended by her and leave. So she had tried valiantly to explain a Traveller's view of the Faeran the night before, asking him to forgive and forget. Please, she had said, I love you Kholi and I must not lose you.

Ana had talked with Buckerfield but he was too busy to chat for too long – lists to made, providores to be visited – and left in a flurry, Ana retreating to sit in the nook, staring out the window.

People toiled up and down the Stairway. The carlin had placed her staff in the ground, pronouncing a few days of blizzard free weather and journeymen had decided to make a break for the top of the Stair. Equally, those who had been imprisoned by snow in the various Inns of Happiness were now arriving in the town, claiming the Stair was passable higher up the crags. A parade of nations rattled past Ana's window: Rajis, Veniche noblemen, Pymm merchants. Shaggy horses and weathered wagons rolled past, brakes on, negotiating the wide way to the mews where if they chose to stay like Ana and her friends, they would leave their animals and vehicles and return up the walkways to the hospitality of the town.

They passed unseen before Ana's eyes, lost as she was in the confrontation with Severine. To the woman, she barely offered a thought. But Liam! She had seen stupendous rage in her fiancée and the foundation of her trust in him had developed a crack.

Trust had been implicit in her love for him. Trust that he would protect and love, that he was undeniably perfect in every facet. It made her realise she had been sweeping along on a tide of infatuation, blissfully unaware of any other side to the Faeran. How stupid, how infantile and naïve! She pounded the table with her fist and Violet, who had been asleep at her feet curled in a sunbeam, shot out spitting.

Ana's awakening to the vagaries of her fiancée's nature had been harsh and sudden. Rage had rarely been a part of her life. Pa had been a happy fellow, sailing with the tide and accepting circumstance. He had a favourite saying – don't bend the river! He had found by such easy and amenable actions, the tide often turned his way. He had a wonderfully pleasant sense of humour, a belief in his fellow man and was known for his kindness and charity. Of course this was not to say he didn't have moments of frustration. But he dealt with it – after throwing down the hammer or the bag of nails. Then he would laugh at himself and begin again.

No – rage was what Ana had seen in Bellingham's face as he pulled and pummeled her! He personified the emotion and it was rage at her indifference to him that prompted his attack on her. Ana couldn't bear to think Liam was tarred with the same battered brush.

Liam left Kholi at the mews grooming Ajax and Mogu and whispering sweet nothings in their ears. He walked in dark lanes and alleys, blending himself with shadow, casting himself invisible, all the time knowing that Severine had merely to raise her ring to her eye in a crowd and he would be revealed like a black dog in snow. He climbed upward to the inn, his breath coming in sharp spurts, the thin air slicing and cleaving.

Thoughts crowded from the corners of his mind. In the dark corner murder paced, heavy with intent. Liam could never allow such an act as Severine's to go unavenged, nor the ring not removed and destroyed. Rough justice, summary justice! He wanted to kidnap her and place her in the Styx Forest where the Barguest could portend her disaster, where the Cwn Annwn, the whole pack of them, could hunt her to exhaustion and death, or where the Baoban Sith could devour her alive.

But Jasper's words so recently uttered came from a more mellowly lit corner, the corner of reason. 'No Faeran would willingly cause a mortal's death.' Wouldn't they? Especially if they knew a mortal had the means to destroy Faeran? What do you say to that, Jasper?

From an even brighter corner, an unfamiliar warmth welled, touching his life at those other shadowy niches. He looked up as the sensation tugged and pulled at his soul as if Severine had him in her sights. There in the window of the inn sat Ana, to all intents and purposes framed in Jasper's dream mirror. She was gazing into space and he was reminded of the first time he had seen her at 'Rotherwood'. A beautiful and bothered girl who with her lack of artifice and her naïve spirit, had attracted his attention and won his heart.

His heart! Again the clapper of a great bell chimed in his chest.

In that instant he knew the game was over, that he hadn't won! He watched the woman who so charmed him, her hand supporting her chin, a troubled frown creasing her brow.

Ana would care deeply if Severine killed him – the only person in his whole empty life who would, he thought, as the resonance of the now familiar bell echoed. And what would she think of his plans for death and revenge? Oh, she would shrink from him as if he was Belial himself he knew, she who was so gentle and such a fragile innocent.

And what of Adelina? Because she had lost the game as well – she and he both beaten by Jasper's infernal Fate and Destiny!

Adelina! He hurried across the street to the back of the Inn, loaded his arms with wood and began to climb to the attic. He needed to talk.

Adelina heard him coming: the solid tread, someone carrying a heavy load. She pulled open the door and watched as he emptied his arms and stacked the wood by the stove. Brushing himself down and washing his hands, he walked to the hanging garment and examined it.

'It's perfect. You have done it just as I thought you would.'

'I was sorely tempted to try it on, Liam.'

'But you didn't, did you?' He glanced at her, wondering if she were amenable to civilized talk, because he needed to...

'No. It is Ana's wedding gown. It belongs to none but her.' Adelina was winding a skein of green silk onto a carved wooden thread holder.

'I admire your honesty, Adelina. Other women would have tried it on and hidden the fact.'

'Huh!' She snorted. 'You should know me by now.'

'Indeed I should. May I sit?'

Adelina gestured to a chair and put the threadholder down. Something had changed.

'Honesty Adelina, is a rare commodity in Faeran as well as mortals. And so while we speak of honesty, let me say I think we need to speak. Clear the air which seems as rank as a bog-mist. For too long we have bickered with each other and I think the time has come to stop.'

'Really. And what has brought on this sudden urge to seek peace. I confess I am surprised. After all, it is you that created the conflict, not me.'

He picked up the threadholder and ran it through his fingers.

'Maybe, maybe not, perhaps we were both to blame. Anyway, I had... a revelation. And for Ana's sake I need to do this.'

He looked so intent, so desperate, that Adelina almost reached out to touch him, to forgive him the games and the barbs. But she still needed answers before she could move forward on a new path...

'You talk about honesty, Liam. Then I shall be honest with you. You would have been a dullard not to know how much I have been wary of you but having said that, you have surprised me, the lengths to which you have gone to prove your devotion to Ana. My knowledge of Others has revealed far less loyalty and dedication.' She blushed slightly. 'It is why I have been circumspect. I wondered why you would want to marry her. You could have anyone.'

'I could but it is her I want. Haven't you ever seen something you wanted so much you would almost make a pact with Beezlebub to get it?'

Adelina didn't answer immediately, just moved the threads on the table, an image of Kholi in her mind.

'Then it must be that you love her. It would be the very least I could hope for. And if you love her, I am thinking that may be why you did what you did in Trevallyn.'

Liam's face shuttered.

'And what do you think I did?'

For a moment there was silence, broken only by the creaking of the door as Violet pushed her way in and padded over to the fire, the door swinging half shut behind her.

'Ah,' Adelina paused, remembering Kholi's request to her. She had said to him she would drop this witch-hunt as she had begged him to forgive her last night.

'You were saying?' Liam stood and walked to the dormer windows where he gazed at the cantilevered rooftops climbing up the slopes.

Adelina demurred. How could she break her promise to Kholi? It had mattered enough for her to beg him to forgive her outspoken 'rhetoric' as he had called it. And she did not, under any single circumstance, want to lose him. He was everything and all to her – the air she breathed, the glue that held her together. But there was just this one question and here was the means to an answer dangling in front of her like a carrot in front of a mule. She took a huge breath as if gasping for air.

'Jonty Bellingham. You were in Orford when he attacked Ana. Did you hear about it there? Truth now Liam.'

He stayed with his back to her and she admired his broad shoulders swooping in a breathless V-shape to his waist and hips.

'Yes.'

'And tell me, did you feel rage on Ana's behalf?'

He swung round, the handsome face filled with furious loathing.

'Rage? Of course I was wrathful! Weren't you, when you found out?'

'Need you ask? By Aine, Kholi and I went head to head trying to think of appropriate punishment. But this is not about us. I'm asking you – how angry?

'Livid, Adelina. I wanted to...' his voice trailed away.

'Kill him?' Adelina spoke softly. A more prolonged silence followed this time. An uneasy quiet.

'Yes.'

He spoke to the window. Outside, the sun shone unbearably bright. The glare off the white rooftops caused Liam's eyes to ache. He knew what Adelina was working towards.

Ana sat lost in the discord that disappointment wreaks. Her confidence, so newly shaped, folded like clay on a potter's wheel and she felt awry, confused. She needed Liam to be perfect. She had thought her father was and he had become ill and died. And if he had not been perfect, what would happen to her life if Liam wasn't either? She felt a tug as the crinkle in her soul curled a tiny bit more. His hidden rage terrified her, bringing to mind the smell, the touch, the sight of the rabid Jonty. Is this what Adelina meant when she asked if I really knew him? She jumped up from the table and needing to talk to a female mind, headed for the attic stair.

'Liam, did you kill him?'

'Actually no.'

'What do you mean, actually?'

'The Cabyll Ushtey killed him. Not me.' He had come back and sat in front of Adelina and looked her straight in the eye.

'But Liam, honesty again, did you contrive the circumstance?'

He shifted uneasily, dropping his gaze.

'Yes. But in the way of the Others, what I did was right. I enacted punishment.'

Adelina's heart sank heavily with the knowledge that all along she had been right. This Faeran was as dark and dangerous as the Lakes at night.

'Better you had just let mortals deal with Jonty's action in their own way.'

'Your justice is weak, Adelina. Your courts might merely have imprisoned him.'

'Yes they might. But it is not for any one individual to decide in such a dictatorial fashion.' She shifted in her seat. 'Think about Ana, she...' momentarily she heard Ana's voice, *'I would have killed him myself.'* No, she wouldn't! That was spoken in the heat of a very bad moment. Anyone who knew her could see she would flee from brutality.

'You were saying?' The crispness had returned to Liam's voice in the face of a guilty finger.

'Ana – she's terribly gentle, Liam, and despises violence of any sort. Ergo she would despise the perpetrator of violence. Better as I said, that you allowed mortals to deal with Bellingham.'

'I dealt with it the Other way. Whatever else you may think I am, I am Other. We have a code.'

'Indeed. An odd, cruel one it is.'

Ana had rounded the last curve and froze on stockinged feet as she heard Adelina's stern voice, through the half open door.

'An eye for an eye, Adelina.'

'Liam, no matter what, you cannot justify the murder of Bellingham. The Cabyll Ushtey... by Aine!'

'He didn't deserve to live, Adelina! He had already raped Tara at the Inn and if Kholi Khatoun had not arrived, he would have raped Ana. He deserved the Cabyll Ushtey! I merely facilitated the event.'

Ana's hand crept to her mouth and she jammed it in to stop the cry that wanted to burst out. In her mind she saw the bloody mess at Buck's Passing and bile rose, choking her. Her Liam, her lover, the hands that had fondled her, the lips that had kissed her, those lips had uttered persuasive words to Jonty, drawing him mindfully to his death. She opened her eyes wide. Now she saw his rage in her mind. Her eyes ached with unshed tears. Turning silently she fled down the staircase, leaving the fractured pieces of trust she had invested in her lover to lie with a loose ribbon that fluttered from her hair to lie on the floorboards.

'I would never ever hurt Ana or allow her to be hurt. You understand that, don't you? If I did,' Liam looked at the Traveller, eyes pleading with her to comprehend, 'then I don't know what I should do. I feel suddenly, and you may smirk, that I have found the nearest thing to happiness I shall ever have. Jasper would say it is my destiny to have this before I die. Please try and understand, Adelina. I am still Other, immortal or not and it is hard to reconcile myself with mortal codes. Aine, I can hardly understand why I feel the way I do, it's all so different. Please give me time.'

'Oh, Liam.' Adelina bent forward and brushed his hand with her own. 'What you did was so, so wrong, I can't condone it, ever. I understand how different we are, but I ask you to think twice about Other retribution, I really do. You must heed what I say. In the meantime, I will keep this secret. We must never tell Ana or Kholi, yes?'

Liam nodded, relief showing in the loosening of his fingers and hands.

'I suppose in a perverse way I am glad you know what happened. I need you to accept my differences and accept my word. In the end, it is all I have to offer any of you.'

There was another silence, punctuated only by the crackle of wood in the stove and the purring of Violet as she lay blissfully stretched out.

'Now,' Liam stood. 'I must find Ana because I need to hold her.' Because he thought, unable to articulate to Adelina, I need to tell her I love her, because not once yet have I actually told her that I do.

Ana had reached the door of the Inn. Pausing to pull on her riding boots, she dashed tears from her cheeks and stepped into the bright light. The thought of rage, murder and death filled her very being as she dragged the door shut. She began walking fast and then broke into a run, acknowledging no one as she sped down the mountainside to the mews. Had Kholi still been there, he could have soothed her hurts and rationalised the overwrought emotions. But he had left not long after Liam and was now ensconced in an inn with some Rajis he knew, buying a red wedding shalwar kameez for Adelina. It was to be a surprise.

CHAPTER THIRTY

'Have you seen Ana?'

Liam found Buckerfield studiously ticking off supplies from a massive list.

'Wedding cake ingredients.' The publican gestured with his pen. 'No. We talked of the wedding feast and then she disappeared to the nook and I went shopping. When I returned there was no sign of her. She's not with Adelina?'

'No, I have just come from the attic.'

'Well she's not with Kholi either. He's at the Flying Carpet with a platoon of newly arrived Rajis. They were haggling and there was a lot of lewd laughter. Do you think she's gone for a walk through the town?'

'Possibly. I'll head off and find her somewhere.'

'Daydreaming, to be sure. She was staring out the window in another world when I left.'

Liam said goodbye and headed out the door. For Ana to walk alone was unusual and her mood had been so withdrawn this morning. As he hurried along he mused on Adelina's plea that he leave Faeran retribution behind. He kept a wary eye on the passers by, searching for black hair, carmine lips and a dangerous gold ring and wondered if he could.

'Hey Liam, you lookin' fer Ana? She ran past here awhile back like the Gabble Retchet were behind. Her face was terrible affeared.' One of the shop owners who so admired her called to Liam. Running as if the Huon and the Wild Hunt were behind? Why? A thread of concern knotted in Liam's belly. The very utterance of Huon's name inspired a fear in all sensible beings. Liam began to hurry.

Ana had run blindly, stumbling and twisting past the newcomers to the town. *Trust, trust, trust, trust.* As she ran, the words echoed in the tap of her boots on the walkways. She doubted she could trust him at all, that she had judged him through the rosy tint of infatuation and lust and she hated him for his lack and hated herself for her own naïvety. Anger and hurt tugged at her as her heart galloped to and fro. Worse, worse than anything, was feeling so utterly let down, that someone else she loved should so deceive her. How could she trust, let alone love someone who could watch a murder happen, who could facilitate murder? She pushed open the mews door and walked hastily amongst the stalls, looking for the animals she had grown to love, nausea in her gullet seesawing like her emotions.

The sanctity of the mews offered peace in which to mull over her troubles – the solid animal comfort a reminder of the safety of home. Oh how enticing home seemed right now! Something familiar. Something she had a lifetime of knowledge about, where life went on in a never ending and well-ordered cycle. Where she didn't have to think or make decisions.

She rounded the corner and came across the beasts. Ajax turned toward her and nickered and Mogu blinked, the brown eyes softening, the closest the argumentative animal could get to a welcome. Ana ducked under the rail and ran her arm down the woolly camel's side, rubbing in between the front legs the way Kholi had shown her. Then under the next rail to Ajax where she flung her arms round his comfortable, massive neck. Something knocked hard against the top of her head and she whipped around to see the lofty greyness of the Faeran horse Florien, as he pushed imperiously at her, and seeing his bridle hanging by his stall, she grabbed it and began to approach.

He snorted fiercely down his nose and backed off, tiny half-rears displaying displeasure at the gall of the mortal woman.

'Florien!' Ana growled at him through a curtain of weeping. 'Stand up!'

He stilled momentarily and dropped his head to blow with disgust down his nose. Seizing the moment, she pushed the bit against his teeth and as he began to fling his head up, she quickly hooked the headpiece over ears that flattened lower by the minute. He ducked and weaved with his head as she tried to latch the throatstrap, until in her anger and so uncharacteristically, she grabbed at the reins and jerked twice, hard on his mouth.

The animal froze to a standstill, so still that Ana should have noticed, especially as Florien was Other. But she was busily engaged pushing the rails away and tugging impatiently again on Florien's tender mouth.

He pulled back sharply, rearing high, hooves combative and passing within a hair's breadth of her head so that she heard the swish and quickly stepped back. It served to fire her anger and hurt further and as he came down, she looped the reins and cracked him hard on the neck as if the animal was Liam and it was his cheek she belted. The two merged in her mind and she pulled again.

'Come on, Florien, I want to ride! I need to get away!'

The horse shot out of the stall, nearly dragging her over, the eyes so often gentle and honest now filled with a grey malice directed single-minded at the mortal and he danced into the sunlight, his splendid coat shining like metal, the silver hooves as he pranced, sparkling like flying knives that could dice and slice.

Ana climbed the mounting block, noticing Florien's wither twitching with a temperamental tic and the sweat beginning to darken the silver neck to charcoal, but some perverse need made her want to ride her lover's horse boldly, against his wishes, to gallop the animal and return him to the mews, dripping and lathered so that she could scream at Liam,

'See, I rode your precious Faeran horse! I mastered him and he is nothing but an average four-legged ride, like you Liam, are a very average two-legged one. So mount up and ride from me because I cannot love someone I can't trust!'

As her leg slid over the glossy coat and she sat astride, she sobbed anew, because a chilling descant rippled through the discord of her thoughts – how Liam had saved her, loved her and caressed her. Further, underneath it all, tribal drums beat a tattoo: the prophecy from long ago back in Trevallyn, saying *go on, go on.* She drove her heels into the horse's side as she, the mortal, gave him the command to move off.

Immobile, ears pricked, the horse stared ahead toward the gate and his dark as death eyes met the amber ones of a black dog, invisible to the mortal. The Barguest gave a low growl, measuring the horse which sidestepped, ears flat back, tail swishing from side to side like an angrily held flywhisk. Ana's heels tapped again.

But he was Florien, Faeran horse, and he reacted to none but Faeran command and he launched himself into a mighty buck, throwing her forward onto his wither so she hit it with a bruising bang to her groin and then he pranced out of the yard of his own volition, Ana trying to find her seat, not concentrating on her reins and unaware that Florien had maliciously and most dangerously slid his tongue over the bit.

He sidled out of the gateway, ignoring his rider, avoiding the Barguest, stepping high like a dancer, and Ana momentarily sensed a peculiar lightness in the horse, as if she rode upon a cloud which could turn from gentle cirrus to threatening cumulonimbus in seconds and it crossed her mind terribly briefly and with a pang of trepidation, that she may have erred by taking him.

She urged him along, thinking he would concentrate and forget his fidgets. Being bareback, she sat as softly as she could, timorous, trying to find his rhythm. But as she endeavoured to focus on the horse, images of Liam crept into her mind again and she felt tears threaten.

She tried to imagine him holding her now she knew what he had done, tried to resurrect the joy, the sensuality. But a sickness lurched in the pit of her stomach as she pictured that smooth, cool voice enticing Jonty with whatever the scum wanted to hear – drawing him closer and closer to the bloody barbarousness of the Cabyll Ushtey. In her agitation she drove heels as sharp as tacks into the horse's sides.

With a shriek, Florien lifted himself to a gallop, nearly unseating her. The more she hauled on the reins in her desperation, the more the horse pulled harder, tongue over the bit and with no control. Terrified, she grabbed a lock of mane as the horse raced across the frosted lower fields, branches whipping against her face, cold air numbing her cheeks and fingers, aware she was now at the mercy of this fleeing, overpowering maelstrom. Her agitation and her broken heart were now completely subsumed by racketing fear as the world whizzed by, the only noise the pounding of the horse's hooves, her heart in bolting accompaniment.

Now she knew she had done the wrong thing taking him! His Otherness was far beyond her powers and abilities. She looked down at the ground rushing in a muddy blur below the sharp hooves, knowing to slide would be like falling under a guillotine, their sharpness shredding her to pieces. Alarm as cold as the iciest wind-driven snow flooded through her, her mind full of the Barguest, of doom, of desperation.

Ana knew how to ride, gripping the horse with thighs that ached with effort, trying to anticipate, trying to ease the horse out of its malicious hysteria – trying to save herself. But it was obvious to anyone the horse carried the rider deliberately to frighten and distress, that the rider had no power over the wanton animal at all.

Each ditch, each log, tested her balance and tenacity to the limits. She could barely see ahead, the whipping wind so cold it dried her eyes, creating distortion in her vision. Vaguely, not far ahead, she perceived a barricade, a dark shape that loomed blurred and indistinct.

A stonewall approached, higher than Florien's wither, grey and coated in ice. At its foundations, a slick puddle of black ice lay disguised in the shadow of the edifice, a dangerous take-off for the most able equestrienne.

Ana identified the fence too late, the wall with its lichen trimmed and snow-rimed blocks like Mt. Goti in her mind. Frantically she squeezed with her knees and leaned low into the horse's leap, trying to gather his attention and stride together.

Florien's hooves touched the ice, sliding, sending his forelegs sideways as he attempted to leap. Ana tipped over his shoulder and hit the top of the wall with a resounding impact that forced air from her chest with a cry, her temple grazing the rocks, blood spurting, pain shooting like splinters of glass and nails through her head. The horse tucked his floundering forelegs tighter to leap over the top of her, hind-legs scrabbling for a surer take-off. But his front hooves knocked her off the wall and he tumbled after her, a dappled silver blur as he crushed her to the ground on the other side. Rushing through her mind as she rolled and tumbled from rock, to ice, to mud and as the horse forced her closer to a smashing, crashing oblivion, was the thought that Pa, her beloved Pa, would find her and make things better. All would be well.

The prophecy whispered faintly, as if it mattered at all, *'time to stop, time to stop.'*

Above them in bare winter trees, birds chimed and in the distance, the Caointeach cried out as she washed her bloody laundry on the edges of the Great Lake, warning everybody of cataclysm and doom.

Hearing this portent of disaster, a flock of black swans took flight from the lake heading south. One, more curious than the others, turned back towards the fields below Star on the Stair and swept the ground with her black eyes, till she saw collapsed figures near a stonewall.

The horse struggled up, his foreleg dangling and shattered. Under him, Ana lay bloodied and battered. Her neck was broken and the seed she and Liam had so lovingly and unwittingly planted within her died as her last breath expired between torn lips. At the gates at the mews, a large black dog howled meanly, adding his vindictive cry to the mournful lament of the Caointeach.

Maeve Swan Maid recognised the doomed horse and rider. She owed nothing to Liam. Not until he called in the remaining favour with the last feather. In that simple, guiltless fashion of the Others, she turned away from the horror below and flew on to join her friends.

Liam had begun to sprint as he heard the cries of the Caointeach and the howl of the Barguest and around him mortals grabbed at amulets and made signs of the horns. Entering the mews, he was met by a frightened ostler.

'Miss Ana sir, she has taken Florien bareback! The horse wern't willing I tell 'ee.'

'I need a mount, Dan, a fast one.' Liam's pale face did nothing to reassure Dan as he bit his lips, aghast at the cry still echoing around the walls of the mountain. He pulled out a feisty bay Raji stallion and threw on a bridle while Liam waited impatiently for a leg up. The atmosphere in the mews crackled. The Caointeach's cry, that wail that everyone, mortal or otherwise, would fain never hear in their lives, had stirred the beasts and the mews was noisy with fret and nerves.

'Which way?' shouted Liam.

'The south road!'

Liam left the mews galloping, his heart filling his chest to bursting.

When he had left her this morning, she had been quiet. There was a vagueness about the kiss on his cheek and the look in her eye had been faraway. But was that not normal for a mortal woman – any woman perhaps? Kholi said women behaved oddly prior to marriage. And, he had added in a voice of great suffering, women were prone to all manner of moods for the smallest reason. But enough to take Florien? Florien was a man's handful, let alone a woman's! Again he heard the echo of the Caointeach, as if the miserable Other's portentous and bowel-twisting wail was bouncing off every single snow-covered rock and crevice of the whole Celestine Stairway.

In the distance, he saw a black swan circle and then fly on. A filthy darkness settled in his belly, reminding him of Jasper's 'destiny' and he gripped with his knees as the stallion propped near a grey stone wall, dancing sideways, dragging away from the bit and reins with fear. Beyond the wall, Liam glimpsed the drooping head of Florien.

He flung himself off the still moving horse and leaped to the barrier, dislodging snow and rock.

Florien nickered, a piteous, pain-filled sound.

'Oh no! My blessed friend, not you!' Liam jumped across to the horse, unaware of Ana as she lay in the mud and snow-filled ditch at the foot of the wall. 'Florien, where is she, my man, where is she?'

As he crooned, Liam felt pointlessly down the horse's leg, over the shattered bone and punctured skin. Without a word, he uttered a Faeran charm, running his hand along the horse's shivering neck. The horse sighed and crumpled to the ground, slowly vanishing like a grey mist as the sun strengthens. And as he disappeared, so Liam turned back to the wall and saw the battered, muddy shape lying in the ditch.

Ana lay twisted and covered in snowy slush. Her eyes were closed as if she were in a heavy sleep. He wished she would wake and just stood for a moment staring, knowing the Caointeach's cry had been for Ana – the gentle mortal who had shaped his heart as if it were clay into a pitcher filled with devotion. Now, like the hard baked pitcher that is dropped on the ground, his heart cracked and shattered.

He said nothing. Moving on jellied legs, he knelt at her side marking the neck at the frighteningly unnatural angle and the imprint of a horseshoe on her forehead. This time there was nothing to be done. No grindylows nor dunters to mesmer. No Jasper to mend her. Her life's breath and her soul had departed long since, leaving her an empty husk, just like the Faeran Severine had killed. He pulled her to him and smoothed the mud away from her face gently, taking a corner of his coat to wipe away the blood that had trickled from the corner of her lifeless lips. He bent and kissed her and just sat for a moment.

His mind tripped over and over the utter regret he felt at never having told her he loved her, tripping and falling, again and again, until he wanted to scream with the sheer pain.

I WOULD ASK YOU, MY FRIEND, to return these little books to their hiding places. For even though Ana is dead, my story must continue.

Follow the bees again. You will come to a tall white Bethlehem lily, the kind we laid on Ana's casket. Underneath its funereal petals you will find a black washi-covered pamphlet, loosely bound. I am too overwrought to do a full binding. And underneath the midnight leather scarab beetle at the foot of the lily, you will find a black washi covered loose-leaf manuscript. Please read on.

CHAPTER THIRTY ONE

'She will have to be cremated, Adelina.'

Buckerfield stood in the room where Ana lay on the bed. Liam had washed her face the best he could but she bore many signs of a thorough bashing from Florien's falling body.

Adelina could not take her eyes off her. Surely she was just asleep. Maybe a little concussed? But no, if she really looked hard, she could see the pallor of death creeping over the exposed skin and giving substance to the truth. Ana's lovely pink lips were a palest lilac colour, and her skin had lost its youthful blush and where not bruised, was the colour of ice.

Adelina looked at Buckerfield.

'But should we not return her to her home? To her family?'

She felt her hand taken. She knew it was shaking because whoever held it, held it firmly between warm, enclosing fingers.

'My shrimati,' Kholi said with a voice as gentle as swansdown. 'It is winter. It would take a month to get back to Orford. It is not possible. And the ground is too hard down in the valley to bury her. It is as Buckerfield has said, she must be cremated.'

'Oh, Aine!' Adelina sank into a nearby chair. 'How did this happen?'

'She rode Florien and tried to jump a wall.' Buckerfield's happy face had collapsed and he neither tried to hide nor staunch the tears that trickled down, catching in the folds of his chin. 'Florien is dead too.'

'Oh my stars!' She stood and walked to the door. 'Where is Liam?'

'He went to the attic. He has hardly said a word, it's as if he has folded in on himself.'

Adelina pulled the door open with a rush and ran to the stairs. Kholi leaped after her but Buckerfield grabbed him by the arm.

'Leave her. She must deal with this in her own way as she has always done. We are here if she wants us but in the meantime friend Kholi,' the big man sniffed and wiped his face with the apron he had untied. Blowing hard, from the confines of the twisted calico he continued. 'We have things to organise. Come with me. I would value your help.'

Adelina ran up the stairs. As she got nearer the top, she slowed until her feet dragged and she walked at a snail's pace. In that room would be the robe made to fit Ana, to mould to her body.

Moving to the door, Adelina heard voices and stopped to listen. A man's voice, deeper and more aged than Liam's and speaking gently. She bent and picked up a blue striped ribbon lying on the top step as she opened the door where the robe swung before her, mockingly beautiful. And to its side a spare man with white hair cut close to his head. Sitting slumped at the table, hands laying out flat in front of him and still covered with Ana's blood, Liam was silent. To all intents and purposes, Adelina hadn't even entered the room.

The ribbon dangled from her hands as she looked at the Faeran she had disliked for so long. The anger coursing through her died a little as she spied the broad shoulders slumped in defeat, the titian hair messy and knotted, the blood and mud-stained garments. There was no need to rant. Nothing she could say would have any more power than the raging pain Liam obviously suffered at this minute. Momentarily, she almost reached a hand to him but then the white haired man stepped forward.

'Adelina, my name is Jasper. I am...'

'Yes, I know. You are the Faeran who healed Ana. How...'

'I heard the Caointeach. And I had a vision and I felt Liam needed me. Perhaps you do as well.'

Adelina bristled and everything she had ever felt about the Others and Faeran in particular, erupted like pus from a nasty sore, her compassion for Liam dissolving in an instant.

'Not unless you can bring her back to life. Or perhaps you can reverse time. Right back to when she first met me at the Stitching Fair. But no, come to think of it, I don't need a Faeran or any Other to help me through this ghastly thing. Your help would be tainted with debt and obligation and I have no wish to involve myself any further with ANY of you! And if Ana hadn't, possibly she would be alive too! Everything I fretted about has come true!'

Jasper touched her shoulder gently.

'My dear! Perhaps now is not the time, but I should say the only thing these two impetuous, unfortunate people are guilty of is falling in love. Each is an individual and entitled to live how they choose.' He sighed. 'I can do none of the things you say. Ana is dead. But perhaps I can help in other ways. May I see her please?'

Adelina was too distraught to argue and turned to show him out. As she went to follow him through the door, Liam turned around.

'Where did you get that ribbon?'

'What?' Adelina scrunched her eyes and spat the word at him, disbelief at the mundane question he had uttered.

'The ribbon – where?'

'It was outside the door. I picked it up as I came in. Why?'

Liam looked at her, eye to eye.

'Because she had it on when I last saw her at breakfast.' His face was as bleak as the Barrow Hills in the middle of winter. 'And so Adelina, I am guessing she had it on as she stood outside the door this morning. Outside as you and I talked about revenge and death and murder. Would that be enough, do you think, to make her rush to the mews and catch Florien and ride as some say, as if Huon and the Wild Hunt were behind?'

A rhetorical question.

Adelina's hand crept to her mouth and she thought how she had told Liam the truth would wound Ana to the core. And then she rapidly followed that crushing thought with memories of Kholi's request that she cease her persecution of Liam, for fear of the possible consequence such an action might have. But surely he had not meant Ana's death!

Adelina suffocated under the weight of thoughts of Ana, ancient Queen of the Travellers. Of Oisin and Niamh. Of Other and fated mortal. As each thought thundered into her consciousness, she was unaware she was crying, her hands clenching the ribbon into a sodden knot.

Behind her, a hand touched her shoulder and immediately a warmth suffused her, flowing gently to her troubled mind and stilling her nervous limbs. Jasper turned her around and looked into the tawny eyes as he rubbed his hands up and down her arms.

'It is no one's fault, Adelina. It is Fate. Be at peace.'

The day of Ana's funeral had dawned quickly and brightly. Adelina was glad of the sun, it lifted the spirits enough to be able to get through what must be done. She looked at Ana as Kholi and Buckerfield began to close the casket lid. Some enchantment of Jasper's had smoothed away the contusions and had given her a gentle blush. Her hair was shining and clean and she was dressed in a fine lawn gown embroidered with softly lustred pearls. Adelina recognised it as Faeran – the quality was unsurpassed. The young woman's graceful hands lay folded gently over each other and her dark eyelashes cast feathery shadows on her cheeks.

'Oh muirnin,' Adelina reached for her hand at the last minute. It was cold – frigidly so and she replaced it and stepped back as the lid was screwed down. She turned to see Liam enter the room, silently and morbidly like a wraith, in time to shoulder a corner of the casket. He looked stricken, as if death held his coat-tails a little too tightly. He had been almost silent since the outburst in the attic the previous day, answering questions in monosyllables.

He shouldered his burden mutely. Kholi and Buckerfield each took a corner but their faces betrayed their feelings like open books. Jasper took the remaining corner on his thin shoulders, his black riding coat, like Liam's, an aptly worn garment.

As Adelina preceded them out the door, she brushed at her hair which she had tied back severely on her head. At her wrist fluttered Ana's blue and white ribbon. She had washed and hand pressed it and tied it in a firm bow, an irregular contrast to her sombre brown garb. Liam noticed it and gestured.

'Why, Adelina?'

She looked at the ribbon.

'To remember, Liam – to remember. And maybe I shall wear it until it falls into ragged skeins on the ground. Each time I see it, I shall remember her on the stair with her hair in that ribbon yesterday.'

She knew he understood she was undergoing penance. That she would forever feel the weight of guilt at Ana's death, just as he would. He scowled at the ribbon as she held the door open.

The cortege paced up the snow-covered slope to the Site of Everlasting Life, mourners heavily wrapped and coated against the grievous cold of the mountains, protected from the corrosive pain of death. At the lych-gate, a woman sunk deep in thick black furs stepped back as the pallbearers eased by.

Jasper's chest tightened in the fiercest grasp of a cramp that threatened to fell him, a rope of a sensation that twisted and spliced. He gasped, stumbled and took one hand from the coffin to rub his chest, mumbling a charm, a protective spell to restore himself. The pain eased but a dark forboding flooded to his very backbone, tinging everything with the ebony cast of death. He knew with the instinct of an elder, that he had just passed something cataclysmic. He tried to glance back but the inexorable drag of the coffin and the other three pallbearers pushed him on. Liam, insulated by his own deeply incised pain, sensed and saw nothing.

Adelina however, saw Severine. Stepping out of the procession, she confronted the woman, just as Severine had begun to draw off her gloves, the sun glinting on a plain gold ring. The fraught sensitivities of the last day welled into a fount of invective.

'Get out of here!' Adelina spat. 'You do Ana's memory no favour. Take your stinking servants and yourself and leave here! Now!'

Severine exhibited mock dismay as people walked past casting curious glances at the two women who bristled like dogs, sizing each other as they circled.

'But Adelina, I only came to pay my respects!'

'Bitseach! Respect isn't even in your lexicon! You make me sick with your falsehoods and your arrogance.' She pointed with a shaking finger, her face red with the effort of containing a voice that would burst free from the constraints of etiquette. 'There goes the sweetest young woman you can imagine and you think to soil her departure with the foulness of your presence? You are insane!'

Severine's eyes hardened to flint, the urge to toy with Adelina changing swiftly to the urge to hit! She took a breath and her hand moved sharply.

Adelina's own shot out and grabbed it before the woman could strike. She dug nails as sharp as claws into Severine's wrist, drawing blood, dragging the woman close so she could whisper in her ear.

'I mean it, Severine. Go!' Her hazel eyes flashed with a green spark and her grip tightened as if she held a knife ready to slash and gouge. 'I'm of a mind for murder. Leave!' Her voice lifted. 'Now!'

Severine pulled her wrist away, wiping at the blood, conscious of more glances and whispers as mourners passed in groups. She began to turn, her shoulders rigid with fury, her glance full of flying daggers, her final words full of innuendo.

'You'll pay, my dear friend, how you will pay!'

She swept away, her furs trailing in the snow like a black bloodstain.

Adelina watched as the carlin lit a flame under the faggots of the pyre with her staff and was filled to the brim with anger, guilt, grief – any number of deep-seated emotions that could crucify and torture. The heat of the fire forced people back to the lych-gate and someone began to play a soft melody on a lute, calming and soothing as the notes wound amongst the mourners and down into the town. They turned from the conflagration, wishing to recall Ana as she was, not what she was to become and they all wandered arm in arm to the Inn of the First Happiness, to think about fate and destiny.

CHAPTER THIRTY TWO

Exhausted, wrung out like a dish-cloth, Adelina sat by the lake with Jasper late in the afternoon that fiery day, and they watched the fine plume of smoke as it continued its heavenly journey.

'Can you help Liam? He is utterly wretched.' She spoke softly as an oriental duck paddle by. The hoary ice had melted in the sun and waterfowl flexed their muscles.

'I have tried but he doesn't care to be helped. It is worrisome. He has repudiated so much of his heritage. If he had not, he may have had something to focus on which could pull him from his mortal-styled grief.'

'Faeran don't suffer the same way as mortals with loss?'

'Generally no. It has advantages. Certainly there are great love stories but they are on the whole the exception. Liam's is a love story, Adelina. Whatever you and I felt, we could never have stopped it. Neither could he and Aine knows he tried to deny it almost till the end! It was fated not to last of course and we knew,' Jasper touched her hand with a light gesture, 'that it was doomed but one cannot change Fate, no matter how hard one tries. One can just limit the damage.'

'Jasper, did he really procure buckthorn potion from you?' She shoved her hands deep in the pockets of her nut brown coat.

'Ah, he told you. Yes, he did. He had some outlandish notion that if he assumed mortality, he could change Fate. That Destiny would alter significantly. In its simplest form the rationale makes sense, except that Fate can never be altered, immortal or no. It is mapped from one's very beginning. He refused to see that in his youthful arrogance.'

Adelina listened with interest, cobbling together the fragments of her knowledge of Others.

'How is it then that you have banes if you are immortal?'

'Simply a method decreed by the Lady Aine during Creation, to prevent overpopulation of Eirie by Faeran. When you think about it, it is actually no different to a mortal death, be it a snake bite, drowning in the ocean or a natural death. You call it an untimely accident and such, we call it a bane. We all, you and I, call it Fate. If there is any difference, it is that Faeran can live hundreds and hundreds of years before meeting their bane. The mortal span is miniscule by comparison.'

'But you are special people, enchanted.'

'Apparently, although being special has meant little in this most recent tragedy.' Jasper shook his fine head, staring into some Liam-filled distance.

'So what will happen to him?'

'Ah. Truth? I don't know. He suffers a pining sickness and already it consumes him, now that he is 'mortal'. It's ironic that an ordinary girl should be so powerful and be unaware of it. Unwittingly she taught him to see the other side, the reverse. Faeran only know perfection and the next most perfect thing to replace the last most perfect thing.'

'It sounds boring and self-indulgent.' Adelina's forthright comment raised the healer's eyebrows.

'Indeed,' he replied blandly. 'And Ana may have had the capacity to change that if she had returned to Faeran with him. But!' He shrugged his shoulders. 'If only I could get him to return with me he may escape the darkness I see coming his way. I have the capacity to see some things and I fear greatly for him.'

'Could you be wrong?'

'I foresaw Ana's demise.'

'What?' Adelina turned to face him fully, the slatted bench dragging at the folds of her coat.

'I saw her in a vision and there was a horseshoe. Liam joked it was a mortal sign for weddings and meant that they were to marry. But in fact when she was found, she had a print of a horseshoe on her forehead where Florien had trodden on her.'

Tears filled Adelina's eyes as she winced, the healer patting her hand kindly.

'So you see, muirnin, I am never wrong. And I always maintained Ana would be his bane, even in death, so I suspect he may pine away for her, like an old dog after his master.'

Further down the bank, loud quacking and honking drew their attention to a fellow with a bag full of bread. He cast pieces in the water and eventually the flock of mixed fowl quietened, concentrating on pecking every last crumb he cast on the surface of the lake. After a while he turned their way and as he walked close by, the strap of his bag broke and fell to the ground with a muffled thud, disgorging objects all over the place. He knelt hurriedly to pick up his possessions and grinned shamefaced in their direction.

'Sorry Sir and Lady. I won't be a minute and you can have your peace back.'

Jasper smiled and waved an understanding hand.

'Take your time. You don't disturb us.' He turned back to Adelina, realizing she had been speaking. She watched the interloper pick up an apple, some pieces of scrappy parchment and a knife.

'We are leaving tomorrow, Jasper. We're going to Veniche for a little while. Kholi says I am not ready for the heated chaos of Ahmadabad. He thinks the gentle waterways of Veniche may sooth me and I have never been there. Kholi will ask Liam to join us, and I suspect he will because we are his link with her. Shall he be alright, do you think?'

'As well as he will ever be until he has worked his way through the black purgatory in which he has placed himself. It will be good for him to be with you. But can you, Adelina, cope with him? Can you coexist with him without blaming him? Because remember what I said about fault and fate, what has happened is no one's fault.'

The clumsy fellow in front of them had piled all his spilled goods into the bag and with a polite salute, departed close by their seat.

'I'm sorry again,' his voice was course and low. 'Have a nice day.'

Jasper nodded at the departing back as Adelina continued.

'I can no more blame Liam than I can blame myself. It is something I must learn to live with. And I have Kholi Khatoun. Liam is not so lucky so we must stand by him as well as we can.'

Jasper smiled.

'I think it would be good for Liam to be with you. You Travellers are kind and Kholi has great affection for the boy... I can see that. And when all is said and done, he won't return to Faeran with me so there really is no choice. Just give him some medic at night in his wine. Here.' He passed her a small, stoppered bottle of some brown stuff. 'It will help.'

He hung on the verge of revealing the chest-cleaving pain of catastrophe that had almost felled him at the funeral. But on reflection, he couldn't bear to detail the awful heart-stopping sensation. Enough that he was aware. He tucked her hand in his arm and they walked back to the town to join in what was left of the gentle wake.

The man with the bag was seated at the inn opposite the lake as they left. Pulling off the knitted cap concealing his bald head and rubbing the itchy spots the wool had exacerbated, Luther, Severine's brutally qualified henchman, gave a satisfied sigh.

So much to tell, he thought and no doubt we shall be on the road to Veniche in the morning.

CHAPTER THIRTY THREE

Adelina sat back against the doorjamb as the caravan was pulled along the highway.

Roads were the same everywhere, she thought, they wander and lead and the predictability of their nature and the gentle swaying of Ajax's rump lulls and sooths. For Adelina and her companions the verges of the highway, the rounded foothills and the soaring slopes of the Goti range provided the detail, the activity; the stuff that took one out of one's thoughts if they became too deep and unbearable.

Liam slumped against the other side of the door – thinner, paler, quieter. Speaking only when spoken to. He allowed life to wash over him. And neither Kholi Khatoun nor Adelina tried to draw him out, enough they believed that he sat with them, travelled with them and went through the automatic motions of living. They could ask nothing else of him yet.

When Buckerfield had said goodbye, he had taken Liam in his arms and hugged him, tears threatening in the big face.

'You'll always be welcome, boy! Come back when you're ready.'

Adelina's eyebrows lifted, even more surprised when Liam actually returned the clasp and said in a quiet voice how he would always be grateful for the gift of friendship. She had expected him to stay within his shell, like a hermit crab from the Pymm shores. Her own farewell to the big publican had been no less easy.

'No heart for snow angels at the moment, Buckerfield,' she said.

'Nope. No heart, love. Maybe next winter, eh?'

He kissed her on each cheek and shook Kholi's hand.

'No nuptials without me, do you hear?' He whispered in Kholi's ear, not wanting Liam to hear, for fear of hurt.

As evening began to fall, they rolled closer to the Luned Forest, home of things eldritch and enchanted, just like the Weald. From atop the befringed and bedecked back of Mogu, Kholi spoke quietly.

'The evening is festooned with golden clouds
the faeries dance in the meadow
and the leaf crowned Näcken
plays his fiddle in the silvery brook.'

And indeed trickling by the side of the Highway was a rill of beauteous qualities, musical and entrancing. Adelina had no doubt it was eldritch... there was a frisson. Sometimes Travellers picked up on these strange phenomena, unlike fellow mortals who would plunge onward, chasing the diamond glitter of the stream until some water wight caught them unaware.

And so out came the silver bells, charms and amulets to protect the journeymen as they travelled and camped. Liam watched the preparations with little animation, he couldn't help – silver was his anathema. And he must sleep further from the caravan than Adelina and Kholi liked because of the self-same talismans, so Kholi erected the pavilion, denuded of bells, and Liam slept like a desert man in his canvas quarters, deeply drugged with Jasper's medication, amidst silk and satin cushions and under a huge woolen throw Adelina had found and reversed her shrinking spell upon.

Luther had reported dutifully back to his employer. His skills as a spy, a thief and an assassin stood him in good stead with his mistress and she trusted him implicitly. He was like a very familiar shadow – sometimes she even wondered if he very subtly led her, rather than the other way round. In any event, what really impressed her was his lack of guilt and the way he approached life with cold, unadulterated equanimity. His face barely sustained a flicker when he stabbed or garroted, poisoned or strangled. She appreciated that – the professionalism. If he had been highly strung, it would have itched her like fleas in her bed. She had found him in a secret sojourn down the darkened canals of Veniche, not long before her husband had died and she reminded herself constantly to thank Behir for the discovery.

As they galloped through the trees and tracks behind their quarry, Severine was not much taken with the beauty of the approaching Luned Forest. Her mind had no time for frippery and she travelled lightly. She had a saddlebag and her ambition – it was enough. She reined in her horse, glancing at the sky and the surrounding leaf cover.

'Luther, we'll camp. It grows dark and tomorrow we'll ride faster and close the distance. I want to confront them well before the marshlands. The Marshers may give them shelter.'

The surly fellow dismounted and began to build a fire. The coney he had killed earlier in the day was spitted and roasting in the blink of an eye and he pulled out Raji flat bread and some spicy paste to spread upon it. They drank water as they ate, saying nothing to each other and then each wrapped themselves in heavy riding coats, using saddles as pillows and the fire to warm them, falling asleep easily. Severine slept the guileless, innocent sleep of the baby who knows all its desires will be met on the morrow. Luther took a little longer, reminding himself to sharpen his knife blade and check the garrotte that was in his own saddlebag.

In the honey coloured stone manor through the Ymp trees in the Barrow Hills, Jasper sat looking at the mirror. Thinking of Liam, he watched but was confronted by a black expanse and when he touched the glass it was freezing. He shivered and walked to the fire, throwing another log on and sending sparks flying out onto the hearth-rug. Stamping them down with bad temper, he poured a mug of ruby wine and re-seated himself in the chair. The mirror remained black.

The fire crackled and sparked and the room warmed. The wine spread through Jasper's veins and he felt himself melting into the upholstered comfort of the red chair and his lids grew heavy. He was not a young man, thus the journey to Star on the Stair and the rampant emotion of his time there had left him feeling a little frail– feeling his age he said to Margriet on his return. On that journey he had wracked his brain on how to entice Liam back to Faeran, back here to Jasper's home, to safety. For there was no doubt, at the funeral he had passed something dark and savage and without conscience and he feared not just for Liam but for all of Faeran. He must crack the vision, expand it, find out what it meant and act accordingly. As his eyelids shuttered down, he glanced at the mirror. By Aine, nothing!

The fire burned and the room was cosy. Coming from the red chair was the sound of gentle snoring. A white head leaned back and eyes were firmly closed as the black mist on the mirror vacillated and wafted, parting and closing, parting and closing. The Forest of Luned glimmered with the lights of the Teine Sidhe, the tiny will o' the wisps who could cause such angst to mortals. Lying on the ground was the husk of a body and in the flickering lights, as the Teine Sidhe darted from one side of the Luned rill to the other, back and forth, titian hair glowed.

A log collapsed in the fireplace with a crack and Jasper woke to find himself staring at the mirror as it revealed its images.

'On my soul', he gasped. 'Liam, muirnin, wait! Wait, my boy, I'm coming!'

LATER, MUCH LATER, *I was to wonder how Jasper missed the fact the duck-feeder was a spy. Was the healer so absorbed in Liam's problems, he was blind to anything else or was it just that he was a frail, old man beset with fatherly concerns? Or perhaps it was Fate playing with the lives of those in the game? Whatever mysteries may have caused such a monumental lapse in his awareness, Luther and Severine were now close on our tail.*

Thus the story continues.

Follow the bees again until you come to the castle. It's easy enough to locate with its white pennoncels with the red crosses flying in the breeze. I stitched the castle on needlepoint canvas with real windows. Well, they are actually the clear carapace of a beetle I found, but it works. Necessity, you see, is the mother of invention.

Can you see Rapunzel in the tower with her long yellow braid? Follow her plait to the castle door which opens and reach your finger round inside the walls and there you will find a book, a thick one which will expand hugely. And secreted amongst thickly worked Pymm knots, forming a forest at the foot of the castle, you will find another journal. You must remember when you return this book to its hiding place, to use a dull needle and tease the knots back into shape. It is a hiding place after all.

CHAPTER THIRTY FOUR

Kholi and Adelina made love to the sound of birds. They made love silently, for fear their wretched friend would hear, and with a desperation to their coupling as if in the moment of sheer abandon, they could lose themselves utterly in the physical heights they climbed, where there is no thought, no emotion, just a free-wheeling sensation of freedom. And for that small moment after, when lying still with hearts pounding and sweat dripping, the mind registers nothing but exhaustion and pleasure. They reveled in the sensation guiltlessly for just a moment.

Liam was aware of none of the pleasurable heights being sought in the caravan. He had arrived at that point between awake and asleep where the mind tries to decide if the day is worth waking for. He stretched lazily, his mind registering the far off trills of birds and for a single moment there was absolutely nothing wrong with the world. And then a tidal wave of awareness flooded his brain, threatening to engulf him in its churning depths. His stomach contracted, his heart-beat became a racketing gallop and his eyes flew open as he realised Ana was gone. Crushed, bruised and dead. Worse than that. Ashes to ashes and dust to dust. She was now blowing along the shelves and peaks of the Celestine Stairway. She was a grain of insubstantiality, a speck of nothing. She had ceased to exist and like her, Liam wished he could render himself into nothingness. For not only did the loss of what could have been the love of his life suffocate him, but guilt at her untimely, terrible death squeezed at his lungs and the final throttle was the thought she died without knowing that he had, indeed, fallen deeply in love with her. He spent moment after moment breathless with loss, to the point where he wondered if another breath would even be forthcoming. And if it wasn't, did it really matter?

The thought took on great appeal. Why does one continue when there is nothing worth continuing for? Surely oblivion is better. He narrowed his eyes. Thank Aine he was no longer bound by the infinite coils of immortality. Outside the pavilion he heard footsteps and then the door flap was folded back and Kholi looked inside.

'Ah, my very good friend, you are awake. Were you able to sleep at all?'

'Yes, Jasper seems to be making sure of that. Is it late?' The mundanity of his words hit him like a sledgehammer. It was as though he existed on two planes, the filthy grief-stricken one and then the one where he related, albeit forlornly, to his friends.

'No, early yet. Stay where you are, Adelina has made some porridge and will bring it to you. You must rest, my friend. There is nothing to do.'

Liam lay back. Truthfully, he could hardly be bothered to get up. At least lying here on his own he could indulge himself. At the moment he was content to travel with Adelina and Kholi for a day or two. It gave him time to think. How to put an end to it all? Because that was the solution. An end. And then, if what the Elders said about souls and the After-life were true, he would see her again. And this time nothing would part them, and he could tell her what he wanted her to know.

Had his friends any idea of Liam's rapid descent into such bottomless depression, they would have been fearful indeed. As it was, light footsteps sounded outside.

'Liam! I found some early strawberries growing by the hedgerow, they have the taste of summer.'

Adelina brought her glowing countenance into the tent along with steaming porridge that he took from her, uninterested in the food and completely careless about approaching seasons.

'When do you want to leave?' He took a mouthful of the porridge and sat waiting for her to answer. His chest was bare but he had kept the covers decorously over his lap. Adelina admired the muscled torso, lightly sprinkled with a soft down over the chest and snaking down to his loins.

'Oh, in an hour or two, maybe longer. Take your time. Kholi has gone hunting for meat and while he is gone I shall tidy my van. I'm afraid I stood at the door and threw things in when we were packing. Besides, occasionally I find a burst of tidying therapeutic. If you want, you can keep me company as I believe there are things of yours under my rubble. Buckerfield brought them down to the mews. Said you shouldn't have to be worried by mundane things.'

As Liam scraped out his bowl, the porridge having filled the aching hole in his belly, he thought of the big publican, a lump in his throat.

'Adelina, you have all been more than kind.'

'Fiddle dee dee. It's what friends are for. No more now. Rest and get up when you are ready.'

She took his bowl and he lay back on the pillows. Friends, he thought. Ana had brought him friends. Loyal, kind friends. Was life worth living just for that? These mortals functioned on a different level to Faeran, finding joy in tiny things and fellowship in like minds. Could he ever find that again? Would it be enough?

A vision of Ana floated before him, lying back on Jasper's linen after making love, beads of sweat between her breasts and along her hairline. She would have been the mother of his children and the love of his life. The thought clanged like the clapper of that giant bell, ringing in his head, setting up a hideous vibration throughout his entire body. He threw back the covers and jumped from the bed. No, nothing would ever be enough!

There was no one to reconcile the mental turmoil Liam underwent. He had, in the fierce desire to lose his immortality, become victim to those most feared of all mortal emotions – inarguable guilt and grievous loss.

Kholi had tracked a quail through the lush undergrowth at the side of the rill. Needs must and before long the unfortunate bird was caught, gutted and plucked and ready to be returned to Adelina for one of her herb-filled stews. The early morning sun filtered through the trees, here in full leaf. So different to Trevallyn and the Barrow Hills where winter's long, cold fingers had plucked every leaf from every spinney and coppice. Here, the Luned arboretum warmed with a perennial spring and glamarye wafted in unseen vapours between the boles of the trees. The foliage dripped with sparkling dew and spider-webs were draped from frond to leaf to twig, with the self-same dew catching the early light and glittering. Like diamonds, thought Kholi.

He wended his way back along the edge of the rill that trickled by his feet. The noise it made reminded him of shards of Veniche glass being rattled and shuffled in a small bucket. It was a sound he wished he could share with Adelina, to explain to her about the glassmakers in Veniche, but she had been adamant about staying to tidy the van. And to keep an eye on Liam.

He worried about the Faeran. There was a dark side to his friend that threatened like a storm on the horizon – one could see occasional flashes of lightening and hear ugly grumbling as cumulonimbus clouds tossed and turned. When Liam talked, which wasn't often these days, Kholi felt there was a chance his friend could pull through his sorrow to the other side. But when he lapsed into that dangerous silence, Kholi truly worried.

Many a mortal had lost a loved one. Many a mortal had sunk so deep into the sea of melancholy they quite simply drowned. Kholi Khatoun feared this was happening to Liam, Faeran notwithstanding. He had not shared his disquiet with Adelina because she sometimes seemed sunk in her own tale of woe – some sort of misplaced sense of guilt, so she had enough to deal with. He would worry and watch for both of them. Rounding a root-trailing tree trunk, he pulled up short.

'My shrimati, I thought you were wanting to stay and tidy.'

He spied his love bending and floating her hands to and fro through the crystal waters of the rill. Her garments in their autumnal russet and amber shades wafted in some Welkin Wind, dancing around her hem and shoulders, giving the unsettling impression of Other. She looked up at him and smiled, raising her shoulders in a small shrug. Her eyes swallowed Kholi whole. Had he time, he would have remembered the eldritch nature of the Luned Forest. As it was, when the golden figure held out a wanton hand, he went ignorantly and blindly.

Adelina emptied her baskets carefully on the floor and began sorting all the supplies she had taken to Buckerfield's. Fabrics were folded and each time she had a bundle she would touch it with the little wand and say 'that is all, be small.'

'It is unusual for a mortal to be able to use Other charms.'

Liam sat on the step and watched the woman move around her cosy space. She smiled at him and told him how she had acquired the spell. He nodded and made no comment, content to watch her as she busied herself. Out of the corner of her eye she glanced at him, noticing the slump to the broad shoulder, the brooding slant to the mouth.

'You know, someone told me grief is a form of passionate sadness,' she offered the words into the atmosphere and they fell like silver knives on Liam – cutting, slicing.

'Passionate sadness!' He jumped off the stoop and strode away, running two hands through his tangled hair. 'Aine Adelina, this was all supposed to be a game, not some life and death struggle with passion and sorrow!'

The pity that had filled Adelina dried up as surely as if the blazing sun beat upon it. And she reacted with anger, calling from the door.

'A game, Liam! It's always a game for you Faeran and then when you win, you leave the prize lying on the ground to dissolve into some dreadful half-life between Hades and worse. Better Ana did die smashed into a million pieces! Have you no shame?'

A deep laugh as empty as a pauper's pocket touched a further taper to her anger, so that she shouted after the back so pointedly turned towards her.

'Why did you have to pick her?'

'Be it her or someone else, Adelina, the results would be the same. It is what we do, it is what we are!' He came and stood looking up at her as the air crackled between the two. 'I picked Ana simply because she was ripe, in every way.' His cruel reply silenced her. 'The fact you entered the game was a bonus, I had someone to pitch against. You know shatranj? Ah, I see you do.' He climbed back up to the stoop and sat down, Adelina retreating into the van. 'But Ana, so lacking in device and artifice, very quickly turned me into the sarbaz. I fell in love with her and struggle and deny as much as I could, in the end, she won. She forced my hand and my heart and I lost everything!'

Adelina's mouth opened like a fish and she threw the bundled robe, hitting him in the chest.

'*You* lost everything! Aine, she lost her *life!*'

'Because she heard you and I talking about death, revenge and murder!'

'Because she heard you facilitated the grisly murder!' She spat back.

'And of course, you had no part in the revelation did you?' He whispered softly, like a serpent around the neck of the woman Eve, from Travellers' tales.

Adelina's eyes looked at him, sparkling as tears filled and trickled over. For a moment he sat very still and then he stood and went to her and put his arms around and held her as sobs wracked forth.

Eventually the storm passed and he smoothed his hands over her beautiful copper hair, to cup her face in his palms. He ran his thumbs over her lips and gently wiped the tears away and all the while she stood, fixed to the spot with her eyes closed.

And then he spoke.

'I loved her.'

Adelina's eyes flew open and she followed his movement as he bent down and retrieved the robe, smoothing it as he had just smoothed her hair. She watched the hands, trying so hard not to visualise them on a woman's body.

'What did you intend to do with this, before it became Ana's.' He kept his eyes turned from her, stroking the robe gently.

She shook herself, aware she had stood on the edge of an abyss and something, some greater thing than either of them could have believed, had pulled them both away from a destructive moment. Aine, mother of the world, she thought, flicking three fingers in a grateful token against her heart. Aloud, her voice a little cracked and hoarse, she answered him, aware he was as shaken as she.

'Well, I am an artist embroiderer. It is what I do. Many months ago, I was approached by the direttore of the Museo di Veniche, to submit a sample of my work for exhibition in their embroidery wing. Originally I had planned to submit the cabochon vest but the chance of owning a spell was too much to refuse. So my submission has been somewhat delayed. And then I saw the fabric at the Faeran Market and I knew it would be my canvas.'

'But it became Ana's robe.'

'Yes. But I didn't mind, she was my 'kindred spirit'.'

'Well then, you may as well take it. Finish it. Do what you have to do. Perhaps it's a fitting way to remember her.'

Adelina sat back on her heels, aware of the sick irony in Liam's voice.

'Yes,' she whispered. 'It's an idea. I could dedicate it to her.'

She lifted the wand and the robe was shrunk down to fit in her wall of drawers. Soon, all that was left was Liam's duffle bag lying on the floor, its contents spilling out. Adelina picked up shirts and breeches and folded them carefully, returning them neatly to the bag and as she straightened up to hand it to Liam, she noticed a black feather on the floor. The sun caught hold of the oily hues implicit in the blackness and she reached down to pick it off the floor rug.

'What's this? Is it yours?'

Liam glanced at what she held and then leaned forward and took it from her. He seemed lost in memories for a moment but then handed the feather back.

'You keep it. It is a swan-maid's feather. Some day when you most need help, stroke it and call to Maeve. She owes the holder of the feather one task. When she has performed it to your satisfaction, give her the feather back and tell her she is free.'

'Me? Can I do that with an Other?'

'Indeed, have you not already mastered a wand and charm? I do not need it. I have my own glamarye. You may put it to good use in the future.'

Adelina thanked him and immediately set about sewing it onto her present garment. Where the toile indicated a water bird floating on a still lake, she stitched the feather carefully into the pattern. It blended beautifully. Biting the thread off with her teeth, she glanced at the sun, now high in the sky.

'Tuh,' she grunted. 'Kholi has been gone over long. I wonder where he is?'

Liam detected a faint whisper of worry and pushed himself up from the step.

'I shall go retrieve our desert warrior, shall I? You put the kettle to boil. I'm sure he will want a mug of that loathsome Raji coffee when he returns.'

CHAPTER THIRTY FIVE

Severine had closed the distance between the two parties dramatically. Arising long before dawn, at that moment when one lone bird whistles to herald the faint brightening of the sky, she and Luther had eaten a sparse meal, mounted and set off at an easy, mile-covering lope. They had no interest in the beauty of the sky as it bled through apricots, mauves, and pinks to eventually become an unsullied blue, devoid of cloud. Nor did they notice the scent of herb and blossom as they cantered along the highway, leaving a skirl of leaves in their wake. Their focus was total.

Immediately ahead, smoke was curling lazily into the sky and it articulated just what Severine hoped for and expected. That Adelina, Liam and the excrescent Raji would be lazy and unaware, ripe for the picking.

'Madame, stay here and I'll scout.' Luther jumped from his horse and tied it to a tree. Feeling in his saddlebags he pocketed the garrotte. They had halted far enough away for the scent of their own animals not to reach the noses of the beasts in the encampment. Stealth was all and Luther was a master.

He crept away and Severine found her stomach filled with butterflies. She dismounted and led her mare to the tree and tied it together with the other, then leaned against the rough bark of the corkoak and gnawed at her black riding glove. If this happened the way she planned, by tonight she would have two Faeran souls, to be sewn into the robe and worn, the essence slipping between the warp and weft and into her skin. Absorbed into her bloodstream, to be carried around her body like life-giving air, filling every cell with immortality. By Behir! She shook her head and jumped from her revery as Luther tapped her on the shoulder, the other hand placing fingers to his lips.

'Madame,' he whispered in gruff tones, 'the Faeran has just left to find the Raji. He goes west along the edge of the rill. It's a simple thing to catch him.'

'Then let's go quickly. We'll worry about the woman later. You know what you must do if the Raji gets in my way.'

Luther led off and Severine followed in his footsteps lightly, her soft riding boots making no sound. Dressed in breeches and with a tight sweater, there was nothing to grab at the undergrowth and cause unwelcome noise. Wisely she had chosen shades of verdancy that blended with the dancing shadows of the shrubbery. She was like a nymph, a woodland sprite – definitely more Other than mortal, she could feel it in her bones, she was sure. She fingered her right hand anxiously, the dented gold band sliding round her middle finger, and mouthed its inscription as she stepped behind Luther. *'My circle is a syphon for a soul.'*

Liam had trekked a half a mile following the rill and the faint trail left by Kholi. His strength seeped away, grief soaking it up like a sponge, but his promise to find the Raji and bring him back kept him walking, albeit slowly, one foot in front of the other. The water chuntered by his side, its crystal depths clear, reflecting the morning light like mirrors from the Veniche markets. Above him the birds chimed and trilled and filled the forest with their melodies. Like the Weald, Luned birdsong had a surreal quality, bell-like, tuneful, mellifluous. The sound fluttered about Liam's ears – descants and harmonies. But suddenly he picked up on a discord… a song reminding him of the melodies of the roanes of Pymm. It set an Other's teeth on edge and they would have travelled far from the song, but to a mortal Liam knew it would sound sweet and enticing, gentle music to dance by. Melody to entrap and ensnare.

Liam ran in the direction of the spine-chilling sound, a terror filling his heart, just for a moment replacing the dark pain. Jumping over the roots and lichen covered logs, he burst into a small clearing by the side of the rill.

'Stop, veela! Aine, an bhféa cuidiú a thabhain doen!'

Kholi-Khatoun was about to reach his hand for that of the woman before him. To Kholi she was Adelina, in the mellow autumnal clothes

– exactly those his lover had been wearing when he left at dawn and especially in her eyes which turned their seductive gaze upon the hapless man and swallowed him whole.

To Liam she was a shape-shifting unseelie veela, one of frivolous Others who hung about rill and stream, trail and track, waiting to ensnare an innocent mortal male. Like the Ganconer, they would seduce the passing innocent with their beauty and a casual bedding would cause a sighing sickness, the unfortunate left to wander the wilds completely out of his mind with love and lust. He would starve, for no food held sustenance, only the love of the veela. He would die of exhaustion because he must wander constantly without sleep, searching for the love of this monstrous Other. Should Kholi's hand touch that of the veela, he would become a lost soul.

'Veela, leave him! Take your hand away!' Liam spoke in the language of the Others, his own hand beginning to rise.

The singing had stopped as Liam had jumped into the glade and the veela cast a look of hatred at the Faeran. She growled, her voice gutteral and gravelly, at odds with the smooth face and the large blue eyes and flowing hair, but should one look closer there flickered a bleached, cruel whiteness, a selfish glint in the eye betraying hunger for a game of seduction and sex.

'I said move away! He is mine and you shall not have him!'

'Liam of the Faeran wants men now, not women?' The veela snarled.

'MOVE! Bain as!'

The woman spat at him and stood: tall, white, blanched with anger. Her mouth curved in a sabre-shaped scowl and her cold eyes cast daggered glances at Liam. But she turned her back and left the clearing, her hair flying whip-like in the Welkin Wind, fading into the shadow of the trees, to prevail again upon some other luckless journeyman.

Liam leaped to Kholi's side. The Raji's eyes were vacant, his expression dull. He could have been a dead husk had one not seen his chest rising and falling like a man who dreams of coupling with the love of his life. Liam wiped his hand through the air and Kholi's eyes filled with surprise as they noted his friend standing in front of him.

'Hah my fellow, it is good to see you out and about. Come to join me, have you?'

'In a manner of speaking,' and Liam relayed Kholi's almost fatal confrontation with the veela.

'Hell's teeth! I swear all I saw was Adelina! By afrits Liam, she sounds like the Aicha Kandida in the Raj – seduction and hate, it's all one. My friend! I owe you my life.' Kholi grabbed Liam and kissed him wetly on each cheek.

'You owe me nothing. It is one friend caring for another.' Liam turned away, not wanting the Raji to see his confusion. Perhaps friends are enough, he thought. Is that what Ana would want? For me to be a part of life with these people? No! I cannot, will not ever imagine wanting to live without her. It is not to be borne. His twisted, dented emotions tipped over the abyss and he thought the final, deadly thought.

I want to die! I truly want to die. Without her I am nothing.

His heart sank, weighted with a creeping blackness that spread, filling every bit of his mind, allowing no space for sane rationale. He had seen Kholi's curved scimitar at his side and imagined how quickly he could end it all by falling on the blade. He was now 'mortal' after all he reasoned sickly, a man who has no bane. And as he turned back toward Kholi, his hand began to waft in the air to mesmer the Raji in order to pilfer the weapon.

But someone had beaten him to it.

He cursed his selfishness, the brooding that had channelled his senses far beyond the clearing. Kholi's scimitar lay on the ground and he leaned back against the massive body of a thug, away from pressure at his neck. Already Liam could see beads of bright blood forming a decoration as Kholi strained his chin upwards. There against his skin, exerting its awful, lethal strength, was the fine wire which was a gittern string. Kholi's eyes were wide, fingers clawing at the taut wire.

The insanity that had gripped Liam moments before switched instantly. Like a firestorm when the wind changes, flames leapt high to demolish all in their path. 'Slash and burn' hammered in his consciousness and he ran forward with a banshee scream. The sucking sound of a sword being drawn filled the glade as he raised his hand in a death-mesmer.

But a high-pitched shout cut across the shimmering sound like the crack of whip... a voice he knew and which filled him with forboding, his murderous hand falling away as if weighted with iron sinkers.

'I think not, Liam. Shall you try any of your Faeran tricks then the garrotte will surely slice through the Raji's neck like a harpsichord string through cheese.'

He swung round.

Severine stood by the side of a drooping waterbeech. She smiled thinly.

'Good day to you, sir. I think now you will agree it is I who have the advantage, so I think we shall have less of your arrogance and bad manners than when we met on the Stair the other day.'

Liam's lip curled at the woman.

'What do you want? It can be nothing from him, surely. A mortal?'

'He doesn't matter, you are right. It's what I want from you that matters. Do you know what I want?'

She laughed and the high-pitched sound fell like icicles around the clearing. Shivers rippled up his spine, as Fate and Destiny conspired against him. Jasper was so right, one could never gainsay them.

'Liam,' Severine continued quite calmly. 'I would like you to kneel on the ground with your hands behind you where they can do absolutely no harm. That's it.'

'Let the Raji go. He can be of no use. I know what you want.'

'Well, you see, I really don't have to do anything you say. If you move, the desert man is dead. You have absolutely nothing to bargain with. Not even your life, because that is forfeit, as you know. So be quiet and let me get on with what I came to do.'

Severine began to strip off the glove of the right hand and Liam's eyes fixed on her slow movements, his heart missing two, three, four beats.

She reached for the middle finger of her right hand and eased the gold ring off.

He thought of Ana, of her begging, 'unmesmer her, Liam, please!'

Holding the ring to the sunlight Severine waggled it around and spoke quite pleasantly.

'Do you know what this is? Ah, I see you do. Then you know what I will do. Does it matter do you think? Are you afraid? Will you be missed?'

Kholi struggled and began to curse in Raji but the garotte tightened and Liam yelled.

'SILENCE, KHOLI. BE SILENT!'

'Yes! Be quiet, you filth!' Severine yelled. 'If you don't then I shall have my man take Adelina's lovely throat and play a gittern tune on that as well. All I want is this man's soul, it's not a lot to ask for, is it?'

Kholi's eyes bulged and he looked across at Liam, horror imprinted in every crease on the man's face.

Slowly Severine brought the ring to her eye and positioned it so she could see Liam through it. She whispered and he waited, Fate ringing carillons of bells in his heart and in his ears.

'My circle is a syphon for a soul.'

It was as if his skin stretched towards her. Momentarily he experienced a harsh ripping sensation, as though all his skin was being flayed, stripped and torn, bloody and soft, from the living body, and he cried out with cruelty of it. It happened with unnatural speed. In an instant, the life force inside him shrivelled to a point somewhere over his heart and as he fell into a far deeper blackness than the grief that had gripped him earlier, he realised he didn't care at all. He should. Oh, how he should. He should care about Kholi and Adelina and what Severine might do, but he knew this was the answer for him.

All his life, things had been less than perfect, less than fulfilling. Until he met Ana. And for just a short moment, a mere speck of time in the infinite passing of life in the universe, it was actually more than perfection if only he'd had the sense to recognize it! As his soul began to curl away from his earthly form and pucker and twist, he realised he had only been destined to hold perfection for a second.

His soul burst into the air with a slight popping sound, sighing as it sped toward the ring in a glistening sable stream and Ana's name flew from his lips, his body toppling forward, eyes screwed shut, twisted with the paroxysm of unimaginable pain.

Kholi wanted so badly to cry out. He uttered muffled cries as he watched Severine slide the soul into a chamois bag.

'What, what?' She broke from her rhapsodical weighing of the bag of souls and turned to the grunting and gesticulating Raji, nodding to Luther to let off some of the tension on the wire.

'Why?' The single word grated from a throat scraped raw.

'By Behir, do you know nothing, you piece of camel dung?' She slipped the ring back on her finger. 'This is a soul-syphon. It gathers Other souls, Faeran ones, on a special command.'

'Why?' He almost cried, so great was the pain and shock of watching his friend empty of life like a pitcher held so that water could be poured out.

'Why, why?' Severine mimicked his accent. 'Because possession of two Faeran souls is the most valued thing in the mortal world. Better than a kings' ransom. Because, you grubby piece of desert dirt, it gives me immortality. Two immortal souls give one mortal infinite life!' She tossed the bag from one hand to another in front of him. But then stopped when she noticed the mocking glint in his eye.

'What!' She shouted, signalling to Luther and he pulled Kholi to stand straighter by tightening the garotte again. 'Tell me,' she snarled in his face, some spit hitting his cheek which twitched as he answered, strong and defiant, the Raji who had stood in front of Bellingham, the day he had tried to rape Ana.

'Then you must search more, woman.' The words croaked out like a man who had wandered the Amritsands without water. 'Because with Liam's soul, you do not have what you seek.'

'What?' She grabbed Kholi's shirt and pulled at it so he stumbled toward her and the garotte cut further so the beads became a steady stream. He swallowed, knowing nothing he could do now would help the situation. His heart ached as he thought of Adelina alone back at the van waiting with the coffee pot for he and Liam to return. He thought of big hairy Mogu, of Lalita.

'WHAT!' Severine screamed in his face, shrieking like the Symmer wind. She had reached the end of her tether.

'Because Liam gave up his immortality!' Kholi inwardly smiled as the woman's jaw dropped, wanting to fatally wound her, to cut out her heart and feed it to the dogs, to strike her fool's ambition down utterly. 'In order to live with Ana for the duration of her life, he took buckthorn potion from the Faeran healer, Jasper. He has not been an immortal for two weeks or more. In your little bag, lady, you hold merely a mortal soul, as short of life as the rest of us.'

'But he is Faeran!' Severine screeched in dismay, her life-long vision crumpling at the edges like Liam's soul had done.

'Yes, lady.' Kholi tried to stand tall over her, as the garotte dug deeper and deeper, cutting so close to his windpipe and the precious life-giving blood vessels in his neck. He girded himself, gathering strength into his deep Raji voice. 'But his soul is mortal. As plainly mortal as you or I.'

Severine's face flushed. She crushed the bag to her chest feeling the glacial cold seep through the fabric. But if Liam's soul was mortal, would it be so frigid and would the syphon have sucked out a mortal soul? No! The Raji lies. It's an execrable trick, some insensible way for the filth to get back at me for killing his friend. She turned toward Kholi and studied him for a moment and then smiled an icy glimmer almost as bitter as the freeze that burned her fingers through the chamois.

'You lie. Luther, kill him.'

Kholi began to struggle as the garrotte tightened. Severine, not wanting to see blood spilled, began to walk away. But as she climbed over a root of the waterbeech she heard a bubbling scream as the Raji yelled,

'You'll find out!'

*O*H MY FAITHFUL READER, *grief freezes my mind as that chamois bag froze Severine's cruel hands. Pack away these books quickly and move on away from it all.*

See the soft taupe butterfly with the gold trimmed wings. Lift the wing. There, another journal. And then follow the shooting gold stars to the clouds, stitched with metallic silver thread in excruciating trellis stitch. My fingers bled... a form of penury. In amongst the clouds, a further book.

I have no words to speak to you at this moment. Read on.

CHAPTER THIRTY SIX

The kettle had boiled dry twice over the fire as Adelina waited for the men to return. On a whim, she took out the robe from the drawers, tapped it with the wand and then hung it from a hook against one wall. She sat gazing at it and then took a piece of paper and some charcoal and began to sketch the gown with its panels, labelling each panel and then drawing them larger and in more detail as she began to sequence her stumpwork designs around the robe, always looking for something to link each piece to the next. It was with satisfaction that she sat back after drawing a flight of bees between one element and the next. Yes, that was it. The vital link defined: more and more little gold and black bees flying from leaf to tree. To fill in time she laid out her stumpwork pieces, to determine how much work she had yet to do. Already she had a supply of wired leaves, berries filled with Pymm knots and silk stitched butterfly wings. As she lifted the last of the beechwood hoops filled with calico and to which she had applied various botanical elements, she came across a small wooden circle with a Raji embroidered on silk in its circumference. She held it up to the light to admire it.

He stood, legs akimbo with red and yellow silk pantaloons and a red tunic belted widely by a bronze cummerbund. His face was beautifully shaped and embroidered on the finest sun-tinted organza, right down to the indigo tattoos on the cheekbones. Atop the head sat a red fez, with a swinging navy silk tassel. Adelina ran her finger down the five or so inches of his length to the tiny brown leather shoes with their quaint, up-turned toes. She delicately touched his hands. One waited, fingers curled.

Adelina's mind drifted to the road where Ana had embroidered Aladdin. She remembered the night Kholi had told the story and how they had sat glued to his every gem-like word. Some two days later, Ana completed her stitching and shyly displayed it.

'Ana! You truly have a great skill. I am so proud of you! Kholi, Liam, look at this!'

'He needs one thing, my shrimati... a lamp.' Kholi said. 'A bright gold one!'

'Indeed he does. And we shall find one. And if we polish it, maybe we will have wishes as well.'

Adelina re-wrapped the tiny Aladdin and felt her teeth chewing the inside of her lip. Ana was a bridge between us all, she thought. She remembered that profound Traveller's saying: no man is an island. Ana had single-handedly reconfigured the geography of their lives. Oh Ana, she thought, did your own life re-configure as well?

She wiped her eyes with her fingers. Hating the solitude, she squirmed on her knees on the floor, circulation stemmed, numbness pervading. Somewhere out of a sudden swirling blackness, she coughed, a sawing pain cutting into her throat. Continuing to cough as if she would turn herself inside out, her heart banging, she reached for a mug of water.

'Oh by Aine,' she gasped. 'I wallow in my own pain too much'

Eventually she could swallow more easily: roughness, prickling and the sensation of wire stuck in her throat easing, to be replaced by unease as she stood in the door of the van. The sun was high in the sky and she cocked her head to listen for any sign of the approaching men. Nothing – just birds and the contented snort of Ajax as he grazed at his tether. Mogu lay on the ground, her legs folded neatly underneath, eyes closed, chewing her cud like a contented house-cow. Ajax whinnied and Adelina looked up.

'Liam? Kholi?'

She jumped off the step to the ground, catching her skirt on a nail as she landed and turned away from the clearing to unfasten the garment and make sure it wasn't torn, nor the feather ripped off. Satisfied, she stood for a moment, wondering why evident relief had not filled her veins, why she experienced a cold shudder and why the hair on her arms stood up and her neck prickled underneath the waterfall of her hair. Someone's behind me, she thought, her eyes opening wide. Someone's there!

She began to turn but her arms were grabbed firmly and a large sweaty and blood-covered hand covered her mouth, so that she smelt the metallic odour of gore. She was turned around roughly and a figure dressed in dark green strode into her vision.

'Adelina. It is good to see you again.' Severine smiled, a thin-lipped smirk filled with an arrogance Adelina remembered well. She tried to answer.

'Now, now, don't speak. Luther is going to muffle you and I am going to make you a drink. I thought to give you a lesson in etiquette, because you seemed so ignorant of it the other day. Or perhaps we could call it payment, for the unexpected turn at the Faeran silk stall.'

Adelina thought back to that flay-filled moment at the market and her heart sank. It had only been a matter of time – she knew Severine would make her pay. And hope sank like her heart, landing with a thump at her feet. Luther's grip was oxen-strong and she watched as Severine busied herself at the fire. Luther had tied the muffle so tight over her mouth, her lips and cheeks numbed and a sharp pain throbbed where he had caught her hair in the knot at the back of her skull. He had bound her hands, wrapped round and round in a thin skein of silk, and she pulled hard against the bonds. Severine saw her and laughed.

'It's no use, Adelina. It's Faeran silk. And we all know how exceptional Faeran silk is, don't we?' The woman filled a mug and brought it over to her childhood companion. Unstoppering a phial, she dripped in some thick black drops that left a smell of aniseed in the air, although Adelina knew it was something far more dangerous. Her eyes sought Severine's and she tried to speak.

'Now, now, it's rude to talk with your mouth full and it is even ruder to refuse something offered in hospitality. Just drink this and you will be fine. I think it's time you had a nice long rest.'

Luther grabbed her hair and jerked her head back and ripped the muffle off, tears stinging her eyes as Severine pinioned her chin with the sharp talons of her free hand. Forcing the drink to Adelina's mouth, she nodded at Luther and he prodded her throat with a dagger. She gasped and as her mouth opened in shock, Severine poured the drink down. Coughing, spluttering, she toppled to her knees with Luther still holding her by the hair. A roaring sound filled her ears as if she lay on the seashore and listened to waves being blown in over damp sand. Her protagonists' faces liquefied, blurring and fading and a rush of something bitter filled her mouth as she sank to the ground.

Severine stood over her, looking at the tawny figure as it lay crumpled. 'There was enough to keep her drugged for a day and a night. Keep her that way, Luther. Take her in the van. Hobble the camel and leave it.'

She mounted her horse, springing with an agility that belied the thin, delicate body.

'I will be in Veniche for a few days and shall make my way to the coast as soon as I am able. You know what to do. Keep her drugged and clean and safe. I need her skill to finish my plan. How I am longing to see her face when the realization that she must work for me finally sinks in!'

Clapping her heels to the horse, it sprang away at a gallop. Luther watched until the horse had disappeared out of sight and then picked up the Traveller, throwing her roughly over his shoulder.

He tied her to the bed, careful to protect the hands his mistress thought so valuable, staring at the voluptuous form which was totally at his mercy for the next few days. Behir, it was so tempting! He rubbed his groin crudely and backed out down the steps. Presently, Ajax had been unwillingly harnessed, kicking and biting, and the van began to sway and creak as it rolled along the road, Luther's whip plying sharp cracks in the air. Adelina's head rolled sideways on the pillow but she didn't waken. Nor did she hear the fraught bellows of the hobbled camel or the bereft cries as Ajax neighed back.

Mogu's throaty cries filled the Luned Forest. Anxious birds dipped and dived between branches and twittered and called restlessly, the tenor of the fettered camel creating trepidation.

She tried to shuffle forward but the rope hobbles from fore to hind leg threatened to tip her over and with her great height and bulk, she instinctively feared injury. So she was reduced to bellows: gut-wrenching, throat-ripping cries that could be heard over the tops of the Luned's canopy.

Jasper urged his horse faster when he heard the roar, his horse stumbling as the sound wound between the oaks, ashes and elms. He pounded into the clearing and pulled to a sliding halt, dust surrounding he and the animal and as it cleared, he saw Mogu, hobbled cruelly. He leaped from the saddle and walked toward the beast, holding out his hand and soothing it with a gabble of soft Faeran words. She curled her lips to show her tombstone teeth and spat, trying to shuffle away but Jasper continued to advance, softly softly, until he was nose to nose with the beast. Gently he touched the cambered face, whispering, and the camel groaned back. The groans became bereft bleats and Mogu dropped her great head and rubbed it against Jasper's arm. He stepped to her leg and slashed the rope with a sharp blade.

'Have they gone, my friend? Have they left you? I doubt they have gone willingly.' He worked at the front knot, undid it and pulled it away, throwing it on the glowing embers of the campfire. 'For Kholi Khatoun would never leave his faithful Mogu.' He pulled the other knot free and threw that with disgust after the rest. 'Mogu, my friend, will you follow me while I look for them, find out where they have been taken? There is time surely to save them all.'

But as he spoke the most awful suffocating despair settled upon him and he clicked his horse to follow, dragging at the reins. Mogu watched. Jasper called over his shoulder.

'Come, my girl, come with me. Help me find them.'

Mogu snaked her head from side to side, a mournful bleat shuddering out. Then she took a tentative step and another, to follow the gentle man who had released her. They trekked along the rill about half a mile, until the sun began to slide down on the afternoon side of the sky and birds flew up with alarm from the thickets. There were signs Jasper recognised. A cracked branch, a scatter of leaves on the ground, half a step in the mud on the side of the rill. Someone had passed this way.

Luminescence flickered through the leafy boughs of beech trees and a tiny breeze rattled the green discs together as Jasper entered the tiny clearing. Wavelets danced across the rill as the breeze skipped to the other bank, a tranquil scene of eldritch beauty. But Jasper's skin crawled as if ants marched across it. The mellow patterns of gold on the ground held no suggestion of sunny comfort for the old man and his heart broke in two as he saw the desecration before him. His horse pulled back, snorting fiercely. But Mogu walked on, up to her master's body and nosed it gently, breathing soft breath all over it until she dropped her nose onto the blood stained chest of her master.

Kholi Khatoun lay on his back, eyes wide, mouth snarling. His neck was slashed wide and his life-blood had drained in a massive pool all around and then soaked into the hungry mosses. Jasper turned away.

Liam lay on his face on the other side of the clearing and as Jasper turned him over, seeing the eyes screwed tight in some terrible reaction to pain, he knew the twisted body was merely a husk. That his death had been by soul-stealing. There was a crackling dryness about him, as if his essence, his life force had been sucked out through a straw. It was something peculiarly Other, this cruel dragging at the spirit. Jasper could barely stand, shaking with the self-loathing and disappointment of someone who has been unfailingly wrong about something of the greatest import, something that could have saved someone's life. It was never Ana who was Liam's bane.

'Never!' He shouted, choking on the words. 'NEVER!'

Another mortal woman, a woman with a skein of dark hair falling down her back had willingly, knowingly killed Liam of the Faeran. He touched Liam's forehead and heard a name sussurating on the breeze dancing back and forth over the rill. Severine, Severine, it whispered.

Weakness overcame him as he viewed the bloody violations and he sank to the ground, head ringing, ears roaring. With frantic determination, he whispered charms and incantations, pushing the frailty back, back until he could breathe deeper and focus on the insubstantial message that floated before him like a delicate river mist.

A vision wafted, stronger and weaker colours undulating. Jasper sighed tiredly, feeling a regrettable punishment approaching, but one he deserved. The prophecy ebbed and flowed like strands of hair streaming behind as a swimmer floats in a river – black, red, silver-blonde. But nowhere was there white marking the colour of age. Immediately and with a sick despair, Jasper knew his role for the foreseeable future was as an onlooker and it chafed him because his pain cut so deep.

As the vision oscillated, a faint shadow appeared like ink bleeding into paper and then out again. A text: the words 'breitheamh na trialach' and then everything smeared, blurred into one amorphous tint to fade into the colours of the glade and the rill.

Jasper plunged his face into the basin of his hands.

Not to seek, not to find.

Only to wait.

And then... to judge.

'Not me,' he said tiredly. 'Not me, Liam. I cannot gainsay a prophecy.' He took the rigid hands of the young man in his own aged ones. 'But your soul shall be returned to you in Faeran and you can receive the farewell you deserve.' He glanced across at Kholi and shuddered. 'And I swear, you and Kholi shall be avenged.'

Bending over the Raji, he smoothed his hand over the bloody scorings at the neck and over the wide staring eyes and the open mouth. Kholi's body became soft, clean and peaceful as Jasper asked Mogu to kneel down. Gently and respectfully, the healer placed Kholi on the camel's back.

'My dear friend, I must tie you on. Please forgive me... I would take you to Faeran, to the Ymp tree orchard where you can receive your final rights. And Mogu can live with me.'

He waffled on quietly, being as kind as if Kholi was alive and merely injured. Mogu bent her neck and sniffed the dangling, inanimate toes. The look of anguish in those huge eyes was almost more than Jasper could bear. He clicked his tongue and she swayed to her feet, Kholi secure on her back.

He led his horse to Liam's body and heaved the stiff, young man over the saddle, again tying him on. A tear ran down the wrinkled face and he scrabbled his hand angrily through the close cropped white hair.

'Oh gabh mo leithsceal, mac an cheana. Gabh mo leithsceal.' He ran fingers lovingly down Liam's dry cheek. 'Sorry, my favourite son, sorry.'

A lone starling trilled as the cavalcade headed across the Forest to the Barrow Hills and the gateway to Faeran in the Ymp tree orchard. Jasper led the way, his horse walking quietly behind. Mogu trudged patiently in their wake, conscious of her precious cargo, awash with loss as she searched the horizon for the broad bay back of Ajax and the swaying, creaking van carrying Adelina.

There was nothing. She trudged on.

CHAPTER THIRTY SEVEN

Waves sucking shingle filled the sea air with a rhythmic, hypnotising sound. Breaking softly, stroking the shore, pulling playfully at the crushed shells and then running back to the sea, like a child teasing another. Creeping up behind, tugging at hair and then running away again, giggling. It was a playful sea that stroked the shore of Mevagavinney. In, out, out in. Occasionally a whole shell would be caught in the watery pull and dragged out to sea. But then the next wave would grab it and toss it back again.

Adelina reclined on a window seat high above the small beach, watching the waves. Her head rested against the cedar window frame and she closed her eyes and listened. In, out. Out, in. Luther had stopped the drugs more than a week ago and her body had taken time to stop its craving. She found the waves helped – soothing, relaxing. And she used her own intrinsic strength to conquer the craving. In any case, the need to outwit Severine was far stronger than the need for drugs. To a point she felt the drugs had helped her, taken the edge off the frantic fear, anger... madness.

Her window sat high up a sheer wall that fell away to a tiny cove only a small distance from the breakwater that protected Mevagavinney from the cold waves of the Southern Ocean. Icy blasts from Oighear Dubh, the land of black ice, had been known to knock waves up as far as Adelina's window.

Severine owned the tiny fishing hamlet: the fishing smacks, the trading vessels, the smugglers' dinghies, the men. Her harbour sheltered them behind the protective bulwark of the stone sea wall. Isolated from the rest of Eirie by a forbidding landscape at its back and an inhibiting sea from the front, it was Severine's own world. Her laws, her subjects. Veniche was her public face, this was her private one. Her secret.

The closest village on the mainland was by sea: Polcarrow... a half day with a following breeze. Or to Frynche on the southern tip of Maria Island, two days in good conditions. But few ventured to Mevagavinney, it had a reputation of all that smelt bad and rotten.

Adelina sighed. Always someone whose hands had been busy, she was bored. Luther brooded when he entered with her daily needs, silent as a religeuse who had taken vows. She asked him where Severine was but he chose not to answer. In truth, his brooding presence stirred a fear in her and for once she thanked Aine for Severine's power over he and so many others.

In the beginning, she was content to lie on her bed and watch the shifting patterns of light on the walls. Or to observe the excellent tapestries. She thought it was a series of Travellers' tales. Of Oenghus and the Swan Maid, Tristan and Isolda, Lancelot and Guinevere. She read them like books and then took to examining each and every stitch and thread, changes in colour and tone. And thought how unsatisfying it must be to create things in anything less than a third dimension.

Time passed.

She found some paper in an escritoire and a soft crayon and began to draw. Designs, one after another. And looking for more paper, she made a discovery that changed her life. Far in the back of the little desk, behind a box of broken pieces of charcoal, lay a pen and a bottle of ink and a pile of the thinnest washi paper.

She began to write – firstly a page that she hid under the mattress, and then another page – always at night when she was left alone without interruption. She had begun the third page when she heard voices outside the studded door of her room and quickly thrust her scribblings under the bed, grabbing charcoal and one of her designs and flinging herself onto the window seat, under the light of a flaring lamp.

The door flew back and Severine swept in.

'Now that is what I like to see – Adelina diligently drawing her designs. Good, good.' She reached and grabbed the pile from the window seat. 'Actually very good! Now I see why they want your work in the Museo.'

She moved around the room slowly, as though searching for anything she felt should not be there.

'What do you need?'

'My freedom.' Surliness gritted Adelina's teeth and set her shoulders square and hard.

'Always straight to the point!' Severine looked at the copper haired woman sitting in the window embrasure. 'So let me be equally to the point. No! Not for a long while. I shall ask you again. What do you need?'

'For what?'

'Has Luther not told you? Luther!' She called out through the half open door. 'Send in the housemaid.'

A young waif of a girl with delicate cheekbones and black hair wound into a bun from which wisps escaped, sidled into the room. Over her arms she carried the robe, her eyes downcast.

'I want you to embroider the robe.' She gestured at Adelina's drawings, 'I want it to look just as you planned... with some variations.

'No.'

'No? What do you mean no?'

'No to everything. I will not embroider my robe for you. Never ever!'

Severine's face darkened, a small tic in her cheek flick-flacking away.

'Luther, bring the rest in,' she called to her man and he entered with a bundle wrapped in a cloak. 'Tip it out.' Her harsh voice slipped over Adelina's skin like a snow-shower.

The cloak was unrolled and Kholi's travel caplet and scimitar fell to the floor. Adelina leaned forward, a gasp escaping, her eyes fixed on the familiar objects.

'I think you will stitch, Adelina.' Severine gestured with her thumb. 'I am sure you recognize these. And just in case you think we found them and lie, perhaps you should see this.'

She walked across the thick Raji rugs, her feet silent, unrolling a small twist of paper. Inside was a lock of blue-black hair, curling back over Severine's finger. Adelina looked at the hat, at the weapon and her eyes dwelt longest on the hair, her heart thumping from where it had sunk, low, so low in her chest. She bent and picked up the rolled caplet and crushed it in her fingers, smelling the love of her life drifting on the air.

'Where is he?'

'Somewhere very safe. And he will continue to be safe as long as you do my bidding.' She turned to the maid, growling. 'Well don't stand like a statue, girl, hang the robe up and be careful with it. It is priceless to me.'

The girl hurried to reach for the hook on the side of an empty armoire and hung the gown where it swung to and fro, mocking Adelina with its beauty. Right now, she could have slashed it to ribbons, torn streamers as frayed as her emotions.

'Where is Liam?' She was so filled with ire her voice shook and it annoyed her, for the last thing she wanted was for the bitseach to think she was scared. 'Is he with Kholi? Is he alright? I swear Severine, on my life, if you have hurt them...'

Severine smirked.

'What? What can you truly do to me as you are now?' She sighed, like a mother annoyed with the whining of a fractious child and tossed her hair back over her shoulder, fixing the ice-floe eyes on the other woman. 'Liam is in the same place as Kholi and he really can come to no harm as I said, if you do as I want. So, I ask you again, what do you need?'

Adelina sat silent for a moment, holding the cap to her lips. Then,

'Everything in my van. Baskets of thread, baskets of stumpwork. In fact the whole wall of drawers.'

'Luther, you hear that? Take the wench and see to it. I want everything set up in here in the morning. Go now.'

Luther and the girl walked out of the room, the door shutting quietly behind them. Severine stood in front of Adelina, smiling thinly as the embroiderer bent her head over the caplet.

'By Behir woman, don't get maudlin. It's a cap,' she uttered dismissively. 'And I swear to you, its wearer can come to absolutely no harm where he is. You keep to your promise and all will be well.'

Adelina could hardly bear to look at Severine. If she did she thought she might jump up, grab the scimitar and swing wildly.

'My horse, Severine. Where is my Ajax?'

'At pasture with some of my mares.'

'And Mogu, the camel?'

'Ah. We had no use for her so we turned her loose in the Luned.'

Adelina's fingers gripped the cap tighter and her knuckles turned white as bone.

'Hate me all you like, Adelina. It is no matter. I am your gaoler and you must do what I want, I truly have the upper hand. You are my servant and servants work for their masters. It is as it should always have been.

Wasn't it you who told me I was a changeling, that I am not mortal? Does that not mean I am therefore just a little,' she measured with her fingers, 'better than you?'

She walked around the room restlessly.

'You will find I am not unkind. I shall send your clothes up from the van and just because I like you,' she mocked, 'I will leave you the hat as a comfort toy. This you don't need,' she held up the lock of hair and threw it into the fire, Adelina gasping as she watched it burn. 'And this,' Severine scooped up the scimitar, 'you must not have. Adieu Adelina!'

The following morning, under a grey and forbidding sky, Adelina watched from the window seat as Luther and some men of equally rough ilk carried in her tall set of drawers and placed it on the floor against a bare stonewall. A trunk followed filled with her clothes and the serving girl carried in a bundle of the baskets from the floor of the van. Everything had been found just as it was before Adelina had been drugged.

'Meriope here will help you unpack. She is a mute, so you won't be able to gossip and conspire.' He tapped the servant on the shoulder, using his hands to indicate time and shouting as if the poor woman was deaf as well as dumb. 'Girl, I'll come back in an hour. See you have everything settled before I return.' He took his overlarge, egg-shaped pate and his thick, muscle-bound body and left the room with his cohorts, the key once again turning in the lock.

Adelina cast a tired glance at Meriope and black eyes smiled back.

'He is wrong of course. I do speak.' The wench's voice was as clear as a bell. Adelina clapped her hands together in delight. 'But it pays for them not to know.' Meriope grinned.

Adelina nodded, enjoying the subterfuge and secrecy. A vision of Liam rose unbidden but she forced it away into the darkest reaches of her mind.

'We had best unpack then, had we not?' Meriope began to open the trunk and shake out the clothes that were crushed and pressed flat with the weight of packing. She hung them on hangers and placed them in the armoire, chatting to Adelina as she worked. 'I was captured in one of their smuggling raids. Now I work as a wench in this house, so we are alike, you and I. Both prisoners.'

'Only you get to move about. I have only this room and my garderobe.' Adelina placed her baskets on the massive table stretching along one wall underneath two of the tapestries. As she lifted one of the woven lids, she saw the tiny wand spiked through a ball of wool, like an old crochet hook. A satisfied sigh soughed away.

'Severine may let you walk outside one day, she is a mercurial person.'

'Mercurial? Mad I say! She thinks to make herself immortal like the Others. More than mad!' Adelina failed to see Meriope flinch, busying her fingers unlocking the drawers and checking the contents were unharmed.

'Mad, deluded – it makes little difference. We must do her bidding.' The younger woman shook out a fine lawn chemise and slipped a wooden hanger through the shoulders.

Adelina snorted as she reached for the whispering silk robe.

'Do her bidding I must but I will get my own back'.

She sat and threaded a needle and began to sew the first element on the left front of the robe's hem. Tonight she thought, I shall write more and shrink what I write and sew it into the stumpwork of the gown. The story of this robe shall be for someone to read in the future. Severine's insanity will be learned by someone somewhere and spread across the land. She heaved a sigh with her last thought. For now, that is all the revenge I am capable of.

So my friend, you can see how it all started. I began to sew all day and write all night and my hands became knotted and tired. My eyes became red and sore and I felt exhausted to the point of collapse and I worried it would be hard to give the robe the attention and skill it deserved. Come hell or high water, I wanted this robe to end up in the Museo. If not, then at least I wanted it found by someone who would appreciate my skill and who would want to hear the story it would tell. It was these paltry conceits, to finish the robe and write the story, that fuelled my fires and kept me going, as you see.

Shrink away those last two books and replace them in their hideaways. Then follow the bees to the fish-pond which I have rendered in Veniche stitch on canvas. I applied it separately as you do in stumpwork and surrounded it in detached buttonhole stitch, hollie point and trellis stitch to look like rocks. Under one of the rocks, which you must unpick, you will find another book. Then count two rocks to the one with the tiny shells nestling in the crevice for there is the next journal. Release it in the same way.

CHAPTER THIRTY EIGHT

Adelina gazed down at her pricked, red hands. Where she held the pen tightly at night, her words running away with her fingers, the joints were swollen and where she sewed during the day, she had pierced herself so often, the skin peeled from the tops of fingers. She never wore a thimble, wanting to feel the silk, the gold purl and the leather and most recently, she wanted to feel the pain. Something perverse and masochistic inside her made her think that pain was what she was due. Why not? Ana had died, perhaps because of an attempt at bald righteousness by Adelina. Guilt was undeniable! In addition, like salt to the worst wound, Liam and Kholi were she knew not where.

Meriope walked in through the door, Luther holding it open and then locking it swiftly behind. She gestured with a finger to her lips. Say nothing! And then,

'The brute has gone. We are free for a little while. Oh, Adelina!' She was aghast at Adelina's pallid face and her red-rimmed, tired eyes. 'What ails you? Are you sickening?'

'No, I just want a change of scene. Some fresh air, a walk even. But the bitseach won't let it happen.' She sighed and rubbed her fingers in the corners of her eyes, reluctant to admit to the writing and concealing.

'We shall see. Now what would you like me to do?'

Adelina directed the girl to make the bed and handpress some clothes she herself had washed and then dried in front of the banked-up fire. Meriope worked quietly, occasionally commenting on a piece of embroidery. As she passed the robe hanging on the side of the armoire, she gave it a pensive look, caressed it with gentle fingers and then moved to the worktable.

'You work very hard.'

'I have to. Kholi's and Liam's lives are at stake.'

Adelina licked the end of some raspberry pink silk thread and poked it through the eye of a straw-needle, missing Meriope's laden down expression. Opening her mouth to continue in some anti-Severine diatribe, her heart skipped a beat as the key rattled in the door and her nemesis walked in, stopping to stare with a finger at her lips.

'By Behir Traveller, you look terrible, in fact you get worse every day! And here was I thinking you would bloom being able to embroider uninterrupted.'

'I am tired and stale, Severine, and my hands are sore. What do you expect?'

Severine walked over to the worktable and inspected the hands of her prisoner turning Adelina's white as a linen sheet face to the window – inspecting, analysing.

'You must get some fresh air, I can't afford for you to sicken, not now. A walk outside. Yes, an hour a day in my walled garden. It is secure and I shall have Luther watch you. You will enjoy the garden. It is, even if I say so myself, quite magnificent.'

Meriope glanced at Adelina and smiled, raising her eyebrows. See, she seemed to say, I told you so. Severine turned to her.

'You shall accompany her. If anything untoward happens it shall be your fault.'

Meriope nodded, silent – the dumb dupe.

Severine walked to the window and looked out.

'It's a fair day. You may go out for an hour now. Luther will escort you. But before you go Adelina, I want you to look at these.'

She placed a chamois bag on the table and pulled open the drawer-string. Tipping it up, two shiny, ebony shapes fell out onto the table, lying in a heap, folds softly forming as they crumpled on top of each other. Meriope's eyes widened and her hands began to tremble, the small tin of pins she was holding rattling ever so slightly.

'I want you to cut these into four and I want you to sew them under your stumpwork on the robe. This is the variation I mentioned when you first arrived here, and it will go severely for you, even for your... friends, if you don't accomplish it to my liking.'

A crash drew startled glances from Adelina and her gaoler and pins flew across the rug, Meriope's face anguished as Severine rounded on her.

'Damn you girl! Useless creature. Get on your knees and pick every one up. When you are done, go with Adelina and Luther to the garden. Luther, get Cook to send a basket. They can eat there. Remember my orders, Adelina. I want to see you started on the black by tomorrow.'

When Severine left, Adelina fancied the air grew warmer and heaved a sigh of relief. Good riddance! And by Aine, a walk in the garden! She bent down and picked up the last of the pins as Meriope struggled with nervous fingers to screw the lid back on.

The walled garden was as Severine had said. Graceful, elegant, with shady nooks and arbours and foaming flowers and shrubs of every shade of white.

'Iontach!' Adelina walked disbelievingly down an allée of weeping silver-pear trees, their snowy blossoms lying across the ground like a piece of delicate organza. That such a woman should create such a garden! Meriope followed behind, on edge and withdrawn as the two came to a seat under an arbour and Adelina gestured that they both rest.

'It is as well here as anywhere. Luther watches from the house. He can see our feet sticking out from under the arbour but he can't see me talking.' Meriope spoke guardedly.

'I am surprised you want to talk. You seemed very upset when you dropped the pins! Oh my, it is quite warm here, isn't it?'

She pulled her knitted sweater over her head and shook out the russet locks. Her eyes began to lose their dull patina as the fresh air caught hold and a soft seabreeze eased over the walls and teased the folds of her toile skirt, now clean and fragrant.

Meriope sat back against the wicker of the charming seat and pushed her sleeves up.

'Yes. I was somewhat overwrought. I will confess I don't like her, despite my attempt at equanimity. She makes me tremble.'

Her hands lay in her lap, clasped tightly, her fingers twisted in on each other and Adelina noticed the fine wrists, delicate and as fragile as porcelain. On one arm the girl wore a bracelet of woven stuff, unusual.

She leaned forward to get a better look as it reminded her of something – something infinitely familiar and personal.

She grabbed Meriope's wrist in demanding fingers and looked at the bangle. Made of rich autumnal hair, plaited to form a circle, it swung idly. And it sang to Adelina, a rich chime setting up in her own heart in response. Because her hair was remarkable – red with glowing gold highlights like Raji tigers. There would hardly have been another person in Eirie with those vibrant hues.

'Where did you get this? Where, Meriope? That is my hair, as sure as Aine is the mother of the world. And I know where I left it last.'

'I know you do. And I will not deceive you. Aine, at last I can tell you, you have no idea how I have wanted to! My sister Lara gave it to me. She got it from you.'

'Oh! The silk-seller!' Adelina's breath sucked in. 'You're Faeran! I knew it, I kept thinking of Liam every time I looked at you.'

'Yes. My name is really Lhiannon and I have been sent here by Jasper.'

'Truly? To rescue us all?'

'No.'

The unequivocal negative floated in the air like a cool draught.

'What then?'

'Oh, Adelina, let me tell you. What I have to say is very very hard.' Meriope-Lhiannon's eyes moistened. It silenced the embroiderer beside her completely.

'The black thing, that… that stuff is not what you think it is. You know Severine has been chasing immortality. Well, she found an old poem, a charm of occult lore.

'From caverns deep, abysses cold
There lies a ring, so very old.
Through its eye the bearer sees souls of Others which are keys
Keys to locks which open a door
from which the bearer can expect more.
More life eternal, evermore.'

Lhiannon shuddered before continuing, her hand playing restlessly with the plaited hair bracelet on the other wrist.

'The souls must part befront, behind.
Till four of the same from two will wind

their power around, around and more.

More life, eternal evermore. You see, it tells of a ring, a soul-syphon, the universal bane to all Faeran... a goblin ring that if held to the eye could suck the soul out of me and all my ilk. If the holder, unseelie Others included, can secure two Faeran souls and wear them on a garment, then immortality will ensue, sucked into the very marrow of the wearer. You may not know,' her voice issued in an almost whisper. 'But Faeran are the only ones of the Others who are immortal. It is why, during the times of chaos, the goblins created such a weapon. You can imagine!' She looked at Adelina's disbelieving face. 'It is true, I speak the truth.' She took another shuddering breath. 'The shapes on your worktable are two Faeran souls and if they are sewn onto the robe, their power will permeate Severine's skin and enter her body. In time she will be immortal!'

'Oh by Aine! How repulsive!' Adelina, agitated, tried to stand but Lhiannon pulled her back down. 'So that is why my robe is such a part of her plan! To have a gown made of Faeran silk and Faeran thread and the Faeran souls as well! She is obsessed! I told you she was deluded.'

'It is more than repulsive and I haven't finished, there is worse yet to come.' Lhiannon took a big breath, her face devoid of colour, her eyes bruised with hurt. 'One of the souls is that of my sister. She so offended Severine when she gave you that fabric, the woman made her pay with her life. She found Lara by the lake at Star on the Stair. The rest was easy. The Faeran traders found her body and spirited it away. No one outside of Faeran knows of the murder. Only you and the perpetrators.'

Adelina's face had mirrored a dozen expressions in the telling and something in her was beginning to slide to the pit of her stomach.

'Whose is the other soul?' There was silence... a weary, unwelcome silence from her companion. 'Oh Aine, I know, don't I? Please tell me it isn't Liam?' Her voice weakened to a whisper, her hope lying at her feet, breathing its last.

Lhiannon looked down and said nothing but a tear threaded its way to her chin and she wiped it off. Adelina tried to stand but her legs folded like paper.

'There is more?'

Lhiannon nodded.

'Oh please, no!' The embroiderer whispered, twisting and crushing the sweater in anguished hands. Her hopes died in that minute, one heartbeat and one breath and everything that she had loved and dreamed of disintegrated, leaving an ugly empty vacuum.

'Adelina, I am so sorry.' Lhiannon placed a tentative hand on her friend's arm. 'Jasper found them. He took them both to the Ymp Tree orchard. Mogu carried Kholi.'

Adelina could not cry. She felt like a dried up oasis in the middle of the Amritsands and a hot Symmer wind swirled through her, crisping the edges of her psyche. Moulding and shaping hatred like a mound of sand before the howling desert wind. Finally she spoke.

'Then if you are not here to release me yet, why are you here? What does Jasper want?'

'The souls. The souls must be returned to Faeran or the bodies will be caught in some ghastly frozen tableau, hunched and crushed in whatever ugly position they died. Never to be laid out and given a Faeran farewell. The water that they float on in their funeral barge would dry up. The flames of the arrows flying towards their floating pyre would burn out. If we buried them, the soil would fly from the sidh and they would lie uncovered. If we built a cairn over them with rocks, the boulders would tumble down revealing their unfortunate empty husks.'

Adelina said nothing for a moment, her face white, her heart crushed into a million grains of sand. But lacking wailing tears, she needed to pitch her gall at something, someone.

'Why isn't your great Jasper here himself? Why can't the old man get the souls through some enchantment or other and free me in the process? Isn't he supposed to be all-powerful, infallible, whatever the damned hell you like?'

'Because the prophecy says not, Adelina, and one must never defy Fate. This is the way it must be!'

'Prophecy? What prophecy? I don't care a fig for some vacuous Faeran prophecy! Aine, I have lost the love of my life!' Adelina stood and began to walk down the allée. Lhiannon hurried to catch up. Her black hair was beginning to slide from its bun and she remained mute in case Luther was watching.

Hatred flooded like white-hot lava and filled every sinew of the embroiderer's body, her legs racing to cover the ground.

'She will pay, Lhiannon. Prophecy or no, she will pay with her life!'

I NEED TO SHOW YOU how shattered I am, to make you understand.

But how?

By the paper that is torn by the nib of the pen as I scrawl the words across. By the agitated spatters of ink?

By the tears that splash and smear my very words?

Would it help to know that I have ripped one sheet of paper already, into tiny pieces of confetti, ripped and ripped as if the paper was Severine and I tore her apart?

Prophecy be damned!

I idealized Jasper of the Faeran! I thought he was infallible, capable of anything, the least being to secure those unfortunate souls, to rescue us, surely that was within the scope of his eldritch skill.

But the old man is confronted by some vapid vision and folds. I hate him! I hate everyone!

CHAPTER THIRTY NINE

Lhiannon and Adelina sat side by side at the work-table.

Adelina had reminded Luther how adamant Severine had been that work with the black fabric begin on the morrow. She was sure he did not want to be the cause of her being unable to start, she said persuasively. He locked them both back in the room.

They sat quietly for a while and then Lhiannon gave a nod – Luther had moved away down the winding stone stair. Adelina opened one of her drawers and pulled out a length of weighty black duchesse satin and placed it beside the souls, flinching in case her fingers touched them, unable to believe one was Liam's. Oh help me, she thought, Aine help me, I cannot do this. Faintness blurred her vision and numbed her hands as she remembered Liam searching for Kholi, of the two being found by Luther and Severine. Of what ensued...

Her hand flew to her throat. By heavens, I know how my love died she choked, evoking what Kholi must have felt and began to cough as if her lungs would fly out of her mouth – gut-wrenching hacks. Blackness swirled and she staggered. Lhiannon placed a hand on her arm and softness crept up to her shoulder, over her breast and into her heart, her focus shifting away from the horror. She glanced at Lhiannon gratefully.

'Take the souls and this will suffice to replace them. Quickly.'

Lhiannon drew out a small grey chamois pouch and with trembling fingers placed the precious things inside and tucked it in her bodice. Adelina watched, her mind running fast.

'You must get away. And I have had a thought.'

She grabbed her toile skirt and slid it around to the image of a waterfowl. There, glowing in the afternoon light was the black feather Liam had given her.

'It is a feather from a swan-maid. Liam said I could use it if I ever needed help. What do you think?'

'Yes. It may work,' Lhiannon was circumspect, 'although swan-maids are not renowned for their love of Faeran. But we have little choice.' She grabbed Adelina's hand in pinching fingers. 'Ssh! Be quiet, Luther returns.'

'Tomorrow in the garden then, yes?'

Lhiannon nodded and picked up scissors, pretending to be industrious. The cold souls burned her breast but her heart jumped at the journey she was about to make. Pray to Aine and any of the Spirits, she would succeed!

The midday sun shone palely in a water-washed blue sky. Adelina had once again not slept, choosing to write with a feverishness fueled by the fires of hatred. To sew that morning had been a trial beyond belief as she cut the satin to mimic the souls and sewed the first piece underneath a design of a black thistle she had placed on the back of the garment. The Raji knots she plied back and forth to give the semblance of the thistle head were difficult and at one point, she bled on the fabric of the robe. She swore and hastily dropped some spit onto the stain, dabbing it gently. In some alchemist's miracle, the blood faded and disappeared and the fabric returned to its pristine form.

She constantly glanced at the sun outside the window, longing for midday and wondering why Lhiannon had not come. They needed to talk for what would she, an embroiderer, know of feathers and summoning swan-maids!

At midday precisely, with the sun directly overhead, the door unlocked and Luther pushed it open. Lhiannon stood just behind him, her arm hooked under the handle of a rush basket. Adelina flung down her sewing and tried not to hurry to the door. Remain the same, she thought, be what you are – sullen, angry – murderous! It was all she could do not to grab her scissors and run screaming at Luther's throat, to stab, stab and stab again...

'Meriope has brought your food. I will collect you in an hour.' He spoke briefly and then strode ahead and they followed, not acknowledging each other at all.

Once the garden gate had shut and Lhiannon had given the signal all was safe, Adelina pounced on her.

'Where have you been? I needed to talk.'

Lhiannon stayed under the canopy of a spreading cherry tree. Its blossom cast a wide white awning over the Faeran girl and she could speak freely.

'Severine was in one of her compulsive moods – polish, polish more and then polish again! She followed my every move until Luther reminded her it was almost midday and you needed your walk and food, to which she gave grudging way. What is wrong?'

'I don't know how to use the feather and we have so little time.' Adelina chafed.

'Worry not.' She grabbed Adelina lightly by the arm. 'Let's go to the pond, there is a willow which will shield us. Quickly.'

The willow branches had just sprouted lime green leaves. Tiny pendules of green-white blossom filled the air with a heady scent, the sounds of bees sucking at the pollen droned lazily from under the weeping branches. The leafy curtain closed about the two women like the folds of a tent. By the side of the huge pond, myrtle flag and water plantain spread over the banks. The racemes of swamp lily spiked into the air and the placid waters of the pond were coated in the dark, floating leaves of the water hawthorn. A secret pond, it was a place for swan-maids and Others.

'Adelina!' Lhiannon's hand gripped the woman's arm. 'The feather, quickly.'

Adelina eased away the threads she had cut earlier and handed the glistening flight feather to the Faeran girl.

'What if she's on the other side of Eirie?'

'It makes no difference. It's the oddity of Others. If you call, they can be instantly here. Now watch.'

Lhiannon held the feather by the sharp quill and carefully brought it to her mouth. She blew gently on its length. Each delicate individual piece of the whole danced and fluttered as her sweet breath drifted over it, to sink gracefully back to form the one long feather again.

'And?' Adelina hands twisted together.

'We wait.'

The air beneath the willow was sweet and clean. Light dappled down and the pendulous branches undulated, finding a puff of air where there would seem to be none. The luminous wings of dragonflies beat in front of the two women but neither noticed, too nervous to speak, too desperate to move. On the other side of the pond, water fowl splashed and duck-dived for a feed of water beetle and worm. Frogs set up a croaking chorus and the mirrored surface was occasionally marked by a series of unexplained concentric rings. Calmness prevailed as Adelina chewed at the torn skin on her fingers and Lhiannon palmed the feather back and forth. A honking cry echoed above the garden and the two women looked up.

A black swan flew over the wall, skimming it lightly. She slid along the slick surface of the pond, feet sinking to paddle through the water, wings folding gracefully. The long neck stretched up, bending at the head, the red beak defined against the sable of the splendid coat.

She glided toward the willow, under the branches and to the shore. A leg stepped out of the pond and as she walked forward she shifted from bird to woman, the winged mantle sliding down her arms, to hang like a magnificent stole from elbow to elbow.

'Thy call was heard, Lhiannon. Although it was not thine to make.' She turned the long white face, utterly symmetrical and beyond beauteous, towards the mortal woman she had met previously. 'So Adelina. Thy soul is as empty as the husk of Liam. Black feathers echo black heart. Thou has inherited the feather, what dost thou want of Maeve Swan Maid?'

Adelina, heart tender and sore, remembered when she had met the woman, as she had sat with Kholi by the lake at Star on the Stair.

'It's simple. Lhiannon has retrieved Liam's and Lara's souls from that witch Severine and must get away. Can you help?'

Maeve Swan Maid moved around them as they sat under the willow. She glided, her black robe trailing behind, the feathery cloak still draping from elbow to elbow. Her cool face eyed Lhiannon.

'If Maeve gives thou flying cloak, thou may not give it back and Maeve will remain here in this garden unable to return to her form. For surely the only answer is that thou fly away.'

Adelina broke in.

'She's slight. Could you not carry her?'

'Stupid mortal! Swan has small strength and would never be able to fly with Faeran astride. Maeve is not a beast of burden.' She snaked her head at them and then turned away.

'But we have asked for your help. You are obliged to honour the debt.'

Maeve Swan-Maid turned again, fury marring the beauty. If she had been avian, Adelina had no doubt she would have approached with wings outstretched, hissing and spitting from the red mouth. As it was, the carmine lips drew back and invective in some form of Other language cascaded down upon Adelina. Then,

'Maeve Swan-Maid will honour debt because she wants to be free of the pitiful mortal. Thy trials are not hers and she would be gone. She knew the love of Liam for the mortal woman was fated. Stupid Faeran! But Maeve will save his soul and that of the Faeran girl's sister because she honours all debts. She is a truly honourable Other. She has an idea. Come tomorrow and the answer will be here.'

'Tomorrow!' Both women broke out in an anguished cry.

'Tomorrow.'

Maeve turned away with finality and stepped into the water, not to be gainsaid. She became a swan as seamlessly as she had become a woman and began to swim away, the wings unfolding as she prepared to take flight. Within minutes she had glided up over the sea wall and was gone.

'Tomorrow!' Adelina whispered, aghast.

Lhiannon merely nodded, taking the embroiderer's hand in her own as they sat and blindly watched the willow billow back and forth.

CHAPTER FORTY

Adelina felt her mood reflected the sky. Utterly grey. Except the sky had streaks of white in it, clouds of stratus which made the expanse of grey look like a piece of Veniche water-wave taffeta, what the cognoscenti called moiré. There was no such relief of unmitigated grey in Adelina's mood.

Within hours she would have lost the only friend she had within this prison. And her life, without the hope of seeing Kholi again, stretched out before her like an expanse of wasteland. She had still not cried. Deep inside, a fire burned to be sure. But it was the fire of hate, of revenge, and that allowed no room for grief. Especially not grief for the love of one's life. Even the uneasy melancholy that had ensued on Ana's death had disappeared as the fires of hate consumed her.

One thing shone like a beacon – the fact the souls would be out of Severine's reach. That she would not achieve her dream of immortality. Not with the souls of Liam and Lara. And as each day passed as she searched for more souls, she would grow older and more vulnerable and it would give Adelina time. Time to avenge Kholi's and Liam's deaths.

Midday arrived and no one came to collect her. She paced nervously, going from window to door. Afraid she would see the swan winging its way over the seawall and out again. She sat and tried to sew but could not concentrate and repeatedly pulled the needle free of its thread until she threw everything down in frustration. As she turned from the window again, she heard the key in the lock and turned, heart jumping.

Luther stood there.

Alone.

'Come,' he ordered. 'And bring a coat, it's cool.'

She grabbed her quilted jacket and hastened after him.

'Where is... Meriope?'

'Fetching a basket of food from the kitchens. She will meet us at the gate.'

Adelina closed her eyes in relief, feeling her way down the cool stonewall at the side of the stair. Her fingers brushed against large Raji carpets in jewel colours hanging on the circular walls. She hated that her prison was so beautifully appointed, so thoughtfully furnished, that it was comfortable, that the gardens were a delight. She wished everything was unmitigated horror, like some dracule's castle, so she could hate more and feed her hate with more hate!

Lhiannon was at the gate and Adelina spoke to her in a surly tone.

'I hope you didn't bring the same apples as yesterday, because they were floury and bitter. If your mistress wants my best work then she should feed me with due consideration.'

Lhiannon hung her head in a suitably chastised manner.

'Your complaint is noted.' Luther pushed Adelina in the gate and gave Lhiannon a little shove after her. 'An hour.'

He glanced at them both briefly and shut the large wooden gate behind him. They heard the key in the lock and knew he went to his place on the widow's walk at the very top of the house where he could watch. Wasting no time, Lhiannon blew on the feather and the two women hurried to the warmer climes of the willow.

An oriental duck swam past as they took their places, neither speaking. The duck's exotic black, white and chestnut plumage might have caught Adelina's eye at another time, but instead she turned inward, not wanting to think about Lhiannon leaving. And then she could bear it no longer.

'I'll miss you and truth to tell, I'm not sure how I will cope without you.' There! She had said it. Lhiannon turned to her, her eyes kind.

'Adelina, if any one can cope it's you. I know things will work out and we shall see each other again. Trust me when I say you'll not be alone. There are seelie Others here. We will find ways. You must rest easy.'

As she reached to tuck her hand inside Adelina's arm, the willow branches undulated aside and the black swan glided through.

'Oh!' Adelina jumped off the seat. 'We didn't hear you.'

Maeve walked toward them, woman not swan.

'Maeve is ever discrete and does not trumpet presence.' She looked directly at Lhiannon, a faint curl to the lips. 'Art thou ready, Faeran?'

'Yes.' Lhiannon stood, the whip-thin body trembling like the petals of a fritillaria.

Maeve took a feather from inside the bosom of her gown and as Lhiannon had done earlier, blew gently down its length. The sable feather extended from its tip and grew, flowing to form a cloak of blackish green hue. It lay as lightly on the swan-maid's arm as her own.

'Thou art lucky Maeve feels sorrow for the souls of Faeran and placed an eloquent case before her sister maids. Another swan-maid agreed to lend her cloak and Maeve shall guide, Faeran will fly.' She passed the soft cloak to Lhiannon. 'Adelina,' Maeve turned to the embroiderer. 'Thou can secure severe punishment for Severine from Others. We can tell thee how or if thou require, Others will do it, for she is a murderer of our own.'

Adelina looked up at the beautiful white face with its calculating eyes and carmine mouth. If it had not been so flawlessly magnificent and Other, she would have thought there was a likeness to Severine.

'No. Her punishment shall be mine to exact. Liam was my friend, Kholi was my love. And had Lara not angered Severine by giving me the Faeran silk, it is possible she may have survived. No! I'll do this, I must! It will help cleanse my soul.'

'And how wilt thou escape this place?'

'I don't know. I am in no hurry. I have the robe to finish in my own way and I must plan diligently. I shall take my time.'

'Then it is time for thee to leave, Faeran. Put on swan's-down.'

The feathery cloak slipped up Lhiannon's arms. Adelina watched as the girl metamorphosed, her body shortening, the arms folding into black wings with white wing tips, her head with its black hair becoming the graceful, long-necked head of the swan. She waddled on red legs to the side of the pond and followed the swan-maid into the water. Briefly turning her head on the long willowy neck, she fixed Adelina with a friendly, very un-swan like eye and honked quietly. Adelina lifted her hand and mouthed 'good fortune.'

The two black swans rose off the water, one after the other into the air. Up over the sea wall and higher, banking along the coastline. Adelina realised she had no idea of Maeve's plans thereafter and prayed to Aine to keep Lhiannon safe.

As she walked away from the willow, she heard running feet and on turning the corner, saw Luther, Severine and some heavy men running down the allée toward her.

'Where is she?' Severine spat the words at Adelina.

'Meriope? I sent her to the potager,' she gestured with her arm to the far side of the walled garden where a tall hedge shielded a vegetable garden from the sea wind. 'I wanted strawberries.' She prevaricated, praying.

Severine reached back and swung with an open palm. Connecting with Adelina's cheek, she nearly knocked the embroiderer over. Adelina saw a universe of stars as the force of the hit scrambled her thoughts.

'YOU LIAR! Luther was watching! He saw one swan come in and two leave. She was a swan-maid, wasn't she?' She hit Adelina again, this time on the other cheek. 'Look at me, bitseach. You knew! She has taken the souls! I know because I went to your room and you thought to cheat me with this?' She screeched as she threw a piece of duchesse satin at Adelina's feet. 'By Behir, woman, I could kill you! You have no idea what you have done!'

'But I do Severine.' Adelina replied with as much calm as she could muster, refusing to place hands against her burning, throbbing cheeks. 'I know exactly what I have done. And I would do it again and again and again. Because you are a liar! Worse, you are a murderer! You can't bribe me with Kholi's and Liam's safety because I know they are dead! So kill me. I have absolutely nothing to live for. Do it!'

Her calm resolve shook Severine. The woman stood for a moment in a quandary, then allowed a vicious smile to wipe clean the uncharacteristic confusion.

'Let me see, what is worse? To end your life or to continue forcing you to embroider the robe. Well for sure, working for me will be purgatory, won't it, akin to being damned? But how to make you? HAH!' Her eyes lit up with the brightness of an idea. 'Bring her, Luther! And bring your harquebus.'

One of the men came up behind Adelina and pushed her hard and she followed Severine to a barred fenestration in a brick wall, through which she glimpsed fields, a sickeningly pastoral scene.

'Look!' Severine grabbed her and pinching with her fingers, pulled her to the opening. Adelina caught her breath. There on the far side of the field, grazing with a herd of mares was Ajax. Her hands came up to her mouth and the tears that had remained dry for days, welled up and overflowed. Her Ajax, the only family remaining. Loyal, faithful Ajax, with the back broad enough to be that of the unseelie Cabyll Ushtey.

'Yees!' Severine drawled. 'Ajax. Luther, fire!'

Adelina spun around as the muzzle of the weapon appeared over her shoulder, aiming at the horses and at Ajax.

'NO,' she screamed, knocking it wide. 'No please! I'll do what you want!'

Severine nodded complacently.

'Indeed! Then you shall sew, Adelina. Because Ajax's life depends on it. Every day you shall take your walk and every day you will come to the window and if you have been good, you will see him there. You hear me?'

Adelina nodded, aware of the stalemate, unable to stop the tears and thinking Severine was worse than any Other she had heard of. Worse than the Hag, the Hunt, the Barguest, Black Annis, all manner of unseelie wights whose purpose it was to maim and trouble mortals even to the point of death.

'Where has she gone?' Severine grabbed the embroiderer's arm and twisted it up her back. Adelina hunched away from the drag on her tendons and nerves.

'I don't know. She had a feather and she called the swan-maid and they planned this between them. She's Faeran, Severine! You have truly aroused their ire!'

Severine laughed, a freezing tinkle that provoked shivers in the embroiderer.

'And you think I care? When I have this?' She held up her finger with the battered ring on it. 'So the girl is Faeran! Crafty chit! Well no matter. She's with a swan. She can only go inland to the swan haunts. My hunters will soon find her and when they do, I'll retrieve the souls and then you shall complete the robe and my dream will come to fruition.'

'Why not catch more souls, Severine? Why chase her? She could be anywhere.'

'Stupid woman! Because she has defied me, stood in my way and I shall punish her! Let it be a lesson, Adelina! Those who deny me, die! I shall catch her, never fear. I have many ways of seeking.'

Adelina, sickened by the self-important preening of Severine, felt the dam wall holding her emotions cracking and collapsing – no Kholi to remind her that self-opinionated rhetoric was ever her undoing. She spewed forth.

'Aine you are full of yourself, cocksure bitseach that you are! And how do you, a mundane mortal, plan to do this? With more Luthers, more men all over Eirie?'

Severine coloured but remained cool.

'In a manner of speaking.' She whistled, a high-pitched sound with tongue against her teeth, a shrill call that peeled shreds from Adelina's nerves. Curious baying, like the sound of wind through large pipes filled the air as a pack of wild white hounds ran into the garden seeming from nowhere. And above them fluttered three black ravens, shape-changing as they landed on the ground to swarthy, black clad men. Severine's own men, Luther included, backed away from them and from the unseelie hounds whose eyes glowed red and who snarled through rapacious teeth. She laughed.

'Do you know the Cwn Annwn? The hounds of the Wild Hunt? The Gabble Retchet, Herl's Rade? They could sniff her out, even that thieving little chit. And my black ravens, the black ravens of Mimring? They can fly anywhere and find her! She doesn't stand a chance!'

Adelina cringed as a hound sniffed her skirts. His hackles stood on high and every thing about him spelled hell and damnation. He dripped saliva from razor sharp teeth, smelling of death and despair. Severine spoke sternly in a fierce dialect and Adelina realised she was speaking Other, disbelief rampant as she felt her hand grabbed by the icy fingers of her adversary, to be dragged to the garden gate. With her other hand, Severine clicked her fingers, spoke Other and the Cwn Annwn and the Mimring Ravens vanished.

'I have studied much over the years Adelina, and money opens many doors, Others included. I have access to things you could only dream of.'

Adelina's unbridled ferocity continued to erupt.

'All except the power of immortality, eh, Severine? Didn't you realise Liam had forgone his immortality? His soul will hardly be of use! What a shame! So near and yet so far.'

A cracking blow on the side of her head let her know she had rubbed too hard and by Aine it hurt! Severine's face filled with fury as she snarled back.

'If what you say is true, and I doubt it, it is of no matter. I shall find another, of that I am positive. Perhaps Meriope's!' She turned to her thugs.

'Take her away!'

Luther and another grabbed Adelina's arms and she was dragged up to her room, head ringing, cheeks stinging. But it felt so good! For she had, just this once she believed, fought back and fought back well. The pain was evidence!

She walked to the window and looked down at the waves and then out over the sea.

Lady Aine, she prayed, look after your servant Lhiannon. Guide her and keep her safe and bless the lives of Ana and Kholi and of Liam and Lara. And Lady Aine, if you have the time, bless me and keep me safe too. For I have great work to do and I need your help.

And so my long-suffering friend, you have now read the first part of my stumpwork robe. You have stepped through the embroidered landscape from the left front of the gown, to the left of the centre back seam. And by devious means you have followed my story, accompanied my heart as it was warmed, and watched as it was cut out and trodden on. In consequence, you have seen me develop a hatred and desire for revenge so intense it could burn things to cinders if it were touched. And to my shame, you have seen how I am guilty of contributing to a friend's death, maybe even contributing to more than just the one death. You can judge.

And I suspect you wonder if my revenge will be any stronger than the mere penning of a few tiny books.

I will tell you this.

My hatred consumes me.

It fills me with a smouldering blackness and each time Severine comes near me she fans the coals that little bit more. Here a spark, there a flame. I swear on Liam's and Ana's souls and on the soul of my beloved Kholi Khatoun that vengeance will be sought.

It merely remains to be seen, dear companion, whether you would journey onward with me, to the other side of the robe. For this story shall end, mark my words, and it will all be the better when it does. For do they not say in Eirie that 'revenge is sweet?'

So repair to the right front of the robe and let us read on...

THE END... for the moment.

REFERENCES

1. *Stumpwork Embroidery* by Jane Nicholas. Sally Milner Publishing NSW 1995

2. *Stumpwork Embroidery. Book Two* by Jane Nicholas. Sally Milner Publishing NSW 1998

3. *Stumpwork Dragonflies* by Jane Nicholas. Sally Milner Publishing NSW 2000

4. *Stumpwork Beetle Collection* by Jane Nicholas. Sally Milner Publishing NSW 2004

5. *Peel tower poem:* 'Invidious rust...' from www.peletower.freeuk

6. Coracle racing inspired by *Folk Customs of Britain* by D. Macfadyean and C. Hole. Hutchinson London 1983

7. Hogmanay fireballs inspired by customs from *Folk Customs of Britain* by D. Macfadyean and C.Hole Hutchinson London 1983

8. The moonlight poem: 'Where moonlight...' from *Leprechauns, Legends and Irish Tales* by Hugh McGowan V. Gollancz London 1988

9. The names Kholi and Lalita and the line 'poor Mr. Kholi, no wife, no life.' From *Bride and Prejudice, the movie*. Directed by Gurinder Chadha, Bend it Productions 2005

10. The meaning of the word "faeran": www.etymonline.com/index.php?term=fear

11. *Irish-English Online Dictionary*. www.englishirishdictionary.com

12. The Inns of the First, Second etc Happiness inspired by the inn in the movie, *The Inn of the Sixth Happiness*. Directed by Mark Robson, Twentieth Century Fox 1958.

13. The Historic Fart from *Breaking Wind. Legendary Farts. Folktales of Flatulence*. Selected and edited by D Ashliman 2000 www.pitt.edu/~dash/fart.html

14. 'Oisin and Niamh' and 'Oenghus and the Swan Maid' from *The Enchanted World... fabled lands*. E.Phillips (Director) Time-Life Books NY 1986.

15. The evening poem: 'The evening is festooned with golden cloud...' poem on the Nökken by Erik Johan Stagnelius. www.home.c2i.net/elysnes/nokken.html

16. *Coping with Grief* by Mal McKissock. ABC Books Sydney, 2001.

17. *Spirits, Fairies, Gnomes and Goblins* by Carol Rose ABC-CLIO Ltd Oxford, 1998.

Printed in the United States
220657BV00002B/8/P